THESE WICKED LIES

THESE WICKED LIES

Book 1

MIRANDA JOY

SpellBound Souls

To anyone who is sick of being put in a box.
Don't let them stifle you.

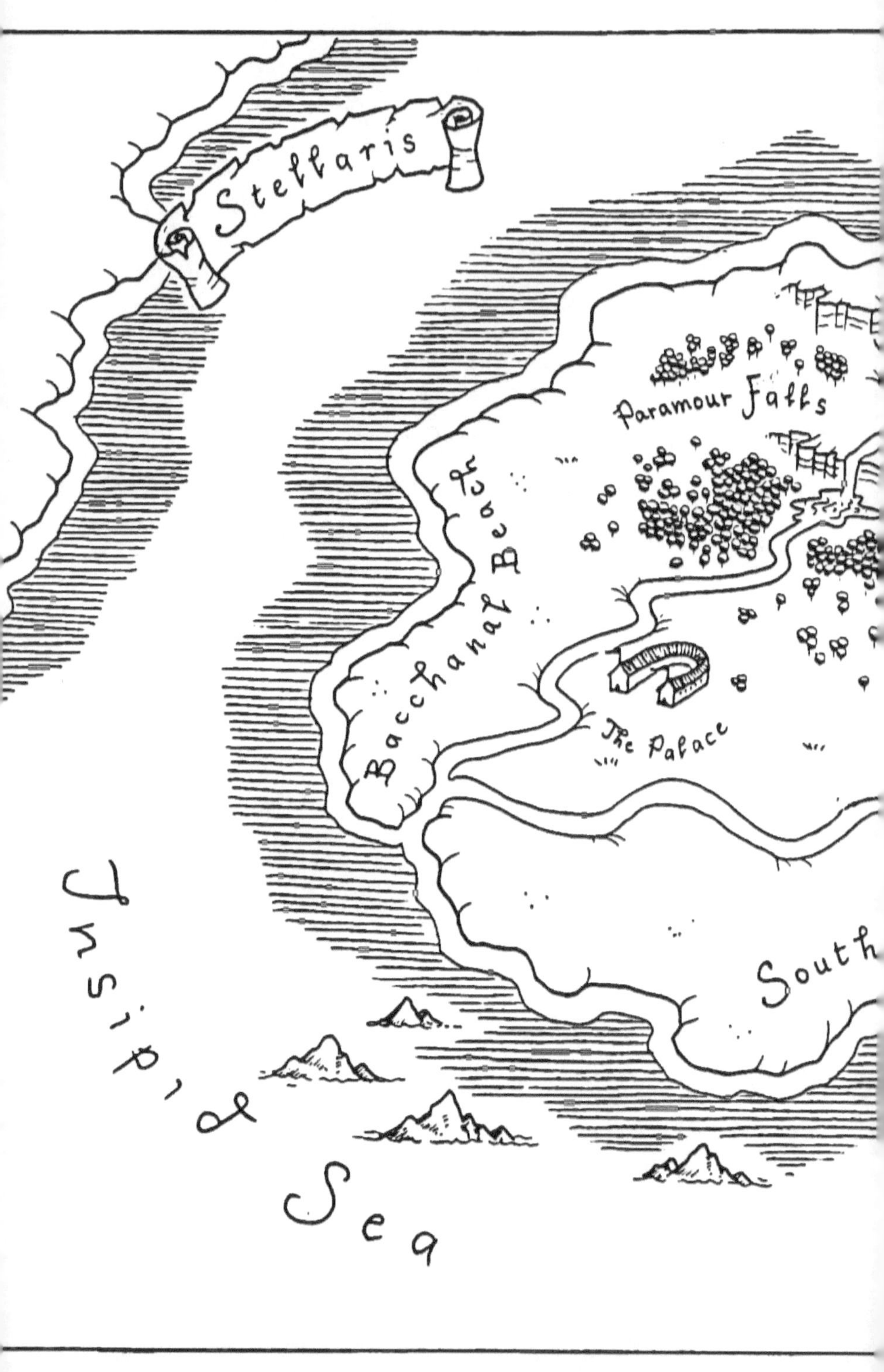
Stellaris
Paramour Falls
Bacchanal Beach
The Palace
South
Insipid Sea

The Prison
To Nevaris
Sands
Hakran

CHAPTER ONE

I'm not in the mood to murder someone tonight, but I must.

My pulse quickens as I gaze at the dozens of sweat-slicked bodies filling the sandy beach, twirling and touching beneath the moon's glow.

I wonder which one I will absorb the life force from.

Palm trees line the jagged edge where sand meets jungle, standing crooked from years of braving summer storms. Though the night air is heavy with moisture, the sky is clear. Stars litter the space overhead, shimmering off the equally dark sea. A raging bonfire sits at the center of the revelry on pale sand, bathing those who dance around it in a warm hue.

Off to the side, closer to the dense forest than the water, I watch from an enclosed ruby-colored tent as bodies squirm in tune to rhythmic drums and string instruments. Squeals and chatter battle with the music, filling the air. Some folks wear the finest garments they own—silk slacks or breezy gossamer skirts in every shade imaginable—but the majority wear only their skin.

Tonight's bacchanal is especially rambunctious. The pleasant weather allows for celebrating on the beach rather than in the palace, like we've been limited to in the weeks past, and the joy is contagious.

I fan myself with one hand, lifting a heavy curtain of hair off my neck with the other.

"I don't know how they stand to have a fire in this heat," Ilona says, her freckled face moist from the humidity. She pulls her fiery red curls off her shoulders, tying them with a strip of cloth. "That cannot be comfortable."

"It's not about their comfort. It's all about the *atmosphere*," I say, reciting my mother's words with an eye roll.

Mother prefers to go all out for the events she hosts; she has a flair for the extravagant. Though she's uncharacteristically late tonight.

It's just Ilona and me sitting on a blanket littered with snacks, in a grand tent watching the revelers. Our stomachs are filled to the brim, and our bare toes wander off the blanket's edge, digging into the cool sand as we watch the night's events. The tent's opaque material is special—a one-way viewing fabric. We can see out onto the beach, but no one can see in.

"Don't you pity them?" Ilona asks, stuffing a chunk of cheese in her mouth, moaning at how good it tastes. "Goddess above, save their poor souls."

I grab a piece of bread off the wicker platter and chuck it at her. She ducks just in time, and it misses, hitting the cloth behind her. Her pale cheeks flush as she swallows her mouthful.

"Oh gosh, Astrid. You know that's not what I meant. I meant save them from the heat, not from you. The poor things will probably die of heat stroke or dehydration long before you even—"

She catches herself rambling and trails off. I snicker. Ilona might be my best friend—my only friend—but she fears my mother and me. There isn't any real reason for it, at least not one she's aware of. It's not like we've ever used our magic on her. Mother only uses her myndox powers on her enemies and disobedient servants—persuading them to do her bidding with mental manipulation—and I only use my vygora powers once a week at these bacchanals, when I absorb the life force energy of a willing participant to transfer to Mother.

It's dirty, useless magic that I neither want nor need.

But if Ilona knew I was responsible for her mother's death, she would have true reason to fear me. Her sentiments would transform to hate in the blink of an eye.

It was an accident. I discovered what I was in that moment, in the most unfortunate of ways, when I was nothing more than an innocent six-year-old with a proud, gap-tooth grin.

I only remember a plump, redheaded woman hugging me—Mother's handmaiden. The hug was enchanting, like warm sunshine on my bare skin. Until the woman went still and the feeling washed away. She went slack in my arms, and I didn't have the strength to hold her upright as she toppled to the ground, shriveled beyond her years as if she had aged decades in those brief moments.

Hours later, Mother found me sobbing on my bony knees at the woman's side, fists clutching her skirts. She took one look at the desiccated face before me, those unseeing eyes, and recoiled.

That was the day we learned I'm a vygora—an energy reader and life force absorber—but not a regular vygora. Transference is unheard of, yet I can absorb and transfer energy from one body to another, much to Mother's delight.

At first, Mother only brought me prisoners to practice my ability on. When the well of prisoners ran dry, she sought volunteers to come to the palace grounds under the guise of these weekly festivities. Over the years, the gatherings have become larger and more exciting—the islanders eager to partake in a bacchanal with their queen. As for Ilona, she never learned the truth about her mother's death. We took her in, and she's been like a sister to me—proof that my callous mother does indeed have a heart despite what the masses assume.

"They're well aware of their potential sacrifice. They choose to be here, Ilona," I say, fingering a frayed edge of the blanket. "I'm not the monster here."

"I love you, I do, but I just find it hard to believe so many people willingly show up each week, knowing they might die." She sighs, but her emerald eyes don't waver from my face. As irrationally fearful as she can be, Ilona always says what's on her mind and keeps it straight with me. At least someone does.

"It's their choice." I shrug, not wanting to get worked up over something I can't change.

"Are you sure your mother doesn't... you know, influence them?"

I sigh. This again?

Mother doesn't use her abilities on innocents. I may have had my doubts in the past, but she's denied it any time I've asked. I truly hope she doesn't invade the minds of others out of selfishness. Then again, she hosts these weekly sacrifices purely for her benefit. She has me drain a willing participant of their life force, only to transfer it to her so she can stay young, beautiful, and powerful.

She is known among the people of the island—and even those living across the Insipid Sea—for making morally ambiguous decisions. Like executing all the island prisoners when I was young. Nobody knows the truth—that she rounded them up for me to practice my powers on.

It worked for us both: she became infamous, and I was protected.

Crime rates certainly dropped after that decree. They began

calling her the Dead Queen because of her supposed ruthlessness. It's a nickname she now wears proudly. But she is capable of compassion. Why else would she take in a young Ilona and shelter her from the truth of her own mother's death?

As uncomfortable as I am with murdering people on a weekly basis to allow Mother to stay young and powerful, I truly believe the island of Hakran *is* safer with her as their queen. Our rule is better than the alternatives.

For example, the countries on the mainland, like Stellaris, are strict and old-fashioned. They don't let women rule or join the guard. They marry off their heirs to other countries for political alliances. It's barbaric and oppressive, especially considering our magic came from the original goddess long ago.

Despite her vices, Mother has been a good ruler. Her mental powers help her rule effectively.

"Of course she doesn't use her power on them." I pluck a purple grape and toss it up to catch. I miss, and it bounces off my nose before rolling into the sand. "She wouldn't do that."

"How sure are you? What if she's manipulating them into thinking they want to be a sacrifice?"

"She's not that powerful. You know she can't affect people beyond her immediate proximity, let alone control the entire village like you're suggesting."

"What if that's what she wants you to think? What if she's got a hold on you too, and you're doing her bidding against your will?" Her voice drops an octave. "I know she's your mother. I mean, she's practically mine as well, *and* she's the queen, but I can't help it. I find it hard to trust myndoxes."

"Why are you doing this again? Is this your way of justifying my choices instead of accepting me the way I am? Am I not good enough for the perfect Ilona? Too dark, too broken, too willing to do my duty and protect my people that you have to change my narrative?"

"Gosh, no," she whispers.

"Then let it go. Stop making me feel bad about completing my duty."

"I just... I've been having this recurring dream... It feels so real. And in it, you're confronting your mother about her lies. I'm not really sure what the full extent of it was... I can't remember. But I have this weird feeling, and then—"

"It's a dream," I say in a flat voice. "A nightmare. Whatever you want to call it. It isn't real."

"But it feels so real. And it's recurring. I keep having the same one!"

"Just because it feels real doesn't mean it is. You of all people should know this."

"Maybe. Or maybe Enira is capable of more than you think. Do you truly believe her power—"

"Oh, does it truly matter, dear Ilona?" Mother's monotone voice reaches my ears, and I look over my shoulder to see her parting the tent's flap and entering. Her ebony eyes pierce me, and her blood-red lips curve up on the side. Tonight, she wears a dress—if that's what it can be called—that matches her eyes. It's constructed of thin swatches, which barely cover her sensitive bits.

Ilona wipes her hands on her slacks and stands, eyes on the ground. "I'm s-sorry, Queen Enira. I didn't mean it."

"Your chatter is bordering on treasonous today. You know how I handle treason, regardless of the mouth from which it spills," Mother says. She waggles a finger before gliding to my side, skirt swishing around her thighs. Pausing behind me, she rakes her ruby nails through my sleek hair. "Darling, you are goddess-blessed with such luxurious locks. Have I informed you of how lucky you are?"

Fighting a scowl, I keep my eyes locked on the revelers outside the tent instead. A droopy-eyed brunette with sun-crisped skin takes off her top. She's so close to us that her elbow swipes the tent's fabric. Her large, bare breasts hang heavily. Reddish-brown nipples stare at me like lopsided eyes, as if they can see me through the opaque fabric after all. "Yes. You have, Mother."

"Oh, what I would give for such hair." Her voice is sharp as glass as she pulls her hands away, reaching for the pile of scarlet fabric on the ground by my side—the veyl I wear during these ceremonies. Tutting with dismay, she shakes out the sand and crumbs. "Ilona, run along, dear. Astrid must tend to her duties. You two have dallied long enough."

"Yes, Queen." Ilona gives an awkward half bow. She's been with us seventeen years now, since we were both six, and still isn't sure how to address Mother. I'd laugh if I wasn't so annoyed at her. Despite our quarrel, she reaches in to hug me, whispering in my ear, "I'll see you later. Remember who you are. The most incredibly strong woman I know."

With a quick wave, she parts the tent's slit and darts away. She'll likely head up the trail to the palace rather than stick around the beach. Like me, she enjoys watching the debauchery but doesn't care to take part. I bet I'll find her sipping a cup of ginger tea and reading a book up in her suite after the ceremony.

"Was that necessary, Mother?" I snatch the veyl from her hands, not looking forward to putting it on. The people don't know I'm the one who performs the transference. Mother keeps me covered, referring to me only as "the vessel" during the bacchanal and transference ceremony. She says it's safer this way, so people don't know what their princess is truly capable of. Plus, it makes her look even more commanding to be fully in control of a being with such dangerous power.

Vain.

Other than Ilona and Mother, and perhaps a few of the queen's closest advisors, no one knows I'm the one underneath these concealing drabs each week.

"It was," she says. "You two have spent more than enough time on gluttony this evening. She distracts you."

"No, actually she keeps me grounded and makes me feel more human, Mother." *Unlike you,* I want to add, but I keep my mouth shut.

"Quit with the dramatics." With her porcelain-smooth skin and severe black bob, she looks like my sister rather than my mother. Perks of receiving the extra life force energy. Though the texture of our hair is similar, my skin is a deeper olive than hers, my eyes a unique shade of teal. Where her features are sharp and angular, mine are softer. Attributes from my father, I'd assume, though I've never met the man. In my twenty-three years, my mother and I have only spoken about the topic a handful of times. Mother claims she had many lovers around the time she conceived me and that it makes no difference which male sponsored my creation. Crass.

"Go. The energy is resplendent tonight. Do not let it go to waste."

It's only one night a week.

It's not all the time.

I'm goddess-blessed.

I can do this.

"Yes, Mother." Groaning inwardly, I stand, slipping the veyl over my head. The heavy fabric covers all five feet of me from head to toe, falling in a pool by my sandy feet. Not a single milli-meter of flesh peeks through; there's not even a cut out for my eyes. Like the tent's fabric, the veyl allows me to see out, but nobody can see in.

"Go, Astrid!" She grabs my shoulders, steering me to the tent's slit and pushing me out into the night.

Outside the tent, the air is only a few insignificant degrees cooler. My thick thighs stick together. Salt from the sea wafts through the air, mingling with the fire's smoky scent.

As I round the tent, making my way toward the bonfire on the beach, my feet drag. Bacchanals awaken my guilt. I don't want to steal the life force of others to keep Mother young and healthy. But I also know it's our best way to protect our rule on the island. The sacrifice of one life keeps many others safe.

Mother once said, "People can fear you, or they can love you, Astrid. One offers protection, while the other makes you weaker. Let them fear you."

If they fear Mother, her power, no one will question her rule. The other countries stay away; we're protected from their potential invasions. The islanders are safe because they remain obedient. Crime is nonexistent. The palace servants stay loyal. Everything runs efficiently.

Turning back toward the tent, I see my mother standing with hands folded delicately in front of her. Elegant. Graceful. She's a stunning woman, but one look at her face reminds me of what she is capable of.

She's the only person I know of who can enter someone's mind and influence their thoughts, shaping their reality until they submit to her control. I obey her because I value my freedom. Some might say that makes me selfish or weak, but I say it makes me smart.

In the past, she's threatened to force me into line if I disobey, but she's never actually used her powers on me.

At least, not that I'm aware of.

I'd know.

Or would I?

Ilona's words haunt me, and I curse her under my breath.

Bodies sway in circles around the bonfire, succumbing to the trance-like rhythm of the drums as I draw nearer, dragging my feet through the sand. Cheers and chatter litter the air, and the energy is ecstatic. Ilona is right. It's strange that each person is so joyous at the prospect of possibly sacrificing their life. It's common knowledge this isn't a normal party, yet they're always utterly delighted.

But there's no way they're *all* under Mother's influence. Nobody's magic is that strong.

Countless bobble-headed partygoers thrash against one another. Scanning the crowd of sticky flesh, I look for someone highly energetic—someone young, with much life to give. On the other side of the fire, near the water, a group of six is fully engrossed in one another as their lips mash and their hands explore. People get carried away during Mother's bacchanals, which works perfectly. Sexual energy is one of the strongest and easiest to absorb because of its intensity.

My cheeks no longer blaze with heat like they did when I was young.

I start in their direction, but movement farther down the beach catches my eye. Moonlight gilds the brunette I saw earlier, the one with the observant breasts, as she straddles a man with thick eyebrows, their mouths merging ravenously.

She will do.

Heading in her direction, I pass the bulk of dancers, thankful to leave the heat of the fire behind, as I slink toward the pair.

"Vessel! May the original goddess bless you!" someone yells over the ruckus. A few more people turn, regarding me with awe.

Conversation picks up a notch as they recognize the symbolic red veyl. A few people bow their heads in a show of respect, and it's quite humorous, considering many are stark naked.

If only they could see it was their princess under this garb. *That* would be a priceless reaction.

Others dance faster, moan louder, thrash against each other harder, all in a desperate bid for me to acknowledge them. To choose them. They *want* me to see how lively they are, that they're worthy of sacrificing their life for their queen.

Ilona's words make me view it all through a new lens tonight, and it looks sad. Pathetic. They truly want to be the reason their queen is young, beautiful, and forever powerful. Week after week, I see so many of the same faces. A few are even nobles from the village.

Ilona's voice haunts my mind: *What if she's manipulating them into thinking they want to be a sacrifice?*

Balling my hands into fists beneath my veyl, I brush off the thought. There's no way Mother could manipulate this many people for so long, and from such a distance. Her power doesn't work like that. As odd as it may seem to Ilona that people would choose to die for their queen, she needs to accept it's true.

My lungs burn for fresh air as I close in on the brunette and her thick-browed man. Their exposed, overlapping thighs are slick with humidity and pleasure. Averting my eyes, I reach one bare hand through the only slit in my veyl, planting it on the woman's back.

She shudders at my touch.

"Forgive me," I mumble, knowing she can't hear me. Even if she could, she wouldn't accept my apology. They always find honor in their sacrifice.

Focusing on pulling her energy into my body, my hand tingles, emanating a soft golden glow where it meets her flesh. The woman gasps at the sensation, throwing her head back with a throaty moan and thrusting her hips forward, as if my touch is as pleasurable as the man's lips were on her neck a moment prior.

My own eyes roll back in my head as a wave of synchronized pleasure consumes me too. There's no denying how good it feels. For us both. I can't stop, can't pull away. The sensation is incredible. Energy absorption is pure indulgence for me. I hate that something so cruel feels so good—and that I like it.

The surge rushes through my veins as I pull all the energy out of her body with a single touch. It continues to pour into me until she's left dry and unconscious, and the connection between us fades away. Drained of her youth, all that remains is a shriveled shell of a human. Her head flops forward, hanging limp, and I'm grateful I can't see her withered cheeks or the final gaze of her vacant eyes.

"Thank you for choosing her, vessel." The thick-browed man places her limp body on the sand before bowing to me and taking off into the crowd.

Waves lap the shore a few feet away, almost inaudible over the chaotic music and shrill revelry around me. I'm tempted to close that distance. To step deep enough into the ocean that it wraps its liquid arms around me, absolving me of my guilt.

But I don't.

Mother's waiting for me.

The sacrifice is over, but the celebration is not. As the wine flows and fire burns, so will the activities of the night. The people will continue to party, thanking their queen and the original goddess for blessing them, while I curse her for damning me.

CHAPTER TWO

After absorbing energy, I'm euphoric. I can think clearer, move faster, breathe better. My senses come alive. With the life force of another coursing through my veins, I am complete.

Making my way through the writhing crowd, I move as quickly as I can with the heavy veyl and dank heat weighing me down. My feet sink into the cool sand with each step, slowing me down further. The night isn't over yet. Now, I must meet Mother in the throne room for the transference ceremony. I can't wait to give her what she wants and be done with it so I can go back to being myself...at least until this time next week.

I want nothing more than to join Ilona in her suite and catch up on the latest palace gossip over a cup of tea. She's befriended most of the kitchen staff and always hears the most interesting tidbits of conversation. Most of their information is false, but it doesn't make the tales any less entertaining. Perhaps tomorrow we will even wake early and ride to Paramour Falls—a set of twin waterfalls hidden deep in the jungle that cascade down into a lovely freshwater swimming hole. One of my favorite places on the island. The heat makes the journey a burden, but the horses don't mind the distance since they're able to wade into the shallow end of the pond to cool down.

As the sand gives way to packed dirt at the edge of the jungle,

I increase my pace. I scurry along the gently sloping, narrow trail toward the palace. I'm in a hurry to finish the night.

The thick, lush canopies overhead obscure the night sky. Without the moonlight or the glow of the bonfire to illuminate the forest, it's almost pitch black, but I've traversed this short distance enough times that I could make it back to the palace with my eyes closed.

The jungle always has a fresh aroma. Rejuvenating, despite the stifling air. The cacophony of insects resonates around me. They don't sleep at this hour.

My hands itch to rip off the veyl so I can run the rest of the way home and be done with the transference, but I must stay covered in case of wandering eyes. Plus, Mother always makes a ceremony out of the transference. She invites her advisors, the diplomats stationed here, and the village's noble families to bear witness as I release the newly obtained energy into her body.

With flowing wine and lowered inhibitions, the transference ceremonies end up being as scandalous as the bacchanals. The main difference is the power divide among the attendees—the bacchanals consist mostly of ordinary townsfolk while the ceremony consists of those with magic, money, or status.

Sometimes, Mother's guests will attend the bacchanal, then the ceremony after. Like they can't indulge themselves enough.

Considering I rarely attend any of Mother's other events, no one notices that their princess never attends the ceremony or bacchanals. I skip most things she hosts—her balls, socials, seasonal dinners, and the like. I go unnoticed as the princess, which is a big reason why it's easy to go unnoticed as the vessel.

Since the guards are rotated out every few years and turnover for servants in the palace is high, it's hard to make friends. At this point, I don't even bother to learn most of their names.

Blades of grass tickle my feet as I emerge from the jungle thicket and cross the manicured lawn. Although the palace, with its rounded mansard roofs and marble and limestone walls is grand, it sits only one story high. The low, sturdy design protects it from the high winds and rains during storm season, while the pale stone reflects heat.

The normal island storms are dangerous on their own, but sometimes they're fueled by wild magic dredged up from the deep sea. The magic fuels the storms in a deadly combination of hail, lightning, fire, and high winds, causing extensive damage and deaths. The wild magic itself isn't deadly—the way it intensifies the storms is. Luckily it's only elemental magic, similar to aethyn power, and nothing like myndox or vygora magic.

The palace, sprawled across the well-tended courtyard, consists of three main wings. The center portion—where the central foyer, throne room, ballroom, main dining room, and largest library are—is slightly taller than the side wings. The wing to the left, where I'm headed, is where the servants' quarters, kitchens, and stables are located. On the opposite side, to the right, are the main suites. The royal wing. There's also a plethora of unnecessary rooms scattered throughout the palace—receiving rooms, solariums, lavatories, smaller libraries, pantries, and more.

Mother loves excess.

Our lavish palace set high on the jungle hill, away from the village center, certainly reflects that.

There's even a subterranean level that houses the war room, sparring areas, and safe spaces in which to practice magic. Deeper yet, there's a level I've never visited: a dungeon of sorts known as the pit. As far as I know, it's unused. I've never been down there because it requires an authorized touch for entry. Only Mother and her commanders have access.

Thanks to aethyns with the power of harnessing water elements, the palace's stone is infused with ice, kept magically cool. A reprieve from the heat.

Mother's voice echoes in my head: *The vessel should enter discreetly like a servant, not through the main doors like a guest.*

I pass the gardens and stables, heading toward the servants' entrance off to the left. Fire-infused sconces, anchored to the marble walls, light the courtyard—lit thanks to aethyn power as well—and illuminate the entrance.

Something catches my eye next to the door, and I pause. The pale orange light of the flames washes over a lean man dressed in unusual clothes. Rather than the typical Hakranian bright colors and thin layers, he's wearing a beige doublet and dark brown breeches. Chocolate-brown waves messily frame his face as he leans against the wall.

I hesitate, eyeing his demeanor, and wonder who the hell he is and what he's doing here.

Another, less malicious, side of my vygora power is the ability to read other people's emotions. It's not as exciting as pulling their life force out, but it's harmless and sometimes useful. Like now.

Focusing, I close my eyes and try to draw his emotions toward me…but instead of receiving a wave of foreign emotion, nothing comes. It's like he's empty of emotion. But that's not possible. *Everyone* has emotions, even if it's subtle like relaxation or contentment.

My brows draw together, and I open my eyes to ensure he hasn't left.

He hasn't moved.

Clearing my mind, I try again.

Emptiness greets me, as if there's a barrier I can't cross. Even with the excess life force heightening my own senses and power,

I still can't draw his emotions out.

What the hell?

I scowl at him from beneath the veyl, but he startles me when he cocks open an eye, grinning right at me as if he can see me beneath the cloth.

"Hello, mi lady," he says with a smirk. His voice is sensual. Though I can't read his emotions with my power, his demeanor and tone tell me he's relaxed—arms crossed, head tilted back, one foot propped up on the wall behind him.

The top few buttons of his shirt are undone, and as he moves the gap in cloth widens to reveal a tanned chest. My cheeks heat.

Great. Naked bodies no longer make me blush, but apparently a fully dressed stranger does.

With a physique like that, I'd say he's a laborer. But despite being a little disheveled, his clothing is too nice. Although it's clearly foreign, it's clean and well-made.

We aren't expecting any new diplomats or visitors from other countries, but even if we were, why would he be out here, alone?

Something is clearly off about this man... If I weren't so intrigued, I'd be more alarmed.

Why can't I pull his emotions?

"You don't belong here," I say.

I shouldn't engage him. Mother would be furious if she knew I spoke from beneath my veyl. The vessel doesn't speak. Someone could recognize my voice. Impulsivity and curiosity win the battle though, locking my feet in place.

His grin deepens, and his eyes crinkle adorably at the corners. "And you do?" He shrugs, standing tall and releasing his arms from where they were folded across his chest.

"Clearly."

"You could be anyone beneath that curtain."

"I'm Queen Enira's vessel," I say with conviction. Everyone knows of the queen's power and of her vessel. She's feared far and wide. I might not be able to draw his emotions toward me, but I bet he would still succumb to me absorbing his life force if I needed to. Perhaps that's why I'm not as threatened as I should be.

"Would the Dead Queen truly let her prized toy traipse through the jungle unattended?"

"I don't have time for this." I step forward, but he moves in front of me, blocking the door with his muscular body. As much as I want to figure out why he's here, Mother will not be pleased if I keep her waiting.

"Seems dangerous, if you ask me."

"I didn't."

"If you were truly the vessel, you could stop…a threat, no?"

"Shoo."

"Did you shoo me?" His mouth quirks with humor as he looks down at me. He's at least a foot taller than I am.

"You shouldn't be back here." If he's here for the bacchanal, he should be down by the beach where the people play, not here by the servants' entrance, especially not if he's visiting Hakran from elsewhere.

"They say Queen Enira covers you because you're hideous. A demon, in fact." Even though his smile fades, there's a twinkle in his eye. His comment was meant as a challenge.

I ignore him, moving around him to get to the door, but he sidesteps, blocking my path again. His scent invades me—something like sandalwood. Intoxicating.

"They say many things," I reply. It's true. I hear most of it, especially with Ilona being so close to the chatty palace staff. I wonder if they'd say such cruel things if they knew the vessel was their princess.

"I think the truth is in what they don't say. That your queen is nothing but a manipulating—"

"Stop!" I raise a hand under my veyl though I know he can't see it. Lowering my voice, I add, "That's treason. She can execute you for it." Mother doesn't tolerate traitorous remarks well. Not that we've had any for as long as I can remember, but there's a reason for that.

Despite the heat, a chill works its way up my spine. My breath comes in quick pants. I didn't think this man was a threat initially, but the way he's talking is making me quite uncomfortable. Being alone with him out here feels like a bad idea.

"Not if you don't tell her." He takes another step closer, he's now so close that his body brushes the fabric of my veyl. He doesn't look much older than me and he carries himself with cocky confidence. "As for what you're hiding under there, I'll find out soon enough."

I stare at him in shock, frozen in place by his arrogance.

Did he just threaten to uncover my identity?

He throws in a casual wink before sauntering off around the side of the palace, disappearing into the deep-blue shadows of night.

Whoever that man is, he's a threat.

As I make my way to the throne room, my head swivels compulsively with the unsettling need to check over my shoulder every few steps.

Scurrying through the vast marble corridors toward the main hall, I pass a few wide-eyed servants and masked guards who nod in respect.

They don't respect me for me; they respect me out of fear of Mother.

My mind flits to the arrogant stranger who seemed to neither fear nor respect Mother. I wonder who he is and how long he'll be here. Secrets live in those golden-brown eyes of his, and his mysterious intentions make me nervous. No way would Mother allow someone she doesn't trust to roam unguarded around the palace.

And why couldn't I feel his energy? I'd think something was wrong with my magic, but with the extra life force swimming through me from the bacchanal, I'm as strong as ever.

I can't help but find myself intrigued. Drawn to the potential danger.

Hopefully he's discreet and doesn't do anything idiotic to end up on the receiving end of Mother's wrath.

I move as fast as the veyl will let me, grateful for the cool stones of the palace walls. Inside, without the thick air of summer pressing on my lungs, I can breathe more easily.

Despite growing up here, I've never quite felt at home in the palace. Perhaps it's the opulence, the vastness. With white marble, golden fixtures, and an excess of columns and windows, it's absolutely stunning, but it lacks something I can't quite put into words.

I rest comfortably here, but my heart isn't attached to the space. There's no ache to return when I spend the day away. No deep relaxation that penetrates my bones after a long day.

No grand excitement breaking up the monotonous days. Perhaps that's another reason I'm drawn to that mysterious man.

Four guards stand outside of the throne room, giving me a small nod of acknowledgement when I arrive. They are dressed in identical midnight-colored leather uniforms with headgear, and everything other than their jaw, eyes, and hands are covered. Male and female guards are virtually indistinguishable from one another. Most of them have similar dark coloring and muscular builds, but I can tell some of them apart by their stature and their eye color.

Newer guards wield basic staffs with blunt tops and minimal functionality—though I'm sure they could still do some damage—or no staff at all. Commanders and the higher-ranking guards wield elemental staffs infused with aethyn power, which allows them to use the elements as weapons.

Most of the commanders and guards are posted near the coasts, with the sentries stationed inside the palace. I've never gotten to know any of them, other than Commander Jamell, who stays at the palace by Mother's side and trains with me a few times a week.

Everyone on the island knows they're here as a precaution. A show of power. If anyone ever tried to overtake the palace, the real threat is Mother. If anyone were to get near her, they would be vulnerable to her effortless mental manipulation.

Or maybe the real threat is me? I'd imagine if the situation were dire enough, Mother would reveal the depths of my vygora powers and allow me to protect us.

They believe I can only read emotions as a vygora, and thus they think me weak. Imagine their surprise at discovering their princess can absorb life force with a simple touch. That the vessel is not a faceless puppet controlled by their queen after all.

Part of me almost wishes we'd find ourselves under attack so I could reveal the truth and allow the two sides of me to merge into one. I hate being torn between personas, not knowing who I really am.

Tonight, I continue playing my role of vessel for Mother and make my way through the throne room toward Mother's dais. Even from a distance, her smile is vicious. Her gold crown glints with black diamonds, which complement the coloring of her onyx throne but contrast severely against the pale stone walls and floor.

A few dozen people stand on either side of the center walkway, watching as I cover the distance. Paying them no mind, I focus on Mother's throne in front of me. Just a few yards ahead now, three steps up.

I can't help but think importing marble to the island must've been incredibly expensive, since it's not found naturally on Hakran. Building the entire palace from expensive stone was merely one way of flaunting her wealth. Shame burns in me as I think of the many villagers living in poverty while we live in excess.

The mass of people is a kaleidoscope of color in the edges of my vision. Their liveliness is at odds with the woman they worship.

Their Dead Queen.

Such a juxtaposition.

Some people bow their heads and chant small prayers to the goddess under their breath. I roll my eyes at their credulity, knowing they can't see me.

Mother stands as I draw near, raising her arms above her head and looking up toward the towering ceiling. A large oval window sits behind her, and moonlight leaks in, highlighting her in silver light. Other than a few sconces on the walls, the window is the only light source. On darker nights—when the moon is hidden behind storm clouds—it's too dark to see the steps in front of me. Luckily, there's enough of a glow tonight to see as I carefully climb, cautious of getting tangled in the veyl and tripping.

Ilona's words about Mother's elaborate manipulation have burrowed their way into my head, unsettling me. Distracting me. I stumble as I step toward Mother.

"Bestowed by the goddess! My vessel. Bring forth the life

force and bless your queen," she says, her voice echoing off the stone.

The crowd replies in unison, "Blessed by the goddess. Long live the queen!" They break out in an uproar of cheers, and the guards situated around the room pound their staffs onto the floor. It echoes like a familiar song.

Clang, clang, clang.

Kneeling on the cool stone in front of her chair, I hang my head in submission. Mother remains standing, giving her speech of thanks to the original goddess—the most powerful being to ever exist—for splitting her power and creating the many old gods and goddesses that used to be worshipped, for allowing those gods and goddesses to procreate and pass their power down to those worthy of the magic, and for giving her such a *blessing.*

Stories.

That's what they are. Myths that the people cling to, that explain the otherwise unknown.

She launches into a speech about how the people must trust and follow her.

I'm glad she can't see my facial expressions under the veyl.

"With the life force energy from our sacred sacrifices, your queen will remain young and powerful—able to protect our beloved island of Hakran from uncertainty or peril. Your queen will ensure the longevity of your kin. With these sacrifices, we attain security. We prosper."

"Riveting," I mumble sarcastically under my breath. Mother's use of the third-person perplexes me.

The crowd roars back, "Security, longevity, prosperity. Blessed be the people. Long live the queen!"

With my head still bowed, my neck begins to ache.

Hurry up already.

Finally, I hear her call to me.

"Come, vessel."

She sits on her throne, and I crawl the two feet forward, trying not to become tangled in my veyl. It has become second nature after so many transference ceremonies, but I still dread this part every time.

Reaching a bare hand out of the veyl's slit, I slide it under Mother's wispy skirts, planting it on the naked skin of her ankle. Once my palm is wrapped around her calf, I focus on calling forth the energy I absorbed from the bacchanal's sacrifice.

From the girl with too much sun and heavy breasts.

Poor girl.

I didn't even know her name; I doubt Mother would even care. Trying not to picture her face, I swallow my guilt as I complete the task.

The unnatural, miserable task of transference.

Absorbing energy from a given sacrifice fills me with pleasure—it's as if the life force is desperate to be consumed by me—but transference is radically different. It's as if my body, my magic, pleads with me not to let the energy go. It's pure agony.

As if it's warning me to stop.

Fire consumes my body as I try to release the energy, as though my organs are melting inside of me. Gritting my teeth, I fight against the pain, forcing the energy out through my palm and into Mother's skin. This is clearly not painful for her.

Blackness swarms in front of my vision, and I begin to sweat despite the cool temperature of the throne room. By the time the feeling ebbs, I'm dizzy.

Dry.

Empty.

The crowd continues to chant behind me.

"Blessed be the people. Long live the queen! Blessed be the people! Long live the queen!"

There's a faraway ringing in my ears, and it invades my head. Normally, I'm tired after a transference, but once the pain subsides, my regular strength and energy return. This time, I'm depleted, lacking the strength to even raise my head and look at Mother.

Without warning, my stomach roils, and a bitter taste arises in my mouth. I dry-heave once before the entire contents of my stomach—half-digested beef and potato stew—spew in a chunky mess inside of the veyl.

The stench is too much—heavy and sour—the veyl suffocating.

A raw, carnal screech of disgust leaves Mother's throat as she places her heel in the center of my chest, shoving me away from her. She pushes a bit too hard, and I tumble backwards down the cold steps. With the veyl's fabric tangling around me, I'm unable to catch myself.

It's a quick fall, but my head slams against the hard floor with a whack.

The last thing I hear is Mother calling for a guard to escort me away.

Then silence consumes me. Darkness feasts on my senses.

CHAPTER THREE

My head pounds out a dull rhythm inside of my skull as I come to. Accompanying the headache is a sore throat and an uncomfortably dry mouth. I'm parched.

It takes me a second to realize my veyl is off. The feeling of familiar silky sheets and the comforting smell of jasmine greets me, relaxing me slightly.

Wait—who brought me to my room?

Mother's been so strict about my staying covered, so she won't be pleased my identity has been revealed. Goddess save whoever took my veyl off.

"Good. You're awake, Princess." The gruff voice startles me, and my heart jumps in my chest as I sit up.

"Oh, Cedrik. I didn't see you there." Our palace healer stands hunched over my writing desk, his weathered face taut with concern as he fiddles with a small vial of liquid. Various bottles of different shapes and sizes are scattered before him. His tonics and potions.

Cedrik is a vygora like me. Rare in a different way, with the ability to read the state of one's body rather than one's emotions. Without any kind of examination or interrogation, he can determine what is amiss with a patient. He's also well-educated in potion-mixing and herbalism, so he can treat almost any curable ailment.

Whereas I feel the emotions of others, Cedrik experiences their discomfort and suffering. I'm surprised it hasn't hardened him. Working at the palace is better than being a village healer, though, or worse, being a city healer in another country. At least here we only suffer from minor wounds or illnesses. Things like cuts or colds or sprains. And much less frequently than the villagers.

"How long was I out?" I ask.

"Not long. Less than an hour," he says. "Here." He hands me a clear, bubbling tonic that smells sharp and bitter. "For your headache. Drink it down."

I oblige, trying not to choke as the repulsive taste coats my tongue and slides down my throat. It's warm and fizzy.

"Eck." Gagging, I make a face and look to my night table for a carafe of water. Cedrik was prepared though, and he hands me a glass. I accept it gratefully, gulping it down and washing away the foul taste.

"You're my hero, Cedrik."

Additional wrinkles appear around his mouth and eyes when he smiles. His is the face of a kind man with a tired soul. Turning his back to me, he crosses the room, grabbing his oversized leather bag from the floor. He rummages around before pulling out a vial of pale yellow liquid and placing it on my desk.

"Anti-nausea tonic. Drink it before your next transference." Packing away the rest of his implements into his bag, he returns to my side, silver-flecked brows drawn tight.

Fuck.

He knows I'm the vessel. I was really hoping he didn't, for fear of what Mother might do to him. She could manipulate him to forget, of course, but unless she actively works to keep her hold on him, it'll fade. If he leaves her proximity, it'll fade. I fear Mother would take drastic measures to keep our secret.

"That doesn't normally happen, now does it?" he asks, ripping me from my spiraling thoughts.

I shake my head. "I haven't vomited or passed out before, but sometimes I feel incredibly nauseated."

"Well, you were fairly dehydrated and exhausted, and that likely contributed to the little episode you had. Next time you feel like that, sit down and take a breather. Let it pass. The syncope and headache can be attributed to whacking your head on the marble. It's lucky you didn't sustain a concussion or injury. That mother of yours—"

"She didn't mean it, Cedrik."

"I'm sure, Princess." He agrees, but the knowing look in his eyes tells a different story.

Mother didn't mean to kick me so hard. She'd certainly meant to push me away from her—it would have been abominable for the vessel to soil the queen with vomit—but there's no way she meant to send me tumbling down the stairs. She'd never hurt me purposely.

Would she?

Ilona's words come back to haunt me. *Maybe she's capable of more than you think.*

But even if Ilona was right, and Mother does manipulate me, that doesn't mean she wants to harm me.

My doors are thrown open with flourish as Mother enters the room, ordering her personal guards to wait in the hallway to give us privacy. The doors close with a click, and she crosses over to my bedside, looking at me without expression. I sit up taller, trying not to look weak, an automatic reaction in her presence.

"Verdict?" She glares down her nose at Cedrik, like he's an inconvenience. Not like he was the one responsible for mending my twisted ankle last month after I fell from my horse or the one who cleared her intolerable head cold a few weeks prior.

Using my power, I pull her energy toward me. She is impatient, annoyed, likely because of my incident…but there's something else, something unsettling. She's on edge, which is unusual for her. Why?

Brushing it off, I close myself off from her feelings.

"It's likely the intensity of the transference is weighing on her," Cedrik says, his eyes meeting mine.

I look away, busying myself smoothing down my long hair before hopping out of bed. The only thing covering me is a thin night slip, so I rummage through my armoire, looking for a robe with which to cover myself. Finding a black satin robe, I throw it on, tying the belt tightly around my waist.

"What does that mean exactly, Cedrik?" Mother asks.

"The energy expulsion seems to be taking its toll on the young girl—"

Mother cuts him off with a loud sigh. "Tell me, what do you propose we do about that?"

"Cease the transferences."

Passing them, I part the floor-length turquoise curtains concealing the casement doors, throwing them open and hoping for a breeze. A wave of hot air hits me, and I regret the decision, shutting them immediately.

I can't wait until the weather cools.

Slinking into an oversized chair, I peer at Mother and Cedrik, trying to seem nonchalant when in truth I'm eager to see how this plays out. If Mother believed I was at risk from the transference, would she discontinue her bacchanals? Would she relieve me of my duties as the vessel? Would she put *me* before her own desires?

"Unacceptable."

Well, that's a no.

Mother digs her blood-red claws into Cedrik's chin, forcing him to look at her. His face pales, and he stutters as he tries to talk.

"She—I—I gave her an anti-nausea tonic to prevent the sickness from rising next time."

"So there will be a next time, yes, Cedrik?" Each time she says his name, it's condescending, a piercing blade.

"Yes, my queen." She releases her grip, allowing him to bow his head in submission. Straightening, he tightens his grip on his bag.

"So there is no problem after all?"

"Other than dehydration and nausea, none at all, my queen."

"Good." She smiles slyly at him.

"If she continues with the transferences, it would be my recommendation she gives less in order to preserve her own energy." He winces at Mother's expression. "Or that she take more life force to sustain you both?" He chokes the suggestion out, as if it pains him to say it.

It's a deplorable option, really. The last thing I want to do is kill more people than I already do.

"Dismissed," Mother says.

He swallows audibly, eyes shifting to me in a quick apology before he hustles toward the door.

"Oh, and Cedrik?"

"Yes, my queen?"

Her eyes narrow as her tone hardens. "You will not remember this visit. Princess Astrid and the vessel are not one and the same. You cared for the vessel, only, and never saw its face."

His eyes glaze over, and he nods slowly at Mother. Unease claws at my gut. This is bad.

I react quickly, drawing Cedrik's emotions out for a quick

reading before he can leave. Pulling his energy toward me, I look for an indicator that Mother's manipulation grips his mind—a void, emptiness, new emotions, anything—but I'm stunned when Cedrik's normal emotions crash into me: fear, loathing, sadness.

A chill tickles my spine despite the night's warmth. I'm picking up no trace of Mother's magic. I'm not sure what I was expecting, but I was hoping for some sort of indicator that he's under her control now. If there was, I would be able to tell who her victims are… but there's no way for me to know for certain.

Cedrik exits the room, doors clanging shut behind him. Mother turns to me, her eyes dark and steely. Something else gnaws at me. Her influence should wear off once Cedrik is no longer in her immediate proximity. So why did she let him put distance between them?

Either she's using her myndox powers as a temporary fix until she can deal with him in a more permanent manner, or her reach extends further than I was aware of.

Is she more powerful than she used to be? Or has she always been this powerful and I haven't noticed?

Ilona might be right about her. Could Mother truly be capable of manipulating all the villagers at the bacchanal? Forcing the sacrificial desire upon them? Have I been blind to her cruelties?

Whispers of her nickname flood my mind: *The Dead Queen.*

Could she be manipulating me too?

I think I'd know. I'd feel it somehow. Wouldn't I?

"Astrid, what a relief you can continue with our transferences," she says, pulling my attention to her. Forcing a smile, I try not to let my thoughts show. I've always had a certain amount of fearful awe in regard to her, but for the first time, I am truly terrified in her presence. She pats my head gently. "I would give much to have such a glamorous mane."

Running her claws through my sweat-matted hair, she works on detangling the knots. It's the only maternal gesture she offers me.

I hate my hair. It's hot, heavy, and stifling. But I let it grow because it earns compliments from her. I love when she plays with it and revel in her regard, but I'm starting to think she does it because she's obsessed with my hair, not because she wants to comfort me.

After everything that's happened this evening, she doesn't seem to care that *I'm* okay. No. She's pleased I can continue gifting her life forces—no matter the cost to me—and she's focused on my hair.

It's not love.

It's *envy*.

Closing my eyes, I steady my breathing as she continues raking her nails through the knots, tugging until they loosen. Finally, after a few tense minutes, she releases her grip on my hair, letting it fall against my back like a thick curtain.

"Thank the goddess, dear," she says dispassionately.

"Blessed by the goddess," I mumble back in response.

"Yes. Blessings," she says. With a bored expression, she exits the room.

As soon as she's gone, I snag the shears from my desk. Sitting on the ground before my floor-length mirror, I begin hacking away at my hair.

Chop.

Chop.

Chop.

With each snip, I curse—at Ilona for being right, at Mother for her apathy and manipulation, and at Cedrik for being cowardly.

Okay, the last one is unfairly harsh, considering I don't stand up to her either...at least not directly.

This little makeover is my way of rebelling against her and showing my disdain. I've never stood up to Mother. Never tried to push her buttons. This will be a good test to push back in a seemingly innocent way, to gauge her reaction. Plus, it's so damn hot, and I've been yearning for relief.

I snip all of my thick, dark locks until I'm left with an uneven pixie cut. Taking in the new look, I smile. Despite the ruggedness, the shorter style suits me. It highlights my round face, drawing attention to my teal eyes. Shows off my collarbone and neck. Already, I feel more attractive—more confident. Truly like myself.

Goddess, it feels so much better.

It's like I can breathe.

When I see Ilona later, I'll have her shape it up for me. She's quite talented with hairstyling and often, out of her own kindness, tends to the hair of the palace staff. I've asked her to cut my hair before, but she had refused for fear of Mother's wrath—noticing her obsession with my hair. Since I technically did the cutting, she has nothing to fear now.

The best part of all is that I'll never have to feel Mother's predatory claws running through my long strands ever again.

CHAPTER FOUR

A few minutes later, I'm standing in Ilona's room. I did not expect her to laugh as hard as she did.

"Gosh, A. What did you do to yourself?" she asks through her hands, attempting to muffle her laughter.

"What, you don't like it?" I fight to keep a straight face.

"Please tell me you'll let me fix it. I mean, it's quite lovely what you've attempted to do here, but I think I can touch it up a bit so that it's not so...edgy?"

"If you insist."

"Thank the goddess!"

"Oh as if you don't know that's why I'm here." I roll my eyes while she continues snickering.

Ilona's room is across the hallway from mine, making it easy for me to seek her out. When we were young, she shared a room with her mother in the servants' wing. After her mother's death, she began sneaking through the corridors to my room. Of course Mother knew the whole time, considering she has eyes and ears everywhere.

Instead of getting angry or kicking Ilona out, Mother took charge of her care. She even assigned Ilona this luxurious room in the royal wing.

The memories are hazy, and my chest twists at the recollection.

I'm conflicted about Mother's recent actions.

How can the woman who cared for Ilona and kept my secret about her mother's death be the same woman cruelly manipulating the entire village for her own shallow gain? My mind battles itself, as I attempt to rationalize the two different women Mother seems to be.

The one I remember.

And the one I see before me.

"You're so pertinacious sometimes; I worry you'd wear it like that just to make a statement."

"Pertinacious? New word from that doozy of a book you're reading?"

"It is." She smiles shyly. "I was trying it out. It's basically a fancy way of saying you're stubborn or resolute when it comes to upholding your choices. It could also be interpreted as—"

"I think you might be right, Ilona," I say, putting a halt to her rambling. Locking the door behind me, I cross her plush white rug—a risky choice of decor considering how often we used to sneak bottles of dark wine into the space—and take a seat beside her on the lavender chaise. Her room is a little smaller than mine and lacks a terrace. Although the furnishings in our rooms are almost the same, her room is full of beige and lavender hues, while mine is full of turquoise and gold.

"About you being *pertinacious?*" She gives me a puzzled look as she enters the bathroom, returning a moment later with shears and a comb. "You're surprised by that?"

"No, you twit." I toss a decorative pillow at her, and she holds up the scissors in defense.

"Careful!" she shrieks. "Don't torment the person about to give you a new hairdo, for goddess's sake."

"As if you can make it look any worse than it is."

We chuckle.

"How much shorter do you want to go?"

"I'm thinking wispy pixie layers." It's already short, barely covering my ears as is.

She runs her comb through my hair, making *hmm* noises as she inspects it. "It's admirable you tried, but I don't think haircutting is your forte. And you did this dry, didn't you? Don't answer that. I know you did. I can tell. We need to dampen this."

She beckons for me to follow her into the bathroom. After moistening my hair in the sink, she gestures for me to sit before her on the marble floor. It's uncomfortable, and the heady mixture of floral perfumes and sprays suffocates me, but I don't say anything. Better to do it in here and preserve her treasured rug from an onslaught of sheared hair.

"So what did you mean I might be right? About what?"

Soft *snips* fill the air, and a few dark tufts flutter down around me as she begins her work. Shutting my eyes, I heave a sigh.

"About Mother." There's a pause. Ilona remains silent as she waits for me to elaborate. "I think her power *is* stronger than I thought it was. I think she's hiding what she can do."

"She does hide what you can do, A, so why is it so far-fetched that she'd hide what *she* can do too?"

"It isn't. Not anymore."

"I know you didn't come to this conclusion based solely on my concerns. So will you please spill the story? What happened?"

She continues to work on my head as I tell her how I got sick during the transference and how Cedrik helped me. How Mother used her myndox power on him. I relay how I felt his regular emotions after Mother invaded his mind–nothing was skewed to indicate her invasion–and how it's impossible for me to know who has fallen prey to her manipulation.

A chunk of hair lands on my cheek, and I blow it off while Ilona scolds me about staying still.

"I'm surprised you haven't already heard the gossip about transference," I say. Ilona is social with the servants, and word travels fast around the palace.

"You know the girls get nervous chatting about Enira. I really don't hear as much as you think I do." Fingers dance across my head as she plays with the style, fluffing it up and chopping at straggling bits. "It's mostly drama such as who slept with who at the recent bacchanal, which servants are slacking, what we think the guards look like under the—"

"I get it. But if you hear anything about Mother, you'll tell me, right?"

"Of course."

She steps into my line of sight, biting her bottom lip. "How do you know her magic held? Or that she didn't harm him after?"

"I suppose I don't, but Mother's awfully calculated. She wouldn't let him go unless she was confident he'd keep her secrets one way or another. We need to talk to Cedrik and find out."

"As much as I'd love an opportunity to say I told you so again, I really do hope I'm wrong, A." Anguish fills her tone. We might bicker like sisters sometimes, but we'd never truly wish each other harm. She's the exact opposite of Mother—she'd never want to be right for the sake of ego.

"I know, Lonnie," I say, using the nickname I gave her when we were young. Normally she cringes and begs me not to call her that, but this time she doesn't protest. Her face contorts with concentration as she maneuvers around me, ensuring my ends are even.

A few minutes later she stands back, admiring her work.

"Goddess above. Maybe I *should've* cut your hair one of

those times you begged before. Forget Queen Enira's wrath, this is a marvelous look!" She claps her hands together and does a weird dance, finally setting the shears down. "This is *so* you, Astrid."

Grabbing my hand, she pulls me to my feet.

"Look, look." She pushes me toward the mirror above her counter. "Isn't it just gorgeous?"

A stranger stares back at me.

My fingers rise of their own accord, tracing the soft curves of my face as I stare into my blue-green eyes, the one feature I actually like. Ilona truly worked magic of her own—not the literal kind, but a beautiful, talented kind. The layers are short and choppy, a little longer on the top, shorter on the sides.

It feels refreshing. Lighter. Airier.

Turning, I grab her and pull her into a tight hug. "Thank you so much. I knew you'd make me look wonderful."

"No. It wasn't me, A. It's *you*. Your confidence and energy are what make you look wonderful."

Breaking away from the embrace, we smile at each other. Ilona is the sweetest person I know.

Guilt tries to claw itself out of my gut, but I force it down. Even after all this time, I can't help but wonder if Ilona would still love me the same if she knew I was responsible for her mother's death. Sure, I was only a child, and it was a tragic accident, but would she forgive me? Would she forgive me for keeping it a secret all this time?

Shaking the thought away, I squeeze her hand. "Are you tired?"

"Not at all. I should be asking *you* that question though. It's late and you've had a long few hours already."

"I'm fine. Let's go get your tea and gossip." She's right, it is late, but tomorrow we can sleep in.

"Tea, sure, but their lips will seal around you, *Princess*. Good luck getting the scoop."

"I'm not even a real princess," I mumble. It's a blessing and a curse that Mother doesn't require any political or royal duties from me. Since she plans to rule for as long as she can, she has no need for an heiress—no need to prepare me for a job I'll never have. It's nothing but an empty title.

The lack of responsibility offers me extra freedoms, such as exploring the island with Ilona and reading, which I'm grateful for, but sometimes it makes me feel a bit useless.

"You *are* a princess. And *I'm* lucky enough that you're my best friend."

"Well, you'll forever be my only friend since everyone is afraid to talk to me apparently. Let's go."

Ilona's nightly routine consists of sipping tea while reading thought-provoking fiction or educational nonfiction books. My routine is similar, though I seek out steamy romance novels and a cozy chair, whereas she can read anywhere and prefers books thicker than my head.

I never used to like hot herbal drinks...but they have grown on me.

Normally, I don't accompany her to the kitchen. She goes on her own, catching up on the latest gossip without me at her side while I take an excessive amount of time choosing my next read.

The servants must know the chatter gets back to me—it's no secret that Ilona and I are practically tethered—but their lips are looser when I'm not around. Ilona says they're wary of engaging in such conversations in the presence of their princess. They fear their words are too inappropriate for me.

If only they knew what their princess read.

Smirking to myself, I lead Ilona out of her room and down the royal hallway into the main space. We cross through to the oversized kitchen by the servants' wing, finding it emptier than usual.

Marnie—an olive-skinned, robust girl in her mid-twenties with thick eyebrows and a heavy bun of dark hair—gives us a lopsided grin. Marnie's only been here three years, but that's still longer than most of the other servants.

She has a compassionate demeanor and a contagious laugh, making her easy to get along with. I suspect part of the reason Ilona enjoys going to get tea every evening is that it allows her to spend time with Marnie, but I've never asked about it.

"Princess," she says to me with a quick curtsy. "Lady Ilona— oh wow! Your Highness, your new hairstyle is quite lovely."

"I appreciate the kind words, Marnie," I say, "but you don't have to call me that."

Ilona clucks her tongue. "You say that as if you won't be queen one day, A."

"At the rate Mother is devouring the lives of others, I won't be."

Marnie's mouth forms a small circle while Ilona snorts a laugh.

"I'd recommend you don't say that, but goddess knows I can't tell you what to do," Ilona says.

Once we both start cracking up, Marnie joins in, loosening up a bit. I probably shouldn't make such comments in front of the servants. Criticism is another thing Mother doesn't tolerate well, and the staff could get in trouble if they repeat my words.

"Where are Deidra and Lila?" Ilona asks, referring to a couple of older, chattier ladies who typically work during the night.

"Ah, hosting Queen Enira's guests."

Ilona and I share a look.

"Where exactly is Queen Enira?" I ask.

"The parlor. It's a casual affair of dessert wine and pastries." Marnie offers Ilona a shy smile. "Would you like me to make your lemon-ginger tea?"

"I'm perfectly capable of preparing my own beverage. Thank you though." Ilona bites her lip and blushes underneath her freckles. It's adorable. Looking away, I pretend to busy myself with a crystal salt shaker sitting on the counter.

"Oh, Astrid," Marnie says quickly, "forgive my impoliteness. May I offer my princess anything to eat or drink?"

Although I cringe at her use of *princess*, I refrain from reminding her I don't like to be addressed that way.

I've always hated the royal terms: *princess, your highness, my lady*. They make me feel disconnected. Separated from everyone else. It's bad enough I'm forced to be the faceless, nameless vessel once a week. The rest of the time, I'd prefer to just be me. *Astrid*. Not a dutiless joke of a princess who everyone's afraid to talk to.

People can fear you, or they can love you, Astrid. One offers protection, while the other makes you weaker. Let them fear you.

Mother and I differ greatly in that regard. She clings to her titles, her self-importance, the fear she instills. Those things define her.

Maybe I don't want to be feared. Maybe I want to be loved, to have more friends.

"No thanks, Marnie. I'm all right." Lifting myself up onto the marble island, I sit and swing my feet, watching as Marnie finishes wiping the countertops across from me. She's done such a thorough job they gleam. It's hard to imagine that during meal-times, this place is bustling with chaos and every surface is fully covered with spices, herbs, and food of all sorts. With all the guards, the servants, and the nobles that circulate the palace, there are always dozens—if not hundreds—of mouths to feed.

"Why is Mother recruiting servants for her casual affair this evening?" When Mother hosts this kind of event, her guests typically partake in activities that don't require food or drink. They are meetings of the flesh, not minds.

Mother was late to the bacchanal tonight, which was unlike her. Now, she's having a meeting of some sort? What is she up to?

Reaching into a high cupboard, Ilona pulls out a ceramic mug and a box of her favorite tea. Marnie must've already set a kettle out before we arrived, because it begins to whistle a moment later.

"I, uh—I figured you were coming, Ilona," she whispers. Ilona blushes again, tucking a lock of hair behind her ear, and I have the sudden sensation I'm invading a private moment.

"Ilona, why don't you go ahead to the library and pick out our books for the evening when you're done. I'm going to swing by the parlor and visit Mother."

She nods, a grateful smile crossing her face.

It will give her and Marnie some alone time. A rarity inside these walls. Plus, she knows my taste in books better than I do half the time. I'm certain she'll pick an enjoyable read.

Leaving the kitchen, I cross through the main foyer—a ridiculously elaborate space with towering ceilings, a massive chandelier, ornate pillars, and two curving staircases. During the day, when sunlight pours through the skylights, it's so blindingly bright that it hurts.

The receiving parlor is set beneath where the two staircases meet, hidden away behind sliding doors. Inching closer, I pause, listening for any sign of conflict. Raised voices. Shattering glass. Anything that would indicate something's amiss.

Mother's coarse laugh greets me, melting together with a deeper voice.

Mother never laughs.

Backing away from the door, I crash into something hard. An arm flashes out, wrapping around my midsection to steady me.

"Hello, sweetheart," a deep voice purrs in my ear. My heart skips a beat with fear and anticipation, as a warm body presses into my backside. The hair on my arms rises, and I'm hyperaware of the thin robe I'm wearing and how intimate this position is.

"Release me," I demand. The man obliges, letting me go with a soft chuckle.

Spinning away from him, I don't hesitate before shoving his chest. My shove has no effect—he's an immovable wall of solid muscle. A moment later, he voluntarily takes a step back though.

Rich brown eyes gaze at me curiously. Wavy brown hair frames a beautiful, newly familiar face, and I'm starting to worry it isn't a coincidence that I've run into him twice tonight.

"Who the hell do you think you are?" I ask, arching a brow and crossing my arms, as if I wasn't just affected by his nearness and relishing the way his body felt against mine.

He lifts one shoulder in a lazy shrug. "A devilishly handsome nobody, Your Highness."

"Handsy, arrogant, and irksome. Truly a winning combination."

"I see you get your manners from your mother." He smirks, locking his eyes on mine for a heated moment before breaking the stare and moving toward the parlor doors. "Now if you'd excuse me, I have matters that require my attention."

"Eck," I say, making a face. "One of Mother's new playthings? Have fun."

The corners of his lips tilt up as he leans in to whisper in my ear. "Not your mother's. *Yours*."

My cheeks flame, and I glare at him as I try to understand

what he's playing at. If he's trying to unsettle me, he's succeeded.

"Watch the way you talk to me, peasant," I say, standing a little taller in an attempt to remind him of my status. He's on my turf, in my home, and he dares speak to me like this? It's infuriating. Yet I can't deny the part of me that enjoys verbally sparring with this newcomer. The thrill. The challenge.

Whoever he is.

"I'm sure your people would love to hear you throwing around that word as an insult, *Princess*. Peasantry is the backbone of your country, is it not?"

Is he seriously trying to bring my country's affairs into this? I clench my jaw, trying to keep my face unreadable and refusing to lash out. He's not merely an instigator, he seems intelligent and sly too. A dangerous combination.

His gaze skims over my thin robe, and I cross my arms tighter across my midsection, covering myself.

The parlor doors slide open behind him, and Mother's floral scent greets my nose.

"Ah, Astrid. I was about to send for you, dear."

Bracing myself, I look past her, pleased to see everyone in the room is fully dressed. In my nightwear, I'm the odd one out. But it's the middle of the night, after all, so what do I care?

At least she's not hosting an orgy in the parlor like I initially assumed.

She squints at my sheared hair, before squeezing her eyes shut and taking a deep breath as if she's fighting the tirade building on her tongue.

"You ruined your hair," she says in a small, strained voice, likely not wanting to make a scene in front of her guests. "You should be utterly ashamed."

When she turns her back to me, the infuriating man sidles up to my side.

"I don't know what you looked like before, but I like the hair," he whispers, surprising me. "It's fierce. Sassy."

Is that a compliment or an insult?

And why do I care?

"Come, Astrid," Mother calls over her shoulder. "Meet the king of Stellaris."

As I follow her into the parlor with the bronzed man on my heels, unease rises within me.

CHAPTER FIVE

My gaze is immediately drawn to an older man with kind eyes and copper skin sitting on one of the three oversized couches in the center of the room, beneath the gilded chandelier. When he spots me, he places his goblet of wine on the table, and stands to attention, buttoning his jacket with one hand in a swift, practiced move.

His companion—a curvaceous woman with deep umber skin—joins him. They smile as we approach, both too polite to glance at my inappropriately informal clothing for more than a moment.

Or maybe they don't realize a robe isn't my usual choice of clothing. Considering their suffocatingly bland outfits, they're clearly not from here. Who wears a *jacket* on a tropical island?

This man certainly has the aura of a king, yet wears no crown.

"Ah, this must be your darling girl, Enira," the older man says in a baritone voice. "Pleasure." He steps forward, pressing a kiss to each of my cheeks before the woman at his side follows suit.

Definitely not a Hakran custom. Mother hates being touched by strangers, unless it's on her terms...or in her bed. I, on the other hand, find the greeting delightful.

"Pleasure is all mine," I say, bowing my head, giving the Hakran customary show of respect.

"Astrid, dear, this is King Emman Vannyk and his wife, Queen Joccelyn Vannyk, from Stellaris," Mother says. Her mouth is still stretched tight, and I wonder if anyone else notices how fake her smile is.

When I sit beside my mother, the king and queen return to their seats on the couch across from us. The man I met in the hallway sits on the couch to my right, next to another young man I don't recognize.

"You can call me Emman. There's no need for formalities," the Stellari king says, shooting me a wink. "This is our son and heir, Zale."

Shifting my eyes to the other couch, I exhale as the man I haven't yet met stands.

Thank the goddess that ass from the hallway isn't the prince.

I spare the stranger a quick glance, and his mouth twitches as though he's fighting a smile.

Prince Zale steps toward me with a forced smile, his body rigid. "Lovely to meet you, Princess." I allow him to greet me with the same double-kiss as his parents, but it's much less welcoming. It seems he doesn't want to be here anymore than I do. He's a perfect mix of them both, with his mother's almond eyes and high cheekbones, and his father's tall stature. His jaw is shaved clean, his suit perfectly pressed.

This guy is prettier than I am.

When he concludes his greeting, I bow my head again, playing nice, mostly for Mother's benefit. I hate political games, and I hate not knowing what's going on.

The handsy guy from the hallway watches, amusement dancing in his golden-brown eyes. His good humor contrasts starkly with the prince's serious, composed demeanor.

Who does this ass think he is, traipsing all over the palace?

Talking to the vessel *and* the princess?

"And who is this?" I ask, staring at the ass in question.

"Apologies, Astrid. I assumed you two met on the way in. This is Dashiel Dargan," Emman says.

I pull the belt of my robe tighter and hold my head higher, though my insides knot themselves.

"If you consider an assault a meeting, then yes. I've met Dashiel." Joccelyn balks, and Emman's brows furrow with concern. The prince is the only one without a reaction.

"If you consider preventing you from falling on your ass an *assault*, then yes, I'm guilty," Dashiel says. Now it's my turn to balk.

Everyone remains quiet, and Mother's eyes do that thing where they close again, like she's trying hard not to snap. I've never known her to bite her tongue, so this only adds to my unease.

"He also propositioned me prior to insulting me and my mother," I say, refusing to look at him. I want to add the bit about him calling Mother names outside the servants' door earlier, because that would tick her off immensely, but then he'd know it was me under that veyl, so I keep that bit to myself.

"Is that true?" Emman asks in a low voice.

"Perhaps there was a miscommunication between us. She assumed I belonged to Queen Enira. I simply corrected the princess, informing her I belong to *her* now." He looks smug as he confidently spins his story for the room. "As for insults, I don't remember any insults. In fact, I complimented her manners, implying she must get them from her mother. Though, I do recall her insulting me."

"Sounds like you two are perfect for each other," Zale says, breaking the tension. "Be a touch less sensitive, Dash. You won't get your feelings hurt so easily."

Much to my alarm, Dash scowls at the prince, but the Stellari king and queen chuckle as if this bizarre exchange is totally normal. Meanwhile, Mother stares at me with disappointment, as if I've done something wrong.

"Are we going to address the bit about him belonging to me?" I ask, refusing to let this strange encounter bother me. "Please tell me you're not marrying me off to some bottom-feeding peasant, Mother."

"Ah, there's that sharp tongue," Dashiel says with a chuckle.

"*Astrid,*" she scolds through gritted teeth. "Are you intentionally trying to discomfit our guests?"

If I'm not mistaken, I think Mother is the only one truly discomfited.

"What brings you four across the Insipid Sea?" I ask Emman, ignoring her and deciding to play nice instead. Ilona would tell me I can catch more flies with honey than vinegar, after all.

There has to be a reason the royal family is visiting, and I'd like to get to the bottom of it. Their presence might explain why Mother has been out of sorts lately.

Stellaris—a country with numerous coastal cities and trading ports—is located across the Insipid Sea, a temperamental body of water known for its spontaneous storms. Even skilled sailors have difficulty navigating it.

The people of Hakran normally keep to themselves, partly because of those storms, but also because the cliffs and rocky sandbars make it dangerous and complicated to return ashore.

Many sailors have declined trade with Hakran, because they fear the destruction of their ships. The sharp, jutting rocks on our side of the sea make trade risky. The price of importation is steep, and exportation is basically nonexistent, which contributes to high rates of poverty on our island.

"Oh, we came to witness the incredible transference we've heard so much about," King Emman says with a twinkle in his eye. He holds up a glass of wine, offering a toast to the room. Queen Joccelyn, Mother, and Prince Zale follow suit. With no glass prepared, I sit back and cross my legs. "To Queen Enira, Princess Astrid, and the vessel. Long live Hakran."

There is no trace of the laughter I initially heard from the other side of the door.

Political posturing it is.

As they continue to make polite conversation about the palace, I assess the energy in the room. With only the five of them nearby, and a handful of guards around the perimeter, I'm able to follow each thread of energy and sort out its owner.

Focusing on King Emman first, I pull the thread of his energy toward me, inviting his emotions in. The man is mostly tired—unsurprising given his long journey here—but he's also amused and mostly untroubled, other than a small hint of nervousness. That could be from anything—being in a new place, meeting my mother for the first time, or any number of things. Nothing sinister stands out about him.

Queen Joccelyn is next. Releasing the king's energy and drawing hers to me, I'm relieved to learn her feelings are virtu-ally identical to her husband's. If anything, the queen feels even calmer, more relaxed.

When I get to Zale, I discover he's even more nervous than his parents. He's uncomfortable and, oddly, insecure. A wave of guilt washes over me at my invasion of his vulnerability, so I shut down our connection, switching to Dashiel instead.

Nothing.

Emptiness.

Like there's some kind of barrier keeping me from reading

him. As if he can feel my eyes narrowed on him, he shoots me a smirk before returning to the conversation.

Ass.

There is definitely something wrong about him.

Lastly, I draw Mother's energy in, picking up on strong agitation and desperation. That is an odd combination for the most confident, collected woman I know.

I close myself off to the connections, glad no one can tell when I'm using my basic vygora powers.

When Dashiel's eyes shift back to me a moment later, I squirm, uncomfortable beneath his gaze. After a few intense seconds of staring each other down, I decide I've had enough.

"Mother, if you would please excuse me, I'm tired and must head to bed," I lie. Ilona's waiting for me in the library and I've already been gone longer than I intended. Plus, if everyone here is going to talk in circles and avoid the important conversations, I have no interest sitting through it. Small talk is as shitty as politics.

"Nonsense, Astrid. The Vannyks journeyed all this way to meet us. Stay," she says. I clench my teeth, feeling stuck.

"Oh, let the dear girl go, Enira," Emman says. "Goddess knows we will be here for quite some time. We will have many opportunities to get to know one another. There is no need to rush our friendships." He grins at me, shooting another wink.

Mother inhales sharply at being told what to do in her own palace. But she smooths out her expression quickly, nodding in agreement. "Yes, yes. You are excused, Astrid. Please be prepared to entertain our guests until further notice."

Did she *let* someone order her around? What is happening?

Swallowing my concern, I smile at everyone before bowing my head respectfully one final time. I scurry out of the room, sliding the doors shut behind me. Releasing a *whoosh* of breath, I mentally thank Emman for sticking up for me.

What a strange evening. No wonder Mother's been on edge today. Considering how little she communicates with the other countries, I can't imagine she's impressed to have a visit from other royals. If I cared more about politics, I'd probably be concerned, but alas, I don't. Mother can deal with whatever problems might arise.

For now, I have a smutty book with my name on it.

CHAPTER SIX

As expected, Ilona is curled up in an oversized chair in the library by the time I get there. One hand holds a book propped open on the armrest, while the other hand raises a mug of tea to her lips.

"How many does this one have? Eight hundred?"

"Nine hundred forty-four actually," she says, grinning at the thick book.

I chuckle to myself before plopping down on a chair near hers, a small side table and lamp between us, and launch into a recap of the parlor visit.

Rows and rows of bookshelves line the space, and it's comforting—like hanging out with old friends. The library has the same white marble floors as the rest of the palace, but the worn rugs and colorful spines decorating the shelves make this room more welcoming. More alive.

A few comfortable chairs are scattered throughout the space. Our favorites are the two chairs across from the main doors, beneath the windows. During the daytime there's plenty of natural light. Now, though, the velvet drapes are drawn, giving it an aura of seclusion.

Another winning feature is that it's almost always empty. Other than a few servants who scuttle about in the mornings dusting, cleaning, and organizing, no one really comes in here besides Ilona and me.

Something about the scent of paper and ink calms the soul.

"And what the hell do they mean, he's *mine?*" I ask Ilona after I relay the events of the evening to her.

"At the risk of sounding patronizing, I think you should've stuck around to find out." She yawns.

"Sometimes I feel like I'm playing a game that everyone is in on but me." I sigh as Ilona hands me her tea, and I take a swig. It's lukewarm, lemony with a hint of mint. "A game I don't care to play."

"At least Queen Enira rarely involves you."

"Unless she needs to use me for something. Which is why this meeting is bothering me."

"Well, they said they're going to be here for a while?"

Nodding, I take another sip of her tea before placing it on the mahogany table between us. "Considering they journeyed goddess knows how far across the Insipid Sea, I'm not surprised."

"The queen is probably so pleased." She snorts a laugh, covering her mouth with her palm, and I laugh with her.

"You should have seen her face when she saw my hair! Oh, it was hysterical." I pick at the velvety fabric covering the armrest. "She's going to have words for me. You know how much she loved my hair."

"I'm proud of you for making a decision for yourself. As much as we fear her, she is *your* mother. She loves you...in her own controlling way. That ought to mean something."

"Invoking her wrath is not my favorite pastime."

"Then let it go. Worrying is worthless. Even if it's bound to happen, there's no sense in prematurely living it out in your head, putting yourself through the situation twice."

"Great advice. Is that from your brick of a book there?" I

point at the hardcover she's hovering over.

She slams it shut, showing me the illegible, warn-out cover. "This old thing? No, it's *Hakran Rediscovered: Island Folklore.* It's about the original goddess and there's lots of lore on the lesser gods and goddesses. It talks about how we used to worship them big time. I wonder what happened."

"Who knows." Though we've all heard some variation of the tales, not many of the islanders are religious. It's common to give generic thanks to the goddess, but no one truly worships her. At least not like they supposedly used to.

"And apparently there were a lot more lesser gods and goddesses than we thought. They were tasked with ruling over various aspects of humanity, such as love, deception, war, luck, death, and so many others."

"I think that's bogus. If there were truly that many gods and goddesses, where'd they all go? And why haven't we heard more about them? Seems like silly stories to me."

Ilona bites her nails as she thinks. "Good questions. I'll probably look for more books on them and the origins of magic next." Her face lights up. "Oh, and there's a Paramour Falls lore that is quite beautiful. I had a dream about the falls…" Her voice takes on a wistful tone as she trails off.

"Fascinating," I say. "And where's my read for the evening?"

Grinning, she reaches beside her and pulls a much thinner book from between the chair's cushions.

"Tonight we have, *Her Warrior of Passion,* chosen by yours truly." The twinkle in her eye tells me it's going to be a good one. Clearing her throat, she begins reading the synopsis in a sultry voice. *"Esmerelda spent every day fearing for her life— her safety—until the powerful, fearless Gideon crossed over her threshold and into her heart—"*

"Are you sure *you* don't want to read this instead?" I tease, snagging the book from her hands. She doubles over in laughter without putting up a fight. It's brave of her to snicker at my reads, considering *she's* the one who picks them out. One might even think she chooses books she's secretly interested in, just so I'll tell her the juicy details. She's always quite curious about the plot. And by "plot" I mean the sexy scenes. Every time I finish a book, she demands I recap the good parts—and there's no laughter then.

"Oh goddess. I could never." Pink blossoms on her cheeks.

"You act like it's immoral, Ilona. Me recapping the fun bits is no different than you reading it yourself." I hand the book back to her. "Here. Read it yourself for once. It's much better when I'm not butchering the *plot,*" I say, giving her a sly smile. I know I've won the battle when she hesitantly accepts the book and settles into the chair. "I'll find something else."

Leaving her to start the book in peace, I head to the romance aisle, and grab a random book without reading the synopsis.

I curl up in the chair next to Ilona, and we share the remains of tea while silently indulging in our stories. Although Ilona is often adamant about how much she dislikes romance novels, she seems to be enjoying it.

Pages slice through the air as we read. I love moments like these, when I can simply exist without being forced into someone else's box. Everything else is on pause, and I have no responsibilities or pressures. I'm not the vessel, not a princess, not even a daughter. Just a girl reading a story.

We read until our eyelids get heavy, then decide it's time for bed.

"I might hold onto this until I'm finished. It's quite good actually," Ilona says. She brushes ginger curls out of her face and bites her lip bashfully.

"Before you get too comfortable, I propose we have our chat

with Cedrik." Shooting her a knowing look, I grab my own book and follow her out of the library.

We pass two guards by the door—faceless, nameless sentries standing in silence. They offer a polite nod as we pass. Taking a right, Ilona and I scurry through the main wing toward the servant's wing where Cedrik resides.

The night is peaceful, quiet. The minty scent of soap fills the air, informing me the hallway was recently scrubbed by one of our hardworking servants. Although Mother has many faults, she does pay the servants handsomely. Most of the palace workers live on the grounds in the servants' wing—some with their families—without cost. If she were truly cruel enough to use her myndox power for personal gain or cruel manipulation, wouldn't she simply persuade the servants to do her bidding without pay or reward?

Perhaps I was too quick to believe the gossip about Mother when I saw her use her ability on Cedrik. Even if her power is stronger than I initially thought, it doesn't necessarily mean she's using it for greed, does it? She was protecting me by influencing Cedrik to forget his princess is the vessel. That's all.

Maybe Ilona was right, but not in the way we initially thought.

Once we talk to Cedrik, we'll see if Mother's manipulation stuck—if she's capable of more than I thought she was. That will at least give us confirmation on one thing. Then I can decide to either let it go and trust her or investigate Ilona's theory. Because if Mother has truly succumbed to the darker side of her power, what's stopping her from using it against us?

I'd rather stop it before it gets that far.

We arrive at Cedrik's door in the servant's wing, but no one answers when we knock.

"He must be tending someone," Ilona says, giving me a worried look.

"Yes, or Mother killed him."

Ilona gasps. "Don't say that."

"You're the one who put these conspiracy theories in my head, Ilona. I'm suspicious of my own mother thanks to you."

I *really* hope she didn't kill the healer. I'm quite fond of him.

A few more guards walk by, their heads swiveling in our direction as they pass.

"There are an awful lot of sentries in here tonight," Ilona whispers to me.

Glancing around the wing, I take in the extra bodies. Instead of the usual two or three, there are six patrolling tonight... and it's only the *servants'* wing. There were double that many in the main wing when we left the library.

Something is definitely off.

"The Vannyks are visiting, remember?" Of course Mother has extra guards in the palace. We have royal visitors from the continent.

"Do you think they're from Stellaris too?" She nods toward a few of the guards down the hall. "They're so...big." Our guards are undoubtedly strong, but they're lean and tall. The guards here tonight are thicker, more powerfully built.

"It's possible," I say. "Leave it to Mother to dress Stellari guards in Hakranian uniforms. What's the point of that?"

"She probably doesn't like their faces," she says. We almost never see the faces of our own guards, as Mother has them wear a protective headpiece that obscures their features. It's partly for armor, but mostly to keep them looking uniform.

I stifle a laugh. "She probably wanted them to match the other guards. Goddess forbid anything disrupts her aesthetics." I can easily see Mother doing that, especially considering she implements dress codes at all of her events—everything other than the bacchanals, that is. She even avoids the library because she considers it an eyesore with all the mismatched books and cluttered shelves.

A young servant girl passes us, and I call out to her.

"Have you seen the man who lives here?" I ask, pointing to the door.

"Princess." She bows her head, eyes wide in shock. "Cedrik? Ye-yes. He's tending to a wound in the stables, Your Highness."

"Thank you," I tell her before shooting Ilona a pleased smile and continuing down the hall. "If she didn't kill him, then she's confident of her hold on his mind." I'd still like to find him to confirm that, but it's the only thing that makes sense.

Shortly after, we arrive at Ilona's door in the royal wing and say our goodnights. Parting ways, I cross the hallway to my own room. Thankfully, Mother's rooms are at the far end of the hall—nearest the main wing. She and I are as far away as we can possibly be from one another in this wing. Empty guest rooms fill the space in between. Though, with the Vannyks here, those rooms are likely in use.

Many guards line the corridor, another indicator of our visiting royals, and the man at my door isn't one I recognize. With wide shoulders and a tapered waist, he wouldn't be easy to forget. And those thighs...definitely thicker and more powerful than what I'm used to seeing.

Trying not to openly ogle—or "admire," as I prefer to say— the guard's physique, I draw my gaze up to his honey-colored eyes. There's a fine layer of stubble on his tan jaw. Even in full Hakranian gear, there's no doubt he's Stellari. I would remember someone like this guarding my door.

These men are definitely easy on the eyes.

Stellaris is growing on me. Perhaps I should visit the mainland soon.

"And who are you, new guy?" I ask in a seductive voice, stepping up to the guard. It's been a while since I've had a man between my thighs, and I'll admit, I've settled for much less enticing guards than this one. "I could use some company this evening."

My smile is sly, leaving no room for him to question my intention.

The guard's eyes shift over me in a slow assessment. He has no staff—elemental or plain—and I wonder if that's a sign Mother doesn't trust him. When I train with Jamell in the morning, I'll ask him what he knows about the new guards.

"I'm talking to you," I say, my voice taking on an edge. Just a few inches separate us now, but he remains silent. I don't miss the way his lips twitch. "All right then. I'll take care of myself."

As I close the door, a hand flashes out to catch it, and the guard enters, a smirk on his face. Shutting the door behind him, he glances around my teal and gold room, as if committing it to memory.

"Lush," he says with approval.

"I didn't invite you in to talk decor," I say, though it pleases me he likes the space. With a four-poster bed large enough to fit five, a shimmering chandelier, and matching drapes and sheets, it's definitely lavish. I love how rich the gold feels and how the blue-green shades balance it, keeping it vibrant.

He reaches up to take his headgear off, but I stop him.

"No. We'll be quick," I say, grabbing him by the wrist and dragging him across the room to my bed.

"What if I want to take my time?" he asks in a husky voice.

Clearly he's not from here, or he'd know the drill.

It's not a secret that both my mother and I enjoy our guards from time to time. She has the same few on her permanent rotation, giving me peace of mind that we at least don't share the same man.

"This is about pleasure, nothing more. The quicker, the better."

"But good things come with time," he says, winking at me.

"Lucky for me I'm not a *good* thing, so I'll come fast." He snickers at my reply as I push him down on the bed. Straddling his legs, I begin working his belt off. He grabs my hands, stopping me, before flipping me over in one quick movement. Grasping both my wrists in one of his, he pins them down above my head.

"What the hell is wrong with—" His lips crash into mine, silencing me. Instinctually, I kiss him back, moaning at how good his mouth fits with mine. He deepens the kiss, letting our tongues dance. His intoxicating scent—something vaguely familiar—fills my nose, disarming me further.

Goddess save me, this man can kiss.

I squirm beneath him, bucking my hips and begging for friction.

When he breaks the kiss, we both breathe heavily, our lips glistening with moisture. The oxygen gives me a much needed moment of clarity, and I turn my head, denying his lips as he leans back in for more.

"Get. The fuck. Off me," I demand in a dark tone. As phenomenal as that kiss was, I don't take kindly to a man trying to shut me up with his lips. I prefer to be in control, and I never kiss the men I bring to my bed. "Try that again and I'll bite your lip until you bleed."

Without hesitation, he stands. Reaching down to readjust himself, he shoots me an amused look. "You could ask nicely, sweetheart."

Sweetheart.

Sandalwood.

That's what that scent is.

"Motherfucker," I say. "Take that off." I point to his head-gear, and he grins.

"You're vulgar for a princess. Has anyone ever told you that?"

Moving quickly, I snag the piece covering his face, swearing when it reveals exactly who I didn't want to see.

Dashiel Dargan.

"Your mother warned me about how *active* the position is. Though I hadn't imagined it happening so quickly."

"You snake!" I screech. "How dare you!"

He holds up his hands in surrender. "Before you throw around accusations of assault again, don't forget you're the one who invited me in here. Demanded, really. If anything, I'm the one who feels assaulted."

"You're not cute."

"You're infuriating," he growls, his eyes flashing with heat.

My lips tighten, fighting a grin at his annoyance. A piece of me is elated that I've gotten under his skin as much as he's gotten under mine. "You didn't seem to think so a moment ago when your tongue was in my mouth."

"You weren't talking then."

Grabbing a pillow from my bed, I chuck it at him. He laughs as it brushes his shoulder on the way past. When he sees me picking up the empty glass carafe next to my bed, aiming it to throw at him next, he stops laughing.

"Tell me why the hell you're here. In Hakran—in my room—trying to weasel your way into my bed."

"Hakran requested additional guards, and Stellaris provided them." He shrugs. "I do what I'm told."

It reassures me that he really is a guard and isn't just pretending to be one to sneak into my room. I should've known based on his physique. Judging by the way he flipped me over and pinned me down, I'd say he's definitely *skilled* at what he does.

"What deal was made?" I ask. There's no way the Vannyks brought over an entire army for Mother to use at no cost. And even if Mother's magic is stronger now, there's no way her manipulation could reach across the sea. She couldn't have manipulated them to come to her. The Vannyks came here on their own, willingly.

"That's a question for your mother or King Emman. I'm not privy to the detailed politics between our countries."

"Still doesn't explain why you're harassing me and sneaking into my room."

He grins. "Do you always invite men to your bed, then treat them like dirt? No wonder they don't come back for more."

"They don't return because I don't want them to." My heart pounds with rage as I realize he knows more about me than he should. "How the hell would you know?"

"Queen Enira appointed me as your personal guard. Like I said, she gave me a *full* rundown of the job description."

"You're saying my Mother assigned me a permanent guard, not even one from my own country, and informed him of my sex life," I say in a flat voice. "Do tell, oh great Dashiel Dargan, why did she choose *you*? What makes you special?"

He ignores my mocking tone, replying in a surprisingly serious manner. "I was Prince Zale's guard. I'm skilled in combat, weaponry, and sailing, among other things. Beside King Emman's own guard, I'm the best from Stellaris. We train all our lives and stay for life, unlike your guards, which constantly rotate out. Most of your men aren't even trained properly at all. They're just an illusion of an army. And the few who are? Your mother can't spare them."

"Men and women," I correct.

"What?"

"Our guard is made of men *and* women, unlike your barbaric country."

"What are you—that's your takeaway?" His brows scrunch together as he gives me a quizzical look. "We have men and women in our guard too. It's just a term."

Okay, clearly my information about Stellaris isn't accurate. Out of all the things running through my mind, my misinformation on their gender roles seems the least imperative though, so I let it go.

I try to consider why Mother would feel the need to bring on more guards—to assign me a permanent one. I've never had someone following me around, since I can destroy lives with a touch. I have no need for protection. Though, if something's going on and Mother needs extra protection—or at least the illusion of it—it would seem fitting for her to include me in that coverage.

So what has her spooked? And what did she trade to gain an entire Stellari army?

Does she realize the man she appointed to protect me is immune to my powers? Something about the situation doesn't sit right with me.

"Thanks for the illuminating conversation, Damien. You can go."

"It's Dashiel. But you know that." He mutters something like "unbelievable" under his breath.

"I said you're dismissed."

"Are you always this much of a bitch?"

Coolly sliding past him, I open the door as wide as it goes. "When I don't like someone, yes, and I especially don't like you." *But I would like you between my legs.*

I flash back to him holding me down, kissing me with fervor. There's no denying how hot it was, and the thought of it brings back a spark of desire. If I wasn't so stubborn, I'd gladly take him back to my bed and have my way with him. But there's no way I'm allowing myself to look weak in front of him now.

As he strides out of the room, he flashes a saccharine smile my way.

"Think of me while you *take care of yourself,*" he whispers in my ear. I shudder, turning away from him and slamming the door so hard behind him that my chandelier tinkles overhead.

As much as I hate being bossed around, I can't help but comply with his order, letting images of his warm honey-colored eyes, muscular thighs, and smug smile push me over the edge before falling into a deep sleep.

CHAPTER SEVEN

Knock. Knock. Knock.

Cracking my eyes open, I groan internally.

Streams of pale pink light peek around the edges of my curtains. It's at least past dawn, but barely. Last night was the longest night ever, and I hardly slept.

"Yes?" I groan. The servants know not to bother the royal family—Mother, Ilona, or me—the day after transference. It's the one day of the week the handmaidens are supposed to be off duty. More importantly, it's the one day a week I catch up on sleep. Not even Jamell expects me for our training session until late afternoon.

Gianna, my favorite handmaiden, calls through the door, "So sorry to wake you, Princess, but you need to get up." Despite the unexpected intrusion, it's a welcome voice. One of the many reasons I adore her is because she doesn't treat me as awkwardly as the other servants do.

Stretching my arms overhead, I reluctantly pull myself from the silky sheets and patter to the door. Unbolting the locks, I swing it open to let her in.

"Good morning!" Her wavy amber hair is piled high on her head, her face painted with impeccable taste. The uniform black slacks and maroon tunic can't hide her ample curves. She always looks so composed and dignified, even in the mornings, and she's quite talented at drawing me out of my morning moodiness.

"Morning. I wasn't expecting you today." Yesterday was such a long day. On top of it all, Ilona and I practically pulled an all-nighter reading. Drawing her in for a quick hug, I stifle a yawn. Once we release, I peer out into the hallway. Dashiel stands there, staring straight ahead and ignoring me. Does he not sleep? "Go ahead and get set up. I'll be right there, Gia."

Moving past me with a nod, she hustles to the connected bathroom, probably drawing me a bath with scented oils, just the way I like. Gia is probably here today because Mother sent for me so she can parade me around like a show horse in front of the Vannyks.

"Have you been out here all night?" I ask Dashiel.

"You ask like you actually care," he deadpans, his gaze flashing to mine. "I could've shared your bed, but alas, here we are instead."

"Don't be dim. I never would've let you stay the night."

"Annnnnd you've just reminded me of how much cozier it is out here. Alone. No great loss after all."

"I was trying to be pleasant this morning."

He shifts his weight, eyeing me like I'm a skittish cat that might bolt or sink my claws in at any second. Good. Let him be wary.

"I traded off for a few hours rest, Your Highness. So be assured I am primed and ready to trail you like a shadow, watching helplessly while you harass today's poor victims."

"Ass," I mutter.

Closing the door, I pad to the bathroom, unsurprised to see Gia lining the counters with my facial products and paints while water runs in the clawfoot bathtub in the center of the room. The aromas of eucalyptus and mint fill the air—an invigorating blend that I enjoy in my morning baths.

Groaning, I bury my face in my hands. "Mother is relentless."

Gianna only smiles, giving me a sympathizing look. As kind as she is to me, she doesn't dare speak ill of Mother.

"I really don't need all that, Gia." Waving a hand toward the small jars of powders and colors. "There's nothing wrong with my natural face."

"Queen Enira ordered it. Sorry, Princess." I can tell she's genuinely remorseful, stuck in an awkward place, and I don't want to make her feel worse. She might be my handmaiden, but Mother is the one who employs her. It doesn't much matter what I want.

In another life, one where Gia didn't feel like my inferior, we'd be good friends.

"Did she at least say why?" Dropping my robe and stepping out of my nightdress, I enter the scalding water with a yelp. She laughs, knowing I enjoy being practically burnt to death during my baths.

"Breakfast with the visiting royals of Stellaris," she says.

I'd wanted to visit Paramour Falls with Ilona today, for an isolated swim in the middle of the jungle, but that doesn't seem plausible anymore. At the least, I'd still like to seek out Jamell for a quick training session before getting glamorized.

"I suppose you won't need my help washing your hair now." She gestures toward her own head, referring to my new cut. "Not that my opinion matters, but I prefer this style on you. It emphasizes your facial structure."

"Of course your opinion matters. Thank you." That's a big compliment coming from Gianna. She's skilled at the art of appearance, a true whiz with hairstyling and makeup. The only reason I hadn't asked her to fix my hair initially is because I didn't want to intrude on her personal time after hours. Plus, Ilona is plenty skilled in her own right.

I'm surprised the two of them haven't become better friends. They seem to have a lot in common. Then again, I don't think their paths cross often.

"You're probably used to people telling you what they think you want to hear, but I do mean it." She chuckles.

"I had no doubts."

Sinking deeper, I accidentally move too quickly, and a small wave of water splashes over the side onto the marble. My skin is glowing red, but already I'm adjusting to the bathwater's temperature. The irony isn't lost on me that I complain about the island's heat yet prefer a hot bath even during the summer.

Most of our luxuries—such as running, heated water—come at the hand of aethyns. It's the most common type of magic, and the aethyns are the hardest-working people on the island.

Normally, each aethyn can harness or manipulate one of the four elements: fire, water, earth, air. I've even heard of some aethyns wielding multiple elements, but I've never met one myself.

Higher-level aethyns can disperse their magic into items. Those individuals are often employed by royals, but even if they aren't, their powers afford them a higher quality of life than ordinary citizens.

Here at the palace, we have a few aethyns controlling each element. I don't engage with them, but they're around. Water aethyns keep the palace cool by infusing ice into the stone, the same way they keep our food fresh with an ice-room. Fire aethyns keep our chandeliers lit and our water heated. Earth aethyns tend our gardens. Air aethyns work as couriers and use their magic to lift items with ease, moving about the palace completing odd tasks.

They're all responsible for the various elemental staff weaponry as well. Of course, their power isn't endless. It's limited and used sparingly. When their magic runs low, they need to spend time around their element to recharge.

There are also etheryn, though there aren't any on the island currently. Myndoxes have mental magic, vygoras have emotional magic, and the aethyn have elemental magic. However, the etheryn have spatial magic. The abilities they work with are the most obscure of all, as they manipulate space, time, or light. Many think them nearly extinct—the theory being their extreme brand of magic is too taxing, took too much of a toll and has wiped most of them out. Others say they exist in hiding. Altering space and time is a dangerous thing, and it makes many people uncomfortable. Persecution is a real concern.

We had our own light etheryn who worked as a seamstress before she passed a few years ago. She spun the material for the tent and my veyl, manipulating light in such a way that one could see out but not in.

Mother hasn't found a replacement.

After a few minutes of scrubbing my body, Gianna finishes setting up the vanity and turns to me with her brows raised and her lips pursed. A telltale sign she's about to divulge some gossip. She might not speak ill of Mother, but she has her fair share of palace whispers to share with me. It's not as useful as the information Ilona gets from the kitchen staff, but it's still entertaining.

"So," she begins, "Have you *seen* the prince of Stellaris?"

"I have."

"By the goddess." She places a hand on her chest. "Isn't he absolutely gorgeous?"

It's Dashiel's face that crosses my mind—his knowing eyes, smirking lips, and artfully messy hair. Pushing the image away,

I picture the prince. Equally handsome but in a more composed and ultimately less intriguing way. He seems fine, just boring. Predictable.

"Yes," I agree. "He is."

"And the guards!" She giggles. "Both the men and women are so fit, so *built*."

Quickly, I sit up in the bath. My breasts are exposed, but I'm comfortable in my body and pay no mind. Gia has been with me for long enough that she's likely as familiar with my body as she is her own. And I was just as comfortable with the handmaiden who attended me before her. Growing up privy to Mother's extracurriculars, and amidst her weekly bacchanals, I'm not shy.

"So there really are female guards?"

"Yes! And they're all so beautiful and strong," she says. "Well, from what I can see underneath their leathers. It is rather strange they're dressed in Hakranian gear though, no?"

I make a sound under my breath, neither confirming nor denying her question, before pulling myself out of the bath.

Gia wraps me in an oversized towel, chatting away as she prepares my face and hair, but I'm consumed about my thoughts of the female guards. It's a great thing Stellaris isn't as oppressive as I thought. But then why does Mother look down on other countries, claiming they're barbaric and backwards?

She hosts enough long-term diplomats to know the truth, so has she purposely been lying to make herself look better in comparison?

Gia finishes preparing me much sooner than usual—thanks to the shorter hair. She fishes around my armoire, pulling out a pair of loose, billowy black pants made of a wonderfully thin material. To match it, she picks out a gold top with thin straps that connect to my wrists in an open-sleeve style, revealing my midsection while fully covering my chest. Then she slips gold sandals on my feet. Finally, I snag a pair of gold sun-shaped earrings and a matching gold choker to finish off the look. I now embody the gilded color of island sunshine on a clear day.

"Ta-da!" Gia says proudly. "What would you do without me?"

"Allow my face to breathe," I say, rolling my eyes. My eyes are dramatically darkened with kohl, my cheeks rosy, lips nude. It's not the worst appearance, but I'm still deeply annoyed about Mother's disruption. I don't appreciate the way she micromanages my life.

Gianna laughs, knowing my displeasure isn't aimed at her.

"Thanks for making this more tolerable, at least. You're good at what you do."

"Don't get all mushy on me now, Princess."

At least now I can converse with the Vannyks and learn more about Stellaris. Plus, if Ilona and I are staying at the palace today, that means we can find Cedrik and see if he truly doesn't remember anything about me being the vessel. If that's the case, Mother's power has transformed and strengthened. If she can alter memories and erase minds, that's truly terrifying.

After so many bland days of listening to Mother drone about island politics, it's almost exciting to have two ongoing mysteries—Mother's agenda with her heightened abilities, and the visiting royals.

A nagging feeling tells me the two might be connected—wrapped around each other like jungle vines—and I'm determined to chop them down.

Instead of heading to the main dining room where Mother waits, I exit the palace, cutting across the courtyard to the servants' wing. It's quicker than roaming through the corridors. I'd rather not risk passing the dining space and being spotted by Mother.

A blanket of morning heat wraps around me, and I mourn the loss of my visit to the falls today. The freshwater swimming hole would've been such a delight; the day is practically made for a swim. It's still early, the sun barely beginning its ascent, the skies clear and azure.

"It's hotter than the devil's balls," Dashiel says from behind me.

"Classy."

"I'm pretty sure this isn't the way to breakfast." I speed up, trying to ignore the bulk of a man who is, indeed, trailing me like a shadow today. "You can't outpace me either, sweetheart."

"Stop calling me that."

Pushing through the servants' door, I take a sharp left toward the winding staircase that leads down to the training space.

Sure enough, as soon as my feet hit the training level, I spot Jamell. Although I don't typically meet with him until later in the day, I was certain he'd be here. He's Mother's favorite commander, so if he's not meeting with her, he's usually here training the other guards.

It's a nonstop job considering how often the guards are rotated out of the palace.

Maybe Dashiel is right and Mother's guard is a facade. Nothing more than the illusion of power. Perhaps if she actually kept her guards in permanent roles instead of rotating them around the island, she'd have a more indomitable group.

The training space has one large room with a bunch of smaller rooms branching off of it. Padded floors and walls cover the whole space, and a section of thick, unbreakable glass windows offers a glimpse inside some of the other training spaces.

On the wall opposite the stairs, a heavily locked and secured door blocks access to the pit. The door, infused with a blend of aethyn and etheryn powers, is soundproof and can only be opened if Mother or one of the commanders touches a palm to its surface. I've never been down there. I don't even think it's in use anymore.

The pit is made of silenxstone—a rare material that mutes magic entirely. Right off the coast sits another empty husk constructed from the same material—the old prison.

There hasn't been crime on the island in a long time, hence no prisoners to keep.

Here in the training room, the dress code is more lenient, and guards are allowed to train without their head coverings. Spotting a few familiar faces, I nod politely. Everyone I pass lowers their head in a show of respect.

I wonder which ones I've taken to my bed.

"How many of these poor saps have you ruined?" Dash whispers in my ear, as if he knows what I'm thinking. He sounds amused, but his jaw is tense, as if he's annoyed.

"You know, you make it really hard to forget you're here," I say. "Jealousy isn't becoming."

"I'm not jealous," he whispers, his warm breath caressing my bare neck. "You couldn't ruin me if you tried, Princess. I'm the one who'd be doing the ruining."

Warmth pools in my stomach, my body aroused by his proximity and words. I step away, putting space between us, and he flashes a dimpled smile.

Jamell's attention finally shifts to me, and he says something to the man he's sparring with before jogging across the room to me. Dashiel backs up, allowing me to speak to the commander without him looming.

Jamell's quite a bit older than me, but it doesn't slow him down. Known for his agility and endurance, he could outlast anyone in battle. I admit, he's a great choice for commander. Mother did well.

"How ya doin', Princess?" His bald head glistens with sweat as he gives me a charming, gap-toothed grin. The age lines, crooked nose—broken more than a few times—and missing front tooth make him appear more menacing than he really is, but I know him to be an endearing man. "I wasn't expectin' ya till later."

I glance around the space to ensure everyone else is out of earshot.

"What's the deal with the new guards?" I ask, cutting right to the point. Mother is still expecting me for breakfast, and I'm already late, so I'd like to make this quick.

His smile fades. "Ya know I ain't s'posed to talk 'bout these things."

"Oh come on, Jamell. I'm your *princess,*" I say with a hint of authority, using an angle I typically try to avoid.

"Ya know I can get in trouble with Queen Enira fer my loose lips."

"I won't tell if you don't." I shoot him a playful wink, and he chuckles, loosening up a bit.

"Fine. Only 'cause yer my favorite princess on the island."

"I'm the only princess on the island."

"There's been...new threats against Hakran, the queen, and, well, I 'spose that means you too." His eyes dart away guiltily. "Look, I dunno much yet. There's a meetin' this afternoon 'bout it."

Nodding, I thank him for sharing what little information he has. It explains why Mother sought additional guards. Now I need to find out what this threat is and what she traded to acquire an entire army.

Another thought hits me: What if she didn't trade anything at all? What if the threat's a lie, and she's using her myndox power to assume control of the Stellari guard? But why?

The problem with my theories is they just don't make sense. I'm fully in agreement with Ilona that Mother's powers are more dangerous than we thought, but I'm not fully sold on the idea that she's some evil entity manipulating everyone within her reach…

We say goodbye, and I hustle back up the stairs, across the yard, and into the main wing, not caring about whether or not Dash is keeping up. Even though I'm quite in shape from all the physical training and outdoorsy adventures, I'm still a little winded from the quick pace and heat. Leaning against the cool palace stone, I close my eyes and focus on controlling the airflow into my lungs.

"Don't hurt yourself."

"For fuck's sake, Dashiel." My eyes flash open. I was hoping I lost him.

He smirks, and for some reason, it enrages me.

Who the hell does he think he is?

"I don't trust that guy," he says, his voice adopting a stern tone.

"Commander Jamell?" I snort. He's literally one of Mother's—and Hakran's—most-trusted soldiers. "Of course you don't. You have some baffling contempt against Hakranians."

"Be careful," he warns.

Ignoring him, I cross the corridor and head into the dining room, already over today and not wanting to face Mother.

CHAPTER EIGHT

The scents of molasses and honey-ham fill the air. The doors are spread open, and I enter at a leisurely pace, as if I wasn't just running around the grounds a moment ago.

The irksome Stellari guard follows me in, sliding the doors shut behind us and standing guard beside the other few men and women already in place.

"Good of you to finally join us, dear," Mother drawls from the head of the table. Her dark eyes flash like midnight storms.

I smile falsely at her. "Good of you to wake me so early for this thrilling occasion."

"Show some respect, Astrid," she snaps, shooting me a warning look. I glance away, taking in the breakfast table instead. Beyond the berry-cakes, sugar-rolls, and stacks of glazed meats, the king, queen, and prince of Stellaris sit around the table in an awkward silence, watching the exchange.

Sudden guilt creeps in. I've embarrassed Mother in front of the visiting royals, and I want nothing more than to make her look good in front of them.

I'm acting like a child.

"Please forgive me," I say sincerely, addressing the Vannyks. "I'm not the most pleasant after a fitful sleep." Looking at Mother, I add, "Apologies, Mother."

Queen Joccelyn raises her eyebrows before looking down at her pancakes and slicing into them. I wonder if she ever speaks, if King Emman lets her. Maybe their country *is* oppressive after all.

"We began without you, not wanting to waste a perfectly fresh meal," Mother says.

Pulling out the chair to Mother's right, I sit next to Prince Zale, across from his parents. It's almost humorous, the five of us sitting at a table that fits thirty people. So unnecessary.

The king offers me a soft wink, and his wife smiles warmly at me.

They seem nice enough.

Prince Zale and I exchange greetings, then proceed to ignore one another as he chews his food and I load up my plate with turmeric-saffron eggs and almond-poppyseed pancakes. Neither of us bother to make conversation.

Yep, the prince has the personality of a dead moth. Even worse, he's using a knife and fork to eat his muffin. A muffin! That's certainly a crime.

A snort comes from the door, before turning into a cough. My head swings around, and I meet Dashiel's amused eyes. If I'm not mistaken, I'm pretty sure he's laughing at my discomfort. The other guards are a few feet away from him, so clearly he wasn't indulging in jokes with them.

Does he find this breakfast humorous?

He might have a better personality than his prince, but there's something off about him. He's too mouthy and arrogant. Then there's the whole issue with me not being able to read his emotions. I don't trust him.

For the next twenty or so minutes, the room fills with polite chatter and the clinking of silverware. I devour my food, giving silent thanks to our talented kitchen staff.

I really should visit Marnie and the others more often with Ilona and tell them myself.

"Astrid, dear," Mother says once everyone's satiated and we're sipping espressos. "The Vannyks will be in Hakran until further notice. It seems there is a threat against the mainland. I have offered our *protections* in exchange for access to their resources and personnel. I rest assured you will help them adjust well. You *will* be nice."

Ahhh, now things are starting to make sense. The threat wasn't against Mother. She didn't seek out help from Stellaris. It's Stellaris that's facing a threat, and they have sought out Mother for help, something she clearly used to her advantage while negotiating.

She had offered them help and protection in exchange for access to their army. They likely have no clue how strong her magic is. How would they? If she's truly manipulating our entire village, she can easily manipulate the Stellaris army as well, and none would be the wiser. I didn't know about it myself until Ilona brought it up and I witnessed Mother use her power on Cedrik. In fact, I don't think I need to see Cedrik to know the truth anymore.

It's all adding up, and it's not looking good.

The Vannyks have made a massive mistake.

"Are we combining courts? What does this mean?" I blurt.

King Emman chuckles while his wife wears an amused expression. "The threats aren't directed toward the people of Stellaris, only the royals. Which is why we're taking refuge here while the remaining armies work to neutralize the threat. The agitators aim is to eradicate those in power—the royals who harness significant...abilities. Myndoxes, vygoras, and aethyns alike," he says. He must consider etheryn extinct too, since he left them off his list.

Magic is rare on its own, and of those with magic in their blood, only few people are truly powerful. Those who are stronger than the rest, such as Mother or the Vannyks, have a tendency to rule. Magic is passed down through bloodlines, so it's easy to keep within royal families. There are, of course, wealthy low-level myndoxes and vygoras within the nobility. Those who don't come from prosperity, like Cedrik, work as healers or guards, among other things.

The power of the aethyns is often too weak to be useful in anything other than infusion. Instead, they find work as laborers or craftsmen, infusing products for anyone who can afford their services.

"Which class are you?" I ask the king and queen. Mother makes a *tsk* noise under her breath and takes a sip from her espresso. It's not necessarily rude to ask what their powers are, but it could be viewed as gauche.

"We're myndoxes, like your mother," Queen Joccelyn says with a bashful look. "Though, not nearly as powerful."

So the other queen does talk after all. And she's a kiss-ass.

"All three of you?" I ask. She nods, smiling broadly, as if she's proud. Although magic is passed down through families, there's no guarantee a person's descendants will inherit the same type of power as they themselves have. Take Mother and me, for instance. She's a myndox who birthed a vygora. It's likely I had an ancestor with similar abilities somewhere in my family tree.

It used to be frowned upon for those with magic to copulate with those without—for fear the magic would be diluted. Over time, the stigma faded. As those with magic began to couple with the normals, the bloodlines did in fact become weaker, which resulted in magic becoming the rarity it currently is. Considering the strength of my power, I'm willing to bet my father, whoever he is, has magic of his own.

"Our power is slightly different," King Emman says. "We cannot influence the minds of others, but we also cannot *be* influenced by other myndoxes." He flashes a blinding smile at my mother, and my brows rise to my hairline as her own lips tighten upward in a fake response.

Mother can't manipulate the Vannyks.

Holy shit.

No wonder she's been so off-kilter lately. She probably had no idea until they got here. Now she's stuck with equal-level royals who are unaffected by her power.

They might not be susceptible to her magic, but their guards are. So far Dashiel is the only one I can't get a read on. He seems to be the exception. So, if there were to be an altercation or power play, I imagine Mother would still win, as the numbers are on her side.

Luckily, royals cannot murder one another to assume their thrones. Lore says the original goddess put natural laws in place forbidding magic wielders from harming one another.

Though we can use our magic to kill regular humans, or we can kill magic wielders without magic.

Another law, according to lore, says that any royal who kills another royal forfeits their own throne and is forbidden from assuming another.

Apparently the original goddess ran into these issues when she dispersed her magic among humans, and she put the laws into place to protect the land and the people from further destruction. It was meant to keep peace throughout the lands and eliminate power plays. However, that doesn't mean there aren't loopholes. Mother could easily have one of her guards assassinate the Vannyks if her end goal *was* to steal their throne. Then they wouldn't technically have died at her hand or by her power.

Is that what she wants though? Another country? For what? More bodies for more power?

Something uneasy stirs in my stomach as I grip my cup of espresso.

Hopefully the Vannyks watch their backs and are skilled in defense, because I'm trusting Mother less and less.

The prince leans across the arm of his chair toward me, lowering his voice so no one but me can hear him. "He makes us sound so pitiful."

"Well, what else can you do that's a little less...*pitiful?*" I whisper back with a chuckle.

"Some secrets aren't to be revealed." He grins at me, and I roll my eyes, polishing off the rest of my espresso in one big gulp.

Maybe I was quick to judge and he doesn't have the personality of a dead moth after all.

No, the personality of a live moth, perhaps.

"Not to sound harsh, but why Hakran? What makes you think we can protect ourselves let alone you?" I ask him quietly.

Out of the corner of my eye, I watch Mother ball her hand into a fist on the table before sliding it out of sight onto her lap. She sucks her cheeks in tight, and I can tell the conversation she's having with King Emman and Queen Joccelyn is bothering her. I'm relieved she's too distracted by hosting our new guests to berate me for my hair or my disobedience.

Maybe I'll like having them around after all.

The Stellari king and queen chuckle softly, their humor an antithesis to Mother's uptight nature. Biting my lip to hide my amusement, I stay focused on Zale.

Good goddess, his cheekbones could cut glass.

"Hakran has nearly impenetrable coasts," the prince says. "Only the coast near the south—South Sands I think you call it—is tolerable for ships, and only when the tide is high enough to maneuver around the largest of rocks. We have guards on the lookout, ready to alert us to any incoming ships, which gives us time to prepare. With both your guards and ours, we have the advantage."

"You know an awful lot about our geography."

"Why, we learned ourselves how difficult it was when we navigated our personnel in yesterday," Queen Joccelyn says, apparently having overheard our conversation. Her eyes flash downward as she grips her husband's hand and gives it a squeeze. Her voice gets quieter. "We lost one of our ships. Our mistake for overestimating our abilities. The Insipid Sea can be quite unforgiving at times, even to the most skilled of sailors. Luckily Queen Enira here came to our rescue in time before any lives were lost."

"It could have been much worse without her help," King Emman says, holding his espresso cup up toward Mother with a head nod.

So that explains why Mother was late to the bacchanal yesterday.

"I'm glad everyone made it safely," I say. It's an earnest statement. I've never been off the island myself, but I've heard about how treacherous the Insipid is. The idea of crossing the sea in the face of storms, sharks, and other obstacles stresses me out.

The storms are deadly enough on land, I can't imagine how perilous they are out on the waters.

The three of them go back to chatting amongst themselves, and I look back to Zale, who's eyeing me with open interest.

"Do you miss your guard?" I ask, tilting my head toward Dashiel, who stands by the door, staring at us with an unreadable expression.

"Dash?"

"I prefer arrogant ass, but yes. Him."

Zale snorts into his coffee before recovering and smoothing his shirt down.

Interesting.

He has a sense of humor, but he tries to stifle it. I wonder if he's more engaging away from his parents. I'll have to find out.

"He's good at what he does. He's also a close friend of mine, so I might not be the best to confide in about him."

"Why, Prince Zale, are you saying you'll run and tell your little buddy I'm badmouthing him? The scandal." I place the back of my hand against my forehead mockingly.

He shrugs as his eyes crinkle with humor. "I'm giving you fair warning."

"You're almost as banal as my mother."

"Did you just imply I'm boring?" He frowns, brows scrunching together as if he can't understand why I'd call him that.

"Join me and my friend on an adventure this week and we'll try to rectify that."

His eyes light up. "I've heard of a place called Paramour Falls. I'd love to see it in person. Do you know where that is?"

"Oh, I absolutely do." I grin, shooting him a playful wink. He clears his throat before glancing away.

I make him uncomfortable. This is going to be fun.

"I'd prefer if you stay close to the palace, Astrid," Mother says, invading my conversation with Prince Zale.

"What about the falls? Ilona and I had planned to visit soon for a swim."

"The beach is bountiful. Perfect for a swim."

"Mother, with all due respect, I understand where you're coming from, but I am a grown woman and would appreciate my freedom to leave the grounds." The water from the falls is much more refreshing, icy cool compared to the tepid beach water in summertime. Plus, there's something marvelous about swimming in the middle of a green jungle; it's like a private oasis.

"Zale's trained in combat as well. They should be fine," Emman says.

"I'd love to see the falls," Zale adds eagerly.

Joccelyn nods in agreement. "Perhaps it could be an opportunity for him to learn the land, Enira."

Mother flinches as if she's been slapped. She's not used to anyone bossing her around or referring to her as simply *Enira*. I'm amused by the Vannyks' laidback nature, thrilled that they can't be manipulated by her power. What a challenge it must be for her.

I glance at Zale, and he offers a shrug.

"Astrid can show him the grounds while she partakes on her *adventures*," Mother grits out, as if it was her idea all along and she wasn't strong-armed into agreeing. Venom laces her words, as if the idea of my explorations is something dirty and incomprehensible.

"Thank you, Mother." Standing, I give her a kiss on the head, reveling in the way she flinches slightly at the public show of affection.

Oh I'm going to pay for this later.

But somehow, right now, having the Vannyks around gives me a strange boost of confidence—a feeling of security. It's like Mother is a wild beast who's finally been tamed and caged.

I hadn't realized how much I feared her until they showed up and offered me a reprieve from her scrutiny.

Zale stands as well, pushing in his chair before rounding the table and bestowing a kiss upon his mother's head in a sweet show of affection. Joccelyn smiles adoringly at him, and I experience a slight twinge of jealousy at their relationship.

I wonder what it's like to have a normal, caring mother.

"Dashiel is the best to have around, Astrid. You'll be perfectly safe with him at your side," Queen Joccelyn says to me, standing to give me a hug.

Oh.

Her compassion catches me off guard, but I recover quickly, hugging her back.

Saying our goodbyes, Prince Zale and I walk side by side out of the dining room. The new bane of my existence opens the doors to let us pass before catching up with us.

"Dash, I hear you and Princess Astrid are getting along well," the prince says, tugging obsessively on his sleeves to straighten them out.

Perfectionist.

"Ah, she told you how she pounced on me last night?"

"I did, and I mentioned it was a disappointing affair," I retort. Dashiel's brows rise, as if he had expected me to deny it or lash out rather than go along with it. Zale chuckles quietly before shaking his head.

"I'd be more than happy to make up for what my friend here lacks," Prince Zale says. I don't miss the way Dashiel shoots him a dark look, and I can't help the laugh that escapes me. The prince has a little bite after all.

"You're bound to put the princess to sleep with your *banal* personality, Zale."

"I'd rather be perceived as vapid or boring than as a disappointing affair."

It's unsurprising that Dashiel was eavesdropping on our conversation at the table. Of course he was.

"Perhaps we could combine forces to please the princess?" Dash asks. "She seems like someone who might enjoy the challenge."

My heart pounds furiously at his implication, and for a moment I wonder if it's a legitimate offer. I wonder if I might accept the offer.

Ultimately, I decide he's probably toying with me, purposely trying to unnerve me. I speed up to put some distance between us, trying to keep my head clear.

Dash calls after me, "Don't worry, Princess, I want to be here as much as you want me here."

"We might get along better if you keep your mouth shut," I say, spinning around to face him. My eyes flash to his lips. Soft, kissable lips that would feel so good on my—

Nope. Not going there.

Shaking my head, I push the thoughts away. It doesn't matter what he looks like. Not with such an utterly arrogant personality.

Goddess have mercy, this is going to be a long visit.

"If he's with me, who's with you?" I ask Zale as we continue heading through the main hallway toward the royal wing, with Dashiel behind us. I'm hoping to find Ilona in her room. "Don't you want your *best guard* all to yourself?"

"My mother was wrong. Dash is only the best if you don't count me," he says. Dash makes a snorting noise.

"Is everyone from Stellaris so arrogant?" I ask, warranting a chuckle from Dash who's now currently walking too close behind me. If I were to stop moving, he'd crash right into me. I look over my shoulder as I continue moving forward. "And you—give me some space, please!"

"*Please?* She has manners?" Dash asks mockingly as he slows his pace to put another foot of distance between us.

"She *did* say please."

"You two are infuriating. I can't believe I thought you were quiet and respectful," I murmur to the prince.

"And *banal,* don't forget," Dash adds, instigatingly.

Zale's lips quirk up in a grin. "Are all Hakranians this uptight?"

"I suppose we are."

"Interesting, considering the activities you all enjoy participating in," Dash says as he steps up to my left side, keeping pace with Zale and me now instead of trailing behind. "I imagined a much more *contented* island of people. Like I said, we can help with that."

"I am perfectly content. Or I was before you showed up." I rub my temples. "I thought I asked you to give me space?"

Dash grins, waving his hand within the scant space between us. "Plenty of space here, sweetheart."

"And I'm not sure what you heard about us over in Stellaris, but not everything you hear is honest. It's often easier to spill a lie than it is to spill a truth."

"I've heard plenty, sure, but it doesn't beat the amount of flesh I *saw* last night on the beach," Dash says. "Or how you tried to devour me in your room."

He was at the beach?

Surely I would've noticed him on the beach. Unless he wasn't in sight.

That would explain why he was at the servants' door randomly. He likely headed back moments prior to me coming across him.

"Were you *lurking* at the bacchanal?"

"Lurking. Gathering intel."

"Anything to add to this, Prince?" I ask, swinging my head toward Zale, who's grinning with amusement.

"Lurking. Gathering intel." He repeats Dash's words while he scratches his chin. "Tomato, toh-mah-toe?"

"You two are quite inclined to get on my nerves today."

Reaching Ilona's door, I nod at another passing guard and lift my knuckles.

Knock. Knock. Knock.

"It's me, Ilona."

"Doors open, A! Come on in."

I swing the door open but don't immediately see her. The bathroom door is cracked open, and orange light spills out.

"Finally! I went to your room, but Gianna was packing up. Said Queen Enira requested you for breakfast with the Vannyks." Her voice rings out from the bathroom. "Have you seen the abundance of scrumptious strength roaming around? Good goddess, I—"

"Ilona?" I call out, my voice a little higher than normal, but she doesn't stop talking. The two men beside me shake with silent laughter.

"—wouldn't mind letting one of them use their *staff* on me." Zale balks as Dash continues to laugh quietly. "And there was this really tall woman with the perkiest buns I've ever seen—"

"Ilona."

"Forget reading *Her Warrior of Passion,* we could be the main characters in our own version of Stellari guards of pa—" Stepping out of the bathroom, she immediately ceases speaking when she sees who stands with me in her room. Her face turns the deepest shade of red I've ever seen, and her mouth widens into an O. "Astrid...why didn't you mention we have guests?" Her voice comes out as a squeak.

I shrug. "I tried to stop you."

"Hello," Dash says with a grin and a wave while Zale stares

at anything but Ilona.

"*Her Warrior of Passion?*" he asks.

Ilona groans, burying her face in her hands. She's dressed in loose pants almost identical to my own and an emerald blouse that brings out her green eyes and contrasts with her fiery hair. It's her color.

The Stellari men look almost humorous next to our light, colorful clothing. Zale in his long-sleeve navy jacket and boots, Dash in his full-body leathers and head covering.

"What brings you here, Prince? To my room?" Ilona asks, trying to play it cool by changing the subject. Based on the way her eyes dart between the two men and she fans herself with her hand, I can tell she's anything but.

"Yes, great question. Why *are* you two here?" I ask.

Dash stares at me. "I go where you go."

Zale sheepishly rubs his neck. "I need a break from politics."

"Are you familiar with riding?" I ask them.

Zale crosses his arms, challengingly. "I could outride you with my eyes closed."

"Doubtful, but this is terrific news. Let's go riding." Fingering the sleeve of his jacket, I ask, "Are you sure you'll be comfortable in this? I can have a servant grab you a change of clothing."

"I'm fine in my own clothes, thank you."

"You'll overheat in that."

"Not worried about *me*, Princess?" Dash interrupts, narrowing his eyes.

"Honestly, no. Even if I was, the leathers were made by aethyns, infused with ice and cooling winds to prevent our guards from overheating. You'll be quite fine, unfortunately."

Ilona snickers until her attention snaps to where we're standing—in the center of the room, near the foot of her bed, on her beloved carpet. "Off my throw! How dare you soil it with your filthy boots!" She plants a hand on Dash and Zale, trying to push them off her carpet. They retreat, murmuring apologies.

"Today is off to a great start," I mumble. "Ready?" Turning to Ilona, I open my eyes wide and mouth to her: *goddess save me*. She nods vigorously, sliding on her slippers and turning off the lamps.

Once we exit the room, she skips to my side and pulls me a few paces ahead of the men. Leaning in to whisper in my ear, she says, "This is going to be a long day unless we ditch these wieners."

"Ilona Ellis Palmetto, did you call them *wieners?*" I double over in laughter before side-eying the curious men. "Let's show them who this island belongs to."

"Which one's Aife, huh?" Dash asks, pointing at the lighter mare with a golden mane, then at the taller one with the coloring of a starless sky.

The stable hand chats with another guard by the entrance, eyeing us skeptically until I wave, assuring him we're fine. Closing my eyes, I inhale deeply, relishing the scent of the stables. Hay and manure. Not exactly delightful, but it brings warm feelings to the surface. Soft whinnies and whimpers flit through the air, bringing a curve to my lips.

"This one," I say. Stepping up to the tall, dark horse at the end of the row, I give her a kiss on the nose and talk quietly to her.

"Pretty thing." Zale nods appraisingly before swiping his gaze to another horse.

"Ilona, don't let them ride Pancake." I point to where Zale's eyes have wandered—to the ruddy horse across the way.

"Pancake?" he asks.

"Let me guess, you named her when you were two?" Dash asks.

"No. Actually I did, and I was seven." Ilona crosses her arms in front of her chest.

"How did you decide on that name?" Zale asks, looking genuinely curious. I admit, he's beginning to grow on me already. He might seem bland at first, but he's actually composed and pragmatic with an ounce of humor. It's a refreshing change of pace from his intense friend I've had the displeasure of getting to know.

"Obviously she's the color of pancakes." Ilona looks embarrassed as she nuzzles her horse's neck with her nose. "And she really likes pancakes."

"How did you figure tha—actually, never mind." Dash shakes his head.

"Can we go to Paramour Falls?" Zale asks, but I deny his request, informing him that we need an earlier head start if we plan to spend the day there. It's a hard ride.

His lips purse, but doesn't put up a fight.

"Enough chatter. Let's get to riding, boys!" I say with a devilish grin.

Ilona and I share a look before saddling up.

We lose the boys in the jungle, twisting and turning with ease through the familiar trails, before returning to the palace to read in the library alone. The thought of them riding around in search of us has us snickering sporadically over the next few hours.

It's a peaceful afternoon until Mother barges in, eyeing the worn books with distaste.

"How you can find relaxation in this horrid place is beyond me, Astrid," she says. She wears a long-sleeve gossamer dress in a deep ruby red that covers her chest and private areas but is entirely see-through around the midsection, legs, and arms.

Gritting my teeth, I hold back a snarky reply. The only thing *horrid* here is her.

"What brings you here, Mother?" I ask instead.

"We are organizing a soiree of sorts in honor of the Vannyks."

I shut my eyes briefly so she can't see me rolling them. She'll use any opportunity she can to host a party. Unsurprising.

"This will be unlike our normal...*affairs,*" she continues. "Proper dress. A banquet. Appropriate dancing."

"So, a ball?" I ask.

"Not at all." Scoffing, she waves a hand at Ilona. "Ball sounds stuffy. You would agree, yes, Ilona?"

"Actually, a ball sounds grand! Gowns and dancing? It's such a fabulous idea, and I've always—"

"A *soiree,*" Mother says through clenched teeth.

Ilona swallows, eyes shifting to the floor. "Yes, Queen Enira. A soiree sounds much lovelier than a ball would."

"Wonderful. We shall host it the day prior to the weekly bacchanal. Two exhilarating events back to back. The people will be pleased. You two will work with the servants to ensure everything is set."

"You want me to plan your ba—soiree? In the next five days?" My eyes widen.

"No. I have planned it. You are ensuring everything meets my standards. You *will* take care of it to my liking." Her black eyes feel invasive as she stares unwaveringly at me. Swallowing, I nod in agreement, although it's the last thing I want to do. Her lips curve upward in a feral grin as she claps her hands together.

"Splendid. You really should not dally, considering you have five days, dear."

She spins on her heel, a tornado of floral perfume and gossamer, and blows toward the door. Pausing, she slowly turns toward us with her head tilted.

"You will allow Dashiel to do his job, Astrid. Do not make a fool of the poor boy."

Seriously? Mother of all people is telling me to be *nice* to a guard?

It isn't until Dashiel and Zale show up two hours later that I begin to feel bad about ditching them.

Ilona and I debate banquet meal options with Deidra and Lila—two of the kitchen servants—as the pair charge in out of breath, slick with sweat, and wearing identical expressions of rage.

"I hope you two got a nice laugh in," Dash says, his eyes flaming. "We spent hours looking for you, thinking something had happened on our watch."

"It's your fault for losing us," I say.

"ASTRID!" His voice booms through the kitchen and everyone goes silent.

Other than my mother, no one has ever dared talk to me like that before, especially not in front of others. My cheeks burn with embarrassment and I'm prepared to berate him for speaking to me with such condescension, but the words stick in my mouth.

"This is not a game to me," Dash says after a beat. "This is my job and I take it seriously. I take protecting *you* seriously."

A weird feeling—almost like guilt—creeps up on me. He's not mad we ditched him; he was worried. He was afraid something happened to us out there. His concern is surprising, and I can't help but find it oddly attractive.

Playing it off before he can notice, I shoot him a nonchalant smirk. "Worried about me, Dashiel Dargan? I'm a big girl."

He rips off his headgear, tossing it aside, causing the two servants to gasp and scatter, leaving the four of us alone. Running a hand impulsively through his messy waves, he shakes his head as though he finds me unbelievable.

"I'm not laughing about this." He steps close enough that I can see the sweat beading on his brow, the flush on his cheeks. I wonder how he got that small scar on his temple—or why I even care. "It's not funny."

"For the love of the goddess, Dashiel. You're so hot and cold." I'm downright pissed at his tone with me, but I no longer feel the urge to reprimand him. Instead, I want to challenge him. "I've known you for like two days and you've cracked jokes the entire time. But suddenly you don't have a sense of humor anymore?"

He flinches almost imperceptibly. "This is different."

"It was a joke."

His face hardens before he steps back, out of my face. "Clearly we don't have the same sense of humor. Forgive me for not finding your safety, or my job, very funny."

"We're all safe." I roll my eyes, trying to downplay my building annoyance at his outburst. "Relax. I didn't expect you to be so uptight about it, okay?"

"Uptight? I'm not—"

"You are. You're being a killjoy."

His brows shoot up to his hairline and his mouth drops open. "You are acting like a child!"

"Oh so now you want to throw insults?"

"No. I'm not actively trying to insult you. I'm simply stating it like it is."

"I'm the *princess*. You're only a *guard,* Dash, you have no right to talk to me in this manner."

"Wow." Disbelief crosses his face. He shakes his head. "I hear you, Astrid. Loud and clear."

My hands vibrate with fury. This man is maddening! "*You* started this."

"It doesn't matter who started what! Will you just listen to me? You have no idea what—" He pauses and runs a hand over his face before lowering his voice. "It doesn't matter. Forget it." He storms out of the kitchen, and my stomach sinks.

For a few seconds all I can do is stand there and stare at the empty doorway he disappeared through.

Finally, I turn to Zale, trying to downplay how bothered I am by Dash. "Your guard has some serious issues."

His nostrils flare. "He's been through a lot. You really should cut him some slack."

"We were only playing around. I survived fine on my own before you two showed up, and I'll be fine long after you leave."

"It's not even about that. His only responsibility right now is to watch over you. It might seem absurd to you, but why can't you at least let him do his job?"

"How am I supposed to know he takes his *job* so seriously? The guy doesn't seem to take anything seriously!"

"I know Dash can be a jokester, a bit of a fool even, but that's his way of trying to alleviate a potentially uncomfortable situation. He likes making people smile and laugh, but it doesn't negate the seriousness of his duty."

Ilona frowns at Zale sympathetically. "We truly didn't mean to upset him."

Zale stares at me, unwaveringly. There's no admonishment in his expression, only true concern.

"We're really, really sorry," Ilona squeaks out. Her pale cheeks flare with color, and she nudges me with her bony elbow.

"All right, fine, I'm sorry too."

Zale nods. "I appreciate that. And Dash will get over it."

"It's been a long day," I say, slicing through the residual tension. "I'm going to my room to cool down."

The three of us walk to the royal wing in awkward silence. As we draw close to our rooms, we run into Dash. His hair is wet from a fresh shower, and his eyes are red-rimmed.

My chest squeezes at the sight of him—this rugged, arrogant guard—and it's hard to breathe. No one speaks for a moment, and I'm secretly grateful I'm not the only one who doesn't know what to say. The dampened mood weighs down on me.

"I'm sorry," I say, at the same time he says, "I shouldn't have overreacted."

He forces a smile. I see the lingering hurt in his eyes, but if he wants to play off the situation and pretend nothing happened, I'll do the same.

Zale clears his throat, but when Dash keeps his attention locked on me, he mutters a goodbye, leaving with Ilona.

Once we're alone, I eye Dash carefully, ignoring the weird energy between us. "Are we good?"

He leans in toward me. "We're good, *Princess.*" His warm breath caresses my ear, sending a tickle up my spine and a flood of heat to my core.

Great.

Now I'm angry, confused, *and* turned on. I don't know how Dash manages to affect me so greatly, but I hate it.

Based on his outburst and Zale's words, I'm almost convinced that he only wants to do his job well. And if it wasn't for the strange way my magic doesn't work on him, I might believe it. But frankly, I do not trust him.

So why do I feel an extreme amount of guilt about upsetting him?

I shouldn't care about him, yet I do, and that's the most terrifying thing of all. Nothing good will come of this, especially since I'm uncertain of his true intentions.

He puts space between us again, gazing at me with a serious expression. Gone is his usually playful demeanor. "And you were right. You are the princess and I'm just a guard. I shouldn't have spoken to you like that."

I groan. "That's not what I meant."

"That doesn't make it any less true."

"Look, I'm sorry for... well, I'm sorry for making your job harder I guess."

"It's fine, really."

"All right." I'm skeptical, but I don't press. "We're going to be spending a lot of time together. I don't want things to be weird."

"Here's an idea to make up for it—take us to the falls? We can all get away and relax for a day."

"All right. But not until next week. Thanks to your prince and his family, we have pressing obligations this week."

"Okay," Dash says, with a stern expression. "And one more thing."

"Yes?"

"No more ditching." We lock eyes, and something intense passes between us.

"Fine. But only if you stay out of my way like a good little shadow. Let me live my life without your constant interference," I say.

He smirks, much more authentically this time, and offers me a hand. I eye it warily before accepting and shaking. "Deal."

CHAPTER NINE

The next five days pass in a blur of golden ornaments, food tasting, and ballroom rearranging.

Yes, we have an actual ballroom, despite Mother's aversion to formal events. She might not want to call it what it is, but based on the dress code she insisted upon, it's definitely a classic ball.

"Look at you, Princess," Ilona teases, eyeing my smokey cat-eye and nude lip combination. It's rare that I wear makeup. The island is so hot most of the time that it melts right off my face anyway. It is inconvenient and unnecessary. But tonight, I took great care in embellishing my appearance.

My floor-length dress is a translucent, flowing gold satin. It sits snugly against my flesh, hugging my chest and hips before flaring around my thighs so I can walk. With a deep V-neck and only two thin straps holding it up, it looks like a mix between a nightgown and a ballgown.

"And yet, *you're* the one who looks like a princess," I say as we walk through the royal wing toward the ballroom in the palace's heart. There's no animosity in my tone; I mean it. Ilona is stunning in her forest-green gown. The tight sleeveless bodice has straps that criss cross over her back, and a multi-layered tulle skirt rustles around her as she walks.

It makes her eyes glow and contrasts with her fiery hair that's flowing tamely around her shoulders tonight. Her makeup is simple and understated; she's been careful not to hide her unique freckles.

"I hate Mother's events. I'm only going for you," I grumble. Her cheeks flush, and her smile grows wider. She's excited that Mother has decided to host a regular ball for once, in honor of our *guests*.

No regular villagers are invited. Only the noble families—those with magic or wealth—are in attendance. Everyone has been granted a plus-one though, so many regular folks have tagged along.

Ilona normally despises Mother's events too. The bacchanals and the parties normally turn into orgies full of inebriated citizens. However, with the Stellari king and queen in attendance, tonight's event is expected to be a bit more...upstanding. And Ilona loves an excuse for a pretty dress and nice pair of shoes.

I prefer my flats and pants, but I must admit I do feel stunning.

"Are you sure it has nothing to do with that handsome prince or your new guard?"

I shoot Ilona an annoyed look as music carries through the empty hallways. "Prince Zale couldn't handle me if he wanted to. And my new guard constantly looks like he's up to no good."

"Well I suppose you can keep an eye on him tonight. Maybe the two of you can get up to no good together. It's been a while since you've taken a lover." She waggles her eyebrows at me. It hits me that I forgot to tell her about how Dashiel and I kissed. With all of the strange energy after his outburst the other day, I've been trying to avoid any conversations with him or about him.

"Oh really? If you want to chat about my love life, how about we dive into yours. How's Marnie?" I ask, trying to change the subject.

She makes a small squeaking noise, avoiding eye contact. "Gosh. I'm not sure what you're talking about," she says, her voice going up an octave.

"Sure you don't." We both laugh. "Speaking of, is Marnie coming tonight?"

Ilona flushes a deeper red and tries to turn so I don't see. "I can't invite a servant."

"I'm pretty sure you can invite whoever you'd like as your plus one, Ilona."

"Your mother—"

"Probably wouldn't even notice with the amount of wine she consumes at these things. Her head will be buried in the sheets or in someone's lap before long."

"Not at the Vannyk's ball!" She gasps, undoubtedly imagining the horrors of Mother's event turning rogue in front of other royalty.

"You're right. She'll be on her best behavior tonight. Unless the Stellari secretly enjoy wild rendezvous of their own?"

"They still marry off their heirs to other countries as political pawns, Astrid. I'm sure they're quite old-school." Her face lights up, and she begins talking quickly, her quirk when she's excited or nervous. "Oh my goddess. What if they want you and Zale to marry for a political alliance! Do you think your mother would go for it? You're an adult. She couldn't say no. Would you live here or in Stellari—"

"Ilona," I say. "Enough of that nonsense. I'm not marrying anyone. Especially not an uptight prince with the personality of a doorknob."

"I resent that statement, Princess," a familiar voice drawls.

"Of course he's right behind me," I say, rolling my eyes. Ilona makes a small choking noise, and her eyes widen in horror. I turn, casual as ever, and offer a small wave to the prince.

He's dressed in a black tuxedo, bow tie and all. His dark hair is styled as always—longer on the top than the sides—and he looks as handsome as ever. He offers me a toothy smile, his white teeth contrasting with his dark skin.

He stands out in his Stellari formal wear. We won't see the men from the island wearing such outfits tonight.

But it's the person standing at his side who truly catches my attention, causing my breath to hitch.

Dashiel.

He wears equally formal attire—a button-up shirt with slacks and suspenders—and with his artfully messy waves, he looks delectable.

Though we've been around each other plenty, our usual banter has been stilted. I'm still not sure where we stand, and I'm not sure how to engage. Goddess forbid I end up offending him again.

"You take longer than the ladies to get ready," I say, crossing my arms, opting to pretend everything between us is fine. Dash's eyes follow the movement before slowly dragging up to my face. He offers a feral grin. "We almost left without you."

"I thought we agreed on no more ditching?" he counters.

I visibly relax at the mention of our deal from the other day. It seems he's no longer irked at me. "And I am a woman of my word."

Zale leans in to give me his customary kiss on each cheek before doing the same with Ilona. When it's Dashiel's turn to kiss us, his lips linger on my cheeks, the heat of his body radiating toward me, like we're magnets drawn together. When he releases me, I feel colder. Emptier.

He gives Ilona a polite, chaste kiss on each cheek. She turns to me with a questioning look. She definitely noticed his affectionate greeting. I'll have to give her a rundown on what occurred with him earlier this week.

"You have a thing for calling me a bore," Zale says with a bit of bite.

"Maybe his lackluster personality is simply to throw you off his scent. It's a facade," Dash says with a smirk.

Zale shakes his head, his lips pressed into a straight line.

"Let's hope you're not betrothed to him," Ilona whispers, but it comes out louder than she intends. Dash bursts into a laugh, and a dimple appears on his cheek. It's spectacularly beautiful to see him wear an expression of such joy.

"Betrothed?" Zale asks in a strangled voice. "Why in the stars would you say that?"

"She reads too many of those far-fetched romance stories," I say. I grab her elbow and resume leading her toward the ballroom.

"Hey!" Ilona's cheeks blaze as red as her hair. "You're the one who told me to read *Her Warrior of Passion.*" She turns to the men and loud-whispers scandalously, "Spoiler alert: the warrior likes to use the back door."

Zale's eyes widen, and he distracts himself by adjusting his tie, while Dash's face continues to crinkle with humor.

"Ilona," I cry out through tears of laughter. If she's trying to embarrass me, it's not working. I'm mostly amused that she's fired up enough to take shots at me. Normally she doesn't stand up to me when I pick on her. "It's called *anal.* Just say it."

"Absolutely not," she says matter-of-factly. "And for the record, I prefer stories of lore and history."

"Sure," I tease, knowing she's lying to herself more than to us.

"Lore?" Dash asks, sharing a look with Zale.

"Yes. Did you know that it's said the original goddess was from Hakran? That the land here is filled with extraordinary magic and mysteries that have been forgotten throughout the years, like—"

"I'm sure they don't care," I say, jumping in.

"Actually," Dash says, eyes shifting nervously, "what do you know?"

There's something weird about the way he asks, but I let it go. "None of the lores are true." Ilona's stories are just that—stories. Fiction. Fairy tales. As we near the ballroom entrance, Zale offers me his arm, and feeling apologetic about calling him bland, I accept it. Ilona takes Dash's, and the four of us enter together.

We're tardy enough that the party is already in full-swing—the wine is flowing and feet are gliding across the dance floor—but we're not too late that Mother notices. She's likely busy mingling and bathing in praise.

With the expansive, open floor designed for dancing, gilded chandeliers, and carved marble columns, the ballroom is much more ostentatious than the throne room. It's meant for entertaining. It's luxurious and overstated.

To our left sit banquet tables with fresh food and cocktails. The serving staff busily moves to and fro, refreshing the tables as they empty. They will ensure the guests have plenty throughout the night. To our right are several gold and white sofas on which people relax. Swaths of color swirl around us as the ball attendees dance the night away.

Beyond it all, along the far wall, glass-paned doors lead out into the courtyard. A few people trickle in and out.

"I love balls," Ilona breathes out.

Dashiel and I snicker while Zale casts us scolding looks. "You two would be perfect together."

Before I can object, Zale carefully releases my arm and switches places with Dashiel.

"Hello, sweetheart," Dashiel purrs in my ear. My skin pebbles, and liquid warmth spreads between my legs, but I refuse to let him know how he affects me. Instead, I huff in annoyance. At this point, I'm more annoyed at my body's reaction to him than I am at him.

"What were they laughing at?" Ilona asks Zale.

"Your love of *balls?*"

"Oh, gosh." She chews her bottom lip, looking amused herself now. "The formal kind. Not the man kind."

Zale's face scrunches with bewilderment. "The man kind?"

"Not a fan of anal *or* testicles, eh?" Dash teases. I swat his shoulder in warning.

"I—well, not really," she says tentatively. "Sometimes, I suppose."

"Well, looks like we have something in common after all." Zale casts Dash a dirty look before smiling at Ilona. I snicker at the exchange. Perhaps the four of us might be friends after all.

We greet the Vannyks and say hello to Mother—who is dressed in something opaque for once—before locating beverages.

Dashiel, Zale, Ilona, and I converge on a set of couches, observing the evening's polite chatter and appropriate dancing. Dashiel sits by my side, with Zale and Ilona on the couch to our right. We have a clear view of the entire room.

"I'm pleasantly surprised," Ilona says, sipping her burgundy wine. "Your mother's affair is incredibly felicitous."

"Felicitous?" Zale asks with a frown.

"It's probably one of her new words." I chuckle. "Which book did you read that in?"

"I thought anal was her new word," Dashiel adds. I snort,

laughing so hard that I almost choke on my wine. Zale sighs and looks at Ilona apologetically. Her cheeks redden but she snickers along with us.

"Felicitous—you know, pleasing. Well suited," Ilona says. Zale shakes his head and starts a new conversation with her, discussing synonyms of *felicitous*.

"You look absolutely stunning tonight," Dashiel whispers in my ear. I gulp my wine, hoping to distract myself from his closeness.

"I know," I say. He chuckles darkly, and his warm breath tickles my ear. "You're too close to me." I scoot a few inches away, putting distance between us.

"I beg to differ. I don't think I'm close enough."

I groan, draining my wine. A servant passes with a tray of beverages, and I flag them down, gratefully accepting a filled glass.

"You're nervous," Dash says. Finally, I turn to meet his stare, and his eyes crinkle with glee. "I make you nervous."

"No you don't." I glance away, looking at Ilona instead. She's deep in conversation with Zale, but I interrupt them anyway. "Would you like to dance, Lonnie?"

She pouts at the nickname before nodding. Excusing herself from Zale, she treads to the dance floor with me. We spin around to a few songs, smiling and laughing until our cheeks are flushed and we're out of breath.

"This is so much fun, A!" She giggles. "I wish your mother would host more events like this. They're spectacular. I feel like royalty."

"You *are* royalty," I say.

After another dance, we return to the couches to take a break. Surprisingly, Zale and Dashiel are exactly where we left them. Dashiel's eyes darken as his gaze roams me hungrily. Riding the buzzy high of the wine and dancing, I saunter over to him with a wink.

"Dance with me next?" he asks.

"My poor feet have had enough," I say. "Maybe next time?"

"We both know there won't be a next time. You'll dance with me tonight."

"Demanding, Dashiel Dargan." I scowl mockingly at him, but my stomach flutters with his demand. I don't want to like his arrogance, but I do. It turns me on.

"Do you dance, Prince?" I ask Zale, turning my attention to him and Ilona.

"Absolutely not," Zale says. He smooths a hand over his jacket.

"So uptight," I mutter with an eye roll. "Of course you don't dance."

If I'm not mistaken, I swear Ilona looks disappointed at Zale's lack of interest in dancing. Perhaps it's all the wine getting to my head, but I wish he'd make an exception for her. I bet if Marnie was here, *she'd* dance with Ilona.

The thought of Ilona and Marnie together, happy, gives me an idea.

"I'll be right back," I say, jumping up. "There's something I have to do." Ignoring Ilona's quizzical look, I scurry to the exit. Dashiel, of course, tags along as I hustle to the servants' quarters to find who I'm looking for.

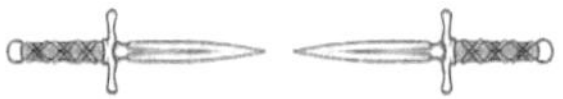

Thirty minutes later, after a bit of tipsy begging combined with Gianna's magic, Marnie's dressed in a pale pink gown, her dark hair loose around her shoulders.

"Are you sure Ilona wants me there?" Marnie asks, twisting

her hands together nervously.

"Trust me." I adjust her skirts one last time, before leading her into the ballroom.

We make our way back to Zale and Ilona, and at the sight of Marnie, Ilona's mouth drops open. "Marnie, what are you doing here?"

Marnie's face drops and she stammers out an apology. "I just—I thought—"

"No. I'm so sorry. I didn't mean it like that," Ilona says. "You look beautiful. I'm pleased to see you. I only meant that I wasn't expecting to see you."

Marnie grins before casting a bashful glance in my direction. I leave the two of them alone, and the men follow me to an empty couch nearby.

"I'll be right back," Zale mutters. I don't miss the way his eyes continuously flicker over to Ilona as he makes his way past them. He cuts through the dance floor, to the other side of the room.

"That was a nice thing you did," Dashiel says, plopping down at my side.

"That's what friends do." I shrug.

"Would you say *we* are friends, Princess?" He trails a finger lazily along my bare shoulder.

"No," I say. He sits with one arm behind me, his legs spread open so his knee bumps my own. I'm tempted to scoot away and put distance between us again, but then I decide against it, secretly relishing his nearness.

I blame the alcohol.

"Good. I don't want to be your *friend,*" he whispers in my ear.

Before I get a chance to reply, Zale sidles up, balancing three glasses of red wine in his hands. They're filled to the brim, and I'm impressed that he hasn't spilled any. But then again, Zale would probably have a heart attack if he spilled something on himself.

The three of us drink and laugh for the next couple of hours, and I'm pleasantly surprised to discover Zale can loosen up a bit.

Everyone seems to be having a wonderful time. I've lost sight of my best friend, but last time I saw her, she was twirling Marnie around to the music. Even Mother wears a rare smile on her face as she floats between various nobles on the dance floor.

"The wine here is delicioussss," Zale slurs. His lips are tinted dark red.

"Are you drunk, Prince Zale?" I stifle a laugh behind my hand. Dashiel's eyes widen in surprise, and it causes me to laugh harder. Before I know it, the three of us are laughing hysterically.

"Nope. I'm not." He stands up, and the way he stumbles says otherwise. "Come on. Let's dance."

"He's inebriated!" I say, hiccuping from my own drunkenness. "The prince is sick of being dull. He wants to dance!"

Dash stands beside him and slaps him on the back.

The three of us meet up with Ilona and Marnie on the dance floor. Zale shrugs out of his jacket, tossing it aside carelessly, a wide grin plastered on his face. I'm humored at how different he is after a few drinks.

After a bit of chatting, I let Dash lead me away from the group. We dance quietly, wrapped in each other's arms, until the buzz wears off and tiredness settles in.

And for once I almost feel like I'm at home.

It's been one week since the Vannyks came and disturbed our routine, but things are almost back to normal today.

I sit alongside Ilona on a snack-filled blanket in our ruby-colored tent on the beach, watching the revelers as they twirl around the sand in the warm light of the snapping, spitting bonfire.

Lights have been strung up from the tent to the platform where the musicians play, beating on their drums and plucking at their stringed instruments. Bare feet spray up bits of sand and muck as they move about. Laughter and chatter ring out.

"Goddess, this week flew by," Ilona says, making a little sandwich of cheese, ham, and crackers.

"At least we're relieved of ball-planning duty."

"It was a *soiree,*" she says, mimicking Mother's flat drawl. We both chuckle.

"It wasn't so bad, surprisingly," I admit. And it's true. Everyone seemed to have an enjoyable time together. It stayed classy, too, which is an accomplishment on its own.

"Where is Dashiel? Certainly he didn't accompany you here tonight. I'm sure your mother would never trust him with that secret."

"She's hosting a dinner for the Vannyks. He got invited and couldn't decline, thank the goddess."

"Oh! Marnie told me the Stellari brought some strange fruit with them from the mainland! Eggplant? Weird name though. It looks nothing like an egg and more like a big, purple—nevermind. Apparently it's a delicacy. Enira instructed the kitchen staff to make a meal in their honor, so I don't think she will be creeping around tonight either."

"Good." I harrumph.

"Maybe I was wrong about Queen Enira." She sighs, looking up at the sloping fabric overhead. "It's just that I've had the same dream a few times, and it feels so real every time."

"It's only a dream." I stand, placing the veyl over my head, eager to get this over with. At least Mother is up at the castle with the Vannyks, leaving me in what almost feels like peace tonight.

Other than the killing-someone part.

I despise taking innocent lives, and I've begun to strongly suspect these people aren't here wholly of their own free will. Despite my hesitations, my body moves of its own accord, pulling me through the motions.

"Yeah...sure, A." Ilona sounds dejected.

"You don't have to wait for me either. Go see Marnie and get your tea if you'd like."

"Okay. What are you in the mood to read tonight?"

"I would much prefer my bed, quite frankly," I say, exhausted from the events of this week.

"Oh thank the goddess." Ilona's whole body visibly relaxes as she brushes the curls out of her face. "I drank way too much last night and want nothing more than to rest. I didn't have the heart to break our evening routine."

She wraps her arms around me, suffocating me beneath the heavy fabric.

"Can't...breathe, Lonnie."

"Oh gosh, sorry. Sorry!" Her eyes widen with embarrassment. "I just wanted to thank you for inviting Marnie. It was very kind of you."

Grunting in response, I reach a hand out through the slit of my veyl and give her hand a squeeze. "That's what friends are for."

Would I still be your friend if you knew I killed your mother?

My own voice echoes in my head—the guilt I try to keep behind bars deep inside me.

"Go. Say hi to her for me, and have a restful sleep."

"Don't forget you're the most powerful woman in Hakran, your mother be damned, A." She leaves in a flurry of fiery curls and lilac perfume.

I smile, downing the bitter tonic Cedrik gave me last week in hopes it will prevent another bout of nausea during the transference. I've been so distracted, so busy with Dashiel and Zale, that I haven't given him much thought.

I hope he's okay.

Trudging through the rest of the evening's motions, I choose a teen male for the sacrifice this time. As I absorb his energy, I keep my eyes closed, trying to fight the waves of pleasure that threaten to drown me.

I don't like this.

I can't like this.

If it wasn't for Mother needing the life force to stay in power and keep our island secure, I wouldn't use this side of my power at all. But I do, for her. I must hurry to the throne room to complete the transference, to allow her to feed off me like a leech.

I leave the swaying bodies, crashing waves, and salty air behind, along with the husk of a boy who will never take another breath.

CHAPTER TEN

The next day, thankfully Mother doesn't send Gianna to wake me up, allowing me to get some much-needed rest. Ilona and I decide to take Dash and Zale to Paramour Falls. It's also better to do it now, while we can, before the infamous summer storms begin rolling through. Not to mention, I need to get away from the palace.

It will be exactly the relaxing day I'm craving. A trip to the falls should make everyone happy.

Summer heat clings to us like leeches the moment we exit the palace. The breeze has died down, the sky an expanse of pastel blue.

We stop by the servant's wing on the way to the stables, and Ilona runs in to grab lunch and water packs from the kitchen.

The stable hand tips his straw hat at us as we enter. "Yer en luck today, Princess Astrid. We've two mares left back 'ere."

That's luck?

"Please tell me they left my Aife," I say, referring to the mare I've had since I was a child. The stalls that normally hold around three dozen horses all sit empty except for two mares in the back. Aife's shiny midnight mane stands out immediately, and I grin.

"'Course 'ey did. Wouldn't take yer girl, Princess."

"Thank the goddess. I didn't realize the guards would be

taking them out today."

"Training for the new lot," he says, eyeing Dash from head to toe with a wary look.

"Is this going to be an issue?" Zale asks, fingering the neckline of his shirt. For once, he's actually wearing something with short sleeves, though it still has buttons and screams *uptight*.

Ilona looks at me with pursed lips.

"Two horses and four of us; doesn't seem like an issue at all," Dash says. He ignores the stable hand's perusing eyes, jogging over to the back of the stable, where Aife and the other mare are.

"Come on then." I loop my arm through Ilona's, and the three of us catch up to him.

"I recommend you two ride together." Zale points at me, then Dash. He turns to Ilona. "You can ride with me."

Putting my hands up, I shake my head aggressively. "Absolutely not. I'm not riding with your mouthy guard."

"Actually, he's *your* mouthy guard now, and your mother requested he stay with you at all times."

"You wound me, sweetheart." Dash's lips tilt up as he clutches his chest dramatically with one hand. "I was under the impression we were making progress."

"I don't need someone to *protect* me," I bite out.

"According to Queen Enira, you do," Zale counters.

"I'm trained. I'm capable of fighting just fine."

Before I have time to react, Dash darts toward me. He shoots a foot out, sweeping both of my legs out from underneath me in one quick motion. My back hits the hay-covered ground, and the breath leaves my lungs in an *oomph*. Faster than I can comprehend, he's on top of me, pinning my arms down over my head. His heavy body presses into me, and I flash back to the night I *almost* brought him to my bed.

If he hadn't tried to take charge, there's a good chance I would've ridden him harder than one of these horses. Then again, something inside of me comes alive with Dash's challenging nature—something that scares me, makes me think I *like* being out of control around him.

"Plenty capable, it seems," he says sarcastically.

His gold-flecked eyes meet my own, searching, reading with a burning intensity, as if he can somehow tell what I'm thinking. His deep, woodsy scent invades my nostrils, and my body softens beneath him. My eyes slowly glide to his lips, just as his tongue darts out and wets them. All of a sudden, it's hard to breathe, and not only because he has me pinned to the ground. My cheeks heat, my legs begin to open of their own accord, begging for him to come closer. My movement seems to snap him out of his trance, because he jumps up to his feet, shifting the crotch of his pants discreetly before extending a hand out to me. Slapping it away, I pull myself up and straighten my top.

"Absolutely uncalled for," I scold him.

"You ride with me, or we don't go."

"A, it's not a big deal," Ilona whispers to me.

She's right, and I *really* want to visit the falls. I need to get away from the palace for a bit, even if we're weighed down by a pretentious prince and his overbearing guard.

"Fine. You're in the back though. I'll be in charge for the ride."

"I've learned my lesson. I'll relinquish control this once." He winks at me, and I swat at his shoulder, my brows furrowed.

"Don't make this worse than it has to be."

Zale waves the stable hand over, and I'm surprised when the man waddles over to make small talk with the prince. Based on how put-together and proper Zale seems, I figured he was one of those royals who refuses to get their hands dirty or speak to the help. Admittedly, it's attractive seeing him roll up his sleeves and maneuver through the stable like he knows what he's doing. It seems he does know what he's doing; I watch in awe as he saddles Pancake more quickly than the stable hand does Aife.

"Are you checking out my prince?" Dash's lips turn up into a lopsided grin.

"Are you jealous?"

"Maybe a little."

"What can I say? I like a man who's good with his hands."

"Oh just wait until I show you what I can do."

"Not going to happen." Tightening my lips, I give him an unamused look before turning back to my horse to prepare her.

After the horses are fully dressed and ready to ride, Zale says something quietly that makes Ilona laugh, and I eye them with open interest.

Placing my foot into the stirrup, I swing my other leg over. Dash does the same behind me. He scoots close, wrapping his hands around my bare waist. I flinch at his touch.

"I've never seen a riding outfit like this," he whispers in my ear. "Can't complain."

It's nothing unusual for Hakran—a thin, gold crop top and riding pants. But I suppose our dress code is a little more relaxed here than on the continent, likely due to the differences in climate. Luckily, he's covered in thick leathers. Knowing we have some layers between us brings me comfort.

Ilona had forced Zale to ride behind her too, and I shoot a sly look at my best friend.

"At least you two won't be able to lose us this time," Zale mutters, irked at being in the back. The need for constant control must be a Stellari trait, much like their arrogance.

Exiting the stables, we ride out into the sunshine and cross the side yard, getting onto one of the jungle paths. Ilona and I have visited enough times to know exactly how to get to the falls, though it's off the main trail.

The steady beat of hooves on dirt fills my ears as the birds chatter in the background. It's one of the most comforting sounds in the world. The thick canopies overhead offer a bit of reprieve from the sun's harshest heat, and we fall into a rhythm.

"So why Aife?"

"What?"

"Why'd you name your mare Aife? I'm assuming you named her, since she's yours."

"In some translations, it means 'warrior woman.' Aife was the stable runt—she almost died when she was young. When Mother let me pick out a horse on my seventh birthday, I chose her and named her Aife because despite everyone telling her she was one thing—a runt, useless, lame—she recovered and proved them all wrong. A true warrior. When I was little, I wanted to be a warrior too."

"But you don't want to be one any longer?"

Frowning, I shift in the saddle, accidentally brushing up against Dash. He hisses through his teeth as his fingers squeeze into my side. The proximity should be awkward—uncomfortable even—but it only ignites a wave of heat inside of me. It's getting more difficult to lie to myself about being drawn to the man. Despite being a bit arrogant, he *is* quite funny, a breath of fresh air compared to the noblemen I'm used to.

Suddenly, I'm far too aware of his closeness. His muscular thighs on either side of me. His strong hands gripping me just enough to keep steady. The unfamiliar yet delicious scent of something spicy mixed with the outdoors. Fighting to keep my breathing steady, I replay his question in my head.

"I am plenty warrior, in my own way."

"You have pretty poor moves for a warrior though."

The lust that was swirling around a moment prior is doused by his words, as if someone dumped a bucket of ice down my shirt.

"Excuse me?" I snap.

He chuckles, and this infuriates me even more. How dare he insult me after I give him something real?

"You could've easily stabilized yourself or broken my hold earlier," he says, referring to when he pinned me down in the stables. "Twice now I've used basic moves on you, and twice you found yourself subdued."

"Maybe I let you subdue me."

He chuckles mockingly, and his breath tickles my nape. "You are way too strong-willed to go down without a fight. Unless you didn't know *how* to fight."

"I do," I reply defensively.

"Most of Hakran's guards don't know how to fight, but you think a princess does?"

"Yes..." My gut sinks as I realize where he's going with this. My cheeks flame with embarrassment and anger, but I contemplate his words. He wouldn't be here if Mother's guards were trained properly, would he? It's further proof her guard is simply an illusion of an army. "You think she instructed Jamell to purposely hold back during my training? Or do you think he himself doesn't know how to fight?"

"Commander Jamell seems efficient. But it's awfully strange that the commander of the Hakranian guard supposedly spent *years* teaching you how to fight, yet you can't break out of a basic pinning."

Biting my lip, I let the thought sink in. Jamell has always been an effective instructor, but I've only ever trained with him. I've never tested my skills with anyone else, never needed to defend myself properly. How would I know if he was purposely handicapping me?

"Hey," Dash says, squeezing my waist gently, "if you'd like, I'll show you a few things."

His words are soft, reassuring even, and I find myself considering his proposal. Maybe he's wrong and a few practice sessions with him will reveal that Jamell has indeed taught me proper skills. But if he's right, and Mother truly has sabotaged my training—one of the few things that truly empowers me, brings me joy—I don't think I can trust her anymore. If she's been lying about this, what else is she keeping from me? What else is she holding me back from?

"I don't need you to show me anything," I snap. "And stop groping me!"

Dash grows silent, scooting back as far as he can on the horse, and loosening his grip on me almost entirely.

My anger is misplaced, I know, but I can't help it. I hate that Dash is so observant. I hate that he's the first person to ask me *why* I named my horse Aife, to ask me if I still want to be a warrior. I hate that he seems to notice me, that he's pointing out things in my life that not even I have noticed—like Jamell's lackluster training.

Most of all, I hate how he makes me feel, because I know he's only going to hurt me later. Nothing good comes of a man with so many secrets; no matter what he says or does to try and wiggle his way beneath my bones, I refuse to let him in.

For the rest of the ride, Dash tries to keep a polite distance—as much as he can on horseback—and every nerve in my body is hyperaware of him.

Finally, after two hours of riding, the thicket of trees and the tangled vines give way to a clearing in the middle of which sits a shimmering pond of crystal-clear water. It's a shallow body of water, only reaching up to my neck at its deepest. On the far side, a wall made of craggy rocks and overreaching greenery stands fifty feet high. Water tumbles down from two separate openings, racing around jutting stones before merging into one thick waterfall and dumping into the pond.

The two streams are what give Paramour Falls their name. They are also known as Lover Falls—where two become one. The two waterfalls begin their descent as separate entities before entwining into one, losing themselves wholly in each other as they cascade down the ridge. Much like two lovers falling into one new life.

Sunlight reflects off the glimmering water, casting miniature rainbows alongside the falls before disappearing into a thin mist.

Zale shed his shirt somewhere along the ride, and his tawny skin glimmers with drops of sweat. His hair is mussed on the top where it's longer, and by his flustered look, I can tell he's not used to the heat. Dash, though fully covered, is the coolest of us all in his aethyn-infused Hakranian leathers.

Conveniently, our water pouches are also aethyn-infused, meaning they refill by drawing moisture from the air. Between the two horses and the four of us, we went through a few pouches before we even reached the falls.

Dismounting, we let the horses wander. They gleefully trot over to the shallow end of the pond, wading in where the clear water reveals a smooth-pebbled bottom. Aife releases a pleased whinny. This side of the pond is shaded by thick palm leaves, offering a radical reprieve from the harsh sun. Closer to the falls, where there are no trees overhead to block the sun, light glitters off the water in a way that's almost painful to look at.

Birds flit around us, tweeting and chirping their contentment.

"I thought this was storm season," Zale says, eyeing the area in awe. "We're lucky the weather has been so kind."

I glance at Dash, who wears a contented grin as he takes in the clearing.

"The storms will still come," I say. "Sometimes the storms stall over the sea before ambushing us. We need to keep our eyes on the sky and watch for darkening clouds or increasing winds."

It looks clear now, but I know better than anyone how quickly that can change.

"I've heard the storms here are different than on the continent," Zale says.

"There's wild magic at the bottom of the sea. Sometimes the storms dredge it up and hit us hard with a combination of elements. There's no way to predict if a storm is normal or elemental, but we take precautions. Elemental storms start like regular storms, but they hit us with a mix of ice, fire, wind, and lightning. Sometimes all at once. They're dangerous."

The prince *hmms,* considering my words with interest.

"Are those oranges?" Zale points to the oval fruit dangling from a nearby tree.

I shake my head. "Kumquats."

"Cum-what?" Dash asks with a smirk, suddenly looking interested in the conversation.

"You're an idiot." I roll my eyes and Ilona snickers. "It's similar to an orange but it's a bit more sour. You can also eat the peel."

"Interesting," Zale mutters.

"Watch for snakes by the brush and under the large rocks, by the way," I call to him right before he sits on a large boulder near the edge of the jungle. He jumps up, glancing down and kicking his boot against the side of the rock before determining it's safe to take a seat. Snakes don't typically come out in the summer heat, but they enjoy curling up for naps under the cool side of rocks and bushes.

Ilona chuckles at the discomfited prince as she removes her pack from Pancake and begins to unload it, spreading out a large, thin blanket by the edge of the pond where it's not too rocky. The packed dirt provides the perfect sitting area. It's a shaded section, so Ilona won't burn. The sun isn't as forgiving with her as it is with me—we learned that the hard way after falling asleep on the beach as teenagers. She cried on the walk home, tender to the touch everywhere her flesh had met the sun. Even after Cedrik fixed her up with his salves, the healing process was intense.

Even after that, she has never hesitated to join me on another beach trip. She's too soft and sweet for this world, but I'm thankful she sticks by my side. The thought of her always being there for me brings a smile to my lips.

"What are you smiling about?" Dash says as he strides over to me.

"That I'm no longer subject to your grubby hands around my waist."

Smirking, he reaches up and pulls off his head covering, tossing it aside.

Deep-brown waves tumble around his face, matching the thin line of stubble that's surfacing along his jaw. This close, I can make out that curious little scar on his left temple, which only adds to his rugged handsomeness.

The sun washes over his bronzed skin like a welcoming embrace.

"Goddess have mercy," I breathe out.

"Yes?" His eyes glimmer with amusement, and I realize I said that out loud. Now he thinks I'm admiring him. He *knows* I'm admiring him.

Ignoring his hypnotizing gaze, I turn my back to him, squinting at the falls instead. Just because he's a beautiful specimen to look at doesn't mean I actually *like* the guy. He can be easy on the eyes and an ass all the same.

It's impossible to deny my body's natural reaction to him, but I'm unsettled that he tried to speak to me—the vessel—outside the servants' quarters on the night of the bacchanal. It was highly inappropriate. And he degraded my mother, Hakran's queen, on her own soil, which is treason. Not to mention I still haven't determined why my powers don't work on him. That alone is enough to drive me mad.

Since the Vannyks are immune to others with myndox powers, I'm beginning to wonder if Dash is secretly a vygora who can block out my power. It would explain why the Vannyks were insistent on Dash guarding me. Perhaps they wanted to even the playing ground.

Despite my distrust and anger, it takes everything in me not to turn and ogle his muscular physique as he sheds his leather.

"You need a bush, A?" Ilona calls from where she's lying on the blanket with a handful of biscuits. Her pants and blouse are discarded off to the side, and she's sporting an emerald two-piece suit that emphasizes her slender legs and toned torso. "You look like you need to relieve yourself."

Zale clears his throat awkwardly as Dash barks out a laugh.

I chew the inside of my cheek. "Just hot and tired. Come on, let's go for a swim."

Seconds after kicking off my own shoes and pants, I realize I haven't changed into my own garments.

"Dammit," I say. Not because I'm wearing only a golden crop top and plain black panties, but because I've been so distracted lately I couldn't even remember to dress properly for swimming. At least I'm not the only one. Turning back, I see Dash and Zale have both discarded their own clothes and are in matching black undergarments that are similar to shorts but smaller and more formfitting.

Way more snug. They highlight everything below the belt, confirming my suspicions that Dash's muscles aren't the only thick thing on him. His thin underwear reveal he's well-endowed. Glancing at Zale, my breath catches as I realize he's equally equipped.

I clear my throat and look away, flushed.

There's no way these two irritating men should be affecting me this greatly. Not with the amount of naked flesh I see on a weekly basis.

"Looks like they brought their *staffs* this time," Ilona says with a giggle as she catches me ogling.

Wincing, I toss a shoe at her. "Oh my goddess, Ilona. Don't ever say that again."

"As if you weren't checking them out too."

I toss my other shoe at her, and she ducks. It sails right into the water.

She doubles over in laughter as I wade into the cool water to retrieve it, treading carefully on the slippery pebbles that line the bottom of the pond. After tossing my shoe ashore, my arms wrap around my body as I shiver. The three of them join me in the water without hesitation.

"Damn, it's freezing," Zale says. Despite his words, he wastes no time plunging beneath the water. When he resurfaces, he shakes out his hair, splattering us with cool droplets.

"Knock it off!" Ilona splashes him. "Some of us need time to acclimate here."

"Aren't you used to this by now?" Dash asks. From the corner of my eye, I notice a large tattoo on his right bicep. As curious as I am to see what it is, I don't dare turn my full attention to him.

"We don't come here as often as you might think," I say.

We trudge deeper into the pond, and once the water is about chest high on me, Zale prowls over to Ilona, snagging her by the waist and lifting her up. He tosses her into a deeper section of the water where she lands with a *splash.*

"Oh she is going to be livid, Zale." He gives me a shit-eating grin as Ilona resurfaces with a growl, pushing red strands out of her face. The water next to me ripples as Dash moves toward me with a predatory look on his face. Backing up, I turn to swim away, but he's too quick. "Don't you dare! Don't you even th— AHH!"

Before I can successfully escape, he grabs me by the waist and tosses me over his shoulder, plunging us both underwater.

Squirming, I try to fight him by pounding my fists on his broad back, but it's no use. Underwater, I move in slow-motion, my blows softened. Fear zips down my spine.

He wouldn't try to drown me would he?

A moment later, before I can fully panic, we resurface, and I gulp for air.

"You complete and utter ass!" I screech at him. "You can't handle the princess like that."

"If Jamell did his job properly, I wouldn't be able to." He winks.

His words make me irate. Smoke would be billowing out of my ears right now if such a thing were possible.

Ilona readjusts her top, and as she ties her soaking mop of red curls into a bun, she glances up at me, pausing when she realizes how angry I am.

"Hey, A, you all right?" she asks for the second time since we've arrived at the oasis. She throws Dash a dirty glare. I told her about everything that happened between the two of us last night before the bacchanal, and now she's wary of him.

"Clearly he doesn't like Queen Enira much," she said, in reference to him calling my mother manipulative the day I met him as the vessel. "He's also much too arrogant in his privileges here. I can't believe he spoke to the vessel so openly! Then tricked you into sleeping with him—"

"Almost sleeping with him," I reminded her. "He's just so… infuriating."

"I definitely don't trust the guy, whether he's Prince Zale's best guard or not."

"She needs to loosen up a bit," Zale calls out, snapping me back to the moment. He leisurely floats on his back, fingers trailing the water alongside him.

"Says the uptight prince!" I was hoping he'd develop more of a personality away from the palace and the prying eyes of his family, but it seems that hope was in vain. He's only proven to be an even bigger jerk than I initially thought.

"I'm not as much of a bore as you seem to think I am," he responds as his eyes flutter shut.

"Snake!" I yell at Zale, pointing just beyond him, then chuckling as he panics, splashing through the water toward us.

He scowls when he discovers there's no snake, and Ilona, Dash, and I laugh freely. The moment is more lighthearted now, so I push away my mistrust and skepticism of these two Stellari men. I vow to enjoy this beautiful day at Paramour Falls with my best friend, prince and vexing guard be damned.

⚔ ⚔

We float around for hours, splashing each other and swapping quips until Zale declares he's hungry. Ilona's face is a deep, sun-kissed pink, so she follows him out of the water, flopping down on the blanket beside him.

"What do you think might come of that?" Dash asks, a mischievous look in his eyes as he nods toward my friend and his prince as they laugh together, sharing sliced veggies and hummus.

"Ilona and *Zale?*" I ask, incredulous.

"You don't think your friend can attract the eye of a prince? That's not very kind."

Snorting, I do my best to give him a serious look. "No. I don't think *your* prince can attract the eye of *my* friend actually." Ilona's been crushing on Marnie for the past year, though she still hasn't openly admitted it yet. As someone who's known her for years, I can tell from her behavior—the way she fancies her nightly visits to the kitchen for tea and chatter, the way she thanked me so graciously for inviting Marnie to the ball, the way she flushes anytime the two of them whisper in hushed voices. I know there's something between them.

"He has a chance," he says, as if he's schooling me on my best friend. "She and Zale talk." He shrugs as if it's no big deal.

Ilona's drawn to personality more than appearance. But it's rare she finds herself drawn to anyone at all, which is why it's doubtful she'd be drawn to the prince. He doesn't seem like her type—she prefers sweet, compassionate people. People similar to her. People like Marnie.

I frown, wondering why she hasn't opened up to me lately. It's disheartening that she hasn't talked to me about her feelings or let me in on the fact that she and Zale talk, whatever that even means. Maybe she *does* like Zale and feels uncomfortable discussing it during this stage. Or maybe she's confused and trying to figure it out. I need to respect it until she's ready to open up.

Plopping into the water, I paddle my hands and kick my feet, swimming toward the falls. The cascading water roars in my ears, and mist fills the air as I get closer. Holding my breath, I cross through the waterfall, fighting against the pressure as it pounds on my back, threatening to hold me down.

With a slick rock wall behind me and a curtain of water in front of me, this secluded little spot is my favorite part of the oasis. There are even a couple of larger boulders situated underwater that provide an area to sit and relax without being fully submerged. It's like a room made of nothing but earth and water.

"Who taught you to swim like that?" Dash splutters as soon as he comes up from beneath the waterfall, having followed me through it. "Let me guess. Jamell?"

Unable to help myself, I chuckle. Dash might be untrustworthy, but he is quite entertaining. A sweet treat compared to the monotony of the island. I'm torn between pushing him away and keeping him close. "No, actually."

"You *are* aware there are more efficient methods of swimming though, right?"

Splashing him, I roll my eyes. "My method is fine."

"You roll your eyes so much they might roll out of your head."

Cupping my hands around some water, I move to splash him again, but he's too quick. He's on me in a flash, pinning my hands over my head as my back presses against the smooth rock wall behind me. It's the second time today we've been in such a compromising position.

Though my brain screams in indignation at his arrogant invasion of my personal space, my body has no problem with his nearness. I find myself straining to press my slick skin against his.

"Three," he says.

"What?" My breath comes out short and shallow, mirroring his.

"Three times I've pinned you down now without you fighting back."

"Maybe I don't want to fight back." *Maybe I like you this close to me.* I'm horrified those words left my mouth but grateful I shut up before the rest of the thought slipped free.

The intensity in his gaze as he stares into my eyes makes me nervous, and I try to look away. Instead, I find myself captivated by the swirls of color in his eyes. There's not just one shade of brown but many, speckled with my favorite color—gold. The gold flecks are like little hints of sunshine in an otherwise dark abyss.

I bite my lip, and his eyes track the movement. I do everything in my power not to arch further into him as he presses closer. At the feel of his bare chest brushing against my breasts, my body shudders. His mouth reaches my neck, planting a soft kiss before trailing up to my earlobe, nibbling gently. I stifle a moan, wiggling beneath his grip.

His hot breath caresses my ear. "I know who you are. *Vessel,*" he whispers.

My lust dissipates, leaving confusion and terror in its wake. My chest constricts in warning. I'm filled with regret about letting my walls down despite the obvious warning signs.

Choking it all down, I try to remain cool. Mother might have prevented me from learning how to properly fight, but she has groomed me to be a princess. My experience with staying calm and collected will come in handy at this moment.

"I have no idea what you're talking about." Wriggling around, I try and fail to pull my hands free from his grasp. "Unhand me."

Pulling his lips away from my ear, he stares down at me with cold eyes.

"How does it feel to be a murderer? To slaughter your own people like cattle?" His voice rises, fueled by anger, loud enough now that I can hear him over the roar of the falls.

"I don't—it's not what you think!" I'm not sure why, but desperation overwhelms me. I'm desperate to escape this vulnerable position but also desperate for him to know that's not who I am.

I hate the bacchanals. I despise taking lives. I only do it for Mother, because she *needs* that life force fuel. There is no other way to serve her, and I've never been able to decline her commands. Not even for my own conscience.

For some reason, it feels crucial that Dash doesn't view me like he views Mother. He's the first man whose opinions I actually care about. As confusing as that is for me, I'm not sure I'm ready to lose whatever it is we have between us yet.

Swallowing thickly, I struggle to remain passive. He can't know who I am. If he truly believed I was the vessel, knew what I was capable of, he wouldn't dare manhandle me like this.

Clearing my mind, I try to draw in his life force energy toward me. Not enough to kill him, but enough to weaken him and get to Ilona.

Ilona. My heart pounds harder at the thought of my innocent friend, alone with a stranger beyond the wall of water.

If Zale has done anything to harm her, I will stop at nothing to end him.

As I focus on pulling Dash's energy toward me, nothing happens. It's like hitting a wall. The same thing happened the night of the bacchanal when I tried to read his emotions. Nothing.

Sweat beads on my neck despite the coolness of the water, and suddenly I realize that night wasn't a fluke.

Dash chuckles darkly, giving me a cruel smirk. "Those tricks don't work on me, *vessel.*"

Screaming won't be any use. There's no way Ilona would hear me over the falls.

"Tell me why," he says.

"Why what?" I spit out at him, still fighting his grip. I lift a knee to hit him in the groin, but he turns, so I connect with the outer edge of his thigh instead. Shifting again, he pins my legs between his strong thighs, blocking me in a tight vice between his body and the wall.

Fear claws at my throat.

"Naughty girl. Jamell really let you down with that training. I warned you not to trust him." His eyes burn into my own as he speaks his next words slowly. "Tell me why you enjoy slaughtering your own people."

Despite feeling defeated, I keep my chin held high and refuse to appear weak. He grips my chin in his hand, forcing me to look at him as his fingers dig into my jaw.

"I don't!" I yell, squirming beneath his hold.

"I won't release you until you give me what I want. Aren't you concerned about your poor little friend, all alone out there with Zale?" he asks, his voice hard. "Tell me why you kill your own people."

"If you touch Ilona I will burn you alive, you fucker!"

"You didn't answer my question."

"Because I need to!" I spit out frantically, desperate to get to Ilona.

"You're that selfish that you think you deserve the lives of others?"

"No! I'd never. It's not for me it's for—"

"Your mother."

"If you already know, then why are you threatening me?"

"I've never threatened you, *Princess,*" he says, lowering his voice so I can barely hear it. I swing my head wildly, trying desperately to get him off me as he leans close to my ear. "I just had to make sure before I did this."

His lips crash into my own, and he kisses me fiercely but briefly. Before I can fight back, he's off me, releasing my hands and backing away.

"You fucking *fool!*" I scream at him, pounding my fists against his slick chest. "Don't you ever touch me again. I will have your head for this."

"No you won't," he says with a stern look as he puts even more space between us. "You'll understand later."

"How dare you! You don't know what I will or will not do!"

"I do know, Astrid. I know that you won't, because *you* are not your *mother,*" he says softly, a sad expression overtaking his face. Turning his back to me, he swims through the waterfall and out of sight, as if he didn't assault me.

A mixture of salty tears and mist coat my face as I cry in my private oasis.

My beautiful, tainted oasis.

No longer my favorite spot on the island.

CHAPTER ELEVEN

As I make my way ashore, the only thing keeping me moderately calm is the sight of Ilona lounging leisurely, her head thrown back in laughter at something Zale said.

Not wanting to alarm her, I force a smile onto my face. Zale seems clueless about what has transpired behind the waterfall, and I prefer to keep it that way. Another lesson I learned from Mother is applicable here: Don't let the enemy see your feelings. Playing it cool will give me the upper hand, so that's what I'll do.

Dash stands to the side, drying himself off before pulling on his leathers. Now it's much easier to avert my gaze. I'm no longer tempted by his sculpted physique and attractive face. I know what lies beneath his outer shell.

Do the Vannyks know their top guard is immune to my vygora powers? Is he also immune to Mother's? What are his intentions?

"What's wrong, A?" Ilona says quietly as she rushes to my side.

"Nothing! For the love of the goddess, stop asking me that." I brush her off, but she follows, lowering her voice so the men don't hear her.

"Oh you are so full of it. You can try to lie to me, but I can read your emotions just as well as you can read any other person's on this planet."

Except for Dash.

"So it's fine for you to keep things from me, but I can't keep things from you?" I bark, nodding my head toward Zale. She stops short, chewing on her lip and looking away. She must know what I'm referring to, and I bet her cheeks are flushing red beneath that sunburn.

"When we're at the palace, we'll talk," she says, and I nod. Appeased, she tells the men she's tired and that we should head back. Gratefulness fills me. Ilona always has my back. These men and their secret intentions won't come between us.

By the time we get back to the palace, my back is stiff from holding myself away from Dash's touch. The ride was incredibly tense, and I'm surprised I even managed to get on the horse with him at all. What I really wanted to do was gut him with a sharp rock and leave his body for the jungle predators.

As uncomfortable as I am with killing, something inside me craves Dash's death. There's an insatiable urge for me to end his life. I've never outright craved someone's death like this, and it must be because he assaulted me. He deserves any harm that befalls him.

When the four of us return to the palace, we part ways, leaving Pancake and Aife in the care of the stable hand. Ilona and I quietly agree to meet up in the library after freshening up.

Mother had told me to be *nice* to Dashiel, and I wonder if it's her myndox manipulation at work, holding me back from murdering him the old-fashioned way. My insides are a bubbling pit of angry lava, yet I'm composed on the outside. Coincidence? It can't be. *Something* is keeping me from slicing his jugular, and it isn't my moral compass.

Trepidation tiptoes up my spine, a wave of exhaustion and confusion washing over me.

Mother wouldn't do that to me—would she? She only wants what's best for me. At least, that's what I've always thought.

Why do I yearn to end another human's life, regardless of what they've done to deserve it? And—though it's a good thing— why can't I act on it?

I grab a fresh pair of pants and a top, choosing to forgo shoes, and quietly slip out my terrace doors. By exiting this way, I can sneak around the perimeter and through the library window with none the wiser, especially Dash. He might be a snake, but he's observant and intelligent. We can't take any chances.

The terrace is barely illuminated as the sun departs, dimming further with each passing minute. The birds sing their evening song in the jungle outside my room, a colorful cacophony.

Sneaking around the soft ground barefoot, my heart racing, I feel like some kind of trespasser or wrongdoer. Part of me embraces the thrill. The rush that drives through my veins makes me feel truly awake. Alive. Usually, I only experience adventure through my novels, and as fun as they are, nothing beats the real-life exhilaration.

The adrenaline doesn't overpower my feelings of disgust and anger for what Dash did to me though. My blood boils at the thought of him spoiling my perfect oasis.

Staying close to the smooth, pale stone of the palace, I pass a line of terraces and windows lined with draperies that conceal what lies inside. A few rooms down, an orange glow leaks from an open set of terrace doors, gilding the now-darkened patio. It's a guest room, but I'm not sure who's staying in it.

I move slowly, careful to avoid the arc of light. I'm almost free of risk when I hear the rumble of a familiar voice.

"—thought we weren't meeting until later. Did anyone spot you?"

Dashiel Dargan.

That son-of-a—

Isn't he supposed to be guarding my door?

He talks in a hushed, hurried tone to someone I can't see. Creeping closer to the side of the palace, careful to avoid the light, I try to make out what's being said.

"—hate what I had to do."

"You can't save them all, Dashiel. I admire your heart, but it's unrealistic," a soft, feminine voice replies. One I don't recognize. "You can still do what you came here to do. Plans change. *Feelings* change."

An exasperated sigh leaves his mouth. "I am *trying*. After today, she hates me. With good reason."

"She doesn't need to like you."

"Logical words, but they're spoken apathetically, Fatima."

Fatima.

Who the hell is Fatima, and why is she sneaking around with Dash?

And are they talking about me?

None of it makes sense, but it hurts all the same. The betrayal slices me in half.

My nails dig into my palms as I ball my fists, counting backward from ten to stay calm before I do something impulsive like burst in there and give myself away. By hearing this conversation, I'm gaining an advantage. If I can figure out Dash's plan, I can beat him at his own game.

He is going down.

"Do what you came here to do," Fatima says.

There's shuffling as someone draws nearer to the terrace. I

back away, pressing into the wall as I try to blend into the shadows, making myself as small as possible. Dark clothes were a good choice.

A swift girl with dark skin and a head of tightly coiled curls slips from the room before dashing away into the dark forest.

My head pounds with confusion. I'm starting to think Prince Zale has no idea what his guard is up to—that this *guard* might not be who he says he is.

Is it possible Dash is working with whoever is threatening Stellaris?

I consider three options: I can relay what I've heard to Mother, take it to Prince Zale, or stay quiet until I find out more about what's going on.

If I speak with Mother prematurely, I run the risk of her harming the Vannyks out of fear of self-preservation. If I speak with Zale and he knows what Dash is up to, I've ruined my chances to gather intel. I put myself at risk.

Ultimately, I decide to do what has served me well all these years with Mother: stay submissive. By acting like everything is normal, I'll gather intel as I go. When it's all said and done, I *will* take Dash's life with my own hands. Even if I can't use my power on him, I'll do it the old-fashioned way. It's how I'll repay him for his traitorous ways.

Thank the goddess I didn't sleep with him.

Allowing myself to breathe deeper at that welcome thought, I continue around the edge of the palace, coming toward the main hall and the library window. Ilona must already be there, because the curtains, normally drawn shut at night, yawn wide, the window propped open for me.

As I approach the window, ready to climb through, a few guards round the corner opposite of me, headed in my direction.

Dammit.

Running my hands through the grass, I find a decent-sized rock about as big as my fist and chuck it into the trees.

"D'ya hear that?" one of the guards asks the other. They turn toward the jungle, swinging their elemental staffs—charged by fire and offering them light—in that general direction.

Taking the opportunity, I launch my body through the library window, crashing into the side table and taking it down with me.

"Ow for fuck's sake!" I yell, rubbing my elbow.

"That was the most dramatic entrance I've ever seen in my life." Ilona jumps to her feet in surprise.

"Hurry, shut the drapes." I gingerly push myself to a stand, holding my right elbow, which took the brunt of the fall. Once the window is shut and we're fully concealed, I relax slightly.

"That entrance was unexpected," Ilona says with wide eyes. "I get you wanted to ditch your nosey guard, but that was…It was something."

Sighing, I flop into one of the wingback chairs. Ilona does the same opposite me.

"I don't trust anyone right now," I say.

Ilona reels back like I slapped her. "Ouch. That hurts, you know. I get that there's a lot going on, but I thought we were—"

"I'm serious, Ilona." I give her a pointed look before she can start rambling. "Obviously you're the only one excluded from my 'do-not-trust' list."

"Is that why you were in a mood at the falls? Something happened between you and Dash, didn't it? I told you there was something up with that man." She shakes her head, and her wild curls bounce around.

"Nothing happened, Ilona," I say through gritted teeth. "He assaulted me."

This catches her attention, and she gasps, pale eyebrows flying up her forehead. Scooting forward to the edge of the chair, she reaches over and takes my hands in her own.

"What do you mean, he assaulted you?"

"Straight-up held me against my will while he berated me, calling me a murderer and a slaughterer, before forcing himself on me." When Ilona's eyes begin watering, I clarify. "It was a kiss, nothing more, but still unwelcome."

"Oh my gosh, A. I'm so sorry that happened to you. I'm surprised you didn't—oh wait, you *couldn't* use your power, could you?"

"Nope." My jaw sets as I cross my arms in front of me. Ilona knows about everything that has transpired between Dash and me, including how I met him as the vessel and how I can't use my magic on him.

"You rode back with him and you didn't even push him off the horse. I'm honestly surprised at your self-control, but I would've willingly left him in the jungle for the snakes had you told me."

"That's the thing; I couldn't harm him. I wanted to. The urge was there and it still is, but I couldn't."

"I take it you haven't told your mother?"

Shaking my head, I relay every detail of the story to her. As I recall the events behind the waterfall, something strikes me as odd. If Dash despises me as much as he seems to, why the hell did he kiss me? And thinking back, I realize it wasn't even much of a kiss. Just a brief, bold touch of his lips to mine. He had me in a position where I was weak and alone. He could've done much more. Yet that was all he did. Not that it excuses his behavior— what he did was plenty terrible on its own. But *why?* What is he playing at? Why did he wait to confront me at the falls?

Too many questions linger, none of the answers making sense.

When I spill about the scene I witnessed on my way here tonight, Ilona's mouth forms a small, surprised circle, and her fingers tap compulsively against her legs.

"I'm going to find out what Dash is up to, and power or not, I'm taking him down. As for Mother, I don't trust her either." I flick the jagged bangs out of my eyes. "We still need to talk to Cedrik. I wish we had done that instead of lollygagging around the island. Maybe then Dash wouldn't have laid his dirty hands on me."

"Hey," she says, "this is *not* your fault. Don't you dare play the what-if game or try to blame yourself."

I glance around the library, grateful for the privacy. We are utterly alone, with nothing nearby but rows and rows of silent books to keep our secrets. It's our private spot. A row of historical books catches my eye, and a thought pops into my head.

"What was that book you were reading the other day? The one about Paramour Falls?"

"Oh! *Hakran Rediscovered: Island Folklore?*"

"Yes. That one. Do you mind locating it for me?"

Moments from this past week flash through my mind: Zale bringing up Paramour Falls, practically begging to go. Dash asking what we know about our lore at the ball. I chalked both instances up to general excitement and curiosity; they are in a foreign land after all. But what if there's more to it? Something neither is saying?

How did I miss the signs until now?

"I know you've had a long day, A, but that's an unusual read for you. Are you sure you haven't been out in the sun too long?"

When I give her a pointed look, she chuckles, rising to find the book. Angry red shoulders peek out from beneath the green nightdress she wears, a shade darker than her pink face. That could be the perfect excuse for visiting Cedrik later—retrieving the cream to soothe her burns.

When she returns with the thick, battered book, I flip open to the table of contents, locating the section about the falls. I whip through the pages, and Ilona scolds me to slow down before I accidentally tear them and I oblige enough to appease her. Finally I find what I'm looking for, and a sense of overwhelming defeat settles in my gut.

"*Paramour Falls,*" I read out loud. "*Where two falls merge and two lips meet, hearts are joined, their power complete. A fated kiss to break the wall, releasing magic, two share all.*" We exchange worried looks, and I continue reading. "It says a lover's kiss beneath the falls opens the doors to power-sharing, where both abilities are accessed by those who join lips." Scanning, I read more about some goddess named Davvinia and her mortal lover, Anwyr, who tricked her into a kiss beneath the falls to activate power-sharing. All so he could achieve immortality and rule like a god.

"Astrid…" Ilona says, but she sounds far away. Her words blur as my ears start to ring.

As far as I know, Dash doesn't have power to share, unless I'm counting his capability of blocking my magic. Plus, I would have felt if I gained new powers, right? So, what was it then? He *stole* a kiss from me. Tricked me. All to what, gain access to my power?

According to the lore, Anwyr was a mortal. He didn't have any power of his own, yet he was able to access Davvinia's. Maybe a fair trade isn't required. Maybe Dash took without giving anything in return.

My throat thickens as panic sets in. Ilona's mouth is moving, her face pale as she connects the dots herself, but I can't hear anything she's saying. Closing my eyes, I work to regain control of my mind.

I need to make sure he didn't take my power.

Please let my magic be there.

I focus on Ilona's energy—on drawing it toward me.

Waves of concern and dread hit me. Following those threads back to Ilona, I exhale in relief. As much as I despise my magic, I've never been more grateful to feel it coursing through my veins, as strong as ever.

Slumping back into my chair, I rest my head in my hands.

"He didn't *take* my power," I say. "I'm able to read your emotions just fine." But can he access it?

This is why Mother didn't want anyone to know I was the vessel. Despite the seeds of doubt planted by Ilona and Dash, I'm still certain Mother has my best intentions at heart. She is protecting me, not stifling me, by keeping me hidden.

"What do we do?" Ilona asks.

"Murder that lying, manipulating bastard!" I screech, my vision going red with anger.

"Hey, hey. Take a deep breath."

Instead, I scream so loud the doors blast open and two guards run in, evaluating the space for any threats.

"GET OUT OF HERE!" I yell at them, causing Ilona to flinch. Fear radiates from her, invading me as if I'm using my power on her. But I haven't opened any connections between us. It stokes my own worry in return.

"Astrid," she whispers, "I've never seen you this upset. I know it's bad, but you're you. You always keep your cool. We'll figure this out together. Stay quiet and breathe."

"Don't tell me to *stay* quiet while some snake is slithering around *my* palace, stealing *my* magic. Worst of all, I was *this* close to liking the guy. This close." I squeeze my fingers together for dramatic effect before laughing hysterically and gripping my hair with both fists.

Hesitantly, Ilona steps up to me, gently pulling my hands from my hair and wrapping her arms around me. I place my head on her shoulder and cry, letting tears overwhelm my vision.

What the hell is wrong with me?

I'm always under control; she's right. Now I'm raging and crying—bawling my eyes out—for the first time in goddess knows how long.

"I think something's wrong with me," I whisper, feeling defeated.

"Come on. Let's go see Cedrik. He can help."

Leaving the library, we scuttle arm-in-arm through the palace corridors toward the servants' wing.

As we round a corner, I slam into someone.

"*Astrid Lucille Sylano!*" my mother bellows. I back up a pace, mumbling an apology to the leathered chest I ran into. Luckily it's not my mother's, only a random Hakranian guard at her side. "I have not raised you to run amuck through the palace halls."

"I apologize, Mother." My head dips automatically in a quick show of respect.

"Where are you headed with such a fire lit beneath your feet?"

"To see Cedrik," I say.

Ilona keeps her eyes downcast, visibly uncomfortable with the confrontation.

"To retrieve a hair-growth serum, I do hope." She runs a blood-red claw through my short locks, her mouth pinched in a frown. "This is a disgrace."

"I like it, *Mother,*" I say, irritation rising. "We're retrieving a cream for Ilona's sunburn."

Ilona shrugs her sleeve down a little, showcasing her reddened shoulders, but Mother's black eyes don't leave my own. If she notices I've been crying, she doesn't say anything.

Because she doesn't care.

"You *will* retrieve a serum for your hair as well, and you will not mutilate yourself like this again," she says, her tone low and threatening.

I nod enthusiastically, in an effort to end the discussion faster, and she seems appeased. Without another word, she resumes moving down the hallway, leaving us behind.

"Goddess, she is in a particularly vile mood this evening," Ilona whispers. She grasps my forearm with both of her thin hands, gasping. "Astrid, do you think that was one of those manipulation moments? Did she just try to myndox you into *fixing* your hair?"

Pausing, I think of Mother's menacing tone as she delivered the order. "I'm not doing it. So no, she couldn't have. Come." Looping my arm through hers, we gently tap on Cedrik's door. A moment later there's some scuffling and a heavy sigh, and his door creaks open.

"Princess! What a surprise." His voice is gruff, harder than his kind eyes and warm smile. He reaches out to gently grab my hand, closing his eyes for a moment. After a beat, they fly open and his face pales.

No doubt he's using his vygora powers on me. The wounds he finds aren't physical this time. I pull my hand free of his, not wanting him to comment on whatever he feels there.

"We're here for sunburn salve," I say, pointing to Ilona. She should've taken care of that first thing; it can't be comfortable. "I can't handle any more upsetting news today, so I need you to care for my friend first."

Cedrik tilts his head in concern before shifting his brown eyes to Ilona.

"Come in, my dears." Holding the door all the way open, he allows us to enter his suite.

I've been here a couple of times over the years. It's a larger space than the other staff is offered, doubling as a clinic. One corner of the room is blocked by privacy dividers—likely where his bed and personal belongings rest. The remainder of the room is filled with shelves of tonics, potions, and salves. The wall with a large window is blanketed with hanging herbs in various stages of dessication, colors ranging from vibrant green to dark brown. A large table and two cots are pushed against the wall to my left, where he treats his patients.

"Sit, sit." He motions toward the cots before shuffling over to the shelf containing small jars and creams. Ilona grabs a seat on a cot, dangling her feet over the side. With a wince, she tenderly peels off her shirt, baring her irritated skin so the healer can easily access the worst of the burns.

Leaning against the door, I cross my arms and ankles, watching the old man work. He mixes a cream with a few drops of liquid, stirring it methodically. Looking over his shoulder, he offers me a soft grin.

"Drops of aloe and lavender," he says.

Once it's prepared, he approaches Ilona and begins slathering the cream on her shoulders and back. She hisses at the initial touch, sitting up taller.

"It will only burn for a moment, dear."

"Thanks, Cedrik."

"My pleasure."

Silence falls on the room as he works, slathering her skin with a generous layer of cream.

"Thanks for your work the night of transference two weeks ago," I say, trying to see if he remembers anything.

Turning slightly, he gives me an odd look. "You mean healing your mother's vessel? I didn't know you cared for it."

As I cringe at the way he says *it,* my suspicions are confirmed. Mother succeeded in something beyond a basic mental influence—she fully altered his memory of that night. The effects of her myndox powers are lingering beyond the typical reach.

Time and distance had no effect on her powers, doing nothing to lessen her hold like it should have.

"Have you seen Mother since then?"

"Only in passing. She has not had reason to seek me out. A favorable thing, I'm certain."

When he's finished, Ilona puts her shirt back on.

"Princess. May I have a word?" His head leans toward Ilona. "Alone?"

After I nod at her to wait in the hallway, she exits obediently, leaving Cedrik and me alone.

"About your...situation," he begins, likely referring to the spontaneous anxiety I've seemed to develop. "Something is...*off* with your magic." His words are slow, cautious, like he's testing the waters.

He doesn't remember the night of the transference, so he won't remember telling me to consume more life force to keep up my power and strength. He doesn't know I'm the vessel— the only vygora capable of transference. Not wanting to get him sentenced to death or subject him to Mother's rage, I pick my next question carefully.

"What do you think the problem is?"

"I'm not certain, but there seems to be something...new... different circulating with your magic. I can feel it, but I am unsure." His frown grows deeper. "There are tonics that might help settle your emotions, numbing agents of sorts, if you'd like."

Shaking my head adamantly, I tell him I'd prefer to keep a clear head. The last thing I want is to numb myself while in the middle of this invisible war that seems to be taking place.

"Thank you, Cedrik. Truly." I give his hand a solid shake, thanking the weathered man and ignoring his concerned expression before turning to exit, leaving him in peace.

Ilona greets me in the corridor. "What'd he say?"

"He has no idea what's wrong with me," I say dryly. "Something's wrong with my magic, and I bet Dash's kiss had something to do with it. He poisoned me with his toxic lips, Ilona."

"I'll help you take him down." The words sound out of place on her tongue, but she succeeds in coaxing a grin out of me.

"You're a true friend. Luckily, I feel a little more stable now," I lie, not wanting her to know how on edge I am. I'm vibrating with anger, sadness, and confusion, like a bomb getting ready to explode.

"Maybe," she says, but her voice is high-pitched and nervous. "So, your mother is capable of more than anyone knows."

"Everyone's a manipulator." My chest burns with fury. I can't trust my own mother. Can't trust the man with the honey-gold eyes and dimpled smile. Can't trust the unassuming prince and his kind parents.

"Hey, you're not alone. You've got me." She pulls me in for another hug, and I breathe in her sweet lilac scent.

I wonder if she'd still say that if she knew what a monster I can be. I can't imagine she'd be so quick to offer me comfort. Guilt threatens to bubble over, but I press it down like I always do.

Breaking the embrace, I push her in the direction of the kitchen. "Go get your lemon-ginger tea. I'll meet you back in the library for a reading session."

"I'd rather not leave you right now, especially since I'm all that you have. You're clearly having a bad day, and I don't want you to be alone. What if you run into your mother again, or Dash, or—"

"Ilona, you're rambling. I'm fine. I'm the most powerful woman in Hakran, remember?" I repeat the line she says to me every bacchanal.

Her lips curve up, but the worry line on forehead stays.

"But—"

"Say hi to Marnie for me."

Speeding past her, I don't give her the chance to object again. She might not want me to be alone right now, but I can't risk her getting caught in the crossfire of the storm that's brewing inside of me.

CHAPTER TWELVE

The library is expectedly empty when I return a short while later, no sign of Dash or the Vannyks anywhere. Then again, I did take precautions by ducking behind pillars and peeking around corners as I made my way through the corridors. A few guards peered my way with open curiosity but didn't interfere. Hopefully they don't tell Dash where I went if he asks.

I pull the doors closed behind me and make my way through the blissful silence toward the romance section. Row after row of stories greet me, the soft orange flicker of the lamps guiding me. As I trail my finger along the shelves, I revel in the textures of the various worn leather bindings. The scent of ink and paper calms my overactive mind.

As I traverse deeper into the library, deeper into the shadows, a rustic yet spicy scent fills my nostrils; it's one I'm quickly becoming familiar with, and it can only mean one thing.

Dash.

No, no, no!

Sure enough, when I turn the corner, I find him with his back to me, idly flipping the pages of a book.

"Hello, sweetheart," he says without looking up.

Calmly, I begin retreating with small, backward steps, unwilling to turn my back on him. He turns to face me, and there's a flicker of concern in his golden-brown eyes.

"Wait," he says softly, reaching out a hand toward me. "We need to talk." He snaps the book shut, tucking it under his arm as he moves toward me cautiously, as if I'll turn and flee at any moment, which, quite frankly, isn't entirely out of the question.

The only thing keeping me in place, subduing the innate desire to chuck a hardcover at his head, is the look in his eyes. He's acting nothing like the man I saw at the falls, and that alone gives me pause.

What if Mother had him under her manipulation?

These webs are becoming too tangled, more difficult to unravel, but I allow my gut instinct to hold me to the spot without fleeing.

"Stay where you are, *Dashiel*," I say, spitting his name out with disgust and putting my palms up in his direction. "Don't you dare come any closer."

He's not wearing the guard leathers and has no face covering. Plain brown pants cling to his shapely thighs, a white long-sleeve shirt fits the ridges of his muscles, and a pair of worn brown-leather boots cover his feet. His hair is tousled—still drying from the bath he must've taken when we returned—and curling slightly at the edges. The bit of sun he got today has deepened his bronze coloring. Despite cleaning up, he still hasn't touched the scruff on his jaw, and I like it.

I like it?

No. No. No.

How can someone so vile be so handsome?

And why must my body react?

Despite my hormonal reaction to Dash, I'm able to keep my wits about me. That pretty face hides a manipulative personality and abusive tendencies. Nothing he can say will make what he did to me okay. Unless, of course, he can prove my mother had control of his mind. *That* is the only way I could forgive him.

I find myself hoping that's the case. Maybe Mother is somehow behind this and he didn't steal my magic for some master plan where he uses it against me and my people.

"Please, just listen to me Astrid." Hearing my name on his lips, the way he begs, is like music to my ears. I hate that I like the way it sounds. He puts his hands up in a submissive gesture. Something about his warm eyes pulls at me. I nod, waiting for him to speak.

Running a hand through his hair, he smooths it back away from his forehead and then scratches at his jaw. If I could read his emotions right now, I'm sure I'd be getting wave after wave of anxiety and unease.

Without the hardness in his eyes, he seems more vulnerable, more like the lighthearted yet arrogant guard I initially met. It's almost like he wears two different masks—the one I saw the night we met and the one I saw behind the falls.

I wonder how many other people have seen that scarier side of him? Which side is really him?

"It isn't what you think," he says. "You have no reason to trust me, but—"

"Absolutely not," I say, shaking my head vigorously. I ball my hands into fists at my sides, swallowing down my anger and fear. "You do not get to stand here and try to *apologize* for your behavior today."

He exhales and looks at me pleadingly. "I'm not trying to apologize. I don't regret what I did today. It was—"

Scoffing, I say, "You are the most vile man I have ever met, Dash. Stay away from me, or I *will* tell your precious prince what you did." I'm hung up on his words. He doesn't regret what he did to me? So not only did he choose to harm me, he enjoyed it?

There's something seriously wrong with this guy.

"I'm trying to tell you, it wasn't what you think."

"Make no mistake, Dashiel Dargan, I ache to kill you for this."

Hurt flashes across his handsome features, irritating me further. He has no right to be upset.

No longer able to look him in the face—a face my traitorous body felt an attraction to—I turn and flee.

"Be careful, Astrid. You can't trust your mother," he yells after me. His voice shakes with ferocity, his words vibrating down to my core. "You can't trust them."

"I know," I whisper, clenching my fists at my side. "I know."

As the next few days blur by, Dash is always nearby, like a shadow cast from the morning sun, impossible to separate from. I spend most of the time in my room, and at least he has the common sense to linger in the hallway and not to enter my space. Just in case, I wear a dagger strapped to my waist, beneath the waistband of my pants.

Of course he's the only person I can't kill with a simple touch. An infuriating fact.

As daunting as his presence is, I can't turn him in yet. If I turn him in prematurely, I'll show my hand, and I won't receive any answers to the questions that are piling up. I can't risk alienating the Stellari royal family, not when their guards are blended so seamlessly with our own.

Plus, I refuse to appear weak in front of Mother. I need to play the game how she would.

Dash is up to something, and I need to know what that is. That makes him my enemy. What's even worse is he's back to his calculated, cool, and controlled demeanor, as if nothing happened.

And that makes him dangerous.

Dash isn't the only reason I'm holed up in my room either. The palace is filled with raging emotions, exploding with no bounds from every direction.

They're muddling my own feelings. Choking me.

Holding me back from doing anything other than existing and going through the motions of everyday life.

It's as if I'm drawing them out unintentionally from whomever is nearby.

Dash did this to me. He broke my magic, and it's unbearable.

Ilona's worried. I feel it palpitating from her when she stands at my door, knocking and calling to me. I inform her I need time alone, only allowing my handmaiden in to feed me.

Each morning, Gianna gives me a contemplative look, as if she's deciding whether we're close enough for her to ask me what's wrong. I'm relieved when she doesn't.

Today she brings me a coffee on ice—preferable in the summer heat—with an egg frittata to perk me up. She rips my curtains apart to let in the morning sun.

"Will you be training today, Princess?" Gianna asks, as she does every day.

"Yes," I say quietly. Maybe that's what I need to quiet my mind. I've spent plenty of days sheltered away in my room. It's time to face my problems head on and figure out a way to manage my erratic magic and emotions.

Jolts of surprise and gratitude rush toward me, and I battle to keep her feelings at bay. Whatever Dash did to my powers, I need to learn how to manage it.

"Oh," she says, clearly surprised I didn't say no again today, "should I wait to prepare your bath then?"

"Yes." As much as I crave a eucalyptus bath with which to relax and reinvigorate myself, it'll have to wait.

Gianna tries to hide her smile as she searches my armoire for an outfit.

"Your favorite pants." She lays out a pair of loose silk pants and a matching form-fitting shirt on the edge of my bed. Both are black with silver stitching. Easy to maneuver in. Lightweight and non-restricting.

"Thanks, Gia." I smile, but my heart isn't in it. Dressing, I conceal the dagger beneath my waistband.

Bouncing lightly on her feet, my handmaiden stares at me with a grimace, as if she wants to say something but is holding it in. A sharp stab of eagerness spills from her, hitting me from the inside out.

Finally, with a sigh, I ask her to spit it out.

"There's talk among the staff," she starts, "that the reason Queen Enira brought the Vannyks here is to merge forces."

"Yes, well I'm sure you've seen the extra guards around," I say. "She's succeeded."

"It's not only that." She hesitates, wringing her hands. "They're saying it's a marriage of *political convenience*. The Hakranian princess and Stellari prince."

I widen my eyes in feigned surprise, but can't stop myself from letting a laugh escape.

"*I'm* the one who started that rumor, Gia," I say. "I'm not marrying anyone. Certainly not a prudish, uptight prince with the personality of a doornail." To think he started growing on me that day at Paramour Falls too, before his friend betrayed me.

Gianna brings her hands to her mouth, covering her own laugh. "But he surely is handsome."

"Looks don't compensate for a shitty personality." Even though we're talking about Zale, it's Dash's face that flashes through my mind.

"You wouldn't give the poor prince a chance even if it was for political convenience between countries?"

"Goddess save me," I mumble to the ceiling. "Absolutely not."

It wasn't the prince I was interested in but his guard.

And he tricked me.

Now I want nothing to do with either of them.

Closing her lips tightly, she dips her chin in a show of respect. An awkward silence fills the air as I finish getting ready and walk out into the hallway.

Sure enough, Dash stays on my heels throughout the walk to the servants' wing and down to the training area below. Since he's dressed in Hakranian leathers, complete with face covering, I can almost pretend he's someone else. Almost.

The only consolation is the fact that I can't read his emotions. After the last few days, it offers a small but welcome reprieve.

When we enter the combat room. Jamell gives Dash a grim look.

"I got 'er. Go wait out there, kid."

Dash scowls at Jamell, clearly wanting to say something. A beat passes before he retreats, heading out the door into the main training area. The heat of his gaze lingers as he peers at me through the window separating the spaces.

"How ya doin', Princess?" Jamell asks, offering up a charming, gap-toothed smile he reserves just for me.

As I smile back, Dash's words flit through my mind.

You have pretty poor moves for a warrior.

Most of Hakran's guards don't know how to fight, but you do?

The smile melts off my face, and I bite my lip, looking away.

"Doin' okay?" he asks, concern lacing his voice. I also pick up on the impatience and annoyance flowing from him. It's impossible to block out, and it fires up my anger.

"Fine," I snap. How dare he be annoyed with me? *I'm* the princess, which means he works for me. "We're working on breaking out of holds today."

He smacks his lips, studying me. "Yah, sure thing. Whatever ya'd like."

"Yes, Jamell, it is what I'd like. I don't want any attitude or holding back on your end."

His brows are drawn upward at my words, and I try to block out his emotions. I force myself to focus on the squishy mat beneath my feet, the pungent scents of rubber and sweat lingering in the air, anything but his unwelcome reaction in response to my words.

After composing myself, we start with some basic warm-up movements. He adjusts my stance and has me throw a few different kicks and punches. We work at a steady pace until I feel a trickle of sweat beading down my spine and my breath comes in short pants.

"All right, if ya wanna pin someone larger, ya gotta—"

"No. You've misunderstood me. I want to learn how to break out of a hold, not how to pin someone down." The words come out harsher than I intend, a side effect of the blossoming rage in my chest.

He scratches his neck, eyes shooting downward.

"You never know what might happen with the current *threats.* It doesn't hurt to work on self-defense." Each word is like a blade, cutting through the air between us.

A small *hmph* comes from his throat as he slowly nods and scratches his cropped hair. "I s'pose. Ya feelin' ok, Princess?"

"If one more person asks me that, I will slit their throat. You included." I don't recognize the angry voice that spoke but realize all of a sudden that it was me. Jamell stares at me like I'm a stranger.

His lips purse, and his anger crashes into my own, fanning my fire.

"Is there a problem, *Commander?*" I ask, so venomously that I could be mistaken for Mother.

Dash has made me paranoid. If it wasn't for what he said about my poor training, I wouldn't feel the need to test Jamell, a man I've known for years. I was hoping to prove Dash wrong, to shut down his theory that Mother and Jamell have purposely held me back from training properly.

But, I'm starting to notice how hesitant Jamell is, how unwilling he is to expand my training or oblige my requests. We've done the same few things throughout the years: strength training and light sparring, with the occasional staff or a complicated move thrown in. I've always felt tough and strong after our sessions, so much so that I have never given much thought to learning true defense.

I never thought I needed to. I definitely never thought Jamell would purposely be holding back from teaching me proper fighting skills.

But Dash's words have gotten to me, and I'm starting to fear he might be right. My stomach sinks with disappointment.

After a few preparatory instructions, Jamell stalks toward me. He looks hesitant before he jolts forward, using his leg to swipe my feet out from underneath me. My back hits the rubber mat flooring, my breath exiting with an *oomph*.

That was the slowest takedown ever, and I still couldn't stop him.

Straddling me with a knee on either side, he gently pins my hands down by my sides, careful not to put his weight on me. It's a lot less intimate than it was with Dash—thankfully—but also a lot less serious. Wiggling to loosen his hold, I'm able to bring a knee up to his groin, causing him to loosen his grip. I use that opening to twist free, jumping to my feet. He has a protection cup in place, and I barely put any power behind that strike. There's no way he should've recoiled so quickly.

He's faking. He has to be.

"Great job, Princess," he says with a gap-toothed grin. Squinting at him, I don't return the smile. Glancing out the window, I find Dash still observing us, an odd expression clouding his features. He's not gloating like I expected.

I whirl on Jamell. "That was utter shit! Did Mother tell you to go easy on me during these sessions?"

"Wha—of course not. I'm not takin' it easy for fear of hurtin' ya."

"So you *are* holding back?"

One.

Two.

Three.

I count my inhales and exhales to keep my burning desire to stab him in check.

His eyes dart around the empty training space, to the door, then back to my face. He pops his lips nervously, and I can tell there's something he wants to say.

"You're one of Mother's best commanders. It's obvious you're holding back. Why are you purposely sabotaging my training?"

His mouth parts like he wants to speak, but nothing comes out.

"She told you to." It's not a question, but his heavy sigh is answer enough. "She also prevented you from telling me—from talking about it. Didn't she?"

The flicker of apology in his eyes tells me I'm onto something. Jamell, a man who is fearless in the face of confrontation, is rarely speechless. He isn't easily spooked, so there's only one possible explanation: Mother manipulated him into staying quiet about her request to sabotage my training.

"Queen Enira is a damn good ruler, and she's ya mother. She knows best." The conviction in his voice tells me he believes his words—that he believes in my mother. The pride radiating from him confirms it.

"Why, Jamell? Why doesn't she want me to able to fight? Able to protect myself?" My voice cracks, my anger giving way to self-pity. He's right. I might not agree with Mother's tactics, but I've always trusted her to do what's right. Training is the one thing that felt like mine—that felt like freedom—and she's snatched that from me.

"It's easier. Safer this way," he says quietly.

Because if I can't fight, if I can't protect myself, she can control me without even using her myndox powers. She must fear me leaving, or worse, challenging her one day, and doesn't want me to have any kind of advantage. She's not doing this to control me as a princess or her daughter, she's exerting control over her vessel. Her subordinate. Her tool.

My eyes flit past the window to the pit's door. I desperately wish I could get Mother down there, beyond the silenxstone. If I could do that, I could mute her powers and keep her contained while I figure out what to do with this new information.

The information that confirms I can't trust her.

"You blame me," I say matter-of-factly to Jamell, and

confusion contorts his face. "You're angry with me because you're forced to appease me with this false training everyday. You think I hold you back, don't you?"

"I—never. That ain't fact." Guilt and fear swarm me, pushing me back toward the edge of anger.

One

Two.

Three.

My breathing accelerates, and I work hard to steady my heart rate. My eyes flutter shut as I try to push the infuriating realizations away.

Jamell is not my ally. He's Mother's.

We're all pawns in her game.

I can't trust anyone.

"Ya doin' ok?" Jamell asks.

The dam breaks, spewing my rage like hot lava across the room.

My own words echo from the hollows of my mind: *If one more person asks me that, I will slit their throat. Yours included.*

Reaching into my waistband, I pull out the dagger hidden away there, lunging at Jamell like a wild jaguar.

Right before my blade reaches the pulsing vein on his throat, a strong hand wraps around my wrist. It squeezes so hard that I drop the dagger with a cry of pain.

"Not a good idea, sweetheart," Dash whispers in my ear before scooping the dagger up and sheathing it in one of the many pockets of his leathers.

"I WILL KILL YOU, TOO!" I bellow at him.

Anger blurs my vision, white-hot with bursting flames of red. I scream and scream until my throat is raw. Even as Dash shifts me over his shoulder like a sack of flour and carries me up to

Cedrik's room. Even as he holds me down and Cedrik forces a sweet liquid down my throat.

I scream until everything around me is finally silent and my body relaxes into a forced slumber.

CHAPTER THIRTEEN

The rest of the week passes at a snail's pace, dragging me along with it. Once again, I ensconce myself in my room, this time with Cedrik's tonic keeping me numb and sleepy. I'm too tired to care about much, but I need to figure out how to control myself without the concoction taming me so I can take action.

I'm sick of being weak, a puppet for others.

When bacchanal night approaches again, I reluctantly drag myself down to the beach.

As Ilona and I sit concealed within the tent, our attention doesn't linger on the blanket of treats before us or the squirming bodies on the beach.

The rhythmic music barely registers, and only the salty air of the sea has an effect on me—calming, grounding. Only two weeks ago, Ilona was opening up about how she doesn't trust Mother. One week ago, I was drawing closer to a mysterious guard. This week, I know unmistakably that both Mother and Dash are my enemies.

"Your mother is late again today," Ilona says, tugging on a few loose curls from her side braid. Her loose brown pants and emerald top make her look like she belongs in a garden among flowers rather than alongside a struggling princess and her wicked mother.

"She's not coming." Once again, she's hosting a dinner to distract my leech of a guard and the visiting royals. Knowing her, she'd rather be down here with the revelers, but apparently, such a rowdy celebration is unfit for the Vannyks.

"She's backed off a lot recently, I've noticed."

"Only because King Emman and his wife demand most of her time."

"I'm glad to see you," Ilona says, her voice soft, nervous. I've been avoiding her all week. Cedrik's tonic is running through my system, dulling everything inside of me, but it's almost time for my second dose.

"Can we not do this?" I ask, defeated. "I don't want to talk about Dash or Mother or what happened at the falls. I don't really want to talk at all."

I've been successfully blocking everything out during the past few days, with the help of the healer's medicinal beverages. Muddling my mind, the tonic makes it hard to worry about things that aren't directly in front of me. I'm a shell of myself, even more than before.

Salmon-colored liquid in a lidded vial rests on the blanket before me, beside a second clear, bubbling tonic. One sweet, one bitter. One helps numb me while the other keeps me from getting sick. I take the pinkish one twice a day now—once upon waking and once after the sun leaves the sky. The clear one is only for bacchanals.

Today's energy on the beach is high and frantic as usual. The night is cooler than usual, with an intense breeze working its way through the island. As good as it might feel, it's an ominous sign. A storm is coming.

The bonfire reaches out to the side like a claw, pushed by the increasing winds. Palm trees sway like dancing bodies, as if enjoying the celebration too. Dense clouds conceal the moon, blending the sky and sea into a wall of darkness.

I'm normally on edge prior to the bacchanal and transference, but something new is clawing at my stomach. Discomfort. As Cedrik's tonic wears off, I'm swamped by disgust at the prospect of stealing a life. I've never *liked* doing what I have to do, but I've accepted it.

Tonight, I no longer feel accepting.

I might even vomit.

Luckily, I have Cedrik's vial of bitter tonic for nausea. Snatching it from the blanket, I pop off the cork and guzzle the contents. Wiping my mouth with the back of my hand, I grab a flute of champagne and chase away the bitter taste.

It only succeeds in adding to the bitterness, and I think, perhaps, I should've chosen the juice instead.

I reach for the vial of sweet liquid and I hesitate for a moment before popping off the top and dumping its contents into the sand.

Ilona watches me warily. "I take it you don't much care for whatever that was?" She plucks a green grape from a vine, rolling it between her fingers but not eating it. Neither of us has an appetite tonight, it seems.

"It doesn't let me feel," I mumble. "But without it...I can't seem to control my emotions at all. I can feel yours. And everyone who's near me."

"Are you sure that's a good idea?" she asks, gesturing to the darkened sand where I dumped the sweet tonic. "There are a lot of people out there."

"I'm just going to get this over with. Meet me after?"

"In my room? I'll pick our books first. Dashiel might enter the library, but he won't bother you in my space." Her words come out in a rush, her demeanor perking up at my interest in spending time together. I nod in agreement, working hard to convince her that everything is okay. We both stand, and I pull her in for a hug. She moves away, giving me a sad smile over her shoulder before exiting. I haven't yet told her about training with Jamell the other day, my breakdown, or visiting Cedrik. I haven't seen her.

She's my best friend, and I should let her in so we can figure out this mess together, but I worry I can't trust her either. If Jamell is under Mother's control, who's to say Ilona isn't too?

Sighing, I snag the sandy veyl from the floor, shaking it out.

"Goddess be with me. Let's get this over with."

There's a rustling behind me, probably Ilona coming back for something, but before I know what's happening, a strong hand presses against my mouth, and I'm held against a firm body. Decidedly *not* Ilona.

Lips press against my ear. I tense. I've readied myself to suck this person's life force to the dregs for daring to put their hands on me when a familiar voice speaks up.

"Please don't scream, sweetheart. I'm going to remove my hand, but you *need* to listen to me."

Squirming against him, I try to pry his hands from my mouth, but he holds fast.

"Please, Astrid." When I don't oblige, Dash sighs heavily and continues talking. "Fine. Just remember I wanted to do this the easy way." He pins both my hands behind my back, holding them with one hand as he gently places a foot on my calves, kicking my legs out from beneath me, forcing me to kneel. I fall to my knees in the sand, and he keeps one of his hands over my mouth and the other around my wrists. His hold is tight yet surprisingly gentle.

"I wanted to have a normal conversation, but you refuse to allow me that courtesy. I'm not fond of handling women in this manner." I'd roll my eyes if I weren't so fearful in my current position. "You don't have to do this anymore. I know you despise what your mother makes you do. You're free of her control."

What is he talking about?

I struggle to ask him, but my words come out muffled against his hand.

"Her influence can no longer reach you. You are free from her grasp, but you *cannot* let her know. Do you understand me?" I try to shake my head, to tell him I most certainly do not understand, but he only sighs deeper. "She can't know you've broken free from her chains. You need to play along for as long as you can. You're smart; think on your feet. Find me in the library, the same row as last time, and I'll have the answers you want."

The pressure on my mouth and hands are gone instantly, and he bolts away before I can even suck in a gasp of air.

I'm utterly alone now. With his words ringing in my ears, I think about what I want to do. Not what he or Mother or anyone else tells me to do.

Peering through the tent's fabric, I watch the writhing bodies near the shore. My people seem so happy—so carefree. But are they really? I'm becoming more certain that they are here as a result of Mother's manipulation. Each week, I adamantly try to convince Ilona they're here of their own accord, but is it me I've been trying to convince?

Even if they do choose to be here, does it make what I'm doing right? Don't my actions go against the will of the goddess who created us all—the true mother, the earth? Do I even want to do this?

Blood as red as my veyl stains my hands. I can't do it anymore. Shaking with terror at my decision, disgust for who I've become, I itch to rip the veyl into tiny pieces and toss it into the sea.

Dash's words play on repeat: *She cannot know you've broken free from her chains. You need to play along, for as long as you can.*

I know what I'm going to do.

Putting on the veyl, I push through the tent's slit. Sand and wind whip at me, and the crashing waves roar in the background. My black pants billow around my legs, confirming the decision to forgo a night slip was the right one.

As I peer into the jungle, I consider what I'm about to do. At first glance, our quaint, tropical island might not seem like a place where one would find a gleaming marble palace with a wicked throne built atop secrets and lies. A throne warmed by a queen with eyes as empty as her heart—the Dead Queen.

There's a storm brewing. Two actually.

One forms high above the waves, in the blue-black space between sea and stars. The other gathers strength in the deepest, darkest corners of my mind. And the most powerful of storms are known to devastate whatever stands in their way—marble, flesh, and everything in between.

Fleeing the bacchanal, I leave the beach behind. The thumping of the drums matches the pounding of blood in my ears as I fly over the packed-dirt trail, darting through the thicket of trees, until I catch glimpses of the palace.

Slowing my pace as I get closer, I act as natural as possible. The last thing I need is a witness to my erratic behavior. If someone were to alert Mother that her vessel is behaving strangely, it could ruin my plan.

I hurry across the grounds, and before I push open the servants' door, I pause.

A couple weeks ago, a handsome, scruffy stranger stood here and ignited something inside of me. He quickly became a friend—or at least had the resemblance of one—and almost something more. He threatened me, stole a kiss, and unintentionally turned my life upside down.

Or perhaps my life was turning itself upside down and he's been trying to keep me from tumbling with it?

Either way, he was right: I left the bacchanal. I was able to resist my *duty* for the first time ever. Mother no longer has a hold over me.

Practically floating through the corridors, I reach the throne room. Sentries, staffs in hand, stand guard outside the doors.

The doors open at my arrival, and I'm beckoned inside. Everything around me is drowned out by the *thump, thump, thump* of blood coursing through my veins. Taking a deep breath, I plod down the long aisle, keeping my eyes locked on Mother's, ignoring the dozens of people eagerly awaiting the transference ceremony.

Her eerie gaze locks onto mine, too dark, too empty to recognize. I wonder how long I've been blind to the monster she has become. This is not the same woman who cared for Ilona as a child and kept my secret all those years ago. That woman was kind, with a soft smile, warm eyes, and a tender touch.

This woman, with her tight lips and midnight gaze has a touch as cold as her heart. This woman is no longer the mother I once knew and loved, and I hadn't noticed. Until now.

It's as if someone pulled the curtain back and I'm seeing what lies beyond for the first time. It's the strangest sensation, as if I'm waking from a dream I'd been mistaking for reality.

Her influence can no longer reach you. You are free from her grasp.

Dash's words echo through my mind. Was he right? Has he

been right all along?

Shifting my eyes around the room, I struggle for breath. The judgement and expectation, the wonder and curiosity, from Mother's many witnesses is stifling.

I hope, for their sake, that Ilona was wrong and they're not all under Mother's control.

Somehow my feet have reached the dais, and I kneel before her. Nausea overtakes me, for an entirely new reason this week. But Cedrik's tonic works well, helping to settle the swirling bile before I make a fool of myself again.

Mother's voice rings out, followed by the peoples' chants.

Blessed be the people! Long live the queen! Blessed be the—

It fades away as I try to quell my shaking hands, lest Mother feel them trembling upon her calves. Dash's voice drowns out the rest of the noise: *You are free from her grasp, but you cannot let her know. She cannot know you've broken free from her chains.*

Surprisingly, his voice in my head calms me. Breathing becomes easier, and my hands steady. Once Mother has resumed her seat on the marble throne, I swallow around the pressure in my throat and carefully reach out to touch her skin.

Head bowed, I remain still, and she growls under her breath.

I'm confident I'm making the right decision. Except, when I try to focus on drawing her life force energy out toward me, I can't do it. She's cruel and untrustworthy, but she's still my mother. I can't *kill* her.

Sweat trickles down my temples, and I worry that once again I've put my trust in the wrong person. Dash told me I was free from her control, and I believed it.

This is a mistake.

She'll always have some sort of control over me, even without her magic influencing me.

I have no way to save myself, but at least Mother won't know I considered draining her life force. At this point, I'm counting on her hatred of humiliation being greater than her contempt for me. She can't let the people—the Vannyks included—know the transference didn't work. She won't.

She'll fake it for self-preservation. To keep her status as someone powerful and dangerous. To appear in control.

I'm counting on it to save my life.

Sure enough, she closes her eyes, and a soft moan leaves her lips as she mimics the action of absorbing the life force energy I normally give her. Only the two of us know the truth: there's none to give, none I share with her. The onlookers don't know any better.

Once a few believable moments pass, I withdraw my hand, flinching at the purely murderous glance Mother flashes my way.

For a moment, I'm fearful she'll plant a heel on my chest and send me tumbling backwards, but she doesn't. With a wave of her hand, she dismisses me. Two sentries escort me down the aisle and back out the doors. Mother will make another speech, then make toasts with the nobles. That should buy me some time.

I rush to the library to meet Dash, no longer caring who sees the vessel bolting through the corridors.

After all, Mother can make them forget.

CHAPTER FOURTEEN

Mother is all about appearances. She didn't leave the transference ceremony early a few weeks ago when I vomited and she sent me tumbling down the steps, so I know she won't tonight either. I can count on her to linger for at least another hour or so.

After tonight, it seems Dash is the only one I can trust, even if I'm hesitant to accept that. Aside from knowing I'm the vessel, he's also the one who freed me from Mother's control, a hold I wasn't even aware of before he came along. I don't want to trust him, but I have to. Surely he has a plan to get me out of this mess, or I'll face Mother's wrath.

As I rush toward the library, I remember I promised Ilona I'd spend time with her tonight. She'll be upset when I fail to show up, but surely she'll understand after I explain what happened. She'll forgive me.

Glancing both ways down the hallway to ensure no guards linger, I'm relieved to find I'm alone. Sliding the library doors shut behind me, I peel the veyl from my head. I scurry through the towering aisles, making my way to the furthest corner of the romance section. Dash is waiting for me, clad in Hakranian leathers, his headpiece resting on the shelf beside him.

"What the hell was that?" I ask without preamble.

"Do you trust me now?"

"Never," I say.

"Your mother is a threat to everyone, even you."

I refuse to share my own fears with him. I refuse to agree with him or side with him. In my mind, he is just as bad as Mother.

"All those sacrifices over the years—the lives you've gifted her—they've enhanced her abilities as a myndox." His eyes flick to somewhere over my shoulder, remaining alert for anyone that might find us. But the library is as quiet as ever. "We weren't certain at first, but now we are."

"Who's we?"

"Emman and Joccelyn. My parents."

"The—wait." My brows pinch together as I process his words. "Your *parents?*"

He gives me a shy smile, and I clench my jaw at him, fingers inching toward my waistband where my dagger hides. I will not let him charm his way out of this, not until I have the answers I came for. "Zale is still the true heir of Stellaris. I followed the path of a warrior. It was a wise move, considering it allows me to move about fairly undetected. No one expects a guard to have such powerful myndox abilities."

"You have a different last name," I point out lamely, still not fully accepting this bomb of information.

"I'm adopted. Though I've never admitted that to anyone." He gives me a soft smile. "Until you."

Dash appears genuine, but fear crawls up my throat anyway. Ever since he and the Vannyks arrived, he has done nothing but lie to me. Or has he? Grudgingly, I can admit to myself that he was right about Mother and the hold she had over me.

But this is yet another fact he kept from me. What else is he keeping from me?

"I don't understand," I say.

"The Vannyks took me in when I was young. My parents died, and the king and queen found me wandering the streets, dirty, hungry, and alone, on one of their many visits to the city center. If it wasn't for them adopting me as their own son—" His story reminds me of Ilona, except, instead of gaining a new mother in Enira, she really only lost her own—and at my hand. It cuts deep. "They took me in, protected me, loved me. With them, I learned how to use my power, and I got a chance for a better life."

"What did they want in exchange?" I ask.

He shoots me an incredulous look. "Not everyone is like Enira. Some people are genuinely kind and do things out of the goodness in their heart. The Vannyks, for example."

"They didn't force you to become a guard? To use you for your abilities?"

"Absolutely not." He chuckles. "I chose that path for myself. They never forced anything upon me."

"So it was fully your choice to assault me at the falls?"

"I told you, it's not what you think."

"Where two falls merge and two lips meet, hearts are joined, their power complete," I whisper, reciting the passage from the Paramour Falls' book of lore and changing the subject back to what really matters.

His expression softens at my words, which is the opposite of what I was expecting. I had anticipated a fearful reaction or aggression at me discovering what he's up to.

"You took my power," I whisper accusingly. Lightning bolts of fury strike through my body, a prelude to the rage I know is coming if this conversation continues.

"No. You've got it wrong." He runs a hand through his messy tresses. "You can't *take* someone's power. You can only freely share it."

"I didn't *freely* share anything with you." My eyes narrow as I cross my arms over my chest.

"No, but I shared my power with *you.*" His voice lowers as he steps toward me carefully, his soft eyes drinking in my reaction.

Chewing my bottom lip, I contemplate this. "That doesn't even make sense."

"*Where two falls merge and two lips meet, hearts are joined, their power complete,*" he says, reciting the same passage back to me. "A willing kiss behind the falls opens the doors to power sharing."

"You insulted me, attacked me, *forced* me to kiss you."

"Would you have kissed me back? Before all that?"

"Yes! I was beginning to like you, Dashiel Dargan, you dirty bastard!"

"Exactly." His eyes drop to my lips briefly. "But I couldn't let you."

We stand there in silence, as if Dash is waiting for something to click for me.

"When *I* willingly kissed *you,* my power expanded into your own," he says.

Something finally snaps into place. "But I didn't kiss you back," I breathe out.

"Exactly. You never shared your power with me, because you didn't willingly kiss me. I am truly sorry if I hurt you—for scaring you—but I don't regret what I did, and I'm not sorry for doing what I needed to in order to protect you from Enira."

The hurricane of feelings inside of me calms, swirling around the edges and waiting to consume me again. It's as if I'm in the eye of my own emotional storm.

He scared me on purpose—insulting me and forcing a wedge

between us so I wouldn't *want* the kiss—so I wouldn't like it. All so I wouldn't return it and unwittingly share my power with him.

He was *protecting* me.

I don't need anyone to protect me, least of all this Stellari guard, but something about his words brings me warmth. My knees go weak at his admission, and I can't help but find it endearing.

"You seemed so certain in your accusations of me being a slaughterer," I accuse, pursing my lips.

"It needed to be believable. You're an intelligent woman. I knew that was a sore spot and figured it would work."

"What exactly is it you can do, *myndox?*" I ask, though I'm certain I already know the answer. The Vannyks are unable to be manipulated by other myndoxes.

If he's more powerful than his family, which I'm starting to sense is the case, it could explain why he's immune to my vygora powers as well.

"I'm impervious to mental and emotional magic," he says, confirming my suspicions. "I can also hear the thoughts of others." Even in the dim light, I see a flash of color rise in his bronze cheek as he glances at me sheepishly.

A mind-reading myndox. I've heard of them but never met one. Then again, he's probably never met a vygora capable of sucking and transferring life force.

Motherfucker.

"You listen to my thoughts?" I ask defensively, my voice rising, summoning my anger.

He shakes his head, hair tumbling around his cheeks. "Not now. Not with my power in you. My—our power prevents it. You're safe from all intrusions." There's something intimate in his words. The way he calls it *ours* rather than *his*. As if he truly has freely given me access to his powers and it belongs to both of us now.

"But before? You did, didn't you?"

At least he has the courtesy to flinch, embarrassment and regret flitting across his face.

"That's how I was so sure you were unlike your mother," he mumbles. He steps closer, and I don't flinch as he reaches out to run his rough thumb over my smooth cheek. His brown-gold eyes bore into my own, and my stomach tosses with anticipation.

Things start shifting into place—all the smirking he's been doing, how he stifled a laugh during the first royal breakfast, how he's been egging me on—he knew exactly what I was thinking. He found it amusing. It also means he probably knows what Mother is thinking. It would also explain why he told me not to trust Commander Jamell—something I'll need more information about later.

"Your intentions might've been…dare I say, *good?* But this is still an enormous violation. There is so much wrong with what you just told me that I—forget it," I say, rubbing my neck. If I take the time to dissect my feelings on what he said, I'm going to lose sight of the more pressing issues. "You did something wrong. My magic is on the fritz, and I'm not certain your power sharing worked properly."

Although clearly part of the power sharing worked. I was able to refuse Mother twice now: once when she ordered me to acquire a hair-growth tonic and again tonight when I didn't accept a sacrifice for the first time in many years. The desire to refuse has been there before, but I've never been able to overcome it. Until recently.

It was a haunting confirmation, one I needed but didn't want. Mother has been invading my mind, influencing my free will to do her bidding, for goddess knows how long. Part of me feels better knowing I didn't truly want to steal life forces, but another part feels utterly betrayed and defeated.

I *am* a murderer.

Dash might've been saying those cruel words to sever my attraction to him and push me away, and he might not have meant them, but that doesn't make them any less true.

On top of that, my mother places more value on me as her subservient vessel than as her daughter.

"What do you mean?" he asks, his brows drawing in tightly.

"I'm unable to hear anyone's thoughts."

He laughs, and the dimple on his cheek appears. "Have you even tried, Princess? You've been guzzling down Cedrik's mind-numbing concoctions like an addict."

"I can't say I have."

"I suppose I'll have to teach you that in addition to fighting now." He winks, and I look away, heat rising in my cheeks.

"It's kind of impossible to overcome all the screaming anger and sadness that consumes me lately, not to mention everyone else's emotions. I don't even have to try to feel them these days, and I can't block them out. It's like you amplified my own magic. It's uncontrollable."

His brows dip, and he cocks his head at me, contemplating my words. "Nothing about your magic should've changed. I swear it. You should've only received a link to access mine."

"Maybe I need to fuel up on life force," I mumble, telling him what Cedrik told me weeks back before Mother manipulated his memory.

"Did you go through with it tonight?" he asks. I shake my head. "I know I told you to play along with her, but I'm secretly glad you did what was best for you."

"Let's hope."

"Did you outright decline the transference?"

"No. I pretended to try, as if I truly meant to deliver a life force per usual. When she realized what was happening, she pretended it worked to avoid embarrassment."

"Okay good. So she's not onto you."

"Maybe not, but she's not stupid. She's going to know something is off, and she's going to be livid."

Dash shakes his head. "You need to visit Cedrik. My parents are keeping Enira occupied, so you have a little time to get there. He'll have a diagnosis for you, one your mother will have no choice but to accept. At least for the time being."

"Cedrik is in on this?"

Dash smirks. "Your mother might be able to manipulate him with her power, but he's from Stellaris originally. He and Joccelyn were close long ago, and luckily he remembers her. Though *that* is a story for another time. Quick version, he trusts my family. We filled him in on everything, and he'll help. He's never liked Enira."

Suddenly, it's as if I'm a stranger in my own palace. The person I was supposed to trust unwaveringly—my mother—has been exploiting my love and loyalty. Cedrik, whom I previously pitied, is strong enough to stand against my mother. And when I thought Dash was abusing me, he was actually protecting me.

He wasn't stealing anything from me—not my kisses, not my power. He was *giving* me my free will back. The free will I hadn't known I'd lost. Though it offers me a semblance of reassurance, it doesn't change that he's been actively involved behind my back in plots that directly affect me.

"You should go, Princess, before someone catches us in here."

My eyes well with tears. I'm oddly relieved though overwhelmed.

Dash still has a long way to go to earn my trust and repair whatever blossoming friendship we had, but somehow I'm comforted to know he's looking out for me. That he's on my side—him, the Vannyks, and Cedrik. I need to be cautious, but it's nice to know I'm not alone in dealing with whatever Mother is plotting.

I'm aware Dash has secrets and plans that I know nothing of, but like I played along with Mother, I'll play along with him, see what I can learn.

I'm not working with either him or Mother; I'm working for myself and my future. Maybe, possibly, Dash will earn my trust along the way, but I'm not holding my breath. I've been tossed around and tricked too much already.

The dam inside me breaks, and the tears begin to fall. I curse quietly.

"It's okay to let it out." He reaches out, taking my hands in his own, giving them a squeeze. I feel soft and breakable beneath his strong, callused skin. "You're not alone anymore."

The tears fall harder at his words. "Did you just read my thoughts?"

"Not at all. I can't anymore. You're protected." He chuckles.

"Then how did you know what I was thinking, huh?"

"You might be a powerful princess, but you're still human, and I know you, Astrid."

"We've only known each other for a few weeks."

"Don't stab me for saying so, but I feel like it's been longer than that. I know you have a dagger tucked in your pants."

I chuckle halfheartedly through the snot and tears covering my face before patting my blade to make sure it's still there. "I'm feeling really... I don't even know what. Sad. Grateful. Overwhelmed. But, Dash, I don't normally cry like this. I'm not a crier."

"There's nothing wrong with being one, you know."

"There wouldn't be if it was normal for me, but this is what I'm talking about. I *can't* control my emotions. It's like I'm feeling everything tenfold, and it's eating me alive. Cedrik's tonic from this morning is wearing off. I don't want to be consumed by myself, but I also refuse to drink more of his medicine and turn into a ghost of myself. I'm sick of being useless, yet I feel useless either way."

"You're never useless, sweetheart." He tenderly wipes my tears away before placing a hand on each cheek and forcing me to look up at him.

"It feels like so much lately. So much that I can't breathe." Earlier, I despised Dash with my entire being. Now, I'm opening up to him in a way I've never explored even with myself.

I blame it on the irrational sorrow pouring out of me, the desperation to be understood and not be alone in the midst of all these cruel games.

"That's the problem with feelings," he says. "We *need* emotions to feel alive. But too few harden us, and too many weaken us. Let yourself *feel,* if that's what you need to do. You have me, and I won't let you drown."

His eyes glisten with authenticity, and I'm glued to his intense gaze. We stand there, only inches separating us, with his hands cupping my face. We stare at each other, stripped naked and vulnerable.

Stepping even closer, he releases my face and trails a knuckle up the side of my arm, leaving a line of goosebumps behind.

"I never wanted to hurt you, Astrid. Please believe me."

Swallowing thickly, I nod. "I think I believe that." And I do, but it still doesn't mean I forgive him. It definitely doesn't mean I trust him.

"I mean it. My family is good, truly good. We care deeply for each other and our people. When we learned about Queen Enira and Hakran, we wanted to help, to free them. I never meant to—to begin caring for you like I do."

"Was there ever even a threat to Stellaris, or was that a lie too?"

"Unless you count your mother, no, there wasn't, but our plan served its purpose. It got us to Hakran."

"Yeah *and* your guards, which are likely under Mother's control at this point."

"Maybe, but she can't manipulate my family, and now she can't use you either. We have a plan; I just need you to trust me. Do you trust me?"

Unable to give him the answer he wants to hear, I glance away. He reads my expression, stepping back and putting space between us. There's a longing in his face, and he looks like he's fighting the urge to grab me and kiss me.

Part of me wishes he would—wishes he would paint over the tainted memory of our last kiss with a new one. But another part of me wants him to keep his distance, while I'm still unsure of his intentions. Talk is one thing, but only his actions will prove what's in his heart.

"Go," he says. "Seek Cedrik. We have plans in motion."

"Can you find Ilona and let her know everything? Please? We need to watch out for her too."

"Of course." He seems relieved that we're working together instead of being at each other's throats.

There are plenty of things I haven't forgotten about—like the curly-haired girl who was sneaking out of his room the other day—but despite everything, I feel like I can breathe a little easier. Like things are finally starting to make sense.

I leave him behind in the dark aisle, but I don't miss the words he says to my retreating back.

"No matter what happens, Astrid, you're not alone. Don't ever stop swimming. Don't let them drown you."

CHAPTER FIFTEEN

Cedrik answers the door after one knock.

"Princess," he says, holding the door open wide and beckoning me in. His head swivels, checking the hallway in both directions before he closes the door behind us. "We haven't much time." Lines mar his face.

Nodding in understanding, I take a seat on one of the cots next to a table crowded with a variety of tonics.

"Listen to me," Cedrik says. "The transference is taking its toll on you. You sought me out due to another dizzy spell. That's the story."

His first matter of business is to ensure we're on the same page, that our stories line up, for when Mother seeks me out, which she will, as soon as she can. She'll want to determine why her beloved vessel failed her for the first time. She can't know I never took a sacrifice—that I purposely refused her demands and am no longer subject to her myndox manipulation.

I'm glad Cedrik has a plan, even if it means he has betrayed Hakran by working with our Stellari visitors behind our backs. But then again, what they're doing is in the best interest of my people. They're really only betraying Mother. Right?

After all these games and lies, I'm not sure how I'll ever fully trust anyone again, but for the time being, I'm grateful to have others on my side against Mother.

"How long?" I ask him.

The lines in his forehead deepen in confusion, so I clarify. "How long have you been working with the Vannyks against Mother?"

Holding eye contact with me, showing not an ounce of remorse or embarrassment, he exhales deeply. "It's not as simple as that, dear girl."

I open my mouth for a retort, but he gently shakes his head. "Please. We are not afforded much time. Your mother knows something is up, and she's planning to imprison the Stellari king and queen, along with their son. Her next step will be to assume control of their cavalry, if she hasn't already. We planned for her to take the army but not for her to imprison the Vannyks. If she succeeds, everyone will be at risk. You need to stop this."

"And how exactly am I to do that? If she's as powerful as we all fear, we won't be able to stop her."

"This is why we need to work together, and quickly." He takes my hands within his grasp.

"Does Dash know?"

Cedrik rubs his forehead. "No. I overheard chatter in the kitchen. It's not the most reliable, but we have to consider it."

"Then we need to warn him—warn the Vannyks so they can be prepared."

"We will. But do not worry much. They're the only hope in freeing the Hakranians. They're the only ones who care."

"Why do they even care, Cedrik? What does it matter to them?" I'm grateful that someone's paying attention to the horrid woman playing with everyone's lives, but we're such a small, isolated island. Mother's games surely don't affect the continent, so what's in it for them? Everybody wants *something*.

Heaviness settles in my stomach, and a wave of heat consumes my body.

"Their ancestors were from Hakran. This land belonged to their family, long ago," he says quietly.

"So they want the throne then?"

Scratching his neck, he glances away. "It's likely."

"Fucking Dash!" He has to know this. Omitting the truth is every bit as ugly as lying. Every time we take one small step forward, we fall three back. It's hard to give him the benefit of the doubt and trust him when he keeps such important things from me. "That's *my* throne." The vehemence of my words surprises me, and Cedrik's eyes widen with my admission. I've never considered taking Mother's throne. Never thought I'd be the one to rule one day. But if she is deposed, I'm certain I can provide better leadership for the island I know and love.

"The Vannyks are good people, Princess. I urge you to work together to take Enira down. What comes after doesn't matter so long as she's neutralized. They're powerful enough."

"How powerful exactly?"

"Their own myndox power runs deeper than they've let on," he says. "With the exception of that guard of theirs, the family can use their myndox powers to cast a barrier of sorts and protect the minds of others. It's weak, and the reach isn't anything to brag about, but it's a start."

So Dash can read minds, and his family can cast protections from invasive myndox powers. I knew there was more to them. I knew it from that first breakfast. Something seemed *off*. Granted, it makes sense why they kept the extent of their power a secret. It gives them the upper hand.

"So for instance, if Zale is nearby, he can protect those around him from Mother's manipulation?"

Cedrik nods carefully. "Temporarily. It breaks the hold she has on them and protects from further influence, but only while they're close. Once they're no longer in proximity, the protections fade." He scratches his jaw, a pained expression crossing his face.

Chewing on my bottom lip, I wonder if I can help the Vannyks take Mother down. Could I use my transference ability to boost their power like I did for Mother? Even if I could, it would require taking the life force of others—likely many others—in order to make a significant difference. Mother's power grew over seventeen years of weekly sacrifices, not to mention all the prisoners I practiced on, which likely kickstarted her surge of power in the very beginning.

Even if it increases our chances of winning against her, I can't massacre people. And if the Vannyks are as kind and just as everyone keeps telling me they are, they'll never accept that as an option.

Cedrik fiddles with some drying herbs on the wall beside his door, drawing my attention back to him.

"If your mother succeeds in locking them away, they'll be useless. And the silenxstone in the pit will inhibit what little protections they can offer."

"When is she planning to imprison them?"

"Tonight."

I've lived in this palace for twenty-three years and can't remember a time when Mother used the pit. There is so little crime these days that the main prison currently sits decaying on a small island to the northeast of Hakran. I'm starting to realize there's no crime because Mother literally doesn't allow it; she uses her power to control her citizens. The last time there were prisoners was almost fourteen years ago, before I cleared them out while training to hone my power.

Was I really training to use my magic though? Or has Mother been manipulating me into giving her life force all along? Has she always been using me? Do I know the truth about anything, or is everything I know based on lies fed to me by the Dead Queen?

"After you speak with your mother, if it's too late and the Vannyks are already imprisoned, you need to get Dash to the cells—by whatever means necessary—and he can do the rest from there."

The implication isn't lost on me. By whatever means necessary I am to become a weapon. I must use my powers if needed to gain entrance to the pit and free the Vannyks. Since the silenxstone will numb my powers once we enter, Dash will need to use his skills as a warrior to take on any guards patrolling the pit.

"If I do this, I'm betraying my mother. There will be no going back," I say.

"You are doing this for Hakran, for your people, Princess. Or should I say, Queen." He smiles broadly, despite the pain in his eyes, and it kicks my nerves into overdrive. The people of our beautiful island deserve freedom. They shouldn't have to gamble with their lives, bowing to a woman who leaves them starving while she feeds on their souls.

"What if I just kill her myself?" I couldn't do it during the fake transference earlier, but with this new knowledge and the affirmation that I'm not alone, I could. For Hakran, I would.

"If she dies at your hand, you will forfeit your seat on the throne, per the goddess's law."

Giving up the throne is a huge sacrifice, one I'm not sure I'm willing to make. I can't simply hand my throne over to the Vannyks, especially when I don't know for a fact they have Hakran's best interest at heart. They're playing their own games, so how can I be certain they're any better than Mother?

Ilona.

Gianna.

Marnie.

Jamell.

Those are only a few of the people who would be subjected to a new ruler. The Hakranian people aren't faceless or nameless—they're mothers, fathers, sisters, cousins, friends, lovers. They deserve better. It's my duty as their princess to protect them.

"I'm not willing to give that up."

"Then we need to do this according to the Vannyks' plan."

"Fine. I'm in." My hands begin to tremble and I say a quick silent prayer to the goddess.

"You worthless imbecile," Mother screeches as she blows through Cedrik's door not even five minutes later. "I've been searching all over the grounds for you. You *humiliated* me."

An inferno rages in her black eyes, and I swallow a lump of pure fear. Dash told me I'm safe from her now. She cannot invade my mind. Cannot harm me. For once in my life, I have the upper hand.

"I'm sorry, Mother." I cast my eyes down and attempt to shrink into myself as a safeguard. I act like the failed transference was a mere accident, that I'm still weak and compliant, but inside my violent wrath flickers to life. "I-I don't know what happened. I felt weird. Sick and—"

Her hand lashes out, colliding with my cheek. My head jerks the side with the impact. Disbelief consumes me, and my mouth drops open as I stare at her, wondering how I've been so blind for so long.

Because she manipulated me, as she does everyone else in her life.

My hand reaches for my cheek, in denial that she just hit me, despite the radiating sting there.

One.

Two.

Three.

As the three of us stand there wordlessly, I count my breaths, nice and steady, fisting my hand around my pants to prevent myself from returning the gesture. Flashes of red invade my sight, and there's a stabbing pain in my chest. Pure, visceral anger swirls inside of me. I'm about to lose any calm I've been pretending to have.

Fuck the throne. I'm going to kill this bitch right now!

"Queen, if I may," Cedrik interrupts the deafening silence and draws my attention away from her. Terror flashes across his features. "Princess Astrid—"

"She is no princess," Mother spits. Her words are poison, her own brand of venom. "*It* is the *vessel,* gifted by the goddesses to ensure your queen is fit to rule for many lifetimes to come."

The third-person reference to herself irritates me more than the words she used. I try hard to stifle the emotions that are desperate to pour out of me. They mingle with her incoming feelings of annoyance, rage, and disbelief. It's as if she can't fathom how or why her little vessel couldn't do its job and serve a life force up on a silver platter.

Without the sweet tonic to dampen the emotions, I need to work as hard as ever to stay undisturbed by the waves of fury rolling off her. I can't let them overtake me.

"Apologies, Queen." Cedrik tilts his chin down and pauses dramatically in an approximation of a respectful gesture. He's faking. It's meant simply to stroke her ego. "She—it is sick. I believe the toll of weekly transferences is too high for the vessel."

"It can take an extra life to keep. That should recharge it, should it not, healer?"

I bristle at the implication that she might force me to take two lives now instead of one. This isn't how I envisioned the plan going, but I should've figured Mother wouldn't be so easy to fool. She's conceited. A narcissist. But she isn't daft.

"I-I—cannot say, my queen." Anger flashes briefly across his features, and I'm glad Mother's eyes are on me. Clearly he didn't anticipate her reaction. We should've had a backup plan. Of course Mother wouldn't believe I was simply sick or that my powers were weakened. She needs me too much—rather, she needs my powers too much. Obviously she'll stop at nothing to *fix* her vessel.

Narrowing her stormy eyes at me menacingly, she glides to the door and flings it open.

"Enter," she commands to whoever's on the other side.

Two girls with tear-tracks on their cheeks enter the room wide eyed. Whatever Mother has in store for them, clearly they're frightened. For good reason, I'd imagine. I don't like where this is going.

Distress and hopelessness emanate from the girls. Their fear mixes with my own, threatening to push me over the edge and destroy my carefully constructed facade of calmness.

The girls are both dressed in plain white frocks, their feet bare. When they slowly raise their heads to take in their surroundings, I recognize one from the kitchen. She's new, and I haven't learned her name yet. She refuses to meet my gaze. The other raises her eyes to mine, terror marring her features.

"Gianna," I gasp, barely recognizing my favorite handmaiden through my flooded eyes.

"I shall let you choose first, dear daughter." She pushes Gianna's shoulder, forcing her to stumble forward. "My treat. One for you, and one for me."

Gianna's eyes go wide at the revelation that *I'm* the vessel and she's here as a sacrifice. In another life, we could've been true friends, but not in this one.

Streams of tears run down my own cheeks, and my hand flies to my mouth. I can't do this. Mother's going to know I'm immune to her powers, because I cannot do this. I'm going to ruin the entire plan, but I will not take these innocent lives only to please my vile mother.

When Mother's glee leaks into my mind, it's the final straw. Unable to hold myself back any longer, I screech, giving in to my desire to take her life no matter the cost.

"You heartless fucking swine!" Lurching toward her, I let the shocks of anger take over, latching onto her arm. She doesn't back away or flinch from my touch. In fact, her villainous smile grows.

"I should mention two things, before you decide on your next move, daughter dearest," she says with a smug look. "One, you cannot take my life force."

Closing my eyes, I ignore her words, focusing instead on drawing her life force out.

But—

Nothing happens.

Despite my inability to go through with it during the transference ceremony, I truly intend to murder this woman—my mother—right here and now. My claim to the throne be damned. I want nothing more in this moment than to cripple her, to watch as her as unseeing eyes focus on the ceiling above me. This wretched, sick excuse of a woman, of a mother.

Flames lick at my insides, my disgust for her burning me from the inside out.

But I hit a wall, like I did when attempting to pull Dash's emotions out.

Something is stopping me.

"Tsk, tsk, tsk." She pries my fingers off her arm with those blood-red claws and pushes me away. I stumble back, confused. My head pounds from the invading emotions of the four other people in the room. "Obviously I have taken precautions. You think me a fool?"

"How?" I shout. Impossible! How is she immune to my powers? She isn't. She shouldn't be. There's something she's using as a shield—a safeguard of sorts—to stop me. I need to find out what it is, but visceral rage clouds any rational thoughts I have at the moment.

Reaching into my waistband, I rip the dagger free, snarling at her.

"Two," she says, ignoring me. "A bloodthirsty guard of mine is keeping your precious, wild-haired friend company. If I fail to return unharmed in a timely manner, she shall perish at his hand." Mother twirls a strand of dark hair around her slender finger, eyeing my own with disgust. My feet turn to lead. Her words crash over me, causing me to hesitate instead of charging at her with my blade. "I *could* force you to complete this task wordlessly, but I find it is much more rewarding to remind you of the power I hold over you. You must not forget who is in charge of your life. Of Ilona's."

Stepping closer, I stand nose-to-nose with the woman who supposedly birthed me—an almost unbelievable feat considering her cruelty toward me. No mother should treat their child like this. I'm shorter, so she looks down, cocking a brow at me. Her putrid breath spoils the air between us. In this moment, I know she's aware I've broken her hold. Worse than that, she knows she's won this battle.

I can't kill her with my power. I can't even hurt her the old-fashioned way, or she will kill Ilona.

Sheathing my dagger, I step back. My eyelids flutter shut, and I silently count down from ten, trying to regain control before leveling a hard stare at her.

"If you allow that guard to touch her. If you harm her—"

"What will you do, *daughter?*" She claps her hands with delight. "Do enlighten me."

My fingers itch to snag my dagger again, but she only chuckles, as if I'm all too predictable. "Go ahead. If I do not return to Bellis within twenty minutes, he has explicit instructions to slit the throat of that freckled girl of yours."

My hands pause as I battle with my own emotions. The angry, impulsive side of me begs to end this. To end her. But my logical side reminds me of the cost: losing Ilona.

I can't lose Ilona.

She has no one else to protect her.

Cedrik shakes his head, eyes silently pleading me not to do anything rash.

Stepping back, I grind my molars together and stare her down, refusing to flinch at the pure hatred on her face.

One.

Two.

Three.

I'm barely hanging on and won't be able to stay in control for much longer. I need to escape before I do something I'll regret.

"If I complete your tasks, Ilona is unharmed," I say through clenched teeth. It's not a question. My eyes squeeze together as my heart pounds furiously in my chest. My head is light, and it feels as if I'm floating. Dreaming. Having some unfathomable nightmare.

"Of course. What kind of monster do you think I am?"

Scoffing, I stare unblinkingly into her emotionless eyes. "The worst kind."

I turn to face Gianna, and my heart twists at what I find in her face. There's no begging, no pleading. Only simple understanding. Forgiveness that I don't deserve. She looks me straight in the eye and offers me a small smile.

"It's okay, Astrid." Her face is red and raw from crying, covered in snot and tears. Black kohl runs down her cheeks, disrupting her normally perfect appearance.

My throat is so thick I can't respond. All I can do is fight my own tears as I return her gaze, refusing to shy away. I tip my chin down until it hits my chest, the deepest show of respect I can give her.

Her life or Ilona's, I remind myself. It's not a decision I'd wish on my worst enemy. It should be more difficult, but as much as it kills me, Ilona will always come first.

As I place my hands on Gianna's forearms, she whispers something so low only I can hear it. "Don't let her ruin you."

With those final words crushing my ribcage, I force an inhale and draw her energy into my own body. Waves of pleasure consume me, warming my veins and temporarily silencing all the other emotions vibrating through the room. My hand glows with a golden hue. Trying to fight the gratification is no use—so I let it in, accept it for what it is at this moment: a reprieve. All other thoughts fall to the wayside as I pull Gia's life force into my own body, sucking her dry of every last drop. Her body drops to the ground in a crumpled heap, her face dry and hollow. No youth left. No life.

In moments, she went from a vibrant young woman with a sparkle in her eye to nothing more than a crumpled piece of paper—used up and tossed aside.

She will never wake me with her cheery, unwavering voice again. She will never draw another eucalyptus bath or bring me another egg frittata. She will never set out my favorite outfit again. I will never share laughter with her again, or indulge in the latest palace gossip.

Gianna is no more.

Because of me.

The other girl trembles so hard her teeth clatter together. She watches in silence, staring at me in fear, begging me with her sorrowful eyes. Not my mother, *me*.

It's like a knife to the gut. I double over, exhaling sharply as the waves of emotion hit me again now that Gianna's life force absorption is over.

"Please, Mother. That's enough. Don't make me do this," I beg. It sounds pathetic even to my own ears, but I don't care. She has the audacity to laugh—hand on her stomach, tears in her eyes, *laugh*—at my request.

"No. Two lives. One for you, one for me. That was the deal. Unless you would prefer to sacrifice your little Ilona."

A choking noise leaves my throat, and I am utterly defeated as I turn back to the young girl.

"What's your name?" I grit out. I mean to ask softly, but I can't. It comes out harsher than I intend, and she takes a step away from me.

"Ch-Chancy," she says, teeth clacking.

Mother shoots me an icy stare, reminding me that Ilona's life is on the line if I don't hurry this along.

"I'm sorry, Chancy. Truly." *I will never forget you.*

Her eyes glisten; her nose is red and covered in snot. Sweat mats her chestnut bangs to her brow. Shaking her head vigorously, she tries to protest, to plead one last time for her life.

Trying not to drag it out and make it more painful than it has to be, I snag her arm in my hands.

Unlike Gia, who held my stare the entire time, Chancy refuses to look in my direction. Hatred exudes from her, sickening me to my core. Howls leave her mouth, slowly fading as I yank her life force away.

Consuming her whole.

Again, I relish the all too brief flutters of gratification. A moan leaves my mouth in response to the heady attainment. I've never absorbed more than one life force at a time. Even as a child, when I would drain the prisoners, I transferred them directly to Mother one at a time.

This is intoxicating. Pure bliss. My eyes threaten to roll back in my head, but I fight to keep them open, meeting Cedrik's sorrowful gaze. A tear falls down his cheek, sobering me slightly, but it does nothing to dull the invigoration.

Thump.

Chancy's body falls to the ground like a rag doll, her white frock swallowing her desiccated body whole.

It's a sickening sight—a girl no more than fifteen, a hand-maiden I could've called a friend or at the very least protected, in another life. Side by side the two corpses lie.

I executed them.

All because I tried to disobey Mother.

Had I refused Dash and accepted a sacrifice at the bacchanal, I could've taken the life of someone willing instead. Even if they were only willing because Mother had influenced their minds, it would've been less painful than this. The person would have at least been under the illusion they were dying with contentment, believing they were giving their life for a worthy cause. They would've gone peacefully.

The way these two girls passed was the opposite of tranquil. It was the most excruciating thing I've ever experienced in my life, and it's something I'll have to carry forever. A penalty I deserve.

I've taken hundreds of lives over the years, but these two feel different. I could've washed the bloodstains of all the other sacrifices off my hands, knowing they were a result of Mother's power over me, but these two were my *choice*. It was a nearly impossible choice, but one I still made. Perhaps I'm truly experiencing how despicable this is because I'm no longer under Mother's control. I hate myself almost as much as I hate the monster before me.

Mother snaps her slender fingers, gesturing for me to hurry.

My jaw clenches so tight a headache builds in my temples. Stepping over Gia's lifeless body, I place a hand on Mother's bare arm, staring at the wall of potions and tonics beside her instead of into her cruel eyes.

As I begin the transference, I meet resistance, as if the life force does not want to leave me, does not want to enter her wicked body. Electric pain shoots through my body, and I cry out, trying not to fight the process.

I control the transferred amount, choosing to give her as little as I possibly can to content her. Just enough to satiate her without her knowing I'm ripping her off. The less I can give her, the better.

When I'm finished, instead of feeling drained, I feel more energetic, my senses more heightened than normal. For the first time ever, I truly carry another's life force in my body. Despite the extra energy, that's anything but comforting. I'm ashamed and appalled.

Gianna and Chancy are dead, and I can't take that back, but I refuse to let it have been in vain. I will use whatever life remains of them in my own veins to exact revenge on Mother.

I am a murderer. A killer. A slaughterer.

I'm no better than her.

A vile, despicable creature. A monster.

The rage, guilt, and shame inside me continue to build, growing and forming into something uncontainable, pressing on my head from the inside out until—

"ARGHHHHHH!" I explode, grabbing my hair with both hands, shrieking until my lungs burn. Tears fall; I'm completely consumed by sorrow and pity. "I will gut you like a boar, you sick woman!"

Picking up one of Cedrik's tonics, I chuck it at the wall as hard as I can. The temptation to use one of the broken shards of glass to slit open her pretty little neck is overwhelming, so I grip onto a chair with both hands, fighting to hold myself back from lashing out.

Goddess have mercy on her poor soul. With a devil of a mother—

Deceitful little swine. If she tries that again, I will rip that redheaded girl's throat out with my bare hands.

Enira will pay for what she did, heartless witch. She will never be my queen.

Cedrik's and Mother's voices swamp my head, overlapping and overwhelming me.

"Stop it!" I screech out, lifting my hands to my ears. "Stop talking! STOP TALKING!"

"A disgrace," Mother says. It's only because she actually spoke the words aloud this time that I realize the voices were in my head.

Dash's magic.

Mind reading.

No.

This is not happening. Not now.

Poor girl. Poor girl. What has her mother done to her?

Pathetic. What a worthless—

"Please! Please just stop!" My voice is pleading, desperate. It's out of place. It's no use. The noise increases, and I realize with revulsion that I can't stop their thoughts from invading me.

It's robbing me of the little sanity I have left.

"Fuck you, Dashiel Dargan!" I screech, my voice raw. I blame him for this firestorm of emotions and voices burning me alive. I sob until I'm hiccuping uncontrollably, gasping for air.

"Queen Enira, I warned you she cannot handle the transf—"

Mother puts a hand up, warning him to stop. "Fix this, Cedrik. I refuse to entertain these dramatics." She turns on her heel, floating to the door.

"You heartless bitch!" I roar, chucking more tonics at her retreating back.

Cedrik steps toward me, but I wave him away, unable to bear anymore of his pitying thoughts.

This room is too small. I can't breathe with Gianna and Chancy's bodies lying crumpled at my feet. I can't be here a moment longer.

Fleeing the room, I leave his sympathy behind, flinching away from every guard and servant I see along the way. I try to put space between us, to mute their voices.

It doesn't work, and various phrases flit through my skull, as if my mind is a magnet attracting their words.

What's wrong with the princess?

She's just like her mother.

Is she all right?

I knew there was something wrong with her.

I would still pity fuck her.

"Shut the fuck up!" I yell at everyone and no one, clawing at my hair. This is an intrusion, a violation—for them and for me. "Stop!"

After the hell I just went through, I have zero trust for Mother. Any I had has been completely eradicated. Begging with the goddess to save me from the invasion of thoughts, I race through the corridors, focusing on getting to Ilona.

CHAPTER SIXTEEN

"Ilona!" I yell, pounding so hard on her door my fists ache. "Ilona! Open up. Please."

Mere seconds pass, but it's enough that I slide to the floor, my body shaking as I sob.

The door flies open. "Good goddess, A. What is the matter with y—" She stops abruptly when she sees the state I'm in.

Oh no, oh no, what did that distractingly handsome guard do this time? I thought he was finally— Ilona's voice rings out in my head, but I don't care. It's music to my ears.

I jump up, wrapping my arms around her and crushing her to me. I walk us backwards into her room before kicking the door closed.

Oh gosh, oh gosh, this is bad, whatever it is.

"You're okay." I breathe into her hair. "You're okay. You're okay." The relief turns to hysteria, and giggles bubble out of my sore throat.

"What's going on?" Her voice is higher pitched than normal, laced with concern, as are her thoughts. They flow into me freely, but I don't mind.

I don't mind.

I don't mind.

She looks awful. Maybe I shouldn't have left her alone.

"I thought Mother—I'm just glad he left."

"Who?"

"Mother's guard!"

Confusion crosses her features, her eyebrows pinched together. "There was no guard here, Astrid." Stunned, I can only stare at her. "Please tell me what's going on. I'm here for you."

I sink into the plush white carpet, and she kneels beside me.

I knew she should've taken Cedrik's tonic tonight. I should've ensured it. This is my fault. Please don't let her lose herself like Enira has. What has that wretched woman done? Please, goddess, don't let Astrid become her mother.

Words lodge themselves in my throat as I forget what Ilona said last out loud, distracted by her intrusive thoughts. Clutching her blouse in my fists, I beg her not to leave my side.

"I'm a murderer," I whisper. The word rings over and over again in my head, mocking me:

Murderer.

Murderer.

Murderer.

With the admission, my hands release her, flying up to my hair, tugging on the short strands. Ilona untangles my fingers, grasping them on her lap instead.

Two innocent girls lost their lives at my hands—I killed them in cold blood. All for nothing. Mother lied about Ilona's life being at risk. And now she also knows Ilona is my weakness and won't hesitate to use her against me in the future. Beyond that, Ilona worries I'm losing my mind. Becoming like my mother.

I've ruined everything. Put everyone at risk.

"Stop... Please stop... Stop thinking... Quiet..." I mumble incoherently, trying to drown out her thoughts with my own voice. The extra life force I consumed seems to have activated

Dash's mind-reading powers within me. It's too much all at once. I need it gone, but I can't make it stop.

"Ilona turn it off."

Please.

Please.

Please.

I'm not sure which words come out of my mouth or stay in my head, which ones belong to me and which ones belong to her. In my hysteria, they all bleed together.

Spots dance in my vision, and I try to blink them away. Ilona wraps her arms around me, saying something I can't hear. I'm faced by an onslaught of her worry and fear. Things I shouldn't hear because she hasn't said them aloud.

Her pity is the worst. She feels bad for me. As if I'm weak and pitiful. As if I deserve her sympathy.

"Why does everyone pity me? Don't pity me! DON'T!" I scream.

"Shhh." She smooths my hair down on her lap and lets me spill more incoherent words.

It's going to be okay.

When I've cried myself dry, she pries herself from beneath me and crosses the room in a flurry. I'm vaguely aware of her exiting into the hallway before returning with someone else.

"Hello, sweetheart," Dash mumbles in my ear as he scoops me up into his strong arms. I burrow my face into the nook between his neck and shoulder. "I've got you now."

Inhaling his woodsy scent calms me. It's not enough to quiet my racing thoughts or slow my pounding heart, but it allows me to relax into his hold. He speaks reassuringly to Ilona before carrying me away. I can't focus on their words. Don't care enough to peek at where we're going. So long as it's away from the noise.

Away from Ilona's pity.

"Silence," I say, nuzzling his neck. Warm, welcoming skin greets my lips, the few inches of skin not hidden beneath his leathers. His throat works as he swallows beneath my lips.

Click.

A door shuts behind us.

Clank.

A deadbolt engages.

Warm light filters around us as Dash clicks on a lamp, still cradling me like a baby against his chest. When he places me gently on a soft bed, I peer up at him through tear-stained lashes.

"I can't hear you," I choke out. Finally, it's quiet. No intruding emotions or thoughts. Only my own sit heavily on my heart. A pathetic half-chuckle escapes my lips, and I'm hyper-aware of how deranged I must seem.

I take a moment to survey the room. It's cozy, decorated in muted shades of grey with a dark rug and drapes—one of the palace guest rooms. *His* room.

I turn onto my side and curl up into a ball as he steps into the attached bathroom. Water runs for a moment before he trods back to me. There's no pity in his eyes as he kneels beside the bed.

"I hate you," I sob. But he's the only one I can't hear—can't feel. The only one who can quell the waves inside of me.

"I know you do." He brings a moist cloth up to my face, gently wiping away my tears and snot.

He hums a soft tune as he continues cleaning me, and eventually the distractions are enough to keep more tears from falling.

"You're okay, Astrid," he says, his eyes flaring with such compassion that my walls begin to crack. When he's done washing my face, he sets the cloth aside and begins massaging my scalp with a tenderness I hadn't expected from him.

He doesn't ask me what happened. He doesn't need to. The concern written on his face is enough to convince me he's probably figured it out.

In the flickering orange glow from the lamp, his eyes turn to honey. Sometimes they're darker, like damp soil, but in the right light, they appear almost golden.

"Gold is my favorite color," I whisper, trying to think of anything other than the atrocities my mother forced me to perform. "It's beautiful. Your eyes are the most beautiful I've ever seen."

"*You* are beautiful, Astrid," he says, a smirk tugging at the corners of his mouth. Even with the scruff growing out along his jaw—and the barely perceptible, ragged scar—he appears younger and more boyish when he smiles. Dash has his own stories, and one day I hope he tells me them. The realization that I want to hear all of his stories rocks me to the core, so I change the subject.

"Ilona got you."

"She said you asked for me."

"Did I?" I don't remember that, but then again I was wailing and spewing nonsense.

A single tear slides down from my cheek onto the soft onyx sheets beneath me. Without hesitation, Dash reaches up and swipes the remaining moisture away with his thumb. He lingers for a second on the apple of my cheek, his thumb rough against the smooth skin. It's a welcome feeling. My eyes flutter shut, and I revel in his touch.

Murderer.

I'm a murderer.

It's my own thought this time—haunting my moment of peace.

"I killed them." My voice cracks, barely audible.

Silence hangs between us as Dash glances away, his Adam's

apple bobbing with a thick swallow. For a second, I almost wish his mind wasn't closed to me.

"Your mother killed them. Not you, Astrid."

"No. I did. It was me. All me." He doesn't know I mean Gianna and Chancy. He thinks I mean the bacchanal sacrifices.

"Shhhh." He runs a hand through my sweat-matted hair.

"She made me choose, Dash. She made me choose between two innocent girls and Ilona's life. We never should've interfered." I can't help but think it would almost be better to still be under her control. Then I wouldn't have this guilt bearing down on me. Drowning me.

I would still think I was doing what's right, necessary even, for my people.

"You are strong, Astrid. Don't let your mother's crimes weigh you down."

Mother's crimes. I snorted. I *chose* to take Gianna and Chancy's lives. Regardless of the circumstances, that was my decision.

"She's going to hide behind her puppets now. She won't give me another chance to get near her."

Sniffling, I lean into Dash's touch until his entire hand cups my cheek. Wordlessly, he crawls into bed beside me.

"Take those off?" I ask, gesturing to the daggers strapped to his sides. I'm sure they can't make lying down comfortable for him. He nods once and stands. I had only meant for him to take the weapons off, but I don't complain as he sheds everything.

When he's left in nothing but his fitted silk undershorts, he slips back into bed beside me, pulling the sheet over us and adjusting himself until he's comfortable. We're sharing the same pillow and staring into each other's eyes. He's so close, the heat of his skin calls to me.

I'm emotionally drained and physically exhausted from everything I have endured during the past few weeks, today especially. There's something comforting, intimate, about the two of us here in this quiet moment. I want to shed all my worries, if only for a little while, so I can exist without feeling the pain and problems that circulate around me.

"I can hear thoughts now too. I can…read minds, I guess." It's a weird thing to admit out loud, but if anyone understands, it's Dash. Another secret between us.

His eyes soften at my admission. "Ah, so it's the silence you're enjoying, not my presence?"

Grinning at him, I shake my head, mussing my hair against the silk pillowcase. "Never thought I'd seek *you* out for peace and quiet."

"You wound me, Princess." He pulls me closer, and I snuggle into his chest.

"I don't trust you, and I think I hate you," I tell him. "But for a little while, can we just pretend?"

"That you don't hate me?"

"That nothing else exists."

He strokes my hair. "It's only you and me, sweetheart."

My body softens into his, and the sound of our steady breathing quells the chaos in my mind. Until another thought comes racing back.

"Your parents!" I panic, shooting upright, remembering Mother's plan to imprison them. I look down into his face. We're mere inches apart, and his breath is warm against my lips. Something deep inside of me stirs, aches to bring him closer until no space separates us at all. But I refrain.

"She took them," he says, closing his eyes. His face has a pained expression.

"Cedrik warned me. I was meant to get to you before she imprisoned them. We were supposed to stop them."

"You couldn't have. She had them captured during the transference. Luckily she thinks I'm nothing more than a guard, one who is subject to her manipulation. It works in our favor."

"We need to rescue them." With the magic of the moment broken, I fill him in on everything that happened. I'm extraordinarily grateful when his expression doesn't change when he learns the full details of the slaughter. Of my choice to save Ilona, thus dooming Gia and Chancy.

"You did what you had to do." He cups my cheeks with both his hands, his face hardening. "You were born to be a queen. You *are* a queen, Astrid. And this is war—war against your people. We will not let your foul mother win."

"So you don't want my throne?" The jest is a cover as I dig for the truth.

He shakes his head. "Hell no. That was a backup plan I did *not* want to follow through with. We were hoping the princess was nothing like her mother so we could help *her* ascend to the throne. Why do you think I got assigned to your side? It was my mother's idea. I never wanted to intrude on your privacy, but we needed to know the truth."

"And?"

"Thankfully, you are the perfect person to watch over Hakran." He smirks, and I scrunch my brow. It should reassure me that all of Dash's supposed betrayals have had a purpose— and none of them seem nefarious. He doesn't want my throne. He wants me to take it, like I'm supposed to.

I should be happy…yet I'm conflicted. Skeptical.

"Then what do you want?"

"What do you mean?"

"I find it hard to believe the Vannyks left their own comforts behind to risk their lives crossing the Insipid Sea to help my small island."

"We are descendants of the Hakranians, you know. Many of the Stellari people have extended family who reside here." With one arm bent under his head he leans back, stroking my hip with his thumb beneath the covers. "Over the past few years, Hakran has become progressively quieter. More closed off. Trades have slowed down. Much of our correspondence is never returned. My parents aren't the type to rule with great shows of power or ego. They genuinely care for people, especially those whose voices aren't always heard. They heard rumors about Queen Enira—the Dead Queen—and we grew worried. We came here together, hoping the rumors weren't true but preparing for the worst. We were expecting to implement change if needed."

"How did you know the falls would work?" I ask. Even though I was born on Hakran, the Paramour Falls lore wasn't one I knew of until recently.

"Like I said, we're descendants of the Hakranians. Davvinia and Anwyr were my ancestors."

My brows shoot up. "You're descended from a goddess?" Not just any goddess either, but the one specifically linked to Hakran and Paramour Falls. No wonder he knew what he was doing when he kissed me.

He laughs, his eyes crinkling slightly at the corners. "I worry about the lack of education and history your damned mother has provided you. All of those with abilities are descendents from a god or goddess. It's in our blood."

"I mean, I've heard that, but I thought they were only stories. No one even worships the original goddess anymore. Not truly. We call for her blessings or curse her, but that's as far as the acknowledgement reaches."

"It's been so long since the original goddess roamed that she has become a myth, and myths change shape over time."

"You don't think it's possible we're from the same—"

"Not likely." He waves a hand, chuckling at my concern. "The original goddess created *thousands* of gods and goddesses. That's how the lore goes, at least. It says the original goddess is the source of all magic and all beings, that she became lonely and created thousands of beings to keep her company, dispersing her magic among them. These lesser gods and goddesses continued spawning and are responsible for creating the humanity we know, including those with and without power."

"Shouldn't there be more like us then? Vygoras, myndoxes, aetheyns…even etheryns? Surely the handful of royal families, nobles, and royal laborers can't be all."

His expression is grim, his mouth a sharp line across his face. "There were. Many more. Before they were slaughtered."

"By who? Actually, never mind. We don't have time for that. Davvinia and Anwyr are your ancestors? So she forgave him for tricking her?" It was mentioned in the lore book that Davvinia was tricked by her mortal lover, all so he could access her power in hopes of achieving immortality.

"Not exactly. Davvinia loved Anwyr with all her being. He had only been using her, manipulating her for her power. She was pregnant when he took her to the falls and accessed her magic. Fearing for her unborn child's life—a child he knew nothing about—she murdered Anwyr in his sleep. It's said she later died in childbirth, as payment for taking the life of another god."

"But he wasn't even really a god."

"No, he wasn't technically, though he had Davvinia's goddess magic running through his veins. Everything comes with a price."

"What's the price of power sharing?" I ask.

"Shared magic is fueled by love, nothing nefarious. It's a very sacred thing." He runs a hand through his shaggy waves sheepishly while I balk at him.

"*Love?*"

"Well, it's assumed only lovers kiss beneath the falls."

"Tell that to poor Davvinia...or *me.*"

He recoils, his lips pulling into a frown. "Astrid, I never meant what I said. I hated it. Hated hurting you, putting you in that position. If there was another way to protect you, I would've done it. But if I told you what was going on, what I intended to do... I heard your thoughts. Knew you felt the same way about me as I did you, even with all the bickering. I couldn't risk you kissing me willingly and opening your power to me."

"Would that really have been so bad?"

"Seriously? You never would've trusted me fully if I accessed your magic." His tone drops into a low rumble that warms my insides, and his eyes search mine. "I *want* you to trust me."

I turn my eyes to the recessed ceiling, afraid to look at him. Afraid of what I'll find in his expression.

Afraid I'll begin to trust him, though I shouldn't. I can't. He's right though. If he would've accessed my magic, it would've been harder to consider his intentions pure. Though I hate how he did things, maybe there was no other way to go about it.

"You're entirely stubborn, woman. You know this."

"I do," I whisper. And then a thought occurs to me. "Dash?"

"Yes?"

"If you're adopted, how do you know the story of your ancestors?"

He inhales a slow, deep breath. "My real parents loved telling me stories of the gods and goddesses, of our own Hakranian ancestors, before they passed. They were amazing, from what I remember."

"That's really sweet." I roll onto my side, placing a hand under my head as I face him. "I'm sorry you lost them."

"Me too, but I'm lucky enough to have gotten two sets of great parents in my life. Some people don't even have one good parent." He winces, as if he realized too late that I'm one of those people he's referring to. I reach out, stroking his jaw reassuringly.

"You're right. You *are* lucky." I'm happy he had that in his life. It must be an incredible thing to have parents who care enough to pass down the stories of their ancestors. I wonder if Mother knows the origin of our bloodline, if she even cares. "I still can't believe you're related to the Davvinia I just read about recently. Or that you're attached to my favorite place on this island."

"Maybe it's meant to be?" A coy look spreads across his face.

I chuckle, and the carefree humor offsets the anger and sadness that overwhelmed me not too long ago, until I realize what he said about how the magic of the falls is fueled. "The magic of the falls and power sharing are sacred, linked by love?"

He nods.

"Dash…you tricked me into kissing you. Assaulted me." Or at least I thought that's what it was at the time. "Your intentions might've been in the right place, but what if it doesn't matter. What if *that* is why my own magic is on the fritz?"

A frown stretches across his face. "I don't think so. My birth mother told me quite a few stories of the falls. If there weren't true feelings or intentions there, then the power sharing wouldn't work at all. That's how Anwyr was able to trick Davvinia despite his nefarious desires—because *she* loved *him*. In our case, I meant well. I meant to protect you. I think the falls knew and bestowed us with their gift."

Sighing, I accept his answer. The falls shouldn't have turned my magic erratic and uncontrollable. That means it must have something to do with the transferences. There must be truth to what Cedrik said, that I need extra life forces to keep up with the amount I gift to Mother. Perhaps that's why I feel so at peace right now, with the extra life force circulating through me.

"Do you forgive me?" he asks, his voice soft.

I don't answer because I don't want to admit it out loud. That I *do* forgive him. That despite everything, all the reasons I shouldn't, I might even trust him a little.

I grab him by the cheeks, and there's no patience, no hesitation as I slam our mouths together, reveling in the way his soft lips contrast with the roughness of his stubble.

Unlike that day at Paramour Falls, I *want* this. If I'm finally being honest with myself, I've wanted this from the moment he opened his arrogant mouth to challenge me. Ever since I saw his infuriating smirk and that one sweet dimple. I've wanted this every time he's been close enough for me to smell his delicious sandal-wood scent. Whenever he looked at me with those gold-flecked eyes that somehow saw the real me beneath all the labels bestowed upon me.

Warmth pools in my belly, dropping lower to my core. His tongue parts my mouth, exploring gently. Deepening the kiss, I moan into his mouth as he leans me back, hovering over me on the bed. It's a kiss, an innocent kiss, yet it's erotic and intimate at the same time. We continue tasting each other, slow and sweet until we're both panting.

He leans back when we finally pull apart. As he wipes his plump bottom lip with a thumb, his eyes trace my features as if he's committing me to memory.

"Does that convince you how I feel?" I ask, my voice huskier than I expected. His smile stretches wide, and his dimple appears as he nods with approval.

I know it's reckless to give into our urges right now. Mother is on the loose, likely assembling a defense against us. The Vannyks wait in the pit, needing to be rescued. Ilona worries in her room alone.

But for the first time all week, I'm okay. It's the first time tonight I haven't been going crazy under an onslaught of emotions and thoughts.

He pulls his shirt off, revealing a muscular chest, and I can't stop staring at the glorious sight. The tattoo on his right bicep catches my attention, and I realize it's a skull decorated with flowers and a line of words. I trace it with a finger as I read it aloud. "Love is the currency of life - Ayana." Bitter envy rises inside me and I sit all the way up. "Wait. Who is Ayana?"

He closes his eyes, exhaling heavily as he rests his head against the headboard. "We don't have to do this now."

"What do you mean we *don't* have to do this?" My heart twists. "Dash, who is she to you?"

When Dash's eyes flick open, they're moist with unshed tears. His voice is hollow when he finally speaks. "Was. It's who she was to me."

I freeze, not knowing how to respond. I had expected Ayana to be an ex-girlfriend or previous lover, but the look on his face alerts me to the fact there's a more painful story there. I'm desperate to know more about him, but not like this. I wish I had asked out of genuine interest rather than jealousy and insecurity.

"It was eight years ago. We were barely eighteen. At the time, I felt so grown, like I knew everything about the world, but looking back, I was so young. So stupid." A tear slides down his cheek, and seeing him so vulnerable shatters me. Now it's my turn to reach out and wipe away his sorrow. "I was supposed to protect her." His voice cracks. "It was my responsibility to keep an eye on her and I fucked up. She's dead because I was distracted for a second. Just a second too long. One second is all it takes."

I think of the time I ditched him on horseback, how he freaked out on me, and colossal shame chokes me. No wonder he was so adamant about taking his responsibility seriously—something terrible happened to someone he was supposed to protect, and he blames himself.

"I am so, so sorry, Dash," I whisper. It's an apology for what he lost. An apology for how immature I was when I made a joke out of ditching him, unaware of how sensitive the situation truly was. No words can adequately sum up my remorse.

"I loved her," he says. "I loved her, and I failed her. She used to tell me 'love is the currency of life. It's the true magic of our world because the more you give, the more you shall receive. Make sure you spend freely and you will enter your grave a rich man, Dashiel.'" He smiles through his tears as he reminisces. "She would have liked you. She would have liked you for me."

Leaning forward, I plant a soft kiss on his lips, because I don't know what else to say. His lips taste like salt and heartbreak, and I wish I could take away his pain.

When I begin pulling back, he reaches up and grips the back of my head, holding me in place. Our faces hover only millimeters apart, so close we share breaths.

"I'm sorry," I whisper, because I can't think of anything better to say.

He kisses my jaw tenderly before moving to my neck, leaving a soft trail of kisses there. "I vowed to never fail anyone like that again, Astrid, and I meant it." His nips at my shoulder. "And I vowed to never stop loving."

My hands make their way into his hair, gripping tightly as I melt beneath the gentle kisses he plants along my skin.

"Dash—"

He must sense the yearning inside me—I'm begging him to stay here with me a little longer to block out the noise, to save me, to let me save *him*—because he nods slowly in consent.

Placing my hands on his chest, I press his back into the mattress before swinging my leg over him. Straddling his waist, I lean in and kiss him. He grabs the back of my head with one hand, pulling me closer, while his other hand grips my waist, digging into my soft flesh as if he's trying to restrain himself.

"Don't hold back," I whisper against his lips. "This is much overdue." The luxury of going slow, of fully losing ourselves in one another isn't an option. As much as I want to be here with him, dragging out this moment, it's fleeting. We're on borrowed time and I'm greedy for all of him.

My words urge him on, and with a grunt of approval, he flips me over in that signature move of his, pinning my hands above my head. Unlike the soft, tender kiss from before, these are the kisses of a needy, hungry beast.

And unlike the first time he was in my bed—when I kicked him out for taking control—I allow myself to relax and submit.

Reaching down with his free hand, he yanks my bottoms down to my knees in one fluid motion before freeing himself. His erection bobs out, nudging me in the thigh. I gasp at the feel of his bare skin against mine.

I've connected physically with many people, but not like this. Whatever *this* is, it's brand new to me. We've stripped ourselves down; we've bared our naked souls to one another, and instead of running away, I want more of him. It's as if I can't pull him close enough.

He catches me off guard by running a finger up my slit, and I whimper at the sensation.

"Dash," I murmur. I'm loving the way his touch lights up every single nerve in my body. His nearness, his teasing, the anticipation—all of these are almost as euphoric as life force absorption. It's all-consuming. Exactly the type of pleasure I crave from him.

Taunting me further, he leisurely presses the tip of his finger inside of me.

"You're so wet for me," he rasps. Just as slowly, he removes his finger, bringing it to his mouth. His eyes hood with desire as his tongue darts out, licking my arousal off his finger. He hums in approval. "And you are absolutely appetizing."

"Stop...playing with me, Dashiel Dargan...before I go back to...wanting to murder you." My words come out barely audible, in soft exhales, as I writhe beneath him, begging for more. *Please—*"

"Please what?"

"You." I can't seem to form a coherent sentence with the anticipation lingering over me.

"Me what? Say it, sweetheart. Tell me what you want."

"I need you inside of me. I need you, Dash."

With a dark chuckle, he plunges into me in one quick move. I moan at the sensation, and he covers my mouth with his, swallowing the noise. My body stretches and adjusts to the new pressure as he nibbles on my lower lip.

"Is this what you wanted?" he whispers, and I claw at his back, urging him on as I beg for more. "Shhh. Take it all." He begins pumping in and out of me, picking up speed as my slickness assists him. We work frantically, as if we know our time is almost up and we're desperate to wring everything from each other. My fingernails surely leave marks as I pull him close, wrapping my legs around his waist so I can take him even deeper. He groans, and it makes my core pulse with sweet satisfaction, my release imminent.

"You're going to make me c—" I pant, unable to finish my sentence as he reaches a hand between us, running his thumb along my nub in sync with his relentless thrusts.

"There you go, baby, cum for me," he says. "Just like that." His dirty talk is my undoing, and I cry out as my muscles pulse, squeezing around him and edging him toward his own relief shortly after.

With a few strong pumps, he empties inside of me. I cling to him desperately, my heart filled with something I can't name. Something more than simple lust. His lips find my throat, and he leaves a line of soft, sweet kisses up to my lips before disentangling from me. Reaching for the damp cloth he used for my tears earlier, he cleans us both up. It's so gentle, so considerate, that I feel like I can't breathe.

"I take a monthly preventative tonic," I mumble awkwardly, referring to the concoction that prevents disease and pregnancy. I fill the silence more to avoid thinking about the weight sitting on my chest right now, crushing me, scaring me. It's not bad, but it's...a lot. I'm not sure I'm ready to name it yet.

Dash chuckles at my flushed cheeks. "That was irresponsible of me to assume, but I'm glad to hear it."

Pushing up from the bed, he extends a hand to me, and I accept, allowing him to pull me to my feet. Swiping at my cheeks with his rough thumb pads, he wipes away the new tears I hadn't realized were there, then smoothes my wispy hair from my face.

"A queen," he says, looking at me with admiration.

A murderer, the voice in my head replies. After hearing Dash's admission, I wonder if he hears the same voice, too. One day, I want to hear the full story. But it doesn't seem like the right time to ask.

Instead, I ignore the cloud of pain hovering over us, and I smile up at him as we both set about getting dressed.

"Dash!" I gasp.

He smirks at me. "I love hearing my name on your lips, but I love hearing it even more when I'm inside of you."

"No," I say, brushing off his comment. "This is serious. We need to go get your parents." I can't believe we were so irresponsible and wasted so much time.

His face drops and he runs a hand over his forehead. "Fuck."

"I know."

"Listen, you can block out the thoughts like I do. I assume it's similar to how you control your vygora powers—turning the abilities on and off."

"I'll try that," I say, my voice sounding disconnected. Hopefully he's right. "We need to go, now."

As I walk past him, his hand flashes out, grabbing my wrist. In one fluid movement he spins me around and gives me a kiss filled with heat and passion. It's like he can tell I'm struggling, but instead of reassuring me or pestering me to talk about it, he's accepting it for what it is. Allowing us to simply be...whatever we are in the moment without any heavy conversations or expectations.

"I'm so glad you're you, Astrid," he says sincerely. His eyes flicker as they trace the lines of my face. "I'm so glad you let me in."

Again, a chaotic mixture of emotion clogs my throat, silencing my reply. But beneath the stress and fear is something sweeter, something more comforting than the pain normally found in its place. I'm not ready to name it or acknowledge what Dash means to me.

Instead of responding, I walk out the door, knowing he'll follow.

CHAPTER SEVENTEEN

The hallway is eerily quiet. Devoid of sentries. Only Ilona waits, twisting her hands nervously, emerald eyes glistening with unshed tears.

Her sorrow-filled thoughts grab hold of me immediately. I battle to keep them away, deflating when I fail. The reprieve I found in Dash's silence is lost.

Something is definitely going on.

She looks terrible. Pale. Nervous. What did Enira do to her?

Dashiel calmed her down. Oh thank the goddess.

I groan at the endless stream of thoughts leaking out from her and slap my hands over my ears as if it will help block the noise.

"I was so worried about you, Astrid." Ilona's voice and thoughts blend together, and it's almost impossible to tell which words she's spoken aloud.

She places a hand on my shoulder, trying to focus my attention.

"Not now!" I shake her off. Hurt flashes across her face. "Please, Ilona. Just go!"

She's my best friend, my sister, and I truly love her, but I can't handle the unfiltered access to her mind right now. I'm used to her ramblings, but this is another level. Dash and I don't have much time; we need to free the Vannyks. I won't be able to focus with her around.

"Give her time, Ilona," Dash says. He pats her arm somberly. "Astrid will explain everything eventually, but right now she's struggling."

She backs up hesitantly, giving him a soft nod. Rejection mars her sweet face. It's gut-wrenching. But instead of being grateful Dash influenced her to back off, I'm annoyed.

He has no right making promises to *my* friend about what I will or won't tell her, and Ilona should trust me. She needs to stay out of it for now.

A moment later, when Ilona's appreciation of Dash's kindness filters into my mind, the anger, frustration, and annoyance burn inside of me. Then a prickle of jealousy creeps up.

"This isn't me," I mumble. I'm not an envious person. I'm normally rational, controlled. But I'm at the mercy of my unruly emotions.

Ilona pauses, giving me a questioning look. Dash whispers to her, "She can't control either of our powers right now. It's hurting her to be around you."

I storm off down the corridor without sparing either of them another glance.

"Wait!" Dash calls. His boots slap against the marble as he catches up to me. "I know you're overwhelmed right now with every—"

"You know nothing about how I'm feeling, Dash." He was only being kind to Ilona and patient with me. I have no right to direct any animosity toward him, but I can't help it. "You didn't even tell me how to turn off their thoughts!"

"You have to shut them out yourself. Focus, like you do with your other powers."

"This is all your fault for giving me powers I didn't want."

My words stop him in his tracks. From behind me, he says,

"Enira was going to turn on you next, Astrid. She already controlled you when it benefited her, but she was going to erase your free will permanently." Pausing, I turn to look at him. His face is filled with regret, and I know he's telling the truth. "Despite how powerful a myndox she is, I can still hear her thoughts. Her plans. By the parlor, when she saw your short hair for the first time, thoughts of controlling you permanently crossed her mind. You pissed her off with that little rebellious act. And again when you were late for breakfast that one morning."

Rubbing the tension out of my temples, I sigh. "You should've told me. I could've left."

"You can't leave. Your people need you."

"That's not your decision to make!" The inferno inside me burns hotter.

I am angry.

So angry.

Sick of people controlling me. Of making decisions for me.

Dash and his family saved me from Mother's control, but for what? To put *me* on the throne instead? To turn me into their puppet? How is that any different from what my mother has done to me?

I can't even stand to be around Ilona, the one true friend I have.

"No! This isn't how I feel! It's not me!" I scream. Dash rushes over to me, his brows drawn.

He opens his mouth to say something, but I stop him with a shake of my head and a raised hand. "Please, Dash. Let's just get your family out. I don't want to talk to you right now. I can't. I-I'm out of control." It's hard to admit, but luckily a small sliver of logic tethers me to reality. It prevents me from lashing out entirely.

He frowns, and I'm not sure if it's directed toward me or himself. I don't care.

We exit the palace without another exchange, crossing through the courtyard.

"What's the plan?" I ask when we reach the servants' door.

"Thought you weren't talking to me." He grins, and any other time I'd think it's cute, but I'm so far beyond annoyed that I stomp my foot like a petulant child.

"Dammit, Dash! Give me some instructions here."

"Let's hope your slimy commander friend is around to get us into the pit. Once we're beyond the pit doors, our powers will be rendered useless by silenxstone." He points to the daggers strapped to his waist—two at each side. "I'm proficient with combat and can take out the guards that will be down by the cells."

"Even if Jamell is in the training room—and that's not a guarantee—how are we going to get him to open the pit for us?"

"You're the *princess*. Tell him your mother needs you to check on the Vannyks."

"For an intelligent man, you grossly overestimate my reach."

"The guards don't know you're the vessel. They still view you as their princess. Use that power."

Unease boils inside of me. This plan is sounding worse by the minute. "Did you forget the training rooms are directly above the one entrance to the pit? You know, the place where all the guards train?"

"This is why you need Jamell to get us in discreetly, so we don't raise any alarms. If he leads us in, no one will question it. Once we exit the silenxstone with my family, we'll have the advantage. Zale and my parents are efficiently trained in combat. They also have the benefit of casting their own myndox powers to eliminate your mother's hold on any of the nearby Stellari guards. That will raise our numbers."

I'm a nervous ball of energy as I bounce on my feet. Much of my rage has dissipated, but trepidation takes its place.

"You have your blade?" he asks. "Just in case?"

My fingers trace the hilt of the dagger inside my waistband. "Yes."

My body trembles with anticipation as the severity of the situation dawns on me.

"Hey, hey. Breathe," Dash says, noticing my state. He draws me to his chest for a hug. I inhale his woodsy scent as I melt into his arms.

Fuck my broken power and these extreme emotions.

I squeeze him tighter. Despite my unpredictability, he's phenomenally patient and able to gauge when I need him to back off and when I need him to get closer.

I hope that whatever is going on with me gets resolved soon and that it doesn't push him away. Whatever is happening between us is only getting started. We're finally building trust after weeks of ups and downs. Not to mention, the sex was phenomenal.

Breaking the embrace, I smirk up at him.

He chuckles. "Feeling better?"

"For now." Maybe if I think about how good he is in bed, it'll help get me through this chaos.

"I aim to please, sweetheart," he says.

"I said that out loud, didn't I?" I ask. He nods, and I groan, rubbing my forehead in embarrassment. "I'm having a difficult time here; don't hold it against me."

"I would never. But I can definitely hold something else against you after we're done here." He winks, and I roll my eyes at the lame joke.

"All right. Let's just get this over with." I wonder what the Vannyks plan to do with my mother when they have her in hand. The Vannyks don't seem cruel, the kind to murder someone in cold blood, and even if they were, they couldn't kill Mother outright. They would forfeit their own throne, if what I've been told about the goddess's laws is true.

If they're not planning to take her life, then what do they aim to do with her?

As much as I want Mother stopped, it comforts me to know the Vannyks will almost certainly allow her to live. I don't want her dead. At least, I didn't at first—not until she threatened Ilona. Even now, despite her threats, I don't truly want her to die. She *is* my mother, as hard as that is to believe sometimes. Maybe she can be saved. Perhaps I can drain her of enough life force to weaken her power so she's unable to cause any real havoc.

I'll have to figure out a way to use my power on her, to get past the barrier she somehow has in place.

It's hard to say for sure what I want.

I'll save that contemplation for later, when it's relevant. Once we safely get Dash's family out of the pit, together we can assess what to do about Mother.

Dash and I silently enter the servants wing and descend the stairs into the training rooms. Only a few guards are milling around. Jamell is near the center of the room, talking to a tall woman with a thick braid of wheat-blonde hair.

"Ay, Princess. I haven't seen ya round," he calls to me, shooting me a toothy grin before waving the woman away.

The blonde woman's thoughts strike me as she walks by without a passing glance.

So this *is the princess. Shame.*

I grit my teeth, trying not to dwell on whatever the hell she means. Jamell's thoughts hit me next, mixed with a few other stray voices, and luckily they are mostly of the observational variety, making them slightly more bearable than Ilona's were.

Jamell internally notes my uptight body language. Dash's daggers catch his eye next, and his thoughts alert me that the weapons aren't standard issue.

Fucking Dash.

He had better not blow this. We need Jamell to open that door for us.

I stride up to Jamell and ask if Dash and I can talk to him in private. He narrows his eyes as if he suspects we're up to something but leads us to the back combat room anyway, holding the door open for me.

Suddenly, amidst Jamell's silent observations, an unwelcome thought from him flits through my mind.

It's been too long since I've seen the princess's delicious curves. I wonder what would feel better—havin' her underneath me, or havin' my hands 'round her throat. Maybe both—

"Stop!" I yell, and both men pause. Panic rushes through my veins.

How could he?

I thought Jamell was a friend. His betrayal slices me.

Dash was right when he told me not to trust Jamell. Not only is Jamell Mother's trusty pawn, he's a predator. A creep. And, based on his thoughts, a sadist. How did I not see it sooner?

I've been so desperate for the affection of a parental figure that I was willing to accept anything without questioning. I genuinely thought Jamell cared for me. But it was nothing more than an illusion.

His thoughts make me feel dirty, like I need to crawl out of my own skin in order to get clean again.

"Sorry I haven't been around for training," I say. I've been quietly stewing for too long. Surely the commander can tell I'm on edge. Thinking up something quickly, I add, "Mother's required my help around the palace."

Jamell laughs, but it comes off rough, forced. "Oh I know how much ya despise ya duties. I'm surprised I haven't seen more of ya around just to work that burden off."

His eyes narrow into slits as he watches me.

I can really give ya something to work it off, if ya spread those pretty little thighs for me. Heard ya nothin' but a whore like—

There's a loud *crack* as Dash's fist connects with the commander's nose.

Blood spurts out, and Jamell's hand flies up to assess the damage while the other reaches for the blade at his side. Before he can unsheath it, Dash is behind him, a dagger at his throat.

Jerking his head back, Jamell tries to crack Dash in the face with his skull, but Dash anticipates the movement and dodges it. This allows Jamell to get free, but only for a second. Ducking under Jamell's swinging arm, Dash captures him in a headlock before placing the dagger back at his throat.

"What the hell, Dash!" My mouth drops open in disbelief. "This is not what we agreed on!"

"Sorry, sweetheart. No woman deserves to be called a whore. Especially not you. It pissed me off." He shrugs nonchalantly, as if he doesn't have a blade to a Hakranian commander's throat. Jamell's face begins turning colors as he tries to pry himself free of Dash's chokehold. Dash eases up enough to allow oxygen back into Jamell's lungs. The commander sputters, gasping for air, but Dash continues pressing the blade to the bulging vein in his neck.

"Unbelievable." I shake my head angrily. "You were right about Mother's army. Look how pathetic he is."

"What if I'm just an incredible warrior?" Dash asks with a raised brow.

"Yeah, you're incredible all right. Incredibly arrogant." I roll my eyes before turning my sights on Jamell. He narrows his gaze at me. His unwelcome lust from earlier is gone, replaced with a potent mixture of panic and hatred.

I bet ya'd scream for ya ma just like that little kitchen bitch did when I had her face down on the counter as I plowed into her from behind.

The fury I've been trying to keep leashed bursts free, but this time, I do nothing to try and stop it.

Dash shoots me a warning look as if he senses what I'm about to do. But unless he frees his hold on Jamell, he won't be able to stop me.

Good.

I don't want him to.

"You are a despicable, dishonorable waste of flesh!" I screech.

I reach for Jamell's knife and, in one quick move, plunge it into his crotch. His leathers are thick and resist my blow at first, but adrenaline fuels me as I use all my strength to press the blade through, piercing his flesh. I'm glad he's not wearing a protective cup.

His screams are glorious. I thank the goddess for the sound-proof walls.

The blade punctures exactly where I wanted.

"That's for the poor girl you dared put your grimy hands on!" I don't know which girl he was thinking of, but with a predator like Jamell, there were probably multiple victims. I wish I could find whoever he hurt and reassure them that Jamell will never touch them again.

I pull the blade free, dripping blood onto the training mat, and plunge it straight into his heart. Not even his thick leathers can save him from my fury.

"And that's for fooling me all these years!" There's a crunch, followed by a squelch, as I push the blade deeper. Crimson liquid leaks out of both of his wounds. His mouth drops open in shock as his legs give out. Dash moves back, releasing the commander and letting him topple to the floor. Jamell gurgles on the blood dribbling from the corners of his mouth. A few moments later, after a final, wet breath, he falls silent.

Dash strokes his tense jaw. He wipes a fleck of blood off his shoulder and says, "What the hell did you do that for?"

"You're kidding, right?" I ask. Outrage continues to swirl inside of me, but guilt isn't anywhere to be found. I thought this man was my friend, but he's nothing more than a predator. "Did you not hear what he was thinking?"

"I blocked him out after he called the woman I care about a whore." Dash nudges Jamell's body with his toe, as if to ensure he's dead. "Remind me not to get on your bad side."

"You've already been there. You're just lucky it was *before* I completely lost control of my emotions." I decide against telling Dash what I heard in Jamell's final thoughts; he's already dead, and clearly we both know the man he really was.

"As much as I love this newfound confidence and acceptance of your unpredictable...power surges, we'll call them, we really need to get you fixed."

"Whatever," I say, tossing Jamell's bloodied blade beside his corpse. "You're welcome, by the way."

"For what?" He scratches his head as if he seriously has no idea what I'm talking about.

"For keeping your hands clean. Now *you* don't have to take care of him."

"I wasn't going to kill him! I prefer not to murder people."

The words strike a chord in me. Suddenly, I don't like the way he's looking at me—with judgment in his eyes.

What must he truly think of me? I've killed hundreds during my time as the vessel, and today I've murdered three people of my own accord. I wasn't under Mother's control.

My stomach churns, and I look away, crossing to the window that gives a view into the main space.

Our skirmish took place in the corner of the room, out of sight from the few lingering guards, so no one witnessed me murdering Jamell. That's a relief. It buys us time to figure out our next step.

I glance back over at Dash, irked to see the judgmental expression still plastered on his face. "Sorry to disappoint you with my murderous tendencies, oh great Dashiel Dargan. Not everyone's as perfect as you!" Annoyance flares back to life inside of me, threatening to consume Dash.

"I'm not perfect simply because I don't enjoy killing people," he says. "I prefer to keep my body count low, that's all. There are normally other ways of dealing with problems."

"You think I enjoyed that? Oh wait—I'm nothing more than a slaughterer in your eyes. I didn't forget what you called me at the falls."

"Astrid—"

"No!" The monster inside me roars back to life as I snatch Jamell's knife from the ground, charging toward Dash. He at least has the decency to look worried as he takes a step back. He didn't have a single ounce of concern when subduing Jamell, Hakran's best, yet somehow *I* am the one who brings fear to his face. It's oddly satisfying.

"Don't do this," he says.

"You fear me." I battle my anger, trying to prevent it from

overtaking me.

"No, sweetheart, never. I just don't want to hurt you." His eyes flick to the blade, then back to my face. The way he stares at me, with such intensity even as I threaten him, does something to untangle the mess inside of me.

Lowering the weapon, I nod in understanding.

"I meant it when I said you aren't alone," he whispers.

I bite my lip and look away. Now is definitely not the time for these sentiments. Especially not when they'll invoke a stream of hysterical tears. I blink rapidly in an attempt to keep the water-works at bay.

"We need to get into the pit." Ignoring Dash's concerned expression, I stride over to the door and pop my head out. I clear my throat and call to the guards, "Clear the training spaces."

Everyone pauses, and a few guards gaze at me with bewilder-ment. Their bafflement and hesitations swarm my mind.

"Now!" I bellow. "As your princess, I order you to leave!" Surprisingly, they oblige and begin to jog up the stairs. The woman with the braid glances my way as she ascends, scruti-nizing me.

I wait until everyone is out of sight before turning back to Dash.

"You were right," I say. "I guess I do have a little bit of power in my title."

His mouth twitches. "If only everything went that smoothly. Now how are we going to get into the pit?" He analyzes Jamell's corpse. Blood pools around the body, soaking into the training mats. The air is sharp and metallic with the scent of murder.

"Easy," I say.

Crouching next to Jamell's lifeless body, I snatch his knife back up and begin hacking away at one of his hands. Unlike my dagger, this blade is sharp enough that with a little bit of pressure and some sawing, I can slice through the bone. A crack fills the silence as I finish slicing Jamell's hand from the wrist.

"I might've lied earlier," Dash says, as he stares at me in astonishment. "I think I do fear you."

My lips lift in smug satisfaction. I raise Jamell's severed hand off the ground and wave it at Dash. "Let's go get your family."

CHAPTER EIGHTEEN

We make it halfway through the main training space before I start crying.

"What did I just do?" I wail, looking at the severed hand I'm carrying. I toss it, aching to distance myself from the ugly thing.

"You just murdered a guy and cut his hand off," Dash deadpans.

My arms tremble, and tears slide down my cheeks as I look at Jamell's hand.

My old friend.

Trainer.

Mentor.

But he wasn't any of that really, was he? His thoughts betrayed him, and he betrayed me. But is that justification for taking his life?

The tears that cascade down my cheeks aren't just for Jamell. I can't help but think of Gianna and Chancy. Those poor girls. Perhaps I am as bad as Mother is. I'm a monster, just like her.

"Hey, hey, hey. Shhhh." Dash pulls me into his arms. My head rests on his chest. His heart beats wildly beneath my cheek. "Why exactly are you crying?"

He knows my emotions are on the fritz, that burning fury can give way to crippling despair without warning, so why is he asking such inane questions?

"Because I just killed him! I can't handle you being angry at me on top of that!" Goddess save me.

The hysteria overflows, and my body shakes violently as I sob against him.

"I'm not angry at you," he says.

"But that's three. That's three now." Three people I've killed today.

Despite my blubbering, Dash cups my wet cheeks in his hands, tilting my head up to look at him.

"You. Did. What. You. Had. To. Do. Do you hear me?" He speaks each word slowly, as if he's attempting to brand the message into my skull.

"I couldn't stand the way you looked at me after Gia and Chancy," I whisper.

He furrows his brow. "And how exactly do you think I looked at you?"

"With pity. You pitied me. Felt sorry for me."

A soft chuckle leaves him, and he brushes my forehead softly with his lips. He lingers there, and his warm breath caresses my face as he speaks. "No I didn't. I regretted not being there when you needed me."

"You can't always be there for me."

"No, I can't," he says, surprising me with his honesty. I'd half expected him to share a white lie. To tell me he'd always be there for me. His truthfulness only endears him to me further. "That's why I need you to be strong—for *you*. You will be a strong queen, Astrid. And nothing will change that."

"Do you know of any queens who go around murdering her friends?" I continue crying as he wipes away my tears for the second time today.

"You're strong enough to make impossibly difficult decisions, and you make them with the people you care about in mind. You'll be the most incredible leader." He rubs my back tenderly, working to diffuse the bomb inside of me. After a few minutes, he pulls back, running his thumb over my lip and leaning in to plant a soft kiss there.

"Maybe I've been feeding you the wrong line. Instead of thinking about the queen you will become, think about the queen you already are. This is your war—your time to prove your mother and everyone else who doubted you wrong. To stand up and fight for your people."

Something inside of me clicks at Dash's words. He's right. This *is* war.

And I am not a vessel.

Not a princess.

Not a puppet.

None of the labels thrust upon me define me.

I am Astrid Lucille Sylano, and I finally have a chance to step into my own skin without being held back.

"Now what?" I ask.

"Now we keep moving forward." Dash retrieves the amputated hand from where I tossed it before beckoning me over to the pit's door. "Comes in *handy.*" He waggles Jamell's lifeless fingers at me before pressing the flesh flat against the enchanted stone. The stone gives, loosening at the edges enough for us to push the door open and enter the dim space.

"You might think your jokes help, but they don't," I say in a delayed response. My heart pounds at being ensconced in silenxstone, but I'll be glad when it silences my power and quells the frenzy inside of me.

"Hurry." Dash pulls me inside as the thick door closes behind us.

Out of the corner of my eye I notice Dash staring at me. "What?"

"I'm proud of you, that's all," he says.

"For being unhinged?"

"For being a badass who doesn't let anything stop her." He kisses my nose and grips my hand, interlacing our fingers. Together we move down the stone stairs, following three curves before planting our feet on a floor similar to limestone but with a deeper blue finish.

Silenxstone.

It's like a dungeon down here. The corridor is wide but low and made entirely of stone. The few sconces along the wall flicker, casting a dim, orange glow. About twenty feet away, the corridor takes a sharp turn to the left.

I shudder. I can't believe a space like this exists beneath the palace. It's dark, damp, and cool. The lower temperature is likely due to how deep beneath the earth we are. Considering how strict Mother is about her aesthetics, I'm surprised she allows such a disturbing place to exist in her palace.

Dash clears his throat dramatically, and I flinch.

"Shhh!" I hiss. It's like he's trying to attract attention. "Are you insane?"

"Maybe a little, Princess." He readies himself, adopting a combative stance as I slowly back up toward the stairs. With another bellowing *ahem,* he calls out, "Come play, you swine!"

The pounding of boots on stone echo through the corridor, building in intensity as someone draws near. Whoever it is, they haven't come into sight yet, but it sounds like there are two people, and they must be close to rounding the corner.

Dash grips a dagger unconventionally in each hand—the blade between his thumb and forefinger. Two guards burst into sight, but before they can fully register us, Dash hurls the blades through the air at them. The daggers spin, handle over blade, before finding their marks in the guards' throats.

It's an impressive move.

The guards drop to the floor as blood squirts out in steady streams from their necks. Despite how gruesome it is, I'm in awe of Dash's display.

"Holy shit," I say.

"I wasn't judging you earlier. Just because killing isn't my first choice, it doesn't mean I'm above it."

"Where the hell did you learn that?"

"I told you I'd teach you a few tricks. You only have to ask."

It's something I will definitely take him up on later. I never thought he was bluffing about his skills, but it's one thing to hear about it and another to see it in action.

"There are only two guards down here?" I ask skeptically.

Pausing with his head tilted, he waits a few moments before nodding. "Yes. The silenxstone and pit door are the main lines of defense. Your mother is too vain to waste guards down here. She'd rather station them up there around her."

"It feels too easy."

"This is the simple part. Getting all of us out alive is the challenge." He points to the ceiling, to where the training rooms lie above.

"Maybe if we're lucky it'll stay empty."

"If only everything went according to plan." He chuckles. "That blonde guard with the braid looked like she was up to no good. I wouldn't be surprised if she ran right to Enira. A friend is setting up a distraction, but she can only borrow so much time for us."

A friend?

She?

Is he referring to the mysterious, curly-haired girl that sneaked out of his room?

With everything going on, I forgot about her.

Jealousy claws at my stomach again—a sensation I'm still not used to—but this time I can't blame my erratic magic. Not within the silenxstone. No, this time the jealousy is all mine.

"Sure" is all I manage to spit out.

I've tried to keep Dash out of my heart, but he's wiggled his way in. During our short time together, I've developed real feelings for him. I've never been drawn to someone like this, and that scares me almost as much as everything else going on.

Dash calls out for his family as we move down the corridor, stepping over the dead guards and the pools of slick, rust-colored liquid beneath them. He stops to snatch up a ring of skeleton keys and then retrieves his daggers, wiping the blades clean on one of the guard's uniforms before sheathing them.

"Zale!?" he yells. "Ma? Pa?"

"Dashiel!" Joccelyn calls back.

Following her voice, we tread deeper into the dank tunnels. The space opens up, revealing a dozen cages.

The cells are built into the silenxstone, with rust-worn bars comprising three of the sides. The room is decrepit and reeks of urine and other foul odors I don't care to dwell on. With only enough space to stand or sit, each prisoner is cruelly restricted within their cage.

The Vannyks haven't been down here long—a few hours at most—and they appear unscathed.

That's more than I can say for the other three prisoners. Two skeletons, long forgotten, lie in cages off to the left. Another prisoner, in the cage next to Zale's, shifts around in the shadows.

"What took you so long?" Zale hisses, warranting a foul look from his father. "I thought you'd come quicker."

"Oh please, brother. We came as quickly as possible." Dash flashes me a sly smile, and I sigh at his crude implication. His humor seriously has the worst timing lately. I'd also rather him not make puns about our sex life in front of his parents.

Zale groans, but luckily his parents seem to miss the innuendo.

"You brought the princess," Joccelyn says. Her tone is kind, but she eyes me warily as Dash fiddles with the lock on his father's cage.

"She's everything we hoped she'd be and more," Dash says. I'm glad the lighting is poor enough to hide my blush.

"Princess?" A deep voice calls out from the other cage. Goosebumps rise on my arms. I ignore the prisoner, wishing Dash would hurry up as he lets his mother and brother out next.

"Mission accomplished," he says when his family is free. He strides over to me and rubs the small of my back. Joccelyn's eyebrow quirks knowingly before she turns away and whispers something to her husband.

"Your newfound *friendship* is cute and all, but maybe save it for later, eh?" Zale says with a scowl, picking off invisible bits of lint from his sleeves. Clearly he's displeased by the imprisonment. If I thought he was unpleasant before, he's even more so now. "No offense, Astrid."

"None taken," I say dryly.

"He's cranky because he missed his snack time," Dash says.

"Maybe if you two weren't so busy doing whatever took so—"

"Boys," Joccelyn calls wearily. I almost chuckle at how normal the two brothers seem as they bicker, even down here in the creepy dungeon.

"—ife?" The low voice calls out again. "Princess?" I'm not sure what the prisoner said, but something about his tone grabs my attention. Everyone else continues to ignore him, talking in hushed tones about the plan for escape. I take a few steps toward the cage.

"Leave him," Dash warns, reaching out for me.

I brush him off, stepping closer to the cage. Within the dim, flickering light, I can barely make out the man's features. It's impossible to tell his age. Dark hair hangs loosely around his shoulders, and a thick beard covers half his face. None of the men wear their beards that long on Hakran due to the heat. Which means either this man isn't Hakranian, or he's been down here long enough that his beard has grown out. Maybe both? His clothing, nothing more than soiled torn rags now, hangs from his body in tatters.

When I look into his eyes, I gasp. Even in the poor illumination, they're unbelievably green—piercing, pleading. A jolt of electricity surges through me, drawing me to him.

I don't know what it is—he's a stranger, after all, and in a terrible state—but there's some sort of charge in the air between us.

"How long have you been down here?" I ask.

He growls and shakes his head. "No," he whispers through cracked, bloodied lips.

"No, what?" I cock my head, trying to understand what he means. He must be delirious. He's probably starving, maybe even sick.

"We need to go," Dash says, grabbing my arm. His family's footsteps are retreating down the main corridor, and I know it's time to move.

"We can't just leave him behind!"

"We don't know why Enira has him down here."

"It doesn't matter," I snap back, gesturing to the green-eyed man, who watches us with open interest. "I don't trust her, and I don't care to be like her."

Dash sighs, cracking his knuckles before turning to the man. "Don't bullshit me. Why'd she throw you in here?"

"The queen—she—" A dry, rattling cough overwhelms him. His eyes flicker to me. "You are *nothing* like that rotten woman."

Gianna's last moments flash through my mind.

Then Chancy's.

Followed by Jamell's face.

I shake my head. I'm just like her. But the prisoner's words hit me with maximum impact, and I almost believe him. Desperate to cling to anything—or anyone—that separates me from my mother, I snag the ring of keys from Dash.

"You could've just asked," Dash says in a flat voice as I fiddle with the lock.

"You would've said no."

"Unlikely. I'd give you anything you want, Astrid." The words are barely above a whisper, but they strike me as if he had yelled them. My cheeks heat, and I work to open the strange man's cage.

"Astrid?" the prisoner asks with confusion.

"That's Princess Astrid to you," Dash says authoritatively. "And very soon *queen.*"

Dash and I help the weak man out of the cage and let him lean on us as we trudge back through the corridors to where the Vannyks wait.

He smells awful, and I try not to gag at the stench. He's much taller than me but a few inches shorter than Dash. We struggle to find a rhythm to our gait.

How long has he been down here?

We stop to snag an aethyn water pouch from where it's clipped to one of the dead guard's belts, and the prisoner guzzles it greedily.

"Oh what the hell is this?" Zale asks when he sees us. Despite his apparent exasperation, he surprises me by taking the weight of the prisoner off my shoulders, gripping the stranger around the middle, and proceeding with Dash to get the man up the stairs. The gesture showcases the goodness of his heart, but it's almost ruined by him saying, "I'm going to smell like sewage now."

King Emman looks between Dash and the stranger and shakes his head. Joccelyn smiles softly, as if she's unsurprised at the sight of her sons helping a dirty, dying prisoner during the worst of times.

"Are you sure you don't want to leave him and just come back for him later?" Zale asks.

"There might not be an opportunity," Dash says at the same time I say, "Absolutely not."

Sadness fills me at the thought of the two prisoners who clearly died a long time ago.

Did they deserve to die? Knowing Mother, it's unlikely.

They were surely loved by someone, missed by someone.

At least we can save this one man. We can prevent him from turning to dust. That's a small comfort. I refuse to leave him behind.

"Your mother and I will exit first," King Emman says to the boys, snapping me out of my thoughts. "We'll cast our power and release anyone nearby of the Dead Queen's mental grasp. As we free our guards, we'll keep them close. Some of the Hakranian guards might join our cause, too, but don't count on it. Plenty will be loyal to the queen even without her manipulation."

"What's your plan for my mother?" I ask. The prisoner

mutters something about "mother," but I don't pay him any attention.

"Without her magic, she's nothing. Just a woman," Emman says. "We need to find her and get her down here in the pit to fully silence her power."

"How did she get *you* down here?" I ask. Silence fills the air. Joccelyn smiles at me.

"The guards came during dinner," she says. "Enira dislikes us around, for obvious reasons. It was only a matter of time before she tried to exert her power over us."

"Make no mistake," Emman says. "We let them take us."

"Why would you do that?" I ask, shocked at the admission.

"To see the pit for ourselves and ensure the silenxstone was real," Emman says. "We need confidence in our plan to go after Enira, and that means learning everything we can about the island. Including her weapons, defenses, and dungeons."

"They weren't in any real danger with me on the outside," Dash says. "Plus, we have you too."

"Stupid plan," Zale mutters as he eyes the stone in distaste.

Emman sighs at his son before saying, "We also needed a valid cause to start this war. A stronger reason than suspicion of or dislike for Enira. She struck first by imprisoning us. Now our strike back will be considered defensive. We can forcibly remove her from Hakran's throne without sacrificing our own rule in Stellaris."

Dash agrees with him, then offers me a soft smile that holds a mixture of sorrow and comfort. I don't have the heart to return it, so I nod solemnly. It might be my mother they're talking about, but I need to protect my people. They don't deserve to be Enira's puppets. This might be their only chance at true freedom, at gaining their free will back.

Eyeing the thick, black door standing between us and the wickedness beyond, I try to prepare myself. We stand wordlessly, breathing heavily, no one making the first move to open the door.

I might have the Vannyks by my side to protect me from Mother, but nothing can protect me from me. I brace myself for the potentially disastrous storm brewing inside of me, the one that will beg for release as soon as I step outside the silenxstone pit.

Once those doors open, I'm walking into two wars.

CHAPTER NINETEEN

The door won't open.

Each of us takes a turn trying to pry it open, and then several of us combine forces, but it doesn't budge.

"It only opens from the outside," Zale says as he rubs his temples. "Way to go, brother."

"Surely you realize *you* missed this key fact as well?" Dash asks in a flat voice.

"Boys!" Joccelyn interrupts. She likely means to calm their bickering, but her voice comes out high-pitched and nervous, echoing down the stone stairwell. I don't need my powers to tell she's stressed about our current situation.

Emman, conversely, is the epitome of unfazed as he switches to king mode. He strokes the stubble on his chin as he contemplates the obstacle before us. With the lack of concern on his face, it's as though he's debating between a cup of black or green tea.

"This *is* unexpected, but do not fret," Emman says. "We are not entirely unprepared for this. We made arrangements for people on the outside to come to our aid should things not work out as planned."

I think of Cedrik and Fatima and wonder who else the Vannyks have helping them. With the Vannyks locked in here, any of the people they were relying on for help are susceptible to

Mother's manipulation. If she gets to them, who will be left to come for us?

A bead of sweat trickles down my spine, but I fight to stay cool and collected. I hope Emman has a proper backup plan, or else the fight against Mother will end before it starts.

"Things never work as planned," Zale mutters. He pinches the bridge of his nose, and I roll my eyes at his disdainful tone. Zale and Dash might be brothers, but the carefree warrior and uptight prince couldn't be more different.

The six of us stand at the top of the stairwell before the stone door, waiting, as if perhaps it'll open if we stare hard enough. Between the mildew and general rotting stench, I'm queasy and becoming claustrophobic. I crave lungfuls of fresh air.

"There has to be another way out," Zale says, interrupting our silent scrutiny.

"There isn't," the prisoner replies. The liter of water he guzzled has apparently cleared up his cough. He doesn't seem to be in as bad of shape as I first assumed, despite the raggedy clothes and stink. Maybe he can keep up on his own now.

"How do you know?" Dash asks, stepping closer to scrutinize the man. The lack of proper illumination makes it nearly impossible for us to distinguish facial features without being uncomfortably close to each other.

"I've been here longer than you," the prisoner says. "Long enough to attempt escapes." The words are directed at Dash, but his eyes lock on mine as he speaks. It's as if he's trying to convey some silent message to me. I shake my head, having no clue what he's trying to tell me.

Dash shoots me a curious look over his shoulder before turning back to the stranger. "Don't look at her. Look at me when I talk to you."

"Dash," I hiss. Now is not the time for him to be a territorial ass, especially not in front of his family.

"How do we even know we can trust this guy?" Dash asks, glancing at me again.

"We can't. We just…try," I say.

"Why'd Enira lock you up?" Dash asks, turning back to the stranger. He's a few inches shorter than Dash, with a slightly leaner build. Muscles ripple beneath his clothes, and I imagine with proper nutrition, exercise, and clean air, he would be just as strong as Dash. There's no way he can try anything in his current state, but there's something about the sharpness of his eyes that's dangerous.

"Same reason she locks up anyone," the prisoner says.

"That doesn't answer my question."

"I don't need to answer your questions, pretty boy." Dash growls at the prisoner's insult.

"Pretty boy?" Zale chuckles, apparently finding humor in the prisoner's challenging quip.

"Don't worry," Dash says mockingly to his brother. "We all know *you're* the true pretty boy."

Zale's glee disappears, and he scoffs at Dash. "You are—"

"Let's focus our energy on the real enemy, sons," Emman says cooly, taking a step between the brothers.

The longer we stay trapped here, the more hostile the environment becomes. It seems as though we've been down here forever, but I think it's only been around an hour. It's hard to tell.

"We're targets in here," Zale says. He steps closer to his brother and the stranger, as if he's expecting them to break out into a physical altercation.

"There will be a shift change eventually, and the new guards will have to open the door to get down to the pit," Dash says.

"Not sure when, but we'll need to rush them when they open the door and make it beyond the stone. In here we're all muted."

"Thankfully," I mutter, grateful to not have my powers right now. "Small blessings from the goddess."

"What?" Zale asks.

"My magic is uncontrollable. I'm picking up on everyone's emotions in extremes, and I'm easily provoked," I say. "It started after our visit to the falls." I narrow my eyes at Dash, not that he'll notice in the dark space. "Combined with Dash's mind reading, which I also can't control, by the way, I'm…rather explosive." Opening up in front of everyone exposes me. It's a vulnerability I'm not used to.

"Oh, honey," Joccelyn says, reaching to pull me into a crushing hug. It's a sweet, unexpected gesture. I can't help but wonder what it must've been like to grow up with a mother like her.

"The falls?" the prisoner asks. His voice is so low I almost miss it. When I pull away from Joccelyn and glance over at the prisoner, he moves closer to me, scrutinizing me. He balls his hands into fists, clenching and unclenching them. "You kissed beneath the falls." It's not a question.

"That's none of your business," I say. How does everyone seem to know about this lore but me? Luckily no one else seems to notice the prisoner's odd demeanor. They're all too busy assessing our situation.

"Reckless. Thoughtless," the prisoner says so only I can hear him. "*Idiotic.*" If I'm not mistaken, his tone is disappointed, hurt.

"It is none of your business," I spit at him before turning my focus to the Vannyks' ongoing conversation. The prisoner's judgment is of no importance to me.

"Will Fatima come?" Emman asks Dash.

Dash shrugs. "She's at South Sands going along with the plan as originally decided. She's aware of your imprisonment though."

Fatima.

The curly-haired girl that sneaked out of Dash's room. My stomach twinges with jealousy once more. Luckily it's something I can ignore when my emotions are under control.

"She'll buy us time at least," Zale adds.

"What exactly is this plan?" I ask. "And who the hell is Fatima?" Dash exhales sharply before addressing me.

"Fatima is a…family friend. She's a four-elemental aethyn, and—"

"All four?" I say, impressed. "That's rare." Although aethyns who control all four elements are no rarer than vygoras or myndoxes, it shocks me to know there is yet another powerful magic-wielder existing nearby.

"It's not as uncommon as you might think," Zale says. "We have a wider range of abilities in Stellaris. Hakran is a little less… *exposed* to diversity."

Oh.

Maybe I'm not as rare and special as I thought. I add it to the list of things Mother purposely kept from me or lied about. I'm beginning to think the island is a prison. One where Mother has built a reality of her own.

Where do the lies end and the truths begin?

"Fatima's creating a storm with the four elements," Dash says, bringing me back to the plan. "Right off the coast of South Sands. It should be strong enough to send your people into shelter."

My gut churns. "Why would you want to do that?"

"According to our information"—he taps his head, reminding me that he can literally read minds—"you have storm protocols in place. The palace folk shelter in the throne room while your mother takes cover elsewhere. An undisclosed location in one of the many private caves around the island."

Nodding, I confirm his intellect is accurate.

The throne room was built in the heart of the palace and reinforced with double-layered stone to protect our people from such storms. Though I know Mother had the new palace built purely out of vanity, she claims it was to provide better protection from the storms.

I've never even seen Mother during a storm. As Dash mentioned, she rides them out in an undisclosed cave. Some sort of secluded shelter. I'm not sure where exactly she goes, and I don't know why she leaves the palace. I've never thought about it before now.

It's certainly odd.

Knowing Mother, I'm sure her reasoning is entirely selfish. She probably hides out in an even safer location, reserved for only her. Or perhaps she thinks she's too good to sequester herself in the throne room among her inferiors.

If Fatima is using her power to create a storm, it'll be virtually indistinguishable from a wild magic storm. With the four elements fueling it, it will seem like a devastating storm, but since the magic belongs to her, she will be able to control it.

The idea isn't half bad. It's a good way to gain control of the island by separating Mother from the people.

Only Fatima, the Vannyks, the prisoner, and I will know the truth—that the storm isn't any true threat.

"You're hoping they'll mistake Fatima's controlled weather for a wild magic storm," I say.

"With everyone in one space, we can cast our myndox ability together as a net of sorts over the people in the palace, breaking the hold Enira has. When we find her, we can overpower her guards and capture her," Emman says. "We can bring her down here to the pit and cut off her magic entirely to free the rest of the villagers from her control."

"How will you find her?" I ask.

Dash smirks. "Leave it up to me." Of course. Our resident mind reader.

The plan isn't terrible. But what about after Mother's imprisoned? What then?

Do I take over the throne and rule Hakran while the Vannyks return to Stellaris? Will Mother simply rot down here forever?

What will happen between Dash and me? I'm not ready to say goodbye to him, but surely he has duties back in Stellaris. He belongs with his family.

This is the first time I've felt so strongly about someone, drawn to them beyond a single night together, and I'm not ready to give that up. I crave Dash. Having him around brings me joy.

"You underestimate Enira," the prisoner says. "You seem awfully confident in your plan, but do you really think it'll be so easy?"

Before Dash can get in his face again, there's a grinding and the stone door begins to move. A ribbon of light peeks in through the crack.

"Get ready," Emman orders. "We need to rush the entrants and make it beyond the stone to overpower them. Be ready to fight."

The door sticks, as if whoever is on the other side is struggling to push it open.

A feminine grunt reaches my ears.

"For goddess's sake, can you help a girl out? I can't do it on my own! This darn stone door weighs a *lot* more than I pictured in my head." The familiar voice warms my insides.

"Ilona!" I yell as Zale and Dash help pry the door open in record time.

The six of us burst out of the pit into the training space, and I shudder with relief at the bright light and clean air.

Wrapping my arms around my best friend, I hold her tight, whispering my thanks in her ear.

"How did you find us? How'd you get in?" I ask.

We break the embrace, and she points to Jamell's stump of a hand, caked in dried blood and tossed to the side of the pit door. She gags, her eyes watering with disgust.

"I can't believe I touched that," she says, scrunching her nose. "I asked Cedrik what was going on with you. I was worried, A. He filled me in on everything, but then a *huge* storm came rolling in, and I panicked. Everyone's gone to the throne room for shelter, but I didn't see you, and I couldn't leave you, and I knew something was amiss, and—"

"It's okay. Thank you," I say, cutting her off as tears well in her eyes. My chest swells with gratitude, mixing with a rapidly intensifying cascade of emotions. "We're so lucky you came for us."

Thank the goddess she's okay, I couldn't live without her.
That man smells awful.

That hand is so gross. I can't believe I touched it! Did she chop it off? How is she capable of such horrible—

"Stop," I say, squeezing my eyes shut. When I reopen them, I glance at Dash, wordlessly relaying my concerns. He nods, gesturing for Ilona to follow him to the other side of the room. Hopefully he can explain that while being near her hurts me, it's not her fault and I will be back to normal soon.

Her sorrow, fear, and desperation slowly start to hit me as the effect of the silenxstone fades. Mostly she's glad we're okay, but I don't miss the judgment radiating off her.

I don't wish to hear that from her.

I get it. I've been blocking her out. And she did just stumble upon Jamell's severed hand. She doesn't know what I do about Jamell, doesn't know *why* I killed him.

But her judgment still hurts.

As Emman and Joccelyn step aside to converse in low tones, Zale approaches Ilona hesitantly. He leans toward her, whispering something in her ear, and she blushes before shooting him a shy smile. She nods, then rushes past me.

"See you later, A. Be safe," she says on her way by. She spares Zale another small smile before disappearing up the stairs.

I wish Ilona could stay, but she's a liability. Thanks to my erratic powers, I'm connected to her in ways that are dangerous for us both. When she's around, I'm distracted by her, and I need all of my focus on keeping my own volatile emotions bottled up as we find Mother. I can't worry about Ilona right now on top of that.

Thanks to their abilities, being around the Vannyks is quiet, bearable. I'm not assaulted by thoughts that aren't my own— only their emotions, which are tolerable considering we all feel exactly the same right now.

Nobody here invades my mind in a distracting—wait.

"Where's the prisoner?" I ask, realizing I haven't heard or felt anything from him.

"Growing fond of me?" the prisoner asks, and I whirl around to find him seated casually on the floor in the corner of the padded room.

Exhaustion etches his face, and in the bright light of the training room, the piercing green hue of his eyes is even more vibrant.

I hold his gaze, and I swear there's a hint of a smile on his lips.

"No," I snap. "Absolutely not." I wince at my rudeness; he hasn't done anything to warrant that attitude. Maybe the reason

I can't feel or hear him is because of how weak he is. I hesitate before asking, "Are you all right?"

Dash sidles up beside me protectively, as if he's afraid the man might set me off.

"Best I've ever been," the prisoner says sarcastically. His miniscule smile disappears as his eyes wander over to where Dash's arm lies around my shoulders.

"Here," Zale says, stepping up next to him. He snags a discarded bag from the ground and yanks it open. A muffin wrapped in paper tumbles out, and he scoops it up, tossing it toward the stranger. "It's your lucky day, *friend*. Someone left their belongings. And can you please, for the love of the goddess, go freshen up? You smell like a pig's ass." He points to a small door beneath the stairs. "Sinks are through there."

The prisoner eats the muffin in three ravenous bites and leaves to wash up, giving Zale a once-over as he passes.

"What?" Zale asks when he catches me shaking my head at him. "The man smells, and I can't tolerate it any longer."

"Whatever." I roll my eyes.

It's almost comical how irritable Zale is. I'd say he's not thrilled about whatever his family's plans are. But he still cares enough to feed the prisoner, even if his approach is a bit harsh.

I wonder what kind of ruler he'll be; clearly not the action-able kind like his father. He'll probably be the kind to throw stuffy balls and diplomatic luncheons. He'll sit on a throne in a pristine suit while others do his bidding.

He'll probably have Dash getting his hands dirty for him.

I snort at the conjured image.

Emman turns to me, clearing his throat and fixing his sleeves. "Once your mother's hold is broken on the Hakranians and she is imprisoned, you should gain the backing to take your throne."

I missed whatever he said before that, but I nod anyway, understanding enough now to trust the Vannyks and aid them with their plan.

Or perhaps I simply despise Mother so much I'd partner with anyone if it meant taking her down and regaining my life.

I never intended to rule, but I know I will do all I can to keep my people safe.

The prisoner returns, seeming more alert and awake now. I'm concerned about my inability to hear his thoughts or feel his emotions. When his eyes meet my own, I'm momentarily sucked in by the depth I find there—the pure, unadulterated hurt and anger.

It's like looking in a mirror, and it's entirely unsettling.

Dash must not be able to hear the man's thoughts either, because he slowly runs a hand over his mouth, glancing between the two of us, jaw clenched. Finally, the stranger breaks eye contact, but Dash continues to stare at him like a predator stalking his prey.

"We should move out," Emman orders. "Fatima can't keep the storm going forever. If we miss our chance, we might not get another one." He turns, beckoning to the rest of us as he treads up the stairs. Joccelyn follows, then Zale, the stranger, and finally Dash and me.

Putting a bit of space between us and the strange prisoner, Dash whispers in my ear, "I can't hear him. I don't trust him."

"Yeah, but I don't trust Mother either, and she's the one who put him down there," I whisper back.

"Just stick by me. Stay alert."

I salute him mockingly, and he kisses my forehead and grips my hand tightly.

We burst onto the main level, and I'm greeted by the whistle of a strong wind rushing through the grounds outside.

"It really does sound like a wild magic storm," I say. I open the small wooden servants' door to peek outside and instantly regret the decision.

The winds are brutal. Trees sway like drunkards as rain pounds down. Flashes of blue and white zigzag across the sky in the distance. I almost lose my hold on the door, but Zale reaches out right before my grip gives, helping me pull it shut.

"Goddess have mercy," Joccelyn says quietly at my side. "That looks ferocious."

"It's coming from the east," I murmur.

"That's a good thing, right?" Zale says.

"You said Fatima was on South Sands?" I ask. I try to ignore the irrational jealousy that spikes when I speak her name, at the thought that she was in Dash's room. With *my* Dash.

And why hasn't he told me about her before now?

I take a few deep breaths to clear the jealousy away, but it's much harder to do without the silenxstone keeping me in check. This negativity spirals quickly. I need to do my best to remain in complete control if we're going to survive whatever comes next.

"Yes," Dash says, snapping me back to reality.

"Shit," I whisper as they put it together. These winds are coming from the east, whereas Fatima's storm should be blowing from the south. This is a *real* wild magic storm.

"How bad is it?" Zale asks.

"The beaches can flood in the blink of an eye, and the winds can down trees. Expect it to start hailing soon. When it does, going outside will be an impossibility. Lightning and fire strikes are rarer, but when they happen, the damage is immense."

"At least everyone is already sheltered," Joccelyn says. I have to agree with that sentiment. I only hope Fatima didn't make the storm more powerful than it'd be on its own. Hopefully she's wise enough to have called her magic off.

"What about the villagers in town?" Zale asks, concerned.

"The village is to the east, at the foot of the mountain. Because they're at sea level in the valley, the risk of flooding is higher. Many of our guards and palace aethyns are under strict orders to assist them and use their abilities to help minimize damage."

"And I thought Enira didn't care," Zale says sarcastically.

"She does, but it's entirely selfish," I say, thinking about it in a new light. "If her villagers perish, so will her source of power." Five sets of eyes swing my way, and my cheeks heat with embarrassment. Even if no one is admitting it aloud, it's clear that on some subconscious level, they blame me for sourcing her magic.

The bacchanals, the transferences, they're the reason why Enira is so powerful.

It sickens me, and I fight the tears welling in my eyes.

It's not my fault! I want to yell.

Dash reaches out, stroking my hand with his thumb, already in tune with my mood swings.

Joccelyn glances around nervously, hesitating before she speaks up. "What of the others around the island?" She must be worried about her patrolling Stellari guards.

"There are emergency shelters built into the cliffs and caves around the island. Many villagers will barricade themselves inside until the storm lets up. The storms are certainly harsh. They come quickly" —I shoot Dash a warning glare, anticipating a bawdy comment, but he grins back innocently with only a wink— "but they rarely last more than a night or two."

"The storm may still work in our favor," King Emman says contemplatively.

"Let's go round up whichever guards are left behind and get

to work then," Zale says. He raises a sharp brow, as if asking what we're waiting for.

The Vannyks stride through the corridor toward the main wing, talking animatedly with Dash. I pause a few paces behind them with the stranger, curiosity getting the better of me.

There was something in his expression earlier, something that called to me. A recognition of sorts. I've never met this man before, yet there's an ominous familiarity between us.

"Why did Queen Enira imprison you?" I ask, leveling an intense stare at him.

"Out of fear," he says, matter-of-factly.

"Fear?"

"She has her reasons, just as I had my reasons for coming here." When I don't reply, he continues. "She has something that belongs to me. Something I came to retrieve." Pain flickers across his face, but he doesn't try to hide it. It's as if he wants me to see it, hoping I'll understand.

"What's your name?"

"Lex," he says. His eyes roam my face, as if he's searching for a reaction from me. The name doesn't mean anything to me though.

Nodding, I reach out and grab his hand. It's hard for me to witness someone suffering so harshly because of Mother, especially when it *is* my fault she's so powerful. I have more than enough life force coursing through me right now; I might as well use it for something good.

"I'm going to help you recover faster," I say. I'm not a healer, not like Cedrik, but maybe some extra life force will give him a much needed boost. Gianna and Chancy didn't die in vain, not if they can help someone else find their strength again.

Though Lex is not on the verge of dying, he's clearly unwell. A little life force could be exactly what he needs to make it through this war and get home, wherever that may be.

As I press our hands together, interlacing our fingers, I brace for the pain I associate with transference, knowing it'll come. But when I focus on relinquishing some of the life force, something unexpected happens.

It's...strange.

My hand shimmers with a golden hue—like it does during absorption—and the energy flows between us without resistance. And it feels...good. Almost pleasurable, as it does with absorption.

It's incredibly effortless.

Gasping, I break the hold sooner than I intended.

"What the hell was that?" I demand. My eyes widen in disbelief as I stare at my hand. Even with the slight boost to his life force, my other magic doesn't work on him. I was able to transfer to him, but I still can't read his emotions.

This man is an enigma.

It concerns me greatly. The transference was easy...*too* easy. Warning signals flare to life inside me. I glance down the corridor, grateful Dash and his family have rounded a corner and are out of sight. I can't imagine it would bode well for Lex if they learn what just happened.

There's no reason I should want to keep this a secret, to protect this enigmatic stranger, but something urges me to keep quiet for now.

I'm about to tell him to keep his mouth shut about it when a gust of wind rolls through the door behind me, slamming it all the way open. Turning, I watch as Lex bolts out into the storm.

"What the hell!" I yell after him just as Zale and Dash stomp their way back into sight. They hurry over, helping me pull the door back into place. Within seconds we're soaked to the bone with icy water.

"The prisoner?" Dash asks, pointing a thumb at the door.

"He just...bolted!" I say, my mouth wide with disbelief. I leave out the part about the strange transference, not seeing the point of getting into that right now.

"Rat!" Zale yells, shaking a fist in the direction of the door. "He knows too much."

"Clearly he has a death wish," Dash says, wrapping his strong arms around me as I shiver. "We can't go after him in this. Let him go."

Glancing one last time toward the exit, I furrow my brow as I try to make sense of why he'd run like that. He had no reason. Nothing about him makes sense.

I begin to worry that perhaps Mother did have him locked away for a reason. I hope my compassion toward him wasn't a mistake.

Dash and Zale's boots clack down the corridor as they lead me away, the whistling of the wind swallowing our steps.

We move through the corridors toward the main wing and quickly arrive in the foyer outside the throne room. The grounds beyond the floor-to-ceiling windows are dark, with only an occasional flash of blue and green lightning slicing through the sky. The rains have extinguished all the lights in the courtyard.

"Whoa," Zale says. "I've never seen lightning that color."

"Like I said, it's a true magicked storm," I say.

"We have nothing like it in Stellaris."

"The storms tend to die out before hitting the land west of here. The magic sinks back into the waters."

"Can you harness the magic?" Dash asks curiously.

"It's not the same magic that runs in our veins," I tell him. "It's too rogue to harness, hence why we call it wild. It doesn't respond to anyone. It's like trying to tame a serpent. In theory, you could, but the chances of being killed by its deadliness are high."

"So it's basically just extra energy rushing over the seas and through the island?" Dash asks.

"Precisely."

"How often does this happen?"

"A few times a year. The worst are during storm season."

"So, now?"

"Yes."

The windows rattle with a gust of strong wind. The rain pounding against the glass turns vicious—threatening to break through.

"Hail," I say. "We need to go. Now!"

Hail slams into the building, growing louder, mixing with the claps of thunder overhead. The glass in the windows is a few inches thick and infused with ice. This serves to keep the palace cool and provide a layer of extra protection from the storms. But despite the protections in place, sometimes the worst of the wind and hail can break through.

As we burst into the throne room, dozens of eyes swing our way: guards, servants, and anyone caught on the grounds during the storm.

Dash's parents, who arrived a few moments before we did, are speaking in hushed tones near the door, and I catch bits and pieces of their plan to spread out and cast their shields over my people to break Mother's hold.

"It'll erase any hold she has, but it won't protect them from falling under her influence again once they're out of our proximity," Emman tells me.

"Maybe we can convince them to stay here while we split up and go for Enira," his wife replies, but I can barely hear them over the tsunami of thoughts attacking my mind.

That's the princess…
…the Stellari king and queen…
I hope Henryn is all right out…
Thank the goddess we stayed in…
…the village. The poor villagers…
This is the worst storm in…
Is the princess okay?
What's wrong with her?
…crazy like her moth…
…help her mother…
…doesn't care to help us…
…where is she when we need…

I wail, dropping to my knees, my hands over my head.

As the Vannyks cast their myndox shields, breaking any hold Mother has, the onslaught of thoughts gets worse. Instead of being confused like I thought they'd be, the people are angry.

Angry at my mother, of course. But also angry at me.

"I didn't want this!" I yell through my tears. "I didn't want this." My eyes swing up to the arching ceilings. I'm afraid to meet anyone's gaze. Afraid to look at the marble throne that sits atop the dais on the other side of the room—the symbol of these peoples' oppression.

…someone should murder that whore…
…put us out of our misery…
Thank the goddess for the Stellari…
…please save us…
…wretched witch…
…curse your fake tears…
…cry for herself…

"—cast your own—" Dash says, stepping in front of me. Grabbing my shoulders, he shakes me gently. I can't make out his words. "—protect your mind. Come on, Astrid." He frowns, his eyes wide in worry.

"I can't," I whisper, but my voice is drowned out by the clapping thunder overhead. The storm is over us now, and despite the stability of the palace, the ground trembles beneath our feet.

The sea of faces stares at me. Some of the people are whispering amongst themselves and pointing in my direction. Many of them look familiar, but the expressions they wear are anything but friendly. Ilona and Marnie cross into my line of sight, making their way toward me. I don't want them to come over here. Hearing their pity would be worse than hearing the vitriol.

"Stop! Stop! Stop!" I scream at the top of my lungs, fisting my hair. Dash kneels beside me, trying to pull me to my feet. I keep screaming until my throat is raw.

She is insane like her mother.

—kill her before she kills us—

—out of control—

We should gut the whore's daughter.

"I'm trying to save you ungrateful peasants!" I screech, pushing past Dash to stand. "I'm nothing like my mother! I am nothing like her!" The rage wraps its tentacles around my throat, choking me until I can no longer breathe, and in an explosion of turmoil, I reach out, grabbing the hand of the nearest person.

Before I can register what's happening, my hand begins to glow with a gold shimmer, and I'm drawing out life force energy. There's a collective gasp through the room, and the thoughts grow in volume, unintentionally urging me to pull harder and faster.

I can't stop; I can't anchor myself to reality any further. The torpedo of thoughts and emotions is too much to stop.

I pull, and pull, sucking out all the life force of the person in my grip, until they fall to a heap on the ground. The man whose life I just stole stares up, unblinking, his body shriveled beyond recognition.

"Daddy!" A young girl cries out, her voice cracking. "Daddy! Daddy, NO!" An older girl holds her back, her face contorted with fear and unmistakable hatred.

The crowd takes a few panicked steps back as someone whispers. "She's the queen's vessel. *She's* the vessel! It's the princess." Panicked thoughts ensue, pelting me at a frantic rate and merging with the acid spewing from their mouths.

"Murderer!" someone yells.

I'm delirious, panting for breath, unable to stave off the onslaught.

"Stop!" I plead. "Stop. Please stop." Dash's face contorts with anguish as tears fill his eyes. He shakes his head, saying something indecipherable.

Something hard lashes out, striking me in the head before falling to the ground beside me.

A faded shoe.

Someone threw their *shoe* at me.

Dash tries to cover me with his body, to protect me, but he can't help me anymore. He can't save me from this.

I don't even want him to.

This *is* his fault, after all. His power sharing is the reason I'm like this. If he had never stolen that kiss from me at the falls, I'd never have lost control of my power. This isn't fair.

I shove him away, and his face twists with pain, but he refuses to back off, instead, he surges forward to continue shielding me from the people as they chuck objects at me.

I grow lightheaded and sway on my feet, succumbing to the pressure inside my skull. Right as I'm about to collapse, a blast of energy shoots through the room. It's stronger than the wind outside as it ripples through the air, rustling my hair as it passes. I watch in horror as the people in the room crumple to the ground, like they're nothing more than puppets whose strings have been cut.

Dash drops, confusion marring his face.

Followed by Ilona, whose curls fan out around her like a puddle of red.

Then Marnie.

Deidra and Lila from the kitchen fall next.

Deidra's teen daughter.

Then the faceless, nameless guards with head coverings.

And the dozens of other servants from the grounds.

Even the Vannyks tumble onto the floor beside me.

Everyone.

Until I'm the only one in the room left standing.

CHAPTER TWENTY

I survey the room, panicking. Fallen bodies litter the grey marble floor. Not a single person is conscious.

"No!" I gasp. My hands tremble. "I didn't mean it. I-I—"

"You didn't do anything," a smooth voice says.

Holding my breath, I turn to see a familiar pair of jade eyes peering at me.

"You—Lex." Terror pulses through my body. "What did you do?" My voice wavers. I had thought *I* was the one who released that wave of energy, but…it was Lex.

Water drips from his unruly beard, and his clothes stick to his muscular frame.

"They're not dead. Just…asleep," he says. "Come." He reaches out a hand for me, but I recoil, almost tripping over Dash.

"No." Kneeling beside Dash, I shake his shoulder, begging him to wake up.

Lex's jaw ticks as he stares at me impatiently. "I'm not going to hurt you."

"Stay the fuck away from me!"

Sighing, he runs a hand over his beard. "I did this to *help* you. To quiet their voices before you cause further mayhem." He points to the lone dead man in the room, the one I killed in my rage.

"How—how did you know about the voices?"

I pull my dagger free, pressing the blade against Lex's throat and backing him up against the wall.

He raises his hands in surrender. "Easy now, luv."

I almost falter at the gentle shift in his tone but quickly brush it off, refusing to let him distract me.

Realization dawns on me. Lex was there when we were discussing the lore, our powers. He even commented on how Dash and I kissed beneath the falls. Idiotically, I mentioned enough minor details for him to put the pieces together.

I've not only made myself vulnerable in front of the Vannyks but in front of this stranger as well. Dash was right—this guy is not to be trusted.

"I can and will kill you," I say venomously. I press the dagger harder against his skin, drawing a thin line of blood. His lips twitch, as if he's fighting a smile.

"Of course you can." There's no sarcasm in his voice as his eyes flicker to the dead man's frame.

"Give me one reason why I shouldn't slit your throat right now," I demand.

"I want to help you. Let me help you."

"What? I don't—"

"Despite lover boy telling you that you can block everything out, you can't," he says. Something akin to concern flickers across his face before he quickly neutralizes it. Oddly, despite his rude personality, I believe that he truly wants to help. "You're volatile. You're losing control, and that's a very dangerous thing."

My hands are clammy, and I readjust my grip on the dagger. He's right.

Dash has offered me comfort, but other than telling me to *"Control my power,"* he's done nothing to help me actually do so. And Ilona cares deeply for me, but there's absolutely nothing she can do—in fact, I can't even let her near me lately.

I need to regain control. I can't live like this.

"What were you doing?" I ask, keeping my face neutral as I continue pressing the blade into his throat. He swallows, and his Adam's apple presses against the blade. "When you ran off?"

"Nothing nefarious."

"So where did you go?"

"Is that really your business?"

"It is if you expect me to accept your help."

"Why don't you continue letting your lover boy help you, if that's going so well?"

"Stop with the belittlement."

"You can't ask that of me."

"I have a dagger to your neck. I can ask anything I please."

In one quick move, Lex shoves me away from him. He ducks left, and in a flash, he's beside me, capturing me in a headlock. The blade clatters to the floor, the echoes resonating throughout the throne room.

He holds me flush against his damp body, and his beard scratches my ear as he whispers. "Be careful with that blade, luv. Some men enjoy the threat of violence."

I squirm, using all of my weight to break his hold. "You—"

"I am not going to hurt you. Relax." He releases me, and I turn, leveling a glare at him.

"When has ordering a woman to relax ever helped the situation?" I snarl.

"Ah, so feisty." His lips twitch. "We really should get going. I've been contained for far too long, and I'm feeling a touch… deficient. I'm uncertain how long my power will hold." He gestures toward the people around the room.

"I'm not going anywhere with you."

"Well then. Good luck when they wake and place their blame on you. Not sure pretty boy's mommy and daddy will be too friendly after witnessing you murder an innocent man. They seem to be very righteous people. Not to mention how you just knocked everyone out."

"But I didn't even—"

"*That* is what the perception will be, and when the thoughts override your own mind once again, how will you prevent yourself from doing it again? Or something much worse?" There's no amusement in his expression, just grim honesty.

Huffing, I stoop to snag my dagger off the floor. I point the blade at him. "Fine. Give me the solution to my problem, and then we'll go our separate ways."

"Demanding, luv."

"I'm not your fucking *luv*," I say, mimicking his accent.

"Aren't you going to ask what I want in return?"

Tightening my jaw, I continue to stare unblinkingly at him. "Fine. What do you want?" I ask through clenched teeth.

He flashes a broad smile at me. "Nothing unreasonable. A change of clothes. A razor. A brush."

"And a lavender-scented bath, a five-course meal, and a foot rub perhaps?" I ask sarcastically.

"Well, if you're offering."

"I'm not." The thought of a bath with lavender oil squeezes my heart. It reminds me of Gianna. Sorrow courses through me, reminding me of precisely *why* I should accept Lex's help: I'm dangerous.

Clearly my people aren't safe around me in this state.

My murderous urges are strengthening; it's becoming easier to lose sight of guilt and empathy.

Lex might be my only option for fixing this.

I jerk my head toward the exit. "Let's go." I lead the way out of the throne room, pausing to check both ways before stepping into the hallway. Only the decorative columns bear witness to me sneaking out with Lex-the-prisoner.

I'm tempted to ask for more details about his imprisonment, but I'm afraid of the answer. Perhaps it's best if I don't know. Based on his little show of power in the throne room, it's plausible Mother simply fears him. If she couldn't control him, of course she'd imprison him.

Maybe Lex and I aren't so different after all.

But there's also the possibility that Lex isn't a good man.

"The storm calmed down a lot," he says from behind me. "How much time before Enira leaves her little nest?"

I shake my head. "Don't be fooled. It's the eye of the storm—a temporary calm before it whips up again. There's always a lull before we get the worst of it."

"Well then, I might enjoy a lavender bath after all."

Annoyance boils inside of me—strong and demanding of my attention.

"You're mad again," he says.

"I'm not. You said your power will wear off soon. We don't have time for a fucking bath." I just want to fix myself, get back to normal, and be done with this.

"I said I'm uncertain of how long my power will hold. You have a penchant for misinterpreting words."

"I do not. And you wouldn't even know if I did." Rolling my eyes, I pick up the pace, leading us to Dash's room. After pushing the door open, I flick on the lamp. It's weird bringing Lex here. I know the room *is* technically a guest room, but it smells like Dash—spicy and earthy—and I want to wrap myself up in the scent.

Opening the dark grey armoire, I snag a pair of black trousers, a white button-up, and some suspenders.

"Nice room," Lex says. "I hadn't thought you to be an over-sized trousers kind of gal though."

"You know nothing about me."

"So you've already said." Offering me a sly grin, Lex takes the clothes from me.

"There's a brush and razor in the bathroom." I jerk a thumb toward the other door.

Without hesitation, he starts unbuttoning his pants in front of me. My cheeks flame with embarrassment.

"Get into the bathroom!" I scold, squeezing my eyes closed before I see something I can't unsee. There's something inappropriate about being alone with another naked man in Dash's room. It spoils the sacredness of the space.

Only when I hear Lex's boots clack away and the door shut do I open my eyes again. Muddy footprints trail across Dash's stone floor, and I sigh, wondering how I'm going to explain this to him.

Not that I owe him anything—certainly not an explanation—but I've grown to care for him during the last few weeks, and I find myself *wanting* to open up to him. That's entirely new territory for me. Other than Ilona, I never let anyone in. With Dash, that's changing. Now that we're on the same page with waging a war against my mother, there's a greater opportunity to build trust.

But what if we lose against Mother? What if she harms Dash or one of his family members...or worse, kills them? What if she throws me in the pit? What if the Hakranian people don't follow us? My people seem to hate me; they're angry at me, for good reason now.

They know I'm the vessel, and there's no going back.

Tapping my foot impatiently, I try to quell my racing mind. Anxiety bubbles up, ready to overflow and drown me.

Focusing on my breathing—*one, two, three, four*—I try to steady my heart rate.

"Lex?" I call.

Inhale.

Exhale.

"Yeah?"

"Hurry the fuck up."

"Miss me already, luv?"

"No. Stop calling me that." I pause, unsettled by the worries pummeling me. "Can you have a heart attack from stress?"

He pops his head out the door, mid-shave. A thin stripe of smooth flesh peeks out through the dark beard. "Yes."

"Goddess save me," I mumble, rubbing my eyes.

"Just relax."

"Stop telling me to fucking relax! Can you hurry up so you can tell me how to fix my damn mind?"

"It's not a quick fix, but yes." His expression is hard. "I'll hurry."

He steps back into the bathroom, leaving the door cracked so I can see him in front of the vanity. I feel a little better. Slightly less alone.

"Lex?" I call again. Lying back on the bed, I close my eyes and begin to count backwards from one hundred.

"Hmmm?"

"Why can't I hear your thoughts or...feel your emotions?" My voice is barely above a whisper.

He doesn't answer. I'm not sure if he heard me, but I don't care to repeat myself. Instead, I focus on my countdown.

I'm awakened by someone shaking my shoulder.

I jolt up, confused, and glance at my surroundings.

Dash's room.

"Dashiel!" I cry out, reaching for him, but instead of Dash, it's Lex standing before me. I flinch, withdrawing my hand.

Lex is barely recognizable. If it wasn't for his striking eyes, I might not have believed it's him at all.

Beneath all that matted hair is a breathtaking man. He's much younger than I initially thought—no more than thirty. His skin is pale from lack of sun exposure, but there are lingering warm undertones. I bet he'll take on a golden glow with a few days outdoors.

He pulls his black hair into a low bun, tying it at the nape of his neck. Dressed in the new clothes, he is nothing like the decaying prisoner I found earlier this evening.

"How long was I out?" I mumble, smoothing down my top as I jump out of bed.

"Only a few minutes. I complied with your demands." Sorting through our previous conversation, I realize he means he hurried. Like I asked him to.

"How do I fix my power?"

"I will tell you in time. Be patient."

"I don't have time for patience!" Hastily, I put on my shoes and begin to pace the room.

"First, you were a fool to trust that boy."

"What boy?"

"Your little lover boy."

"Dashiel? He's hardly a *boy,*" I scoff. Lex can't be much older than him. "You are so damn condescending."

"We all have our flaws, luv." Yanking a decorative pillow from the settee beside the patio doors, I whack Lex with it. "And that right there is yours, it seems. Aggression. Violence. Though I must say, I am enjoying this tremendously." His eyes darken as he peruses my body.

"My name is Astrid! For godesses's sake. And don't look at me like that."

"Do you always curse the goddess?"

Closing my eyes, I inhale deeply, counting to four before exhaling. My blood is on fire. Sparks flare to life behind my eyelids.

"Relax." He reaches out to touch my shoulder, and I flinch away, my eyes widening.

"Don't tell me to *relax!*"

"This is a particularly fun state you're in," he says, his eyes flashing with heat.

Losing it entirely, I whip my dagger out again, pressing it against his throat. My hand shakes—not with fear, but with fury. There's still a thin red line on his neck from the last time I pulled this move on him.

"It's like you enjoy pissing me off."

His eyes crinkle with humor. "I warned you earlier—some of us rather enjoy the taunt of a sharp blade."

"You're sick. I don't have time for your bullshit. My people need me. Tell me how to block out their intrusive thoughts and fix...my intense feelings," I say, my voice cracking. "Tell me how to fix it. Please!"

"Put the dagger down...*Astrid.*" He says my name for the first time genuinely. I appreciate him taking me seriously and showing respect. I hadn't quite expected it from him, and it eases my mind.

I comply with his command, sheathing the dagger.

"I do apologize for riling you up," he says.

"Do I have too much life force? Or not enough?" I squeeze the back of my tense neck as I continue striding back and forth.

"You think *your* magic is the cause of your distress?"

"Isn't it?"

One of his dark brows rises in surprise. "Absolutely not. You are a… vygora—an extremely powerful one. You're *meant* to absorb life force. It keeps your power at its highest and your senses their sharpest. It is absolutely not the source of your troubles."

"How would you even know?" My eyes roam the angles of his face for any hint of dishonesty. How can I trust he knows anything about my power?

"Because you and I are the same," he says. He grows quiet, his eyes focusing on a spot above my head, as if he's contemplating something. A nostalgic look crosses his face before he schools his expression once again.

"Like me, *how* exactly?"

"I'm…a special kind of vygora, too."

"Everyone seems to be *special* lately," I say. Clearly Mother was lying when she told me she and I are the most powerful beings around. The Vannyks, Dash included, are powerful in their own right. Fatima, whoever the hell she really is, has full elemental control. And after witnessing Lex's display of power in the throne room… Well, I no longer feel that unique.

"You and I—we're different from the others," he says, inspecting his nails. "Granted, our power isn't identical, but you could say it is quite *similar* in nature."

Despite everything, I have no doubt he's right. I witnessed his power rippling through the crowd in the throne room. Everyone dropped almost simultaneously without him even touching them.

Excitement surges up my spine at the memory. It surprises me. Logically, I should fear Lex. But I'm thrilled to discover his power is similar to mine.

Cedrik is the only other vygora I've ever met, but he has nothing on Lex. Lex is a force to be reckoned with.

Yet, I don't fear him.

I'm annoyed, yes. But afraid? No.

"If it's not the life force energy causing my imbalances, then what?"

"*Where two falls merge and two lips meet, hearts are joined, their power complete,*" he says, reciting the now overly familiar passage to me.

"So Dash's power *did* do this to me?" I shake my head. I'm hurt that my initial theory was correct. I asked Dash point-blank if the power sharing made my own magic erratic, and he was adamant it didn't. But that is when all my problems started. My magic was fine, normal, before that kiss under the falls.

Did Dash lie to me purposely? Or is he truly ignorant?

"Yes and no," Lex says, sliding his hands into his pockets. "I'm sure your little—*Dashiel* didn't fully understand the lore. Stories turn into myths—they change over time—but their origins stay the same."

"Explain. The short version so we can get to the fixing." Glancing at the door, I can't help but wonder if Lex's power is still holding strong. Part of me yearns for Dash to come rushing in and kiss me, to tell me Lex is wrong, but another part of me knows Dash fucked up. Even if it was an accident.

"Power is only to be shared freely between the fated. Soulmates, if you will," Lex says, and the intensity of his gaze causes my skin to prickle.

"What happens if you share with one who isn't your... fated?" I scrunch my nose at the prospect of *soulmates*. Nobody has a soulmate. People fall in and out of love all the time. Most loves are meant to be temporary, and I don't believe the soul is meant to be tied to only one person for all of eternity.

"It tears you apart from the inside—driving you insane."

"That's why Davvinia killed Anwyr?" I ask, gaining a new perspective on the lore despite my own personal beliefs.

"Actually, that's why Anwyr killed himself. To free himself of the corrupted power swimming through his veins."

Goddess above.

It's interesting to hear this variation of the story.

"So I'm like Anwyr in this story?" If I share Anwyr's fate, this is worse than I thought. Not only am I a danger to those around me, I'm a danger to myself.

He shrugs lazily, as if it's up to me to determine.

"Okay, given I believe your claims, how do I cut the connection between Dash and me?"

"Time and distance. Ideally, the farther apart you are from one another physically, the quicker the connection will fade. Otherwise it could take weeks, so long as you keep your hands and lips off each other. If the power is not recharged, the line will fade out until it's severed completely."

"Recharged?" I balk at his implications.

"Lover boy *really* fucked up his lore, eh?" Lex says, smirking. "The magic stems from...intimacy. Love or lust in any form enhances the power sharing bond."

So that's why I lost it in the throne room. It was *after* Dash and I had sex, which means our power sharing was intensified. No wonder it was overpowering.

A few key details definitely got lost in Dash's version of the lore.

"So all I have to do is stay away from Dash and not...kiss him, or touch him? At least until it fades?"

Lex scowls. "If it's not too difficult for you."

"How long will it take?" I ask, ignoring the foul dip in Lex's attitude.

"The more distance you put between you, the quicker it'll fade."

"I can't exactly leave. Not during all of this." I wave my arms.

"It's either that or you face Anwyr's fate," he drawls, giving me a pointed look. I hate how alluring his accent is. I hate how everything sounds good coming out of his mouth, even my impending death.

I rub my forehead. "So I'm supposed to just *leave?* What about subduing my mother? Taking my throne? What about my people?"

"Don't stab me for saying so, but the timing is interesting to consider."

I scrutinize him, searching for the true meaning of his words.

"It *could* be an innocent mistake on lover boy's behalf," he says. "He isn't from the island, after all. The lore *may* have gotten distorted, or... But, as I said, his timing is curious." Lex cocks his head as he shoves his hands deeper into his pockets. "But perhaps I'm wrong."

It's too late. Lex has successfully planted the seed of doubt in my mind, and now I'm questioning Dash's motives even further.

What if Dash *did* know the truth of this lore the entire time? What if he's been manipulating me, getting me out of the way so his family could claim my throne without breaking the goddess's laws? What if he purposely shared the one-sided kiss, not to *save me* from sharing my power with him but to save *himself* from suffering the ill-effects, knowing we're not fated?

Could Dash be secretly cruel enough to lead me on and drive me to my ruin, all to steal my throne?

Could he knowingly send me to my death?

I thought I knew him, but maybe I don't.

What if he purposely gave in to our intimacy, knowing it would push me over the edge in a perfectly timed move as his family closes in on Mother? With both Mother and me out of the way, the Vannyks would be heroes rising to save Hakran's people.

My stomach clenches with nausea as I realize that I have no way of knowing his true intentions. Everything between us could be fake.

"What's your problem with him?" I ask weakly. Lex has been belligerent toward Dash since we freed him from the pit. He's called him names, and now he's purposely provoking my mistrust.

"I don't have time for petty grievances with people who don't matter."

Scoffing, I cross my arms. "It seems you have plenty of time to instill uncertainties though." A new thought flashes through my head, and I let it guide my next question. "Why didn't I hear *anyone's* voices at first? With Dash's power? It took some time for me to read their thoughts, and it's getting increasingly worse."

"The magic builds inside of you like a tumor. It's not meant to run through your veins. Your body rejects it, and it will continue to battle against you until it consumes you entirely. That's precisely why the fated are the only ones meant to share magic. Their magic signatures match, drawing them to each other."

"How much time do I have?" At this point, it doesn't matter

if I believe the fated theory. If I don't break our ill-fated power sharing, I *will* die. It will kill me, or I will kill myself to escape the chaos. *That* is something I know because it's eating me alive.

"I guess you'll have to put as much distance between you and lover boy as quickly as possible." Lex sighs, pinching the bridge of his nose. "I have a place where you will be safe to wait out the bond as it breaks."

"Go with you? Absolutely not." Brushing a few stray bangs out of my face, I glare at him.

"Then I best be going," he says, heading for the door.

"Wait!" He pauses, so I continue. "Aren't you going to help us take down my mother first?"

"You could die at any time, and you're concerned about that?" he asks with an inscrutable expression. "Your priorities are wrong, luv."

"This might be our only opportunity. She knows we're onto her, that I'm no longer controlled by her. Once she discovers the Vannyks are free, if she doesn't already know, she will strike with full force. Our only chance to knock her down is to hit her first, before she realizes we're coming."

"That wasn't part of any deal we made."

"But your power, it's—"

"If you think my power is what you need to defeat her, you're sorely mistaken."

"You can help! We can work together. Please. The people need me." I'm begging, and at this point, I don't care how weak it makes me seem.

"Stop worrying about everyone else and put yourself first for once." He stares at me intensely as if trying to convince me of something. I'm too conflicted by his response to say anything else. How would he know whether or not I put myself first?

Turning on his heel, he walks out the door.

I collapse onto Dash's bed, staring at the sleek chandelier overhead as I contemplate what I should do. If I stay, I'm no help to anyone. I've already taken a little girl's father from her in front of the entire palace. They've seen me lose my mind once, and I'm bound to do it again. Right now I have a moment of peace; no one is around to assault me with the contents of their minds. The moment those in the throne room wake, I'll be lost to the monster inside me again.

I'm not my mother—I refuse to be like her—but if I stay, I could become worse than her.

As the guilt and anguish threaten to pull me under, I make my decision.

I need to go.

For Dash.

For Ilona.

For the Vannyks.

For all the people of Hakran.

Lex is wrong, I don't need to put myself first. I'll put *them* first by sparing them from my wrath.

Surging from the bed, I rush to the door and throw it open.

But Lex is already gone. His muddy footprints are the only things left behind.

CHAPTER TWENTY-ONE

The palace is eerily quiet, other than the wind howling outside.

It doesn't seem like anyone from the throne room has woken yet. I'm still stunned by the grandiosity of Lex's power. Something about him intrigues me—he's an even bigger mystery than anything I've encountered yet—but I'll likely never see him again. I'll never get to ask about his experience as a vygora. He might be the only person I'll ever meet who understands what it's like to wield such a weapon inside of them. Or teach me how to better manage my power.

But he's gone now, and it's for the best…except for the part where he was offering me respite from the poisonous magic inside me.

I'm tempted to run to the throne room—to try to wake Dash and Ilona—to shake away the loneliness settling into my bones. But even if I could block out the peoples' thoughts and emotions, it would be a poor idea. If I'm there when the people wake, they'll surely unleash their fury on me.

I killed an innocent man in front of them. I proved to my people that I am as wicked as my mother.

On a more personal level, my ever-changing perception of Dash is giving me whiplash. I'm doubting his intentions once again, and I don't think I can face him yet. It horrifies me to consider he's been deceiving me all along.

Dash claims that he has only lied when it was in my best interest. Was that a lie too? How can I trust anything he says?

The foundation of our relationship is weak—destined to crumble beneath us.

Perhaps when I dissolve our power sharing bond entirely, I'll be able to think properly for myself. As it stands, I barely know my own name right now, which only adds to my resolve to put some distance between Dash and me.

I need to accept Lex's help.

Panic builds, and I bolt out into the wet night. Braving the storm outside seems safer than facing the one in my mind.

We're still in the eye of the storm. The lights around the grounds are out, but in the silver glint of the moon I can make out a few downed trees and belongings strewn about. The horses across the property whinny in their stables, and I pray they're all right. If I wasn't in such a bind, I'd check on Aife and offer her comfort.

Wind caresses me, and stray water droplets from the nearby trees spray me.

Almost immediately, I spot Lex standing in the center of the yard.

His hands are shoved into his pockets as he stares up at the night sky. The clouds have parted enough to reveal a deep black canvas littered with stars. The peace won't last. The other side of the storm will come soon, unleashing more destructive power.

It's the only peaceful moment I might get.

"I thought you might change your mind," Lex says without removing his gaze from the sky.

"Everyone's an enemy," I whisper, finally admitting it out loud. Though, I'm not sure it's true. Ilona is my friend, my sister, even though I can't stand to be around her right now. She's not an enemy though. And Dash…well, I'm not positive about Dash yet, but I don't trust him right now. I can't rely on either of them the way I need to.

Dash once told me not to trust anyone, and I can't help but wonder if his words were a warning. Was he referring to himself?

Hakran's people are my enemy now—and they think I'm theirs. Once the Vannyks wake and think *I'm* the one who unleashed the wave of energy that knocked them out, they'll turn on me too.

Now everyone is going to think I'm just like Mother—my biggest enemy of all.

Lex is the only one offering me assistance, and I have no choice but to trust that he can help.

"Why can't I feel your emotions or read your thoughts?" I ask for the second time.

"There's a reason for everything," he says, finally meeting my gaze. It's a non-answer if I've ever heard one, so I'm surprised when he continues. "I meant it when I said you never needed that boy's protection. You can use your own energy to create a barrier."

"Stop attacking Dash," I say defensively. "This isn't even about him. I really like him. He is a good guy." It's as if I'm trying to convince myself rather than Lex. He doesn't need to know about my reservations, the doubts that *he* planted. Besides, even if Dash has been using me this entire time, it doesn't diminish the good he's done. If he *is* trying to eliminate me and steal my throne, it's because he wants to protect Hakran. Dash might be betrayal wrapped in an attractive package, but somehow his desire to help my people softens the blow. "I'm only going with you long enough for my sanity to return."

Lex nods slowly.

"I'm useless. It's debilitating," I say. The thin red line on his neck is a reminder of my dangerous temper. "The Stellari have a plan to bring Mother down without me anyway, and my people hate me. I have no real purpose here right now."

He squints at me, frowning. "Don't underestimate yourself."

The Hakranian people might think I ran away, leaving them to fend for themselves during their most vulnerable time, but they'll understand. When I return and give them the full story, they'll know I did it to protect them. I'm nothing like Mother. Even if it takes time, I'll earn their trust as their ruler.

A rustling at the edge of the jungle snags our attention. A faint line of orange orbs illuminates a row of guards headed this way.

Elemental staffs.

The guard with the braid must have alerted someone about our atypical visit to the training room earlier. Otherwise, they wouldn't risk rushing to the palace right now; they would've stayed in their shelter.

"Shit," I say.

"Come on," Lex whispers, beckoning me to the side of the palace. We're careful to avoid any light leaking from the windows. Shrouded in darkness, we quietly make our way to another part of the jungle. Lex grips my hand firmly as he tugs me forward.

Despite the unwanted contact, I let him lead me. I'm not afraid of him; I just don't know anything about him. If it weren't for the connection we have as vygoras, I don't think I would've gone with him at all. Rather, I would've disappeared into the jungle on my own, finding some place to hide out in secret.

But I can't deny it: something about him draws me in. I feel safer with him by my side.

Pain speaks to pain, and right now our hurt is speaking the same language. It's not trust between us but some sort of silent understanding.

Once we're out of earshot of the guards, we break into a run. I curse as I stumble behind Lex. How he's moving so nimbly in the almost pitch-black brush is a mystery. Trying not to think about snakes or other nocturnal creatures, I let him pull me along as quickly as I can manage.

"Here," he says breathlessly after we've been flying through the jungle for a while. Pressure builds inside my lungs, and I gasp to catch my breath. I'm in shape, but that much running would humble anyone.

"Where is...here?" Everything is black, the stars and moon shrouded by the thick layer of branches and vines overhead. I can't see them, but I know they're there.

The lush freshness of moisture and the bitter tang of decaying bark mix into an aroma I'm familiar with and love almost as much as the salty sea. We're somewhere deep in the jungle, off the paths.

Lex grunts, and it's followed by a scraping noise, like two boulders grinding together. Then he grabs my hand and pulls me along. The air grows earthier, mustier. The music of the jungle—water dripping from branches and birds cawing—is muffled. There's no breeze, so we must be inside of something.

Tentatively, I reach above me, and my hand meets rough stone.

Releasing me, Lex makes another sound of exertion, and the grating fills the space again.

"Are we...in a cave?" I ask. "You expect us to hide out here for how long exactly?"

Chuckling, Lex pulls out a small orb, illuminating the space. It's the inside piece of a lamp—an aethyn-spelled bulb that contains fire. Smart thinking on his part, except we could've used it to see through the jungle. Maybe then I could've avoided some of the tearing and scraping on my arms and pants. I can tell without even looking down, by the way the air hits my bare skin in random places, that my favorite bottoms are shredded.

We are indeed in a cave. Apparently the scraping and grunting was Lex moving a rather large boulder into place, where it now serves as a door. How he moved something so massive is beyond me.

"It's entirely impossible you moved that boulder on your own, so I'm going to ignore that," I say.

He grins mischievously at me. "You better get used to the impossible, luv, because when we come out the other end of this cave, you will no longer be in Hakran."

"I—what?" I close my eyes and shake my head, murmuring a "never mind" before reluctantly following him through the cave.

The top of the earthy passage is only a few inches above his head, and I can touch both walls when I spread my arms out.

Lex pauses, and I swear he stops breathing for a second as he looks around with a flash of discomfort in his eyes. I'm much shorter than him and *I'm* getting claustrophobic. It's a tight fit, and it's deeply unsettling. A joke about his claustrophobia is on the tip of my tongue, until I realize I rescued him from a small cage. One he was in for goddess knows how long. His trauma is not something to joke about. Instead, empathy surges within me, a warmth I thought I lost.

Wanting to distract him, I say, "You smell better than earlier," but I cringe when I realize how rude it sounds. For reasons unknown to me, I feel the need to lighten the mood. To help him relax under the circumstances. It pains me to know that my mother might've traumatized him. He's unbelievably strong and confident, but even the sturdiest men can fall.

I refuse to see Lex brought down.

His eyes focus on me, and a chuckle escapes him. Relief flows through me. I'm glad to temporarily distract him from his invisible wounds.

"Imagine how lovely I'd smell with a lavender bath," he says. I laugh, and we share a small smile before continuing on our journey.

Holding the orb of light aloft, he leads me through the narrow tunnel in silence.

After what seems like forever, we finally reach the end.

A wooden door stands between us and whatever is on the other side. Lex twists the iron knob, pushing the door open and ushering me through.

"Holy shit," I gasp.

"Welcome to Nevaris," he says with a sparkle in his eye.

Lex is right. We're definitely not in Hakran anymore.

Dawn spreads its wings just over the horizon, and a soft pink light washes over the land.

We're up high.

Much higher than any of the cliffs or hills on Hakran. The ground beneath us is rocky, with vibrant green grass sprouting up all around. The mountain we're on slopes down toward what appears to be a small village nestled on the edge of water. Not seawater though. The air isn't salty and heavy like I'm used to. Instead, it's fresh, with a hint of fishiness.

A green-blue lake stretches into an enormous oval, with the tallest, grassiest mountains rising up all around. Some of the mountains reach up into the clouds, their peaks blanketed entirely. It's as if the mountains stand guard, protecting the quaint village and lake nestled at the bottom.

Some of the buildings appear to sit flush with the water, as if you could walk right out the door and into the lake itself. It's nothing like the colorful seaside village of Hakran, with it's multi-storied wooden structures and dark, sloped roofs.

It's unlike anything I've ever seen before.

"Welcome to my home," Lex whispers in my ear. I turn to find him staring at me with an amused expression.

"Where the hell are we?" I've never heard of Nevaris. Though I can't help but wonder if maybe Ilona has read about this village in one of her books.

My breaths come out in small white clouds, and the air is sharp in my throat.

"Far enough away from Hakran," he says.

"It's cold." I shiver, wrapping my arms around myself. Without hesitation, Lex starts undoing the buttons of his shirt.

"No, that's fine. I'll—" Words leave me when he pulls his shirt off entirely. His muscular chest is marred with pink and white scars. The marks are old, and I wonder if they're from before he was imprisoned. There's a dark tattoo of two crossed swords inked on his left pectoral, along with some words on his inner right bicep. My mouth goes dry as I accept the shirt, trying not to gawk.

Dash's shirt, I remind myself.

Punching my arms through the sleeves, I'm grateful it's already warm from Lex's body.

"Thanks," I mumble, but it comes out hoarse. Clearing my throat, I turn back to the village.

Without a response, Lex begins trekking down the sloped hill. He walks sideways, rather than with his toes pointing forward, and it looks ridiculous.

Walking normally, I only make it a few steps before I lose my footing. I tumble down a good portion of the hill before coming to a stop on a flatter expanse.

Pushing myself to a stand, I swipe at my grass-stained arms with a scowl. Lex snickers behind me, but when I turn to him, he swallows heavily and pretends to look serious.

There's definitely a twinkle in his eye.

Ass.

For the rest of the way, I walk sideways with him, having learned my lesson. I don't lose my footing again.

Once we reach the bottom, I realize the village is much larger up close. It's bigger than the village back home but not quite as large as I'd imagine a city to be.

To our right, a good distance away, lies a row of docks, littered with fisherman who load small vessels up with lines and rods. The lake is so smooth that it appears almost glassy, reflecting the towering mountains and trees in perfect harmony. The shore on the other side is barely visible.

A cobblestone path pops up beneath us as we continue to trek toward the city. A wooden sign with white paint labels it as Main Street.

Vendors appear to be setting up shop along the path. A variety of small booths and colored tents cluster around. Tables are being loaded with goods. I'm amazed at how tall some of the buildings are. Three, four, some even five stories high, nestled into the hillside.

The architecture is like something out of a fairy tale—classic wooden paneling with steepled roofs and jutting balconies.

Despite the chill in the air, this place is cozy…homey.

At first, as we move side by side through the village, no one pays us any attention.

Then a robust woman with rosy cheeks and grey hair glances our way. She does a double-take, dropping and splattering the eggs she was preparing to set out on her table.

"Lexyll," she gasps. Running toward us, she ignores me completely as she wraps her arms around him. "Oh I prayed the original goddess would bring you back to us."

The woman's reaction sparks curiosity in the rest of the shop-keepers and vendors, and soon about a dozen people swarm us, their booths and goods forgotten. No one pays me any mind, as Lex—or Lexyll, as the people call him—is fawned over.

Grimacing at the group, I close my eyes and prepare for the onslaught in my mind... but nothing comes.

When I realize I can't hear their thoughts, an exasperated laugh bubbles out of me. Maybe I'm far enough from Dash that the power sharing bond has been cut.

At the sound of my laughter, the red-cheeked woman glances at me, eyes widening as her face pales.

"Aife?" she says with uncertainty.

"What?" Did she just call me by my horse's name? "I'm Astrid."

She chews on her lower lip, nodding sadly before glancing away.

"This is Princess Astrid from Hakran," Lex says in a flat voice. "She's here temporarily." She and Lex share some sort of silent communication. The woman opens her mouth but shuts it when he shakes his head gently at her. "Just her."

After a beat of silence, the woman swallows and changes topics. "The harbingers kept watch over Nevaris while you were...indisposed." She glances at me with uncertainty. "They'll be delighted to see you. They're still in Harmony House."

"They'll have to entertain themselves a while longer while

I finish business, Beatrice." Lex glances at me. Thanking the woman, he gives her another hug. She spares me another glance, like she's debating saying something, but finally shakes her head sadly and leaves us.

Before we can make it anywhere, more gawking people swarm him, embracing him and praising the goddess. There's no end of curious glances directed at me, and Lex continues to introduce me before anyone can ask who I am. I smile politely, unsettled by the attention.

"Either this town is much smaller than it looks, or they've missed you," I whisper. I can't imagine what it must feel like to be so adored. So loved and welcomed. Lex isn't exactly an unlikeable guy, but based on my limited interactions with him, he seems rude and dangerous. I'm surprised so many people seem to love him.

"Why can't it be both?" he says with a smirk.

"It's hard to imagine anyone missing you."

"Says the woman who missed me in those few minutes I stepped away to shave."

Rolling my eyes, I ignore his teasing and follow him down the path. "How long exactly have you been gone?"

"Too long."

Another non-answer, but this time he doesn't give me the satisfaction of elaboration. "What're the harbingers?"

"Who," he says, staring straight ahead, a grim expression on his face. "*Who* are they? is the proper question."

"Well, who are they?"

"Friends."

"All right then," I say with another eye roll.

Leading us past a hodgepodge of wooden cottages and lodge-style buildings, he stops in front of a small shop with a hand-painted sign that says Fara's Fragrances above the door. He turns into the alley beside it and beckons me to follow.

I hesitate but only for a moment. I've already come this far with Lex, so I might as well see it all the way through. I follow him up a rickety set of steps to the top level of Fara's Fragrances. There are three stories. The top story appears to be an attic of sorts.

When we reach the top of the stairs, Lex opens an unlocked door, revealing a small studio apartment with big windows and a surprising amount of natural light for an attic. There's a thin layer of dust on the white sheets draped here and there throughout the space.

"It's modest, but it'll do until you're ready to return."

My brows rise to my hairline. "You expect me to stay here?"

"Sorry, luv. I know you're used to that extravagant palace, but marble and silk are hard to come by in Nevaris." His expression turns hard, and his jaw tightens. "We're a modest bunch of working folk."

"No it's not—never mind. How long until the power-sharing bond is severed between Dash and me?" I ask. "I can't hear anyone anymore. Does that mean I've put enough distance between us to break it already?"

"Excited to get back to lover boy?"

I curl my lip at him in annoyance. "Obviously I am. It's better than being around your moodiness." What the hell has him flipping from the village's golden child to an asshole for no reason? He has no right to be bothered by Dash, yet he continues taking jabs at him at every opportunity.

"Don't take it personally."

"Kind of hard not to," I mutter. "My magic doesn't work here. How?"

"Nevaris is protected. There are wards in place to shield my—the people from external magic."

"Oh." I catch the way he says *"my"* before correcting himself, but he continues talking before I can ask about it.

"Your power won't work here, but mine will. I can read your magic signature and see if it's still tainted by lover boy's magic. Luckily for you, the wards will subdue the effects of your own magic, so you can relax knowing any attitude you have is entirely your own now."

"You have poor self-awareness if you think I'm the one with an attitude."

Scowling, he rips the dusty sheets from a sofa-bed, a low table, and a bookshelf. Some of the tension in the room dissipates at the sight of the colored spines before me.

I stride closer, and a smile grazes my lips as I read some of the faded titles. "You like romance?"

"They don't belong to me. Consider them yours."

His words are a sobering reminder that this is—or *was*—someone's apartment. That Lex had a life here who knows how long ago, before my mother took him as a prisoner.

We've both been subjected to her imprisonment but in different ways.

"I've never met a vygora like me before," I say, softening my tone. It's my way of making an effort to show my appreciation at his provision of sanctuary. "Can you transfer life force energy too?"

"No. I cannot. But I *can* absorb it without touching others. I can control how much I take—just enough to temporarily render one unconscious, as you saw."

"You could kill them though, if you wanted?"

"Yes."

For the first time in his presence, fear pricks at my skin. He can kill an entire room of people without even touching them—the extremely powerful Vannyks included.

Even Dash was susceptible to Lex's magic…and he's supposed to have the ability to block vygora magic. My own powers don't even work on Dash.

What am I doing here with this man? I know nothing about him, yet I followed him here to this village far away from everyone I know. It sounded like a good idea at the time, and I'm desperate for answers, for help, but I'm beginning to worry about the choice I made.

Lex moves to the small kitchenette and opens a few cupboards, then peers into the icebox with a tight expression. "I need to take care of some things. I'll be back with food."

"I'm supposed to just sit here like a prisoner?"

He looks affronted. "Who said anything about imprisonment? I am not your keeper. You're free to do whatever you wish."

Perhaps it was a poor choice of words—he *was* a prisoner himself recently. Sighing, I rub my temples with my fingers.

An apology sticks in my throat, so I give my thanks instead. He nods, fiddling with one of the front windows.

Eyeing the uncomfortable sofa-bed, I contemplate a nap. We've been up all night, and the events of the past twenty-four hours come flashing back with waves of stress and exhaustion.

As soon as the storm on Hakran ends, the Vannyks and Mother will have their showdown. Hopefully Mother will end up in the pit this time. Perhaps by now, the people in the throne room have woken and discovered my disappearance.

Dash and Ilona might be disappointed when they figure out I ran. Surely they'll worry for me, but they'll understand. They have to. If Dash's power sharing was truly a mistake, he can't be mad that I chose to break the bond to quite literally save lives.

And if it wasn't a mistake... Well, then he'll be grateful for my disappearance.

Now that the Vannyks have begun using their myndox powers to break Mother's hold over Hakran, they'll surely win over my people. When I return, I'll assume my rightful spot as queen—as heir to Mother's throne. I never wanted to rule, but Dash has given me hope that I can be the kind of queen I choose—a kind, caring queen. If there is such a thing.

I'll talk to the Vannyks and explain what happened, convince them that the murder in the throne room was a fluke. If they back me, perhaps it'll help me win my people over.

I miss Dash. Though we've only known each other for a few weeks, I'm used to his presence. I miss his spicy, woodsy scent. His strong, callused hands. The way his eyes always search for me in a room. Watching me as if I'm the most fascinating creature he's ever laid eyes on.

His lips on mine...though I haven't experienced *that* nearly enough.

"I'm glad your anger is subsiding, though I'd rather not feel your lust for lover boy," Lex says, drawing my attention back to him. He's leaning against the door, giving me a bland look.

"Excuse me?"

"At least, that's who I assume it's for?" His brow quirks up in question, and I can't stop my eyes from roaming over his bare chest. The shirtless suspender look is awfully attractive on him. He's already gorgeous after a bit of cleaning up and a shave. I can't imagine how mouthwatering he'll look after a few weeks out of the pit. Some sunshine, exercise, and solid meals will only enhance his appeal.

My cheeks heat in embarrassment at how quickly I went

from daydreaming about Dash to daydreaming about Lex. What the hell is wrong with me?

Stop ogling him, I scold myself.

"Did you just read my emotions?" I ask.

"I told you I could read your magic signature to see if his still taints yours. It requires reading your emotions to do so."

"You said you could, not that you were going to! Give a girl warning before you invade her personal space!" I scold, grateful he said something before my thoughts took a more explicit turn. Granted, he can't tell *exactly* what I'm thinking—he's no mind reader—but his ability to read my feelings is almost as invasive.

Goddess, is this what it feels like to be on the receiving end of my magic? It's annoying.

"Noted." He puts his hands up in a placating gesture. "I will give a direct warning next time. To answer your question, the bond isn't broken. It'll still take time, even with the distance. At least here you're safe from the ill effects."

He reaches for the doorknob to leave, and I call out to him, causing him to pause. "Why are you doing this for me?"

"Because...I know what it's like to lose someone you love. I'd hate to see that happen to you. I wouldn't wish that pain on anyone." The statement is made with the utmost sincerity. I could've easily murdered Ilona, Dash, or anyone else in my fits of rage. I could've taken the life of one of my friends. He's keeping them safe from me, so I won't do something I regret.

Lex's honesty is admirable. He saw my monster, and instead of scaring him away, it lured him in. I understand why I recognize the darkness in his eyes now: our monsters are the same.

His jade eyes linger on mine, and an electric charge passes between us. There's no challenge in his gaze, no mockery, just pure truth and pain.

I've been nothing but rude to Lex, and maybe he's deserving of a little more kindness. Maybe I *can* trust him. Wading through betrayals is exhausting, and the quiet here is a blissful reprieve. Even with Dash it wasn't this calm. Dash's lies—regardless of his intention—always hung over us.

Either way, I vow to be kinder to Lex. At least for now.

Finally, Lex shutters the emotion on his face and exits the apartment. The door clicks shut behind him.

I can't help but wonder who he lost, and how he lost them.

CHAPTER TWENTY-TWO

After Lex left, I took a nap. Now, I'm much too antsy to stay cooped up in the unfamiliar space. Contrary to Lex's belief that my unease is due to my luxurious upbringing, it's not. It's impossible to relax with my homeland in peril. I'm on edge because of that, not because of the lackluster apartment.

Leaving was the best thing I could do. Without my unpredictability getting in the way, Dash and his family can take on Mother. I know it's for the best, but guilt about leaving Ilona starts to sink in. Doubts about whether or not Dash will trust me—whether I can trust *him*—creep in. Worst of all, new worries form about Mother harming Dash or Ilona.

It's reassuring that the Vannyks are prepared to take Mother on without me. They're confident they can secure Hakran's freedom. But I still worry.

Another concern I have is whether or not my people will accept me as their ruler after the outburst I had in the throne room. I pray to the goddess they'll understand once they hear the full story.

I'm not the murderer they think I am. I'm nothing like the Dead Queen. I'll prove it to them.

Light filters in through the threadbare curtains as the sun creeps toward its apex.

Stretching my arms overhead, I wince at the crick in my neck. I might not need many luxuries, but I do miss my bed.

A pile of neatly folded clothes on the table beside me catches my eye, and I furrow my brow. They weren't there before.

Upon inspecting the trousers, forest-green sweater, and thick wool socks, I realize they're just my size. These will be much warmer than what I have on. Near the door, there's even a pair of leather boots that fit perfectly. I slip out of my thin, worn-out clothes and appreciatively put the new ones on.

Lex must've stopped by while I was asleep. Either he's skilled in the art of moving silently or I slept much deeper than I anticipated.

Maybe both.

When I notice a basket of apples resting on the counter, I realize he brought food too. In the formerly empty icebox, there are now chunks of cheese and thin-sliced meats.

My stomach rumbles at the sight.

Silently, I thank the goddess that Lex brought fresh food and clothes as I indulge in a snack. It was a kind gesture.

It was a huge risk for me to run away with the prisoner from the pit; it could've been a terrible choice, but so far, I have no regrets. The last thing I want to do is wait around like some damsel in distress though. As soon as the power-sharing bond is broken, I will return and win over my people.

But for now, the only thing I can do is distract myself.

After I eat, I decide to explore Nevaris. I exit the apartment, shutting the door behind me. Thumping down the stairs in my new boots, I inhale the clean, pine-scented air and use my fingers to smooth out my messy hair. The alley is narrow, barely wide enough for the rickety steps to fit. Despite being a little rundown, the area is clean.

I round the corner to the main cobblestone road, pausing to take in the shop on the first floor.

Fara's Fragrances.

As I'm debating whether or not to go in, the door opens and a delightful floral aroma leaks out into the streets. A chipper girl about my age, with onyx braids down her back, steps into the street. There's a woven basket in her hands, covered with a cloth.

"Ahh—Astrid?" she asks, disbelief in her voice, as if she's both thrilled and terrified. "Of *course* you're Astrid. Silly question. It's marvelous to meet you."

Her eyes flash with recognition, and I wonder if we've somehow met before.

There's a small bounce in her steps as she draws closer, and a smile stretches across her face, emphasizing her apple-like cheeks. As she wraps her arms around me, the handle of her basket digs into my back. I go stiff.

I'm used to people greeting me with respect or silence. Normally I'm given a deep nod of acknowledgement, not a hug.

She doesn't seem to notice my discomfort as I awkwardly pat her on the back. Her flowery scent is overpowering, tickling my nostrils. I hold my breath until, finally, she pulls away.

"This is for you," she says, thrusting the basket at me. I accept it reluctantly. "I was on my way up to visit you, new neighbor! I'm Fara, and this is my shop." She points at the sign above the door. "Though you probably could've guessed based on the name, huh? I live on the second floor, so I guess that makes us neighbors! It's swell to have you around."

Her rambling reminds me a little bit of Ilona. Fara is like a more outgoing version of my best friend. Ilona is sweet, of course, but shy around strangers.

And as nice as Fara seems, she isn't Ilona.

"Aren't you going to peek?" she asks, waving a hand toward the basket.

I pull back the white cloth to reveal a dozen rectangular pastries. They're warm and smell sugary sweet with a hint of apple and cinnamon.

"Thank you, Fara," I say, forcing a smile.

"They're my speciality! Apple strudel. I hope you think they're superb."

"I'm sure I will."

"I figured if you were with Lex, there's a chance he forgot to feed you." Her body vibrates with giggles, and she claps her hands in front of her as if it's impossible to stay still.

"You didn't pop into the apartment by chance earlier, did you?" I ask, thinking back to the newly stocked food and change of clothes. If it's so unlike Lex to care for a guest, perhaps it wasn't him after all.

"Me? Oh no, I've been busy mixing oils this morning. It's a lavender and bergamot day with—anyway, why do you ask?"

"Does Lex normally forget to feed his guests?"

"Well," she says, her voice dropping a few octaves. "Considering Lex's visitors normally come in chains or...without a head, he doesn't normally *need* to remember. I'm sure you can understand why I worry about his hospitality."

My face scrunches at the gruesome implication of her words, and she laughs heartily.

"Don't let his coldness scare you away. He's been through a lot, and he's sacrificed much for us. I can't imagine what he went through in the time he was gone, but I'm sure it hasn't helped his attitude any. Give him a chance, please."

"He seems fine. He's nice enough, really," I say. "He's letting me intrude in his living space, after all."

Her brows draw together as she contemplates something. "That's not Lex's apartment. I mean, he owns the building, so I guess it's technically his, but he lives over in Harmony House. He didn't tell you that?"

I shake my head, looking past Fara and down the shop-lined street to where vendors stand among their booths and tents, talking animatedly to shoppers. A few people seem to be bartering, but most heads are swiveled in my direction, watching with open interest.

Fara glances over her shoulder, following my line of sight, and releases another belly laugh. "Excuse them. They're not used to the excitement. Lex has *finally* returned with his—with a guest. The villagers in this end of Nevaris are mostly bored folk who love any excuse to flap their lips."

"How long has Lex been gone?" He seems rather important to the village, but perhaps it's because it's such a small town. It seems like a place where everyone knows each other. It's even smaller and closer-knit than the island of Hakran.

I still don't know how long Mother had Lex locked up—or why. Lex's answers were cryptic.

"It's been—" Fara starts to whisper.

"Talk about flapping lips, Fara," the rosy-cheeked lady from earlier says as she waddles up to us. "D'ya think Lexyll would appreciate you blurting his business?"

"It's not like that, Bea. You know how he is. I was just giving Astrid here a rundown."

"Astrid." Beatrice eyes me warily. "You look like someone I once knew."

"Aife?" I ask, remembering that she called me my *horse's* name earlier.

When she doesn't respond, Fara tries to fill the silence with chatter about the weather.

"That's my horse's name," I say. "I've never met anyone with the name before. Funny coincidence."

"There's no such thing as coincidences," Beatrice says before shuffling off down the cobblestone path. Without stopping, she bellows out, "If Lexyll wanted to share, he would! Leave it, Fara."

"Beatrice runs the farm," Fara whispers when the woman is out of earshot. "Her husband Tomas passed away last year, and it's been hard on her. I can't imagine it's easy for her to look after all the animals without him. She has two grown boys that help as much as they can, but they have their own children to look after."

Fara keeps talking, giving me insight into the various villagers set up around the street. I nod here and there to pretend I'm listening, but I'm eager to slip away and explore on my own.

"—and the turkey ate the cow with ten toes. I married him yesterday," Fara says, jerking my attention to her.

"What?" I ask, confused.

"I knew you weren't listening." She tilts her head back with a chuckle. "Anyway, I'm sure you have things to do, and my oils need me. Enjoy the strudel, preferably while they're still warm. That is, if they haven't already gone cold with all my yapping. Pop in anytime, neighbor! It's a pleasure finally meeting you."

Finally?

I only arrived a few hours ago.

Relief washes over me when she doesn't stick around for a response. With an animated wave, she slips away into her shop. Although she's plenty nice, I'm not feeling particularly social. I'm not here to make friends and chat about the weather; I'm here to bide my time until I can return and resume my position as the queen of Hakran.

It's strange; I've only imagined Hakran run by Mother. I never thought I was worthy of the throne. Honestly, I never thought I even wanted it, but I'm starting to realize those weren't my own thoughts. They were ideas planted there by the mother who has taken advantage of me at every turn. The woman who has deceived me my entire life.

A light breeze rolls through the street, ruffling my hair. I shiver, wrapping my arms around me. It was kind of Lex to provide me with the warmer clothing.

I like the coolness. It's refreshing. And Nevaris is utterly peaceful. I'd love to bring Ilona here one day; she'd adore the quaint shops and chattering townsfolk.

Walking in the opposite direction from the vendors, I head deeper into the village, passing more wooden houses built into the side of the hill. With their steep, arched roofs and multiple levels, they give the village layers.

The homes are mostly in shades of brown—made with natural, unaltered lumber—but some have splashes of pale yellow or soft pink accents here and there.

Peeking through the alleyway on my right, I spot a few vessels tied to private docks, bobbing almost imperceptibly in the water.

A few people scurry past me, dressed in long-sleeved tops or thick skirts. With my borrowed outfit, I fit in. Almost. Curious glances still flash my way.

One impatient woman tugs at the hand of a small child of maybe about five years old. Out to the side, she's holding a basket of jam jars, being careful not to knock them about too much.

"Mama! I want to feed the ducks!" the child cries, resisting his mother as she pulls him along.

"Vincent, get over here," the mother yells at a slightly older boy with messy orange hair. The older boy catches up to the pair, and his mother releases the smaller boy's hand long enough to swat the older one on the back of the head.

"Ow!"

"What did I say about wandering out of sight?" she scolds.

"I was right there, Ma." He points at the lake, visibly huffing as his younger brother wails.

"I want to feed the ducks, Mama!" the younger child wails.

"Oh goddess have mercy on me! Will you two behave for a single day?" They carry on quickly toward the vendors, and I chuckle as they continue bickering, their voices fading with distance.

I wonder if that's what having a normal, caring mother is like.

The further away from the town center I tread, the more spaced out the houses are. The homes grow larger, and some have yards with free-roaming goats and sheep that bleat as I pass.

Eventually, the street forks off into two paths. On my right the cobblestone path continues, leading to the waterfront and the rolling farms beyond. On my left the path gives way to packed dirt, sloping upward into a tree-lined hill where prickly conifers obstruct my view of what lies beyond.

I continue on the stone path, along the shore.

Clutching the basket from Fara, I pass roaming farm animals and green pastures. The scent of cinnamon and apple wafts up, reminding me of the treats inside. I pull back the cloth and take out one of the flaky pastries, biting into it as I continue my stroll.

Fara was not exaggerating.

It's my first time experiencing a strudel, but it's delightful. It's still lukewarm. The pastry is sweet with a flaky outside and a soft apple explosion inside. There's a hint of spice, and I wonder what exactly it is.

I should stop by and thank Fara when I return, because I'm pretty sure it's the best dessert I've ever had.

As I continue down the winding path along the lake, I enjoy the clean, pine scent. The air is becoming less fishy the farther away I get from the docks. A short while later, I spot an unusual sight. A large, white mansion sits on the water, with its turrets and spires reaching into the sky.

It's in the same architectural style as the rest of the village, but it's reminiscent of a castle. It appears as if it's floating.

I have to squint against the harsh glare of the sunlight reflecting off the water, but after a moment, I realize the building isn't actually floating; it's perched on an almost imperceptible chunk of land, practically flush with the water, giving off the illusion of floating. Only a single stone bridge stretches from the land to the castle.

"For me?" a smooth voice calls. I jump. A man around my age with tousled, honey-blonde locks and a broad grin pops up next to me. I didn't even hear him approach. At first glance, he appears harmless. A second glance reveals he's equipped with daggers at his side and a sword strapped to his back.

His boyish looks and saccharine smile are definitely a facade; his stealth, combined with his weaponry, indicates he's perhaps a guard or a spy.

As he gives me a once-over, his smile grows wider. There's a slight gap between his front teeth, but it adds to his appeal.

"Are you going to respond?" he asks, cocking his head. "Or are you mute?"

"Is there a third option?" I say apprehensively.

"What did you have in mind?" He wiggles his eyebrows suggestively as he circles me, like a predator stalking its prey.

I don't reply as I glance toward the castle. The man follows my gaze. "I'll give you a tour for a strudel."

"What makes you think I want a *tour?*" I scoff.

"The way you're staring at the house with such open interest." I tear my eyes from the castle, looking at him instead.

House? More like a mansion. "Well, what makes you think I even have a strudel?"

He chuckles as I grip the basket tighter, ensuring my treats are fully concealed. "I can smell Fara's desserts from a mile away. Why do you think I came over here in the first place?" He reaches toward the strudel, licking his lips dramatically.

If he is a guard, he's unlike any I've ever met, with his cheekiness and lively spirit.

"Fine," I say, extending the basket toward him. He reaches in without looking, grinning in triumph when he pulls one free. "Do you always proposition strange girls for castle tours?"

"Only when they're not so strange," he says with a mouthful. I cringe as crumbles tumble out of his mouth. "Lex already vouched for you." He takes another enormous bite and tries to speak as he chews, but I can't tell what he's saying.

"Gross." I scrunch my nose and glance back at the mansion. "Lex lives here?"

"Sure does," the guy says. "I'm Callan, by the way. I'd shake your hand, but Lex might kill me if I touch you."

"What?" I ask, frowning. Why would Lex kill him for touching me? Perhaps he's only kidding, but Lex isn't the humorous type, and I doubt he would make such a joke.

Callan cocks a brow but doesn't say anything else. He beckons for me to follow him and leads me toward the bridge. It's made of stones, resting only a few inches above the water line. At only a few feet wide, it's a fairly narrow crossing. It's almost like walking on water.

"Lex is home, by the way." Callan winks at me over his shoulder, and my frown deepens.

"Please don't tell me he's a freaking king or something." I groan. The last thing I want is to drag *another* nation into Hakran's issues. But my guess is that Hakran and Nevaris already have issues of their own, considering Mother imprisoned Lex. He seems to be someone of importance.

After what seems like a mile, we finally reach the end of the bridge, and I'm grateful when my feet hit solid land.

"He's definitely not a *king*." Callan snorts in amusement.

"A prince?"

"Nope."

"He's definitely not a normal villager if *this* is where he lives," I mutter, gesturing toward the mansion that sprawls before us, taking up almost all of the small island.

"Lex is anything but normal," Callan says.

I roll my eyes, deciding to let it go. I'm still too emotionally raw to deal with anyone else's riddles and games. As soon as this bond with Dash breaks, I'll leave and never see Lex again anyway.

But if Lex is here, that's a good thing. I can ask him how long he thinks it'll take before the bond is broken. The sooner I can return, the better for everyone.

I follow Callan to a tall door with a wrought-iron knocker. He pushes through without knocking—an indicator he either lives here too or he's extremely welcome—and he holds the door open for me.

"Welcome to Harmony House," he says.

Harmony House.

Beatrice mentioned this place. She said, *"The harbingers kept watch over Nevaris"* from here, and Lex called the harbingers his friends.

I wonder if Callan is one of them.

But that still leaves the question: what the hell is a *harbinger?*

CHAPTER TWENTY-THREE

Inside, the house is simpler than I'd expected. Or perhaps I'm used to Mother's flair for showy aesthetics and luxury.

Dark hardwood floors contrast with white pillars and high, carved ceilings. I can see through the open space and out the windows to the water beyond. A single set of stairs curls up to a loft-style walkway adorned with iron railings.

It's surprisingly cozy for how grand it is. Then again, everything in Nevaris seems welcoming.

Piano notes waft through the air, accompanied by a rich, deep voice. The music slams into me, eliciting goosebumps.

"Whoa," I murmur. I'm overwhelmed with familiarity, as if I've dreamt about this place before. I've never been here though; I'd remember a place like this.

Callan chuckles at me before striding toward an open doorway on the left side of the room. I follow him, and the piano notes grow louder. We enter a gorgeous formal sitting area with creamy accents. The far side of the room boasts a grand piano, which is set in the center of a raised platform beneath a circular wall of windows.

My breath catches as I take in the elegant man whose slender fingers dance across the ivories with ease. His eyes are shut as he plays a passionate yet haunting tune. Whatever he's singing about doesn't matter; I can't pay attention to the words with how transfixed I am.

"He's decent. I know." Callan grins, nudging me with his elbow.

At the sound of our arrival, Lex's eyes flash open, and he cuts his song short. His piercing eyes lock onto me. Butterflies flutter in my stomach, but I manage to school my expression.

"What brings you here?" Lex asks in that appealing accent of his. "Have I not provided you with everything you need?"

"I—yes. Thank you." I'm unsure of what to say. *Why* am I here? Suddenly I can't explain why I thought it was a good idea to show up here. I'm at a loss for words, distracted by Lex in his sharp suit and styled hair. The mansion seems emptier without the music filtering through it, and I mourn the loss of his beautiful song.

"I offered her a tour in exchange for some of Fara's strudel," Callan says, gesturing toward my basket. I grip it tightly in front of me like a shield. "She has more if you'd like one."

"No thank you," Lex says without taking his eyes off me.

As he rises from the bench, his shirt strains against his toned chest. The top few buttons are undone, and I catch a glimpse of his crossed-sword tattoo. Despite his lax approach to buttoning, he's much more refined than the man I met in the pit. His hair is immaculately styled into a low bun. A five-o'clock shadow clings artfully to his jaw.

He adjusts his cuffs as he prowls toward me, his eyes devouring me. "Glad to see you in something more appropriate," he says with approval.

"Who do you think you are, my father?" I scoff. How dare he criticize my outfit choices? Is that why he brought me new clothes? Was a little bit of midriff and arm too much skin for him? "Not that it's anything to you, but I love my Hakranian clothes."

"I meant appropriate for the weather," he says, arching a brow in amusement. "Your previous ensemble wasn't suitable for a mountain."

"Oh" is all I can say as my cheeks flush with embarrassment.

"Enjoy the tour, luv," he calls as he strides past me, exiting the room.

I stand there, wondering if I should go after him to ask about the power sharing bond, but I can't force my feet to move. Lex's presence has rendered me motionless.

"So, this is the piano room," Callan says, spreading his arms dramatically as he breaks the awkward silence Lex's abrupt departure left us in.

"I figured as much," I mutter, glancing around. "What's with all the flowers?" Floral arrangements in all shapes and sizes fill every surface in the room. Some appear to have been professionally arranged, while some are a mishap of colors and styles.

"The villagers picked flowers for Lex, to showcase their delight. It's a Nevaris tradition to gift flowers or foods."

Fara did say something about Lex that stuck with me: *Lex's visitors normally come in chains or...without a head.* It seems Lex is potentially violent and unhinged, yet the villagers care for him enough to showcase their pleasure and admiration. It's a paradox.

I lean in to smell a bouquet of yellow roses, and chatter reaches my ears—a soft, feminine lilt and a deeper, hushed tone. The voices grow louder, until a tall woman with white-blonde hair and porcelain skin enters the room, followed by a muscular man with dark, upturned eyes and hair so black it's almost blue. They wear casual clothes, with daggers strapped to their sides like Callan.

When they spot me, they abruptly stop talking.

"Callan, you didn't tell us you were bringing a friend 'round today," the woman says. A sad look flickers across her features before she composes herself and greets me. "Hello." It's curt but not unfriendly.

"I'm not his friend. I'm Astrid." The words are bitter as they leave my mouth, but to my relief, Callan snorts a laugh before I can feel guilty about being rude. Perhaps Lex was right about my attitude problem.

"I know." The woman smiles, and it lights up her face. "I'm Loisia—Lo for short. This is Sora. He's not much of a talker." She juts a thumb in his direction, and he grunts in acknowledgement. "Sorry to interrupt your little powwow, but the three of us need to go." She shoots Callan a serious look, and he nods grimly.

"Feel free to give yourself that tour," he says, flashing me an apologetic smile. "Thanks for the strudel!"

Before I can reply, the three of them turn and walk off briskly, their boots clacking in harmony. Sora turns at the last second before rounding the corner. Wordlessly, he glides over to me, slipping his hand into my basket and snagging a strudel.

My brows lift at his forwardness and lack of manners, but he doesn't acknowledge me as he strides after his friends.

"Sure," I say to his retreating back. "Help yourself to my strudel."

Sighing, I plop the basket of pastries down on a side table that isn't completely crowded with flower bouquets.

I should really find Lex and see how long it'll take to break the bond.

As oddly charming and quaint as this town is, I don't belong here. Hakran needs me to step into the role of queen, so the sooner I can win my people over, the better. Plus, I don't want to leave Ilona and Dash without answers for any longer than I need to.

It's only been half a day, and I'm already on edge from missing them. As soon as I can guarantee I won't rage out and murder anyone else, I'm gone.

With that thought, I mosey around, exploring the house as I search for Lex. All is silent on the first floor, so I head upstairs, tracing the iron railing with a finger and admiring its intricate details.

My thoughts wander back to Lex at the piano, and I wonder how long he's played. What else he's good at with those slender fingers. My stomach twists itself into knots as my thoughts take an unexpected turn and an image of Lex shirtless, on top of me, flashes into my mind. I inwardly curse myself, shaking the image away before it goes any further.

I'm oddly drawn to Lex. I can't help but wonder if our energies call to one another because we are vygoras? I don't feel drawn to Cedrik though, not even a little bit, and he's a vygora too.

Then there's the mystery of how my magic flowed into Lex so easily during our transference.

Is it because of how powerful Lex is? Perhaps that's why I'm drawn to him. But it seems like *more* than that.

At the top of the stairs, in the loft, I pass through an informal sitting area. The aesthetic is softer than downstairs, with beige carpet and low ceilings that make the space feel more intimate. I follow the only hallway until I come upon an open door.

Cautiously, I peek my head into the room. It's a large bedroom with plush carpet, a stone accented fireplace, an oversized bed, and a small sitting area. Arching beams overhead give it an airy feel.

Across the room, glass doors reveal a patio overlooking the lake. Lex stands with his back to me, leaning on the iron railing as he sips from a glass.

"Lex?" I call, trying not to sneak up on him. Slowly he turns to me, his green eyes dark and stormy.

"You shouldn't be here," he says, chugging his beverage before entering the room. Crossing to the small table beside the fireplace, he grabs a decanter filled with the same dark liquid, refilling his glass and slamming it back.

"Drink?" he asks without looking at me.

"Sure," I say hesitantly.

I step closer to him, and our fingers brush as I accept a freshly filled glass of amber liquid. My body tingles at his touch, and he pauses, letting his hand linger like he feels it too.

He releases the glass and jerks away, tugging at the collar of his silk shirt with a sigh. It almost appears as if he's rattled by my presence.

Why would he invite me to have a drink with him if he's uncomfortable around me?

I sip the beverage, and wince. The liquid burns as it slides down my throat.

Whiskey.

I've tasted it before, but I'm not partial to it. Lex watches as I work to hide my disgust.

"I should've known you wouldn't like that," he murmurs.

"That would've been presumptuous of you. And it's just fine, thank you."

"Lies," he says, trying to hide his smirk behind his glass. When he finishes swallowing, he slowly licks the last drops off his lips. I track the movement a little too eagerly. "Stop looking at me like that, luv."

"Like what?" I ask, but it comes out breathlessly. Suddenly, it's too hot in the room—too intimate. Even though there's a good foot of distance between us, his presence is electrifying.

This man is totally different than the one I met in the pit. His musky pine scent is heady.

An ache builds between my legs, and I squirm in response.

Shit.

I'm attracted to Lex.

I try to hide the realization behind another gulp of whiskey. My cheeks heat with a mixture of lust and embarrassment. I'm not normally shy, nor do I have any problem going after what I want. But this desire is entirely unwelcome. It's confusing, especially while I'm trying to build something real for the first time ever—with Dash.

Dash and I haven't labeled our relationship. Never declared monogamy. Yet I still feel guilty about my attraction to Lex.

My head buzzes with whiskey as I stare at Lex's sharp features. His demeanor is so cold and off-putting, yet his actions are kind. The contradiction turns me on. It unravels me.

"We can't do this, Lex," I say, stepping backward to put some distance between us.

He laughs. It's the first time such a positive expression has crossed his face. When he's done laughing, he swipes his thumb across his bottom lip, staring at me like I'm the most amusing creature he's ever seen.

"*We* are not doing anything," he says, his voice tinted with humor. "Lust is nothing to be ashamed of."

I don't know if I'm more horrified that he noticed what I was feeling or that he called me out on it directly.

"Lust?" I ask incredulously. "You're wrong." I shake my head.

"Astrid," he says. "I don't need to use my power to see the way you're writhing like a cat in heat." His eyes spark with need as they slowly trail down my body. I'm frozen in place, feeling vulnerable beneath his gaze.

"You're wrong."

He shrugs in response, not taking his eyes off me. I huff at him, hating myself for being so obvious and hating him for being so observant.

So attractive.

This has to stop. I don't even know anything about him.

"You live like a king. You're worshiped by the villagers like one. But you're not." I gesture around the lavish room, trying to ignore my incredibly inconvenient attraction to him. "So who exactly are you, Lex?"

He moves until he's directly in front of me, and I'm forced to tilt my head up. This close, I can see the various shades of green and grey swirling around his irises. Our chests rise and fall in sync.

"There are other beings far more powerful than your measly kings and queens," he says. He reaches out, leisurely tracing my jaw with his finger. It's innocent enough, but my body shudders at his touch. I squeeze my thighs together, trying to ignore the heat building there.

I have a sudden urge to strip my clothes off and press my body against his.

To let his slender fingers dance across my body like they did the piano keys.

To press my lips to his and see if they're as soft as they appear.

Instead, I say, "Your inflated sense of self-importance is sickening," and roll my eyes dramatically. Normally arrogance is a turn-off, but Lex wears it well. It only adds to his appeal.

"It would be an inflated sense of self-importance if my words were false." He's so close that his warm breath tickles my face, carrying the bitter stench of alcohol.

"Are you *drunk?*" I ask, slamming my own empty glass down on the table beside us and breaking the spell between us.

"Barely."

"Don't lie to me."

"I've never lied to you," he growls, locking eyes with me again. "It takes more than a few glasses of whiskey to intoxicate me."

"Then tell me honestly why my mother threw you in the pit."

"Because Enira fears me." His words are low, like a warning to back off from the conversation. I ignore the threat and press on, my head swimming from the alcohol. Perhaps I shouldn't have chugged such a large quantity of whiskey so quickly. Unlike Lex, my tolerance is quite low.

"If you're so almighty and terrifying, how did she overpower you?" I ask.

Sighing, he breaks his glare from me, running a hand through his perfectly styled hair and messing it up. It falls free of where it was tied at the nape of his neck, resting around his shoulders in thick waves.

There's something incredibly satisfying about getting under Lex's skin, seeing him come undone. There are so many different sides to him: the prisoner, the terrifying vygora, the caring man who gave me the shirt off his back and offered me a safe place to stay.

And I've yet to witness the murderous tendencies Fara spoke of. All in all, I'm intrigued. I should step away, but he's sucking me right in.

Most fascinating of all, he's *always* calm and in control, no matter what circumstances I've witnessed him in. It's as if his emotions never truly affect him, which as a vygora, I know is false. We feel things much more acutely than other people.

"She caught me when I was at my weakest," he says, snapping my attention back to him. There's danger in his eyes, and I yearn to see him lose control, to let the beast inside of him free. "I was searching for something she took."

"Something that belongs to you?"

"Yes," he whispers.

"Did you find it?"

His jaw tenses, and he glances away without answering. He suddenly shifts from dangerous to vulnerable, and it beckons to me. I step forward, and before I know what I'm doing, I reach my arms around him. He surprises me by hugging me back. We fit together perfectly.

Slowly, I tilt my head up to look at him. My tongue darts out to moisten my lips, and his pupils dilate. His hardness strains against his pants, pressing against me, begging for this as much as I am. My heart rate increases, and just when I think he's going to close the distance between us, he tenses up, pulling away.

"No. Like you said, we can't do this. I refuse to take advantage of your current state." He adjusts his pants, hiding the proof of his arousal, and I'm desperate to draw him back to me, to resume whatever was happening between us.

I'm intoxicated.

But not because of the whiskey.

Because of him.

"You don't have to be decent with me. I'm an adult. I can make my own decisions," I retort. When he doesn't reply, I add, "It was just a hug." I throw in an eye roll for good measure, pretending I'm unaffected by his rejection.

"Then maybe I refuse to do this to your little friend Dale or Dan or—"

"Dash," I say irritably, hating that he brought him up right now. The spell shatters completely. Guilt and shame claw at my chest.

I've been so worried about not being able to trust anyone else that I've failed to realize I can't even trust myself...at least not right now. Not with everything going on. I was so desperate to escape the plaguing emotions that I'm falling for anyone who offers me an escape.

Dash was an escape from Mother's manipulation and my own mind. Lex is an escape from everything else in my life.

How can I trust my feelings toward either of these men? I've gone almost my entire life without finding attraction deeper than skin-level, and now I'm battling with my attraction toward *two* different men.

One man I know nothing about, and one I can't fully trust.

I back away toward the door, interrupting whatever Lex is about to say. "I need to go," I whisper.

Lex calls after me, but he doesn't follow me as I run down the stairs and out his front door. My borrowed boots slap across the stone bridge as I run. I don't stop until I make it all the way to the apartment.

I secure the deadbolt and chain lock behind me, then, panting, sink down onto the floor. The tears fall, and I let them, knowing it won't do me any good to hold them in.

This time, the tears are for me.

CHAPTER TWENTY-FOUR

I hole up in the apartment for the next few days reading romance novels and contemplating my life distraction-free. I'm biding my time until I can return home. Fara and Lex come knocking, but luckily, when I don't answer, they leave me in peace. This morning, Fara left a red knit sweater and a fresh basket of strudel outside the door. It was kind of her, but I still didn't feel like engaging in small talk.

At night, while the village slumbers, I amble along the lakeside, lost in thought. On my own, free of my clamorous magic and Mother's influence, I'm able to really *think*.

One night, I wander along the crooked cobblestone path, led by only the silver luminescence of the moon above. A few houses have sconces that flicker as I pass, but they do little to keep the shadows at bay. Unfamiliar with the path, I stumble a few times on jutting edges, cursing the goddess each time.

I make my way to the empty docks, then sit on the edge, letting my feet dangle over the water. The lake is tranquil, lacking the powerful pounding waves and stinging salt spray of the Insipid Sea. Both bodies of water make me feel small, insignificant, but the lake is inviting instead of intimidating.

Cool air stings my lungs, and I shiver, wrapping my borrowed wool blanket tighter around me as I think about how I ended up here. So much has happened in such a short time, and I don't know what the future holds. I hope Ilona is okay. I can't imagine how she's faring without me there to guide her. I pray to the goddess that Dash and the Vannyks can protect her by subduing Mother. I'm not sure what they plan, but they seem confident.

Lex also seemed fine with leaving them behind to take care of the situation. It could be because it's not his problem, but then again, *I'm* not his problem and he's gone out of his way to help me. After escaping from the pit, he could've run far away without looking back, but he stopped to help me. He also could've gone after Enira, but he didn't. Something tells me he wouldn't have let Enira walk without punishment, so he either knows something we don't, or he has faith in the Vannyks' ability to subdue Enira.

And on top of everything, I miss Dash. When I first met him, I thought he was nothing more than an arrogant nuisance. Granted, I still think that most of the time, but somehow he wiggled his way under my skin with his stupid smirk and ill-timed jokes. He brings a spark of light to my darkness.

Stretching my arms overhead, I lay back on the dock. The abundance of stars above twinkle as if they know secrets of the night but are unwilling to share. A soft breeze caresses me, bringing with it a fresh pine scent. Being at the lake reminds me of a certain green-eyed stranger. Calming and oddly familiar.

I can't place my finger on it, but something about Nevaris feels homier than Hakran. It's probably because there's no Enira here. No cold, faceless guards running around. No debaucherous bacchanals or orgies on the lakeside. Every day, floral scents waft through the streets, homemade baked goods are brought to my door, and children play happily outside, their scolding mothers never far away. My evenings are filled with silent reflections. It's the kind of place that wraps its arms around anyone who visits, begging them to stay.

The thought of leaving makes my chest tight, but I chalk it up to nerves. I don't belong here. Hakran is my home. My people, my friends, are relying on me. I worry if I stay here any longer, Nevaris' embrace will tighten, and it will only be harder to say goodbye to the sliver of peace I've found here.

I need to leave.

The next day I decide to visit Lex in Harmony House. I've been patient, and I've given it time; hopefully the bond with Dash has faded enough to return home. Even if it hasn't been broken entirely, perhaps it's weak enough that I'll be safe from the ill effects. I can certainly refrain from acts of intimacy with Dash until the bond dissolves, that way I don't recharge it.

I'm ready to go home. I'm tired of everyone else making decisions for me, and I'm sick of sitting around worthlessly. I've spent four days doing absolutely nothing eventful.

I am soon to be the *queen* of Hakran. I am not just my mother's pawn. I don't belong to Dash, and I'm not a slave to his power-sharing bond gone wrong. My emotions are not my master.

As the only vygora with the power of transference, it's time the people see me for who I really am, without the veyl or the influence of my mother. Maybe my people will never embrace me the way I want, but I no longer care. I will be a better ruler than my mother, and that's what matters most. They can hate me, but I'll still protect them.

I make it to Harmony House in record time and burst through the door without knocking.

"Great security," I say sarcastically.

Callan stands in the foyer with a sandwich held up, about to take a bite. His eyes widen at my arrival. "Astrid! What brings you here?" He flashes me a dazzling smile.

"Where's Lex?" I ask as Lo and Sora, wearing identically stern expressions, enter the room.

"Up in his roo—" Callan starts.

"He's busy," Sora says over him. Lo shoots me a look of pity. Suspicion rises, and something about the look on Lo and Sora's faces unsettles me.

I follow Callan's tip, racing up the stairs in search of Lex.

"Wait, Astrid! You don't want to—" Lo calls up the stairs after me, but the blood pounds in my head, silencing her voice.

I get the impression they're hiding something from me, and I don't like it.

Lex's bedroom door is closed, and I barge right in. "Lex! I think it's time that we—" My voice catches at the sight before me, and heat rushes to my cheeks.

Lex stands shirtless on his balcony with his back against the railing, and a fully nude woman stands beside him, raking her fingernails down his arm.

My feet are frozen to the floor, and I'm unable to look anywhere but the place where the woman's nails graze Lex's skin. Envy and disgust coil tightly inside of me.

Lex's eyes lock onto mine from across the room. He raises a glass of whiskey to his lips, ignoring the woman as she leans closer, whispering something in his ear. Her pert breasts rub against him, and a low growl escapes me. When she angles her lips toward his mouth, Lex's face flashes with annoyance and he puts a hand up to block her.

"Out," he barks.

"Sorry," I say. I'm obviously intruding on an intimate moment, and I don't even know why I'm still standing here, torturing myself. I have no right to be jealous over a man I don't even know. I begin turning toward the door.

"Not you, luv" he says in a softer tone. His voice hardens again as he addresses the nude woman. "You, Ana. Now."

"You have serious intimacy issues, Lex." Ana scoffs. Ignoring his request, she trails her fingers down his toned abs toward his waistband, reaching for his zipper. Lex's hand flashes out and catches her wrist, causing her to screech in pain.

"I told you not to *fucking* touch me," he says. His accent is even more pronounced with his angry, carefully articulated words. A tingle goes down my spine. This is a hint of his darker side, and I'm captivated.

When he releases his grip on her wrist, she jumps backward, cradling her hand to her chest in disbelief.

"I told you to leave." Lex finishes his glass of whiskey before entering the room and placing the empty glass atop the fireplace mantel. His body language makes him appear indifferent, but his tight jaw betrays his mood.

Ana dramatically flings her dark hair over her shoulder before snatching her clothes from his bedroom floor. She doesn't even bother to put them on.

"Like I said, serious issues, Lex." She frowns at him before turning her attention to me. She looks me up and down, seeming more concerned than judgemental. "Good luck with him. He'll ruin you, sweetie."

She stomps out of the room in all of her naked glory, slamming the door violently behind her. The force of it causes the chandelier to sway, filling the room with a soft tinkling.

"I'm sorry. I didn't mean to—I shouldn't have..." I begin,

but I'm not sure what to say. My confidence deflates. Why the hell did I think barging in here was a good idea? Finally, I say, "I should've knocked."

"Yes. Probably," he says, stepping closer and eliminating the distance between us. He must've spent the last few days outside, because his olive-brown skin simply glows, and he looks even healthier than he did during our last encounter. I fight to keep my eyes locked on the sharp angles of his face instead of staring at the scars decorating his chest.

"I didn't mean to ruin your frolicking," I say awkwardly, gesturing toward him and the bed.

His lips quirk at the sides. "Frolicking? I'm not certain that's the word I'd use."

"Your entanglement. Engagement. Whatever you want to call it."

"Absolutely nothing happened between Ana and me," he says. "I... belong to another." My eyes widen in surprise. He pours a new glass of whiskey, sipping it nonchalantly, as if he hasn't just pierced my heart with two simple words.

It's not my business, and I shouldn't care. But then why does it hurt so much to hear him say that?

No wonder he rejected me before.

I clear my throat, feigning composure even though he's rattled me. "It's time for me to leave, Lex. I can't stay here any longer. I don't belong here."

"I disagree. But I won't stand in your way if that's truly what you desire."

A lump forms in my throat. I swallow through it and nod.

"Would you like me to check on your bond?" he asks. I'm grateful he's acknowledging our agreement this time, asking for my consent before using his power on me.

"Please," I whisper. I'm scared that if I try to say anything else I'll lose hold of my facade.

Lex places his glass on the table beside me and steps in front of me as his eyes flutter shut. After a few seconds of silence, his eyes whip back open, and he stares at me with an indescribable intensity.

My breathing increases, and I twist my hands together nervously.

"Fascinating," he says with a smirk. "Are you nervous, luv? And is that a wee bit of jealousy I detect?"

I scowl, refusing to respond. Denying it won't make a difference, not to a vygora. It was a terrible idea letting him read my emotions in this state. Clearly I haven't been making smart decisions around Lex lately.

"You still have a bit of connection with…him." He grimaces, grabbing his whiskey and chugging the remainder before placing the glass back on the table.

"Why is it so hard for you to say his name?" I ask, frowning at his glass. How much whiskey does he drink? "What do you have against him?"

"I have nothing against him."

"Then stop being a dick!" It comes out fiercer than I intended. Despite my growing attraction toward Lex, I'm still protective of Dash.

"Are you happy with him?" Lex asks, catching me off guard. I search for any sarcasm or mockery but find none. It seems like a sincere question.

"We only met a few weeks ago, and we haven't had the easiest time together," I reply truthfully. "We haven't really gotten the chance to be happy together, but I think we *could* be, and I'd like to try."

Lex turns away from me, approaching his dresser and snatching a silky shirt. He puts it on, leisurely taking his time with each button before replying. His voice is strained as he says, "Well, then I think it is time for you to return to Hakran."

I'm relieved he relented without a fight, but I'm also disappointed he's letting me walk away so easily. Lex is an entirely unpredictable man, and he constantly perplexes me.

I have to remind myself that he's taken, that there isn't anything between us other than a weird vygora connection. Even though that's a lie.

"How long until the bond's broken entirely?" I ask, my voice slicing through the tension.

"It's faded a good amount since you've left. It's still there, but it's very weak. As long as you keep your physical distance from *Dash,* it should disappear entirely soon." He retreats to the balcony, leaning over the railing and gazing across the lake.

I follow him, admiring the landscape before us. On the other side of the water, mountains climb into the clouds. It looks almost fake, the blue of the sky too vibrant, the water too calm. Nevaris truly is a stunning little place, and I've grown fond of the fresh air here. I'll miss the little things like the sounds of farm animals and the way the breeze chills my skin, carrying earthy scents of fish, pine, and wildflowers. I'll especially miss Fara's strudel.

Part of me wishes I would've spent more time enjoying the scenery instead of hiding away in the apartment, but another part of me is glad I didn't get any more attached to the little village.

"Will I be able to visit?" I ask. "With Dash and Ilona?" I pull my attention away from the lake and catch his expression twisting into something sorrowful.

"You're always welcome here, Astrid." His eyes soften, and something lingers between us, a static charge in the air.

Even though I initially thought I was attracted to him because of his vygora powers, it's more than that. Since the moment I met him in the pit, even when he was weak and dirty, something inexplicable has been pulling me toward him.

It's different from my connection with Dash. Dash irritated me at first, then he dug his way into my heart with his good looks and charm. He's fun and lighthearted, but I constantly worry about what he thinks of me.

With Lex, I can be myself. It's like he accepts the darkness inside of me without judgment because it mirrors his own. We both live in the shadows. Being around him is exhilarating and calming at the same time.

It's unfair to compare the two men. They're not in any sort of competition, and they're both incredible in their own way, and they bring out different sides of me.

Nevaris is not my home, and Lex is nothing more than a stranger. A *taken* stranger. One who will never be more than a friend. I simply helped him, and he returned the favor.

Next time I visit, with Ilona and Dash, everything will be back to normal and Lex and I will laugh about this.

"Are you ready to go?" he asks, interrupting my thoughts as he rolls up his sleeves.

"Yes." *No.*

We leave the room and head downstairs into the foyer, walking past the chaise where a still naked Ana sits on Callan's lap. They laugh about something together.

I guess she didn't take Lex's rejection to heart. Good for her.

Lo leans against the front door, talking quietly with Sora. She offers me an apologetic smile, her eyes shifting between Ana and me.

Does she think there's something between Lex and me? Did she think whatever was going on between Lex and Ana would bother me? It neither involves me nor affects me, especially since Lex is *taken*.

Except that, well, it does bother me. It's not supposed to, and Lo is certainly not supposed to think so, but my chest burns at the thought of Lex belonging to someone else.

Sora's calculating gaze meets mine, and he narrows his eyes, scowling, before adjusting the dagger attached to his leather pants. *Okay then.*

I wonder what exactly it is that the harbingers do. I still never figured out Lex's deal here.

"Leaving already?" Callan says as he plays with Ana's hair. The pretty brunette lets him, smiling sweetly. I wonder if it's common for them to share women.

"Yes," I confirm.

"Will you return?" he asks, smiling hopefully. Something familiar flickers inside of me, but I tamp it down, chalking it up to nerves.

"I don't know yet." And it's the truth. I'd like to bring Ilona and Dash, but I don't know what's going to happen when I return to Hakran. I'm not sure if my new role as queen will allow me time to step away from the island.

"Did the big bad Lex scare you away? This one is nicer," Ana says, slapping Callan on the chest. She giggles. "You can give him a go when I'm done."

"No thanks," I say. Lex growls and glares at Ana. Callan whispers something in her ear, and her face pales as she mutters an apology to me.

The dynamics of their little friend group is getting stranger by the minute.

I stride toward the door, but Lo doesn't budge. She continues leaning against it as she whispers something to Sora, who shakes his head aggressively.

"Don't," he says, the single word slicing through the air. Lo shrugs.

"I need to show you something before you go," she says.

"Loisia," Sora hisses, glancing at me. "Terrible idea."

Lex remains impassive but refuses to meet my eyes.

Callan lifts Ana off his lap, swatting her on the ass. "Time for you to go, gorgeous."

She mockingly pouts, but when she notices Callan is no longer smiling, she locates her clothes and gets dressed. Everyone ignores her as she waves and trots out the door.

"It's up to Lex," Callan says to Lo and Sora, who are staring each other down heatedly.

"You know it's a mistake," Sora says. "Lo needs to respect that."

"Maybe we need to let her make her own decision," Lo grits out. Three sets of eyes swing my way, but Lex continues to look anywhere but my direction. "Have you even told her anything?"

I *knew* they were keeping something from me. I scrutinize Lex, realizing how utterly exhausted he looks. He's as devastatingly handsome as ever, the epitome of grace, but there's something hollow in his expression, a sadness in his eyes that I've recognized from the moment I met him.

"Stop talking as if I'm not here," I say, a sense of foreboding building in my stomach. "Does this have something to do with why my mother locked you up?"

"Yes," Lex says. He strokes his jaw, finally looking at me.

"Who *are* you?" I ask him straight up this time, sick of the games. I want answers. "If not royalty, then what?"

"I am Lexyll," he says simply, "God of War."

I wait for him to give me something else. The room seems to

hold its breath, waiting for my reaction. After a beat, I burst out laughing.

"*God* of war?" I choke out between laughs. Irritation flashes in Lex's eyes, and Sora pins a death stare on Lo, who continues to eye me with pity. When no one joins in with the laughter—not even Callan, who scratches the back of his head and frowns—I realize it's not a joke.

I stop laughing, and Lex cocks his head, waiting for me to respond. Slowly, things fall into place. It all starts to make sense:

How quickly Lex recovered after being in the pit.

His power display in the throne room.

How I can't use my powers on him.

How the villagers adore and fear him.

"And you three are his harbingers," I say incredulously, waving toward Callan, Lo, and Sora. "What the hell does that mean?"

"Harbingers of Death." Sora's voice is low and methodical as he answers. "Yes."

"We're warriors. We lead Lex's legions," Lo says.

Legions.

Of course Lex—the god of *war*—has legions.

But where the hell were they while he was trapped in Mother's pit? It doesn't make sense.

"I thought you were a vygora," I say stupidly.

"Technically, I am," Lex says. "That's the type of magic that flows in my blood."

"But you're a *god*." I still can't get over the revelation.

"Only a few of us remain alive these days, but we exist." He rubs his brow, as if he's annoyed. "All power comes from gods and goddesses."

"Holy shit, are you—are we related?" I ask, horrified. If Lex is a god, one with similar power, does that mean I'm one of his offspring? Is that why my magic reacted the way it did to him? Oh goddess, if that's the case, I totally read our vibe the wrong way.

My face pales, and I feel like I'm going to faint.

Lo mumbles something under her breath, shaking her head while Callan barks a laugh that echoes through the foyer. Even Sora's brows rise in interest as he takes in my question.

"Absolutely not." Lex's green eyes sparkle with amusement. "I have no children."

"Just tell her, Lex," Lo murmurs. Sora elbows her in the side, and she grunts. Callan shakes his head.

"Tell me what?"

"Astrid—" Lex runs a hand across his jaw, as if he's searching for the words.

"Aife," Lo interjects.

"Excuse me?" I ask, bewildered.

"Aife," she says, "is your real name. Not Astrid."

My breath catches in my throat, and my mouth goes dry.

Impossible.

I have no idea who she's talking about, but it's not me. She's wrong. I am Astrid Lucille Sylano, Princess of Hakran.

Aren't I?

CHAPTER TWENTY-FIVE

The five of us stand unmoving, waiting for someone to speak.

"Lo is right," Lex finally says with a seriousness that deeply unsettles me. "You *are* Aife. Goddess of Death. The Deathbringer. And you belong here in Nevaris."

Deathbringer? Goddess? I can't vocalize any of my thoughts, because I'm completely stunned.

The others watch me cautiously, and after a long minute of processing, I double over in laughter once again. "Unbelievable. You hate Dash so much that you're trying to trick me into staying here, away from him, with the most ridiculous story I've ever heard? And you couldn't think of a better name for me than the one I gave my horse?" Narrowing my eyes at Lex, I shake my head angrily.

Callan raises a hand. "Orrrr maybe Lex hates Dash because he's sleeping with his—" Lex exhales loudly, cutting Callan off, and shoots a look that tells him to shut up. Callan shrugs. "What? It's true."

Sora sighs, muttering under his breath about how ridiculous this is. Lo trots into a room on my right. There's a scraping noise and a loud bang, and then she returns carrying a gold-framed painting.

"Here," she says, turning it toward me.

The two people in the painting look identical to Lex and me. In the portrait, we stand side by side, looking equally fierce. My hair flows around my shoulders in the image, but those teal eyes and that round face are unmistakably mine.

"What is this?" I ask quietly.

"The truth," Lex says.

"No." I shake my head violently. "No. You had someone paint that after I arrived."

I glance at each person, waiting for someone to crack and admit it's all an elaborate joke. A ploy to keep me here in Nevaris for some reason.

"I'm sorry," Lo says. She worries her bottom lip between her teeth. "Maybe Sora was right. You weren't ready for the truth."

"No shit," Sora says, glaring at her.

"I know who I am, and it's not this Aife person," I say, my voice cracking. "I'm sorry if you thought I was, but I'm not. I remember my whole life on Hakran. I've never even left the island." I chuckle again. Another realization strikes me, inciting a bit of anger. "Lex, were we... *together?* What the fuck were you doing with Ana?" Out of all the questions I have, that's the one that slips out.

Callan has the good sense to look bashful as he scratches his neck. "Eh, that was my fault actually. I sent her up with the intention to *relax* Lex."

"You seem jealous," Lo adds thoughtfully. "That's a good sign!"

"Nothing happened with Ana," Lex says, pinning me with a dark look.

"Even if it did, Lex has nothing to apologize for," Sora cuts in.

"I have always been loyal to you, Aife," Lex murmurs, a pained look on his face. "When I went searching for you, I had no idea that you'd have a life of your own. That you'd no longer have our memories." His eyes shine with sorrow, as if it hurts him to admit these things out loud.

"Sora's right. You don't owe me any apologies." I sigh. "Like I said, I'm not your... whatever. I *do* have plenty of memories— memories of my entire life, from childhood and beyond. I'm not Aife."

"Those are false memories. Enira planted them, manipulated your real ones," Lex informs me. Bile rises in my throat.

Impossible.

I've lived on Hakran for as long as I can remember. Except, when I try to think back, I don't recall much other than a few prominent memories—such as murdering Ilona's mother. I know my past, know the story of my life, but I can't picture it. I can't recall any significant moments.

"What do you remember about your life, luv?" Lex asks, with an unexpected tenderness.

"Everything!" I want to shake Lex until he realizes how ludicrous this is.

"Do you truly? Are your memories specific, or are they hazy?"

"When I was little, I killed Ilona's mother by accident."

"And what happened after?"

"Mother took Ilona in." I try to think back, to remember exactly what happened, but it's jumbled. I can't conjure the same prominent image as I could with Ilona's mother's death.

"What else? What else do you remember?"

"Plenty of things." I scoff. But when I fail to picture any specific days or events, I begin to panic. The blood drains from my face, and I begin to consider that Lex is telling the truth. A tear breaks free, trailing down my cheek. "What happened to my memories?"

"Enira," Sora says, crossing his arms and leaning against a pillar.

I swallow the lump in my throat. Something Lex said echoes through my head: *"She has something that belongs to me. Something I came to retrieve."*

Was that something *me?* Was he searching for me all along?

"Why would my mother do that?" I hate how weak my voice comes out.

"Enira is *not* your mother," Lo says softly. "She's the Goddess of Deception."

"Is everyone a fucking god or goddess all of a sudden?" I say, throwing my hands up.

"I'm not." Callan beams and raises a hand before pointing to Lo and Sora. "They're not either."

Lex shakes his head before speaking. "Years ago, Enira found our village and began using her power to manipulate our people—good people who didn't deserve their fates in her hands. She sought to make a home filled with pawns. To play with however she desired. But you bartered with her behind my back, and struck a deal to protect Nevaris. I didn't know it at the time. Enira broke her hold over Nevaris's people and simply disappeared one day, but so did you." He rubs his forehead. "I searched everywhere, discovering Enira in Hakran shortly afterward. What she failed to do in Nevaris, she succeeded to do in Hakran.

"She constructed an elaborate illusion where she can act out all of her wicked fantasies. Enira is the biggest narcissist. Being a goddess isn't enough. She wishes to be *the* goddess, and she will do anything to pretend that she is. She wanted a throne, a city, then more power, but it's never enough for her. She wants to command everything and everyone. When I came looking for you, she used my one weakness against me to subdue me and lock me in the pit. Even the powers of gods can't penetrate silenxstone."

His one weakness.

Me.

"You loved me." For some reason the thought of being loved, truly loved so deeply by Lex that he'd sacrifice his freedom, is like a punch to the gut. It hurts, but at the same time it consumes me entirely. My chest tightens.

"As if you care," Sora says, scowling. "You hated him." I wait for Lex to deny it, but he doesn't.

"We wanted to look for you." Lo changes the subject, making a rude gesture at Sora. "But Lex bound us by oath not to follow him when he went searching for you. He prevented us from leaving, from using the legions for anything other than Nevaris's protection. As his harbingers, we had to oblige those wishes, no matter how unfair or *idiotic"* —she rolls her eyes— "they were."

"Asinine," Sora says.

"But my horse's name is Aife," I mumble, still in some sort of shock.

"You probably remembered your real name somewhere in your subconscious," Callan says, offering me a half-smile. "Maybe deep down you still have your memories."

"Callan's right. Your true memories are likely still intact," Lo says. "I don't think they were erased but buried beneath the illusions Enira planted in your mind."

"Maybe," Sora says. He mindlessly fingers a jagged scar on his neck, but when he catches me staring, he adjusts his black turtleneck so the old wound is covered, then glowers at me.

I turn to Lex. "You kept this from me, Lex."

"You wouldn't have believed me. I was hoping if you returned home to Nevaris, that you would regain your memories. I was giving you time to recall your life on your own without interference."

"Was anything you told me the truth? About Paramour Falls? My bond with Dash?"

"All of it." Lex's eyes spark with anger, but he keeps it under control. "I have *never* lied to you."

"But you didn't tell me the whole truth either."

"I'm telling you now!" He yells. It's the second time I've seen him enraged—the first when Ana touched him. "It's only been *five* days since I was freed from that damned prison cell, and for three of them, you've ignored me entirely. Be realistic, Aife."

"It's *Astrid*," I spit. Misplaced nostalgia slices through me at hearing him call me Aife. Even without my memories, something inside me responds to his words. I've had these unexplainable feelings ever since I came to Nevaris, like I've dreamt about this place before. It's familiar yet unknown at the same time. "You were just going to let me go? Let me walk away after all that time you spent looking for me?"

"You don't even remember me," Lex says, his voice cracking. "You said you could be happy with Dash."

"Plus, you hate Lex," Sora mutters, raising a brow.

"Shut the fuck up," Callan says, crossing over to Sora and punching his shoulder. Sora reaches for his dagger, but Lo's hand flies out, stopping him before he can unsheath it.

"Can you two just…not?" Lo asks the two men. "Not right now."

I stare at Lex, ignoring the other three. "You really thought I'd be better off with the woman who manipulated me for years? You were just going to hand me back over to her?" It's almost impossible to comprehend I have a lifetime of false memories and the woman I've called Mother isn't really my mother at all. But then again…the more I think about it, the more it makes sense.

Enira has never seemed maternal toward me. She's easily used and disregarded me.

How could Lex let her have me if what he's saying is true?

Lex's hands ball into fists as he struggles to remain impassive. "It's not about what I want. It's about what *you* want. What you need." Without another word, he exits the foyer, entering into one of the side rooms. Lo chases after him, telling me to wait. Sora grumbles to himself.

"The good news is we have spies stationed in Hakran now," Callan says. "I'm thrilled to report that Enira was successfully imprisoned by the Vannyks. Her powers are snuffed out with the silenxstone. With the direct line to your mind broken, she can no longer control you, and there's a chance your original memories could return."

"Shouldn't they have already returned if her magic is subdued?" I ask.

"Eh," Callan says. "Maybe it takes time?"

"They might never return," Sora says, contradicting Callan's optimism. "There are rumors she has an additional power source backing up her magic. But that's unconfirmed at this time."

"Unreal," I say, closing my eyes and rubbing my temples. After a pause to collect my thoughts, I address Sora. "You said we hated each other?"

He snorts, regarding me through narrowed eyes. "One of *you* lacked love and respect."

"Then why did he come for me?"

"Because we cannot allow *Enira* to control the Goddess of Death." He shakes his head in disbelief. "You were a liability under her influence. Liabilities must be neutralized."

Neutralized?

"As in killed? Are you saying Lex would've killed me if I

hadn't broken free of Enira's hold?" I shake my head. "No way."

"Aife, look—" Callan runs a hand through his golden hair.

"Yes," Sora says.

Unfuckingbelievable.

"I need to return to Hakran," I choke out after a moment of silence.

"Relax," Callan says. "Sora's just a cranky fucker. He's still pissed about the time you almost beheaded him. Lex would never hurt you. *Never.* No matter what." Callan gives Sora a rude gesture.

Sweet relief washes over me. But...wait. "I tried to behead Sora?" My eyes dart back to Sora's, and his fingers absentmindedly reach up to the collar hiding that hideous scar.

"For good reason." Callan laughs. "He totally deserved it." Sora doesn't respond, but his eyes darken.

"Either way, I need to return to Hakran," I say, bringing us back to the most important topic.

"Please don't go, Aife," Lo calls out as she returns with Lex.

"It's *Astrid,*" I snap. She flinches at my tone. "I appreciate you telling me the truth, if that's what it even is, but I have no memories of this. Hakran still needs a leader—they are still my people. I have a duty to them. And I can't leave Ilona alone."

"You're not meant for mere queendom. You're a warrior—a goddess. Deathbringer," Callan says, as if he's trying to convince me not to go.

"*You're a slaughterer,*" Dash's words ring in my mind. He said he hadn't meant those words—he was only trying to piss me off at the falls—but he was right. What would he think of my true identity? Will he accept me as a goddess of *death?*

I don't think he will, but even so, I'll need to tell him. Withholding information is essentially the same as lying. It's a form of manipulation, and I've had enough deception to last a lifetime. The last thing I want is more secrets hovering over me.

"I'm still leaving." Lex nods, his body rigid as he heads out the front door with Sora and Lo on his heels.

Callan waits until they're out of sight, then reaches out and taps my shoulder. "For what it's worth, Lex *never* hated you. He loved you—*still* loves you. Don't listen to anything Sora says. He's a coldblooded bastard who wouldn't know love if it punched him in the dick." He doubles over in laughter. "You two never got along."

With that, he heads out the door.

Lex never looked at me with loathing. Even during the few times he was short with me, I never sensed any animosity there.

Why would it matter to him whether or not I'm happy with Dash? Or that I'm safe and protected? Why else would he despise Dash so much?

Of course the man still loves me.

Lex offered me a place to stay and brought me clothes and food. He didn't take advantage of me even when I was clearly open to exploring the connection between us. He could've but he didn't, because he knew when I found out the truth, I'd hate him for it.

Despite Callan telling me not to worry about Sora's words, I can't help but wonder: Did I truly hate Lex? Why?

I wish with my entire being that I could remember Lex. My heart breaks for him—the man I don't know. I don't find it in me to be angry at him for not telling me the truth immediately, especially since he was right; I never would've believed him.

Even though I'm Astrid now, it proves he still knows me well. Perhaps Aife and Astrid aren't that far removed.

CHAPTER TWENTY-SIX

Within the hour, I'm making my way back through the tunnel to Hakran, with Lex and his harbingers leading the way. I learn from Lo that the tunnel is powered by etheryn magic. That's what enables us to traverse across immeasurable distances with ease. I'm still unsure of where exactly Nevaris is. It's nestled into mountains and covered with conifers, so I assume somewhere north, on the mainland, but I can't recall much about mainland geography. I've explored every inch of Hakran—the island isn't that big—but nothing beyond.

Lex shares that the Vannyks likely don't know that Enira and I are goddesses. He also claims to have overheard them speaking in the pit. They aren't willing to kill her out of fear of losing their throne. That's what I was hoping for previously, but now, I want the bitch dead. If they won't do it, I'll do it myself.

After I get answers from her.

I don't care what Ilona, the Vannyks, or anyone else thinks. This is between Enira and me.

As we near the end of the tunnel, Lex asks to read my emotions one last time. Callan, Lo, and Sora go on ahead, giving us a moment of privacy.

It takes Lex no time at all to pull my emotions toward him.

"The bond is very weak." He runs a thumb over his bottom

lip, refusing to look at me. "It should fade entirely soon. Perhaps even by the time you're back at the palace."

Since I met him, I've thought of Lex as calm and collected, when really, he's a man in pain. Now that I know the truth, I see it in the way his jaw locks up. The way his eyes focus on one spot for far too long. The way his sentences are sometimes short and clipped.

"I'm sorry," I whisper. It's an apology for everything and nothing all at once.

"He's a lucky man." He finally looks at me, and his gaze is electrifying. "You are the most beautiful woman I've ever known. Truly beautiful, all the way down to your core."

My stomach twists at his words, and gratitude clogs my throat. There's no way I could ever hate a man like Lex. I don't believe it.

"I have to tell Dash who I really am," I say, feeling the urge to open up to Lex. "I don't expect him to be thrilled that I'm a goddess of death."

"*The*. You are *the* goddess of death."

"Even worse! I'm a one of a kind slaughterer!" I scoff, throwing my hands up. A bit of rage builds inside of me, a faint reminder of my now-fading bond with Dash.

"You are not a slaughterer, Astrid," he says, calling me by the name I know best. I appreciate him for it. He reaches out, gently rubbing my shoulder and my skin tingles beneath his touch. I shudder, hoping he doesn't notice. "You do not kill for sport or fun. You are a warrior, a ruthless protector of the people you love. Deathbringer to those who threaten the people you've sworn to protect. Even if you choose to protect Hakran now instead of Nevaris."

"Wording it differently doesn't change the reality of what I am," I whisper.

He steps forward, cupping my jaw and forcing me to look up at him through my tears. "In that case, you are a vicious, ruthless murderer."

When he smiles, I chuckle in return. "Gee thanks for the confirmation."

"You're right. Wording it differently doesn't change the reality of who you are. Labels won't change anything about you. Dash should love you more *because* of who you are, not despite who you are. If he doesn't, then he's the wrong man for you."

My heart pounds fiercely as Lex strokes my cheek with his thumb. Neither of us makes an effort to pull away.

Something raw and electrifying pulses between us, and I want to wrap my arms around him—to pull him close and cry into his shirt while he holds me. I cried in front of Dash, but it was because of my out of control magic.

This feels different. Much more real.

It's further proof that the memory of Lex lives somewhere deep inside of me. I *know* this man. I simply don't remember him.

"Why did Sora say I hated you?" I ask.

Lex's brows tighten together, and he curses under his breath. "We've... I've made mistakes."

"Were they unforgivable?"

"That's not for me to decide." His eyes darken as they roam every inch of my face.

"I'm sick of everyone being so cryptic."

"Aren't you fed up with everyone creating their own narrative for you?" he asks, his voice a low rumble, sending prickles down my spine. "Of everyone telling you who you are?"

"Yes."

His face softens at my answer. "That's precisely why I give you the answers I do." He reaches out, tenderly grabbing my hand, and I interlace our fingers together on instinct. A shock-wave courses through me where our skin meets. "I refuse to lie to you, but I also refuse to tell you *my* truth. I can't risk influencing your narrative with my biased perceptions of the past. You need to discover your own truth."

Tears well in my eyes, and I look away, trying to avoid the soft glow of light from the orb in his other hand.

"Do you know the hardest part about this goodbye?" he asks. I shake my head, wanting him to continue. "That it's only tempo-rary, but that I don't know when we'll meet again. It wrecks me to wonder whether you'll remember me. Remember *us*."

I crack, and the tears finally burst free, streaming down my face. "You think we'll see each other again?"

His face morphs into a kind smile, one that makes him look younger, softer. "I'll make sure of it."

I remember the pain in his voice when he said Enira took something that belonged to him—something that mattered greatly to him. And my first day in Nevaris, he said he lost something he loved and didn't want what happened to him to happen to me.

He won't force me to choose him, even though it clearly hurts him to let me go. He's letting me choose Dash, Ilona, and my people, because he knows that it would tear me apart to lose them.

I step closer to him, brushing my chest against his. My head tilts up. Lex might fool everyone with his detachment, but he doesn't fool me. The man feels everything I do—probably more.

He lets the orb of light crash to the ground and grazes my collarbone with his fingers. Goosebumps rise on my arms, and my body hums with energy.

It's thrilling.

I want more.

"Lex," I whisper. A hungry look crosses his face, and everything around us disappears as his mouth slowly starts on the journey toward mine. I ache for him to close the gap. To use his lips to *make* me remember him. I want him to kiss me senseless, until I don't care whether I'm Astrid or Aife. I want to be so blinded by love, or lust, or whatever this is that I choose to stay with him.

I crave his kiss, his touch, because I know it will change everything.

It doesn't matter why I hated Lex before. I don't care if he ruined me—if he turned everything I held dear to ash. In this moment, I'd willingly let him destroy me again, because I know he wouldn't leave me broken.

He'd help me rebuild stronger than ever.

That's the kind of man I know Lex is, deep in my heart.

Right before our lips meet, Callan's voice rings through the tunnel. "Are you two coming or what?" It startles us, and we jolt, ripping apart.

The connection we had a moment ago is still there, but it's been spoiled by the interruption. Lex clears his throat, grabbing his light from the ground. "Would you like me to accompany you to the palace?" he asks, his voice pained.

"No." I sigh. It's something I need to do on my own. I almost lost myself in Lex a second ago. I was close to letting it happen. But I'm glad nothing happened—at least not yet. The last thing I want to do is lead Lex on or hurt Dash unnecessarily.

There are things I need to figure out first.

"Thanks for your help, Lex." We stand there in the too-small tunnel, still not quite knowing how to say goodbye.

For a moment, I harbor one last hope that Lex will grab me and pull me into a soul-shattering goodbye kiss. I'm partly disappointed when he doesn't, partly relieved that he has such incredible self-control. Goddess knows I'm hanging on by a thread right now.

We make it to the exit and emerge into the sticky heat. I'm grateful Lex gave me something thinner and cooler to wear before returning.

"Ugh," I say as my face flushes. The familiar scents of rich earth and salty air fill my nose.

"Sure you don't want to come back to Nevaris?" Lo asks, grinning sadly. She pulls me into a hug, and I don't fight it. Apparently, I'm turning into a hugger. Deathbringer and hugger, who would've thought? "Don't give up on him." Releasing me, she smiles one last time before heading back into the tunnel.

Sora watches her go, then turns to grimace at me before heading after Lo.

"I know you'll be back," Callan says, blinding me with his too-perfect smile and patting me on the head. "I know it. You are going to remember everything. I can't wait." He heads to the tunnel, stopping to take in the vivid scenery. The jungle is drenched in every imaginable hue of green, with flecks of vibrant color scattered about. Even the cave is covered in green moss, camouflaged almost entirely.

Callan whistles. "Damn this place is wild." He nods at Lex before leaving the two of us to our farewells.

Once we're alone, Lex reaches into his pocket and pulls something out, handing it to me. It's small and smooth. I turn the stone over in my palm, wondering exactly what it's for. It's pale blue, almost grey, with flecks of white, and it's attached to a thin black string. A smile grazes my lips at the unexpected gift, and I immediately slip it over my head and tuck it into the neckline of my shirt, letting it fall safely between my breasts.

"Celestite," he says. "They're new. I had Callan forage for them." He tugs on a black string around his own neck, revealing an identical stone, one I hadn't seen him wearing earlier at Harmony House. "If you ever need me, rub your stone between your palms. Mine will heat up in response, and I'll know to come to you."

"And what if you need me?" I tease half-heartedly.

"We both know I'll always need you before you need me." He gazes at me with so much affection that I can't breathe.

I don't reply because I can't.

It stings.

Now that I've seen the truth, I can't unsee it. Walking away from Lex pains me, but I do it anyway. Not because I want to but because I need to.

I need to figure out myself—my past and my future—without the distractions and temptations of Lex and Nevaris.

Maybe one day I'll return.

Without another glance back, I begin my trek west, toward the palace.

CHAPTER TWENTY-SEVEN

I never imagined leaving Lex behind would be so incredibly difficult. It's a wound inside of me, ripping wider with each step.

I'm no longer denying my attraction to him or blaming it on circumstance. I wish my memories would return as badly as he does. I wish it were that simple.

Lex is tortured. I knew it the moment we locked eyes in the pit. I've always seen the glimmer of a threat inside of him. But even through his own anguish, he's willing to sacrifice his happiness for my own.

I finger the cord around my neck, vowing not to use the stone to bother him. Not unless I can commit to him. He doesn't deserve for me to lead him on, and until I can figure out my place in Hakran and acquire my missing memories, I need to leave him be. I need to discover who I am before I can give a piece of myself to him.

Shaking off those bleak thoughts, I trek through familiar vines and bushes, finding one of the many worn dirt paths that will lead me to the palace.

I'm relieved Enira is imprisoned and the Vannyks have been working to reinstate peace among Hakran. They have the people's trust now, and that should only make my transition into power easier. If I can win the Vannyks over, they will back my claim to the throne, encouraging the people to do the same. Except...the thought of ruling Hakran doesn't fill me with peace or elation. It feels all wrong.

I'm not a princess. Not meant to be a queen. I'm a goddess, even though I don't really know what that entails. It's like I'm a child playing dress up, and I don't quite fit into the gowns.

Hakran was never mine to rule.

But at the same time, these people still mean something to me. I can't leave them to fend for themselves. Many of them are impoverished, struggling, and without a ruler, it might only get worse. I need to help them find their footing and rebuild. I owe it to them to see this through.

Finally I emerge from the overgrowth, sticky with sweat. The palace sparkles, looking like a mirage against the bright green backdrop of the jungle. It's so bright that I have to squint before averting my eyes altogether.

I can't wait to see Ilona and Dash.

Oh *Dash*.

Even though I don't know what I'm going to say to him. Our time together was wonderful, but it was fleeting. I still hold affection for him, but I expect he won't feel the same when I tell him who I really am. Plus, with Lex in the picture, it's... complicated now.

Hell, I'm even excited to see Marnie, Zale, and Gi—

Gianna. Poor, sweet Gianna.

She definitely did not deserve her fate, and that's a guilt I will carry for the rest of my life.

I head toward the palace entrance, opulent curved doors made of gold, and I notice an abnormal number of guards milling around the property. None are wearing face coverings any longer, and most appear to be from Stellari, but a good number of Hakranians are sprinkled in among them.

I wonder what the Vannyks did with those who stayed loyal to Enira after being freed from her manipulation. Are they beside her in the pit? I can't imagine the Vannyks would harm them, but they also couldn't have let them go free.

"Princess?" a guard yells. "Princess Astrid?"

"Thank the goddess. She's alive! Someone get the king."

"I'm fine," I say to whoever's listening. "There's no need to bother King Emman." He must be in charge temporarily, waiting for me to return. I bet he's eager to tend to his own country; that might be a further incentive for him to support my claim to the throne.

I enter the palace just in time to see Dash bolting through the corridor. The sharp angles of his face are contorted with concern and disbelief.

"Dash!" I rush toward him, and in a flash, he's crushing me to his chest. His sandalwood scent washes over me. He's warm, comforting. I missed him more than I realized.

"I thought I lost you," he whispers, peppering kisses into my hair.

"Lost me?" It hits me suddenly that Dash might have thought something sinister happened to me. After all, I never sent word that I was okay.

"Did he touch you?" Dash asks, backing up and assessing my state. "Are you hurt, sweetheart?"

My stomach clenches at his term of endearment, but not the same way it used to.

Gripping his hands, I shake my head. "I'm not hurt."

"I'll kill that sonuvabitch," he growls.

"I'm fine," I say. "He didn't hurt me. He helped me."

Dash looks taken aback. "What do you mean he *helped*

you?" He lowers his voice, probably in an attempt to keep our conversation private despite the numerous lurking guards. I eye them warily. Although the presence of so many Stellari guards is to be expected after what happened with Enira and her followers, I still don't like it.

"I'll explain everything. Where's Ilona?" I'd rather explain it to my two best friends at the same time.

"She's—" Dash sighs, scratching his neck.

"Don't you dare tell me something has happened to her, Dashiel Dargan," I warn, releasing his hands and stepping back. Tears pool in my eyes.

"Not like that. She's fine. It's just that—" He pauses, and relief courses through me. She's fine. "Enira told her you...you killed her mother?" It comes out as a question, and I cringe.

Enira told Ilona I killed her mother.

That bitch.

My memory of that event is clearly false; I was never here as a young girl. I never could've killed Ilona's mother... At least not how I remember. Enira likely fabricated the entire story, but until I acquire my memories, I can't promise Ilona with unwavering certainty that I didn't do it.

I don't know what I did as Aife. Who I killed as Deathbringer.

"No," I say, exhaling the word. Ilona will *never* forgive me for keeping such a secret. It doesn't matter if the memory was planted. There was a time I believed it to be true and purposely hid it from her.

I've been played by the goddess of deception, and even now, when she's deep in the pit without her magic, we're still pawns in her game.

"I told Ilona that it can't be true," Dash says. "That it's nothing more than a desperate ploy for Enira to manipulate her, but

I worry she believes it. She's secluded herself in her room, away from everyone except that kitchen girl."

"And Enira?" I'm relieved Ilona at least has Marnie and isn't alone in all of this. I need to see her, explain what happened.

I can't lose her.

Even if our pasts are manufactured, some of our time together was real. I know her, and she knows me.

Dash's brow furrows, probably because I called Enira by her first name rather than *Mother* or *queen.*

"She's in the pit," he says carefully. "Half of her guard rebelled against us, despite being released from her hold. They seem to truly believe she's a good, just queen. We're holding them in the old prison off the coast for now, but Enira is here in the pit. Not many lives were lost, but it was… We can talk about it later. First, I need you to tell me what happened with that bastard."

"Lex," I say. "His name is Lex, and he isn't a bastard."

Dash snorts in disbelief. "Please don't tell me you went with him willingly after what he did to your people. You're not that stupid, Astrid."

"*Excuse* me?"

"I didn't mean it like that." He rubs his temples. "I only meant that you must've had a good reason for leaving."

"I want to talk about it with both you and Ilona, but—" I also need to talk to Ilona about her mother before I bombard her with any of my own grievances. "Can we go somewhere, just the two of us so I can explain?"

Nodding, Dash grabs my hand and leads me through the hallway. I vaguely recognize some of the guards milling around. Some of them look at me with fondness, while others scowl. All of them incline their heads with a show of respect as we pass though.

"Dash?" I ask quietly. "Are the people—does everyone think I am as bad as Enira?"

He curses under his breath. "They know who you are, Astrid, and many are not happy. They saw you kill that little girl's father in the throne room during the storm."

They know who you are.

I want to laugh at the absurdity. They only *think* they know who I am. They've cast a role upon me, just as Enira did.

Bile rises in my esophagus, and I swallow down the bitter taste. How can these people—these strangers—claim to know who I am when *I* don't even know who I am?

They've seen me at my absolute worst and have drawn conclusions about who I am based on that?

"Did anyone have any old memories return?" I ask. Could Ilona possibly have remembered something about her real past?

He looks puzzled. "What do you mean?"

I don't bother responding. If my memories haven't returned, it's safe to assume no one else's have either. And Enira is wickedly smart. She probably switched out the palace staff and guards every few years so she wouldn't *need* to alter their memories. It's possible she only altered the memories of those who have been here for an extended period of time—Jamell, Cedrik, Ilona, and me.

Dash leads me to the library, and I'm grateful for the familiarity of the comfortable space. It's as peaceful as ever.

Does Lex have a library? The books in his spare apartment were entirely to my taste…but of course they were. They very well could've been my books. I'd never live somewhere without books, so I bet Harmony House has a library worth salivating over.

I'm trying not to think about Lex, but it's impossible not to.

Dash grabs a seat in an oversized chair, and I take the one to his left.

"Astrid." He leans forward, resting his elbows on his knees. There are bags under his eyes, and he looks exhausted. "A lot has happened in the few days you've been gone."

I finger the cord around my neck absentmindedly as I wait for him to go on. Instead, his gaze catches on the stone, and he pauses.

"What is that?" he asks.

"Just a stone I like." The lie slips out before I can stop it. He'd hate knowing that Lex gave it to me, and I want to tell him the important things before we get into everything else.

He grimaces. "Lex gave it to you." His voice is flat, and his eyes spark with irritation. It's almost as if he's listening to my—

"I heard the truth in your thoughts."

Dammit.

"How dare you!" I snap.

"I hadn't intended to! Hell, I shouldn't be able to," he says. "What did that bastard do to you?" He kneels in front of my chair, reaching up to cup my cheek in his palm.

"He didn't do anything to harm me, Dash." Sighing, I remove his hand, patting it softly as I grip it tenderly on my lap. "Get that out of your mind. I already told you he *helped* me."

He purses his lips and watches me skeptically. Without hesitation, I relay what Lex told me about the power-sharing bond. I inform him of how power is only meant to be shared between the fated or else it can drive one insane. I tell him the truth about how Anwyr really died, how the bond recharges through intimacy, and how it fades with time and physical distance. I open up about how badly it had hurt me to hear everyone's thoughts, how it put me at risk of harming the people around me—like that poor man in the throne room. I tell him that Lex gave me a safe space to let the bond fade.

But I don't tell him about Lex and me just yet.

"Our bond is broken," I whisper carefully. "If it's not fully gone yet, it will be soon." I'm self-conscious in his presence now that he can hear my thoughts.

"Broken," he repeats. He pulls his hand from my grip and stands before me. I squirm uncomfortably. "So he whisked you away, to what? To save you from *me?* Then he gave you a precious stone to wear? Please don't tell me you're blind to his intentions."

"He has no intentions, Dash. I'm not some poor damsel in distress. It was my decision to step away in order to protect myself—to protect all of you." I leap from the chair, annoyed. And oddly, I find myself grateful it's a regular, mild annoyance rather than the all-consuming rage I experienced last time I was here. I grab the celestite resting on my collarbone. "This is just a way to stay in touch should I ever need assistance."

"You don't need *him* to protect you. I can protect you plenty." He reaches for me, and I swat his hand away.

"Didn't you hear a word I said? I don't need either of you to *protect* me." I pop my hip and place a hand on it. "I'm perfectly capable of looking out for myself."

Lex never made me feel small or weak, but somehow Dash has a knack for it. I freeze up, fearful he's listening. When I glance at him, it appears he is deep in contemplation.

"Are you listening to my thoughts?" I ask nervously.

"Absolutely not." He frowns. "I wouldn't purposely disrespect you like that. Surely you know that by now. I only did it at first when I had to be sure you were pure. I've only ever wanted to protect you." His voice cracks on the last bit.

"Thank you," I say, though I'm filled with uncertainty. I've only been back for a few minutes, and already we've gotten testy with each other. Something has changed between us. It's more than my relationship with Lex. Dash and I built our relationship on lies. It's too easy to mistrust one another. More importantly than that, he could've killed me with his reckless abuse of power sharing; that will always linger over us.

It's hard to trust someone who can freely access my thoughts, especially since he's done it before without permission when it suited his needs. He might mean well, but it puts me at a serious disadvantage in our relationship, and I don't like that.

I caress the celestite, thinking about how Lex said I can learn to use my power as a shield—create a barrier to keep out other vygoras and myndoxes. Until I have my own defense against Dash's abilities, I won't be fully comfortable with him.

Dash watches my fingers trace the necklace, and a crease forms in his forehead.

"I need to speak to Ilona and Cedrik," I say, eager to get to the bottom of all the lies and chaos in my life.

"The healer?" Dash's eyes darken. "I thought you weren't hurt. If that—"

"Stop," I tell him, putting a hand up. "Leave Lex out of this please, Dash. I swear to you he hasn't done anything."

Dash paces before me. "I swear I'm not listening to your thoughts, sweetheart, but I *know* there's something you're not telling me."

"There is," I admit. He pauses, concern written on his face. "Enira isn't my mother." The words tumble out before I can think of the best way to explain. It still seems unreal.

His body visibly relaxes, and a soft chuckle escapes him. "I know."

"What the hell do you mean you *know?*"

"I only learned it the other day." He puts his hands up in a gesture of surrender and flashes me his signature smirk. "Don't attack me. Unless you get naked first."

"You are incorrigible." I laugh, and it lightens the mood slightly. Even though things might not ever be the same between us, I still enjoy his poorly timed humor and cringe-worthy comments. Light-hearted Dash soothes some of my unease.

"I heard it in her thoughts. The woman has some sort of vendetta against you, only I'm not sure why. If it wasn't for your magic, she would kill you, but it's too valuable to her. I don't know who your real family is or how she stole you away from them, but I do know with certainty that Enira is not your mother and she despises you."

He doesn't know how I ended up here.

That means he doesn't have any more answers for me, but he also doesn't know who I am.

Lex said I went behind his back to save Nevaris—Enira never *took* me—but what deal did I strike with her?

Did I offer her access to my power in exchange for her promise to leave Nevaris alone?

Did I *let* her erase my memories? Was that part of our deal?

There has to be more to it.

"How did you apprehend her?" I ask, wondering how the Vannyks managed to outsmart her.

"I mentioned Joccelyn and Cedrik were close friends," he says slowly. "He's been working on a potion for years, one that temporarily mutes magic."

I gasp. "Like how the silenxstone does?"

"Sort of, but it's not as effective. It wears off quickly." He runs a hand through his wavy hair. "Once we woke in the throne room after the storm" —he shoots me an incredulous look but doesn't snipe at Lex or scold me for my murderous outburst— "my family was able to break most of Enira's hold over the people. Some of the guards knew where she was hiding out. They knew how and when she took her meals. We slipped Cedrik's potion into her food, hoping it would work."

"And it did?"

"Well, we combined it with a sleeping potion just in case, which was a smart call. She's immensely powerful, Astrid. More so than we previously thought. She's dangerous. We gave her such a strong dose of the sleeping potion that she should've been knocked out for an entire day. She woke before we even had her cell locked."

I want to yell, "*Of course she's stronger than we expected; she's a fucking goddess!*" But I'm not ready to tell him about who—or what—I am yet.

"You don't want to kill her?" I ask.

"No. But she *will* rot in that pit forever if I have any say in her fate."

"She—she altered some of my memories," I finally tell him, faltering slightly. "At least, that's what Lex thinks."

Dash stares at me with disbelief, squeezing his hands into fists. "And you trust that bastard?"

"What is with you two and the name-calling?"

His eyes narrow as his head tilts to the side. "Oh, so he called me names?"

"What the fuck, Dash. I just told you Enira is not my mother and my memories are missing, and that's what you're worried about?"

"And I told you, I don't trust that dirty prisoner." He pins me with a hard gaze.

"I don't care!" I yell. "I do!"

He flinches as if I've slapped him, his eyes widening in hurt. Dash and I have struggled to build trust for weeks, and here I am, admitting I trust Lex after only a few days with him.

"I need to go."

"Wait," Dash says as I turn to leave. "Don't go. Please."

"I need to talk with Cedrik." If Enira's hold on him broke, he might remember the circumstances of my arrival here. There's a chance he has insight into my true past. I was hoping he might even know of a way to get my memories back.

"He's gone."

"What do you mean *gone?*"

"He accompanied my family back to Stellaris. My father is extremely unwell. His...situation is progressing rapidly. It's at the point where Zale is preparing to inherit the throne very soon. Cedrik returned to help keep him comfortable. He's better than our own healers back home."

"I had no idea," I said, shaking my head. Poor Emman. "Is that why I hadn't seen much of him or Joccelyn while they were here?"

Dash nods, his brows drawn tight. "He has good days and bad days. He's fine on the good days, but the bad days are becoming more frequent. He doesn't want anyone to know he's ill, so he downplays his pain and stays out of sight."

I wrap my arms around Dash, letting him squish me to his muscular chest.

I've definitely turned into a hugger.

"I can't believe you stole my healer," I say when we break apart. "What if someone here gets ill?"

"The village healer is staying in the palace for the time being." He brushes the bangs off my forehead and plants a tender kiss there. "You don't have *any* memories from your real family?" I shrug at him, and he exhales loudly "Do you know how to get them back?"

"That's the key question in my life right now. The silenxstone broke her basic hold over me and most people, but for some reason it didn't mend my memories. Sora said she might have another source of magic."

"Who the hell is Sora?" Dash growls.

"Seriously?" I huff at him. "Since when are you so jealous?"

"Since the woman I love ran off with another man."

Ouch.

Guilt fills my gut, and I hate that I hurt him by leaving, even if it was for the best. I need to hold off on telling him the truth about Lex for a little while longer, until I can sort out the other problems in my life. My guilt overshadows the admission of his love for me, but I can't deal with that right now, so I change the subject.

"If Cedrik isn't here to help me figure out my past, we need to figure out what magic Enira's using to strengthen her hold on me."

"Would it be so bad if you never remembered?"

My eyes narrow at the suggestion. "Yes. Yes it would be. This is my *life* we're talking about."

"You might have a false past, but you can build a real future. Your—Enira, I mean, is imprisoned. You have me."

"I'm getting my memories back, Dash. No matter what it takes."

"Okay. Okay, fine. I understand," he whispers, giving me a soft smile. "I support you with whatever you choose to do."

With everything else happening in this conversation, I almost missed something important.

"Dash..." I begin carefully.

"Yes?"

"You said King Emman left." I narrow my eyes at him, putting the pieces together. The guard outside requested the *king's* presence. "Which king is here?"

His face pales. "It's only temporary. I'm placating the people until you assume your rightful position on the throne."

My eyes flutter shut, and I shake my head vigorously before opening them to glare at him. "Unbelievable. I guess you got what you wanted after all?"

He reaches for me, but I put up a hand and take a step backward. "You know this isn't what I wanted. Not like this. I'm only trying to help. I love you, Astrid."

His words suffocate me. Maybe before the power sharing debacle I would've relished those words. Returned them even. But now they feel all wrong, as ill-timed as his jokes. But instead of laughing, I'm cringing.

When I don't return the words, his dimpled smile drops, and a frown forms in its place. It's the expression of a tired man, a stressed man. One who likely waited sleeplessly for the woman he loves to return.

Only, she returned as a different woman. On the outside I look the same, but on the inside, everything has changed.

Perhaps I'm being unfair to Dash. I don't want to hurt him—he's one of the best men I've ever met. He's attentive and cares deeply for others, but I can't give him what he wants, especially not if I can't trust him.

"I can't do this," I whisper, afraid to meet his eyes. "I need to see Ilona." My heart races as I bolt from the room, desperate to see my best friend and rattled by how wrong Dash's words felt in my ears.

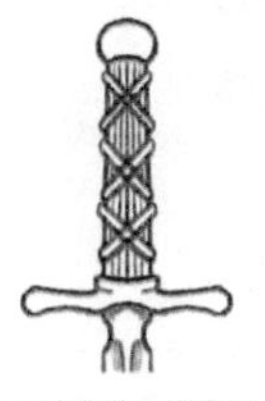

CHAPTER TWENTY-EIGHT

Ilona knows I killed her mother now. It's a secret I've hidden from her our whole lives, but I don't even know if it's true or not. I don't know what to tell my best friend. Until I retrieve my true memories, I'm stuck in a weird limbo. It's a guessing game about what's real and what isn't.

Without pausing to knock on Ilona's door, I burst into her room.

As soon as I enter, she levels a glare at me from where she's sitting on the bed with Marnie.

"You should really lock your door," I say. "Goddess, I've missed you."

Crossing over her white fluffy carpet, I open my arms to embrace her, but she shakes her head and scoots back on her bed, all the way up to the headboard.

Marnie stands, her eyes bouncing between Ilona and me. Marnie's always shown a certain respect toward me, so I doubt she's willing to cause a confrontation, but she looks torn between speaking up and staying quiet.

"Ilona doesn't want to see you," she says quietly. "You shouldn't barge in like that."

"You are in no position to tell me what to do," I say dryly. My lips tighten as I stare her down.

A beat passes, and no one moves.

"Maybe I should just go," Marnie finally says, breaking the awkward silence. Turning to me as she passes, she quietly adds, "Princess Astrid, please, think of what's best for her."

When the door clicks behind me, signaling Marnie's exit, I loudly exhale all the air in my lungs.

"Ilona, please. You're my best friend."

She plays with the edge of her blanket, her big, green eyes welling with tears. "Am I though? Friends don't lie to each other."

"I never lied to you!"

"You killed my fu—mother!" Almost hearing the curse come out of her mouth alerts me to just how livid she is.

"It wasn't like that, Ilona. I don't even think it's true."

Her red curls hang loose around her head, knotted in some sections as if she hasn't run a comb or oils through it in a few days. Purple bags sit like bruises beneath her eyes, and her creamy skin is even paler than normal—almost translucent. She looks the worst I've ever seen her.

A single tear slides down her cheek, then another, until streams fall, trailing over her freckles.

"I thought I lost you too," Ilona whispers. "I saw that man beside you. Saw him raise his hand right before we all fell. Then you were just *gone* when we woke, and—"

"He didn't harm me," I say.

"Stop!" she yells, and I cringe at the way her high-pitched voice rings through the room. She never raises her voice like this, and it pierces my heart. "Stop being so bossy, and *stop* interrupting me. I know I'm not as eloquent as you, that I ramble, but just—just let me get out what I need to say for once! Please." Her voice cracks on that final plea, and her desperation makes me recoil.

"I'm sorry," I whisper without breaking eye contact, even though her words make me want to look away. It's awful seeing her this worked up.

All because of me.

Do I really interrupt her that often?

Am I bossy?

Maybe I haven't been as good a friend to Ilona as she's been to me.

"I thought you were gone, and I felt like I couldn't breathe. You're the only person I have. The only person," she whispers. "I know you hate your mother, but at least you have one. Mine died when I was a little girl. I was left behind with only you. Then *you* were gone all of a sudden too. When I went to visit Queen Enira out of pity, or respect, or I don't even know why—she told me that *you* are the reason my mother is dead.

"You saved me once, Astrid. But now, I learn *you're* the one I needed saving from. You've broken me, and this time you can't be the one to fix me. I'm really alone." She sniffles. Snot and tears cover her face, but she holds her head high, staring at me from across the bed.

"I truly am sorry for everything. I've always loved you like a sister," I tell her softly. "I wish I could take your pain away."

"Well, *I* don't wish you could," she says, her eyes wild and red-rimmed. "The pain is a reminder of what I've lost. A reminder not to make the same mistakes I have in the past. Don't you care about what *I* want?"

"Of course I do! What if I wasn't the one who killed your mother, Ilona?"

"Can you look me in the face and tell me truthfully that it wasn't you?"

"I—no. No I can't because I don't *know* if it was me." I press the heels of my hands into my eyes, rubbing away the forming tears, trying to keep myself from falling apart. In my head, explaining this to Ilona was so much easier. But now, it doesn't feel like enough.

Everything is such a mess, and I feel so lost in the tangle of lies everyone spun around me.

"Even if that's true, you still never told me." Her breath stutters as her tears slow. "You kept this from me purposely."

Her words are a slap across the face. She's right. Even if some version of my memory is true, Ilona is so tenderhearted and understanding that she would have forgiven me. And then she would have had closure.

But now? Now she's learned the supposed truth from Enira, and I've lost her trust completely.

"You're not alone, Ilona. You have Marnie. And you're a grown woman. You're free to go wherever you want. Become whoever you're meant to become." I stare at her through my curtain of tears, silently pleading with her to forgive me.

Whether or not our memories together are true or false, it doesn't matter to me. She's my best friend, and I need her. I love Ilona so deeply that nothing will ever change that for me.

I wish the same was true for her.

"You're my best friend," I say. "I—this—there's so much more to the story. If you'll just give me a chance to explain—"

"Please," she croaks, cutting me off now, and it strikes me how unfair I've been to her. How insanely disrespectful I've been with my interruptions and demands. "Just leave."

I don't want to leave her, but I exit the room with my head held high. I'll wait her out. I'll give her a few minutes to cool down, and then I'll share my side of the story and all will be well.

As I exit her room, I realize I can't hear her thoughts anymore.

The power sharing bond between Dash and me must be completely gone. Not that it matters, because now Ilona doesn't want to be near me at all now.

I hate the irony of it.

I lean against the wall outside Ilona's room and slide to the ground with a heavy exhale.

"She's stronger than you give her credit for," Marnie says, appearing at my side a minute later. We've always been kind to one another, but we've never had a chance to connect. I don't blame her for having reservations about me, especially with how deeply I hurt Ilona. "Don't you think she gets sick of being cast aside?"

I turn sharply to face her, taking in the way she stands with her hands on her hips. I scoff. "I don't cast her aside."

"Are you sure about that? She's always there when *you* need to vent about your mother. She's there for *you* each week at the bacchanals, even though that ruckus makes her uncomfortable. She accompanies *you* wherever you want to go, whenever you decide. But when have you been there for her?"

"I've always been there for—" As much as I don't want to believe it, what she's saying is true.

I *have* made everything about me. I've been a selfish friend lately. It was all too easy to push her away when her thoughts and emotions were too much for me, but I never stopped to think how she might feel. I conveniently left her out, in the name of protecting myself.

No wonder she's so unwilling to forgive me for this final blow.

She's one of the few people I trust, and in a sick twist of fate, she probably doesn't trust me anymore.

"What does she need from me, Marnie?" Marnie is clearly vexed, but there's nothing unkind about her demeanor toward me, even as she puts me in my place.

"To not be around you right now. Ilona has a huge heart. It's inevitable she'll forgive you for whatever it is you've done to her, but she needs some time to herself first." My eyes widen when I realize Ilona hasn't actually told Marnie what happened. There might be hope for our friendship. Ilona is still protecting *me*, even after everything.

Ilona *is* an incredibly selfless, kind friend. A friend I don't deserve.

"I think you're right, Marnie," I say reluctantly, using the hem of my shirt to dry my tears. Forgiveness is more than I deserve.

"I care for her, Princess Astrid. I do. So, I'm sorry if the words came out harsh, but I'm not sorry for saying them."

Taking a deep breath, I nod slowly. "As you shouldn't be."

She steps up to Ilona's door, and I call out to her just as she places her hand on the knob. "And, Marnie?"

"Yes?"

"Please don't call me Princess. Astrid is fine." She offers me a sympathetic smile before disappearing into the room.

Prior to this conversation, I wouldn't have walked away. I would've refused to take an answer I didn't want from Ilona. But now I see how bad of a friend I've been. If I want to earn Ilona's friendship back, I need to respect her wishes, no matter how hard it is for me. Because right now, it's not about me.

It's about Ilona.

Holding my head up high, I retreat, leaving her in the solitude she desires.

CHAPTER TWENTY-NINE

After my reunion with Dash and Ilona, I don't have the emotional capacity to see Enira, nor do I have the mental fortitude to confront my people.

I need to do both, but not in this state. Entering my room with the intention to clean up and gather my thoughts, I plop facedown on my teal sheets and release a heavy sigh.

I need a minute.

The familiar lingering scents of frankincense and lavender fill my nose, sneakily luring me to sleep.

I don't mean to nap, definitely don't intend to sleep through the night, but somehow I do.

The next morning, sunlight seeps around my curtains. It's well past dawn.

At first, I'm confused as to why Gianna let me sleep in so late. Then reality comes zipping back to me, and I mourn her loss all over again.

"No!" I angrily punch my pillow.

After throwing on fresh clothes, I exit my room to find Dash. He can take me to Enira.

I'm tempted to check on Ilona, but I fight the instinct, knowing she needs space and time to heal.

I force my feet to move down the hallway, ignoring the various guards that gawk at me. At least they still bow their heads as I pass, acknowledging me as their superior.

When I knock on Dash's door, he doesn't answer. It's unsurprising. Of course he's not here. I peek through the skylight above and realize how high the sun is in the sky. It must be close to noon. At least the extra sleep did me some good; I'm refreshed and clear-minded.

As I cut into the main wing, a couple of guards pass me, accompanying some villagers through the main foyer and into the throne room.

I watch, perplexed.

A man with sun-leathered skin and chipped teeth spits at me as he passes. "Ye wretched hog. Worse den yer mother." A guard jerks him aggressively by the arm, giving him a verbal warning as he jostles him toward the doorway. Luckily, the spit didn't hit me. It landed about a foot away, sparing me the full humiliation.

What are so many villagers doing here in the palace?

Creeping closer to the throne room—careful not to get too close to the townsfolk—I peer in. Dash sits on the throne, looking more handsome than ever.

Poised.

Regal.

Even without a crown, in his simple black Stellari clothing, he looks like a true king.

I've never seen him looking so pristine.

Where is the handsomely disheveled man I've come to know? It's like I'm viewing an imposter.

He addresses the crowd of villagers, and his voice bellows with authority. Yet somehow, he manages to sound compassionate at the same time. After observing the proceedings for a short time, I realize the people are presenting various issues to him.

"We need to rebuild with better materials! Once and for all," a hunched man yells as he hobbles toward the throne. A chorus of "Yeah!" rings out around him as the people agree. "The storms keep comin'. Keep on hittin'. They ain't gonna stop. It's killin' us goin' in circles with all the damned labor."

A plump woman joins the man. "We rebuild over and over again just to get teared down again!"

"I hear your concerns," Dash begins, his voice silencing the clamoring. "I understand your concerns. They are valid. It makes sense to provide Hakran with sturdier materials. Together we will rebuild a village that is better able to withstand the storms."

"Thank the goddess!" the robust woman cries out. "That cheap whore loved to keep us weak. We'd all work while she sat pretty up in this marble fortress. And that murderous daughter of her—"

"Enough!" Dash's voice booms through the room. It's enough to draw all eyes back to him and shut all open mouths. "Enough with the slander—"

I scurry from the doorway, having heard plenty. The last thing I want is for someone to catch me eavesdropping. I knew the people were going to despise me, that it'd take time and effort to win them over, but seeing it first hand cuts deep.

Meanwhile, it's like Dash was meant to sit on Hakran's throne. Were my suspicions correct that putting him on the throne was the Vannyk's goal all along? I've certainly proven to everyone I'm unfit to rule.

The villagers have clearly come to like and respect Dash, and in a short time. How could they not? To their knowledge, he freed them from Enira and saved them from me.

Clearly he's taking care of Hakran just fine without me. And Ilona...she seems better off without me too, especially now that she and Marnie are closer than ever.

Did I rush back here for no reason?

I don't know who I am or where I belong anymore. Hakran never quite felt like home, and now that I'm back and the people I care about seem better off without me, I'm not sure it will ever be my home. I was adamant about protecting the Hakranians, but maybe they don't need me after all.

Maybe I should've stayed in Nevaris. But without my memories, that doesn't seem right either.

I need answers first. I need to remember. There's only one person in the palace who might be able to give me anything useful.

It's time to talk to Enira.

When I reach the training floor, it pulsates with energy. Hakranian and Stellari guards alike run drills, more vigorously than I've ever seen before. Clearly, Dash wasted no time before implementing proper training for the remaining Hakranian guards.

It's bittersweet seeing Hakran thrive under his leadership.

I have other problems to focus on anyway. The sooner I get my memories back, the sooner I can reclaim ownership of my life.

"Where is the commander?" The clanking of weapons slows, and the guards pause, slowly bowing their heads one by one. Many hesitate, their disdain toward me obvious. Based on the way a few of them grit their teeth and share disgusted looks, I surmise they are only obliging because Dash warned them to show me respect.

I search the room, trying to locate whomever is in charge down here. One of Dash's first actions as king would almost certainly have been to promote a new elite commander—one he trusts.

"Here." A lanky man with a shaved head steps toward me, bowing deeply. "Welcome back, Princess. But please forgive me, for your visit is quite unexpected."

"Who are you?" He looks Hakranian, but I don't recognize him. I'm surprised Dash didn't choose a Stellari guard as his elite commander. Perhaps choosing this man was a show of faith.

"Commander Felipe, at the palace's service," he says. Turning to the ogling guards behind him, he bellows, "Back to work!" They immediately nod their acknowledgment and resume their sparring.

The place reeks of sweat and musk, a sign the guards have been working harder than ever.

"It's been a busy few days." Commander Felipe grunts.

"I need to see Enira," I say, cutting right to the reason I'm here. "I need access to the pit."

He purses his lips, eyeing me cautiously. "All right," he finally says.

The commander leads me to the pit, and I'm immensely grateful Dash persuaded the guards to assist me. Dash is proving to be a brilliant leader. I shouldn't be surprised. I've always found him to be incredibly alluring, intelligent, and charismatic, but it's still a shock to see that the mouthy, arrogant guard I knew has morphed into a respectable royal.

It fills me with a bitter swirl of awe and envy. Dash knows who he is, he knows his place, even though it's temporary.

Felipe places his hand on the door to the pit. The stone responds, loosening so he can push it open.

"Is she the only one down here?" I ask as I step inside.

"Not anymore." Felipe kicks me in the stomach, and I stumble, falling and smacking my head against the wall. "Rot with your whore mother, you vile girl." It dazes me, and for a moment I'm confused about what's happening. "Bradenson was a good friend of mine, he didn't deserve to die, you bitch." He pulls the door shut as I scramble to my feet.

But it's too late.

"Felipe!" I call out, pounding on the stone door. It's useless. The place is utterly soundproof.

He must be referring to the man I killed in the throne room. If only I could express my regret and sorrow—show the people the truth, that I haven't ever meant to hurt anyone. Not like that. It wasn't me. It was my out-of-control emotions, fueled by a corrupted bond.

I scream, fed up with the recent disruptions in my life.

Over a dozen guards saw their commander lock me in here, and yet none of them are coming to help. Dash is the only one who'd come looking for me, and he's currently indisposed. The only consolation is that he *will* find me. Eventually. The guards can't lie to him, not when he can read their minds.

He'll know the truth, and he'll come for me.

The thought calms me, so I resolve myself to do what I came here to do: talk to the woman who caused all this pain to begin with.

I head down the stairs, deeper into the pit. It's as dim and dank as I remember, smelling like mildew and human excrement. Knowing Lex was down here in these conditions for so long breaks my heart a little.

There's no way he deserved that.

For how many years was he here? He never did say.

"Enira, you blasphemous woman!" I yell as I enter the room with cages too small to be considered true cells.

"*Daughter,* finally," she says nonchalantly. In her wispy black gossamer gown, with her hair in loose curls, she almost looks too magnificent to be locked away in such a dreary place. As I step closer, I can see the kohl beneath her eyes is smeared and she lacks her signature red lipstick. That tells another story.

She *is* weak down here.

Vulnerable.

And she knows it.

I have the advantage.

A grin sneaks onto my face, and despite the grim situation, I can't help but laugh.

"Do you even have a daughter, Enira? Truly?" Exhausted with all the mind games and secrets, I cut straight to the point. No sense in toying with her like she does with everyone else. Especially since she's already at my mercy. I might be locked down here, for now, but she doesn't know that. For all she knows, I'm simply paying her a visit and can leave at my own discretion.

Her lips pull back, revealing a predatory smile. "And ruin this perfect body?"

It's answer enough. Of course she's too vain to have children.

"I always wondered why you were such a shit mother," I say, fighting to keep my voice steady. "You don't have a single maternal bone in your body. My life is nothing but a game to you."

"Games are *fun,* dear." She inspects her nails. "Though, providing for you has proved to be the opposite of fun. It has been a lot of work, really."

"Then why do it?" I ask, even though I know why. She wanted my power.

"You still do not remember." It's not a question. She raises her brows and laughs sharply. Placing her face between the bars of the cage, she wraps her fingers around the rusted metal. "I see you have met our dear Lexyll." She tilts her head toward the cage I freed him from. "How does it feel to be reunited with your *lover?* He is quite a fine specimen, I admit."

Her taunting misses the mark. She thinks I don't know the truth, but I do.

"I know who I am," I say. "Cut it out, Enira. It's over."

"Oh. But is it? Do you *truly* know who you are? Or did someone *tell* you who you are?" She's poking at me, trying to get a reaction. "Pretty little puppet. That is all you are." She turns her back to me, and I have the urge to reach between the bars and snatch her dark hair. But I refrain. For now. I am downright pissed, and my patience is wearing thin, so I'm not positive my self-control will hold up much longer.

"That Dargan boy is keeping your throne nice and warm for you, is he not?" she asks. She didn't get the response she was hoping for with her comments about Lex, so of course she's trying to get to me with Dash instead.

When I don't reply, she smiles smugly. "Do not tell me you thought the Vannyks were helping *you* take my throne?" Her head tilts back as she releases a full-on belly laugh. It's the hardest I've ever heard her laugh. It echoes eerily, bouncing off the stones. "You ignorant girl. The Dargan ancestors owned this island. It has been their goal for decades to sit a dirty Dargan upon my throne. Who do you think I stole it from initially?"

I work hard to remain impassive.

She just wants to get a rise out of me.

She's trying, desperately, to manipulate me in a new way, without her powers. Manipulation is all she knows. This is her last resort.

Yet…she still successfully rattles me.

"Why do you think he did not *let* you kiss him at Paramour Falls?" she says tauntingly. "Yes. Yes. I know all about that, darling dearest."

To protect me. Right?

"You truly think he does not know the truth of his own ancestors' lore?" she hisses. "You do not think the Dargan boy knew his magic would ruin you?"

The first part of what Enira says matches up with what Dash said about him being a descendent of Davvinia and Anwyr.

I believe what she's saying, that Dash's family had this land first…but the rest of it? No. There is no way Dash was purposely trying to ruin me.

Please don't let it be true.

Lex planted those seeds of doubt first, but Enira is watering them.

"Does your *lover* even belong to you anymore either? Or did I ruin him for you?" Her hollow laughter rings out in the open space.

I growl. "You are so disgustingly vain, Enira. Doesn't it get lonely being hated by everyone?"

"Not when you have the power of deception on your side." She taps the rusty bar with a blood-red nail, smirking at me.

The Goddess of Deception.

But me?

I'm supposed to be the Goddess of Death.

Of fucking *death*.

And I will make Enira pay with her blood.

"What was our agreement?"

"You still do not remember." Enira *tsks*. "You had something I wanted. Something you managed to take from me a second time." Her eyes dart toward the empty cages to my right.

"Lex?" I ask, confused. She can't possibly think he belongs to her.

"Oh, I finally got *plenty* of him these past few years. Though, I must admit it is not as enjoyable when it is one-sided."

My insides snap in half. I lunge at her, reaching through the bars and snagging a chunk of her thick hair in my fist, pulling her toward me. She screams as her forehead cracks against the metal bars.

"Quit fucking with me, Enira. Tell me how to get my memories back," I hiss in her ear as I yank her head against the bars a second time. Blood trickles from a cut on her head, and she grins as it drips down her cheek. "Will killing you do the trick? I might just do it anyway and find out."

"You think I would make it so easy for you?"

I release her hair, and she staggers back, smoothing out her dress as she reclaims her balance. "Would you really be willing to give up your throne?"

"Not everyone values power above all else. I don't give a shit about the *throne!* This has nothing to do with that!"

"In this world, you are nothing without power. Why do you think I took Hakran? Why do you think I took from you and everyone else around me?"

"Because you are a selfish, despicable narcissist. Look around, Enira. Where is all your mighty power now? What good is it doing for you?"

"If you think my games are over, you are wrong, dear," she says with a waggle of her finger. "Even if you kill me, your memories will not return. I have taken precautions to ensure that."

Gritting my teeth, I weigh my options of testing that theory and taking her life now. I can't be sure it'll work, and until I'm sure, I can't risk it.

"No. You're so vain you thought yourself untouchable. A mistake on your part," I snarl. "Now you've lost everything. Everyone. No one bows to you anymore, *Dead Queen.*"

"You know much about mistakes, do you not, *Aife?*"

I take a deep breath in, trying hard to cool my anger.

"You do not remember what brought you here to me. How you became nothing more than my pretty little puppet," she says in a sing-song tone. "For two people who supposedly hate one another, you both seem keen on sacrificing your freedom for each other."

Lex's powers are unbelievably strong. He's able to avoid magic manipulation, yet he still ended up as Enira's prisoner.

He said it was because she exploited his weakness.

Me.

"Lex agreed to become your slave in exchange for my freedom," I whisper. It's only a guess, but Enira's sly grin is confirmation that it's correct.

Lex was never coming to *neutralize,* like Sora claimed. Sora seems determined to drive me away from Lex, but right now that doesn't matter.

"It was a trick," I say. Somehow Enira remained in control of us both.

"He bartered for your freedom, but he failed to negotiate for your memories." She snickers. "Technically, I held up my end of the bargain. You had your freedom. You could have walked away at any time. Your fool of a lover was too blinded by his love to make a better deal."

My stomach churns with nausea and anger.

Lex you beautiful idiot, you shouldn't have come for me.

Of course Enira tricked him. That's what she does. It's her specialty.

"What was *our* bargain?" I ask, gripping the bars of her cage so tightly the rust cuts into my palms.

"You, my dear, gave yourself up in order to protect the lovely Nevaris from my 'games,' as you like to call them." She tilts her head, giving me another birdlike smile. "So willing to walk away from Lex. So desperate to escape him that you came to me instead. You *agreed* to give up your memories. Nevaris is a charming village, but was it really worth it in the end?"

No.

I wouldn't have done that.

There's no way.

"I made a mistake." My voice comes out flat as I entertain her revelation. Why would I do that when Lex and I could've teamed up together to take her down? The *God of War* and the *Goddess of Death* surely could've found another way. Something about my decision doesn't make sense.

"One I benefited from greatly," Enira says with a cruel smile.

I'm reeling from this new information.

The only thing my conversation with Enira has confirmed is that Lex hasn't lied to me. Somehow, this mess is all my fault. Enira is using another magic source to prevent my memories from returning. As much as I want to flay the woman, make her beg for mercy, I need her alive for now. She's the key to retrieving my past.

I just need to figure out how to get it out of her.

Dash *will* come looking for me soon, and perhaps I can discuss it with him.

Unless Felipe was acting on Dash's orders. The thought sickens me, and I jolt away from Enira's cage. There's no way.

Trepidation fills me. I hope Enira was lying about Dash. But her brutal honesty thus far doesn't bode well for me.

I bolt through the corridor, desperate to try the door again even though I know it won't budge.

Enira's voice calls after me, "You might not be in a cell, but you are still in a cage, Aife!"

I look forward to the day I can end her pathetic life.

After spending the next hour exploring every nook and cranny of the pit, I find nothing useful. Dash doesn't want Enira dead, which means someone will bring her food and water eventually. But even if I can overpower whoever comes down here next, how can I get out of here unscathed? The guards might not be under Enira's manipulation anymore, but that doesn't mean they'll look out for me. Especially not if Dash is a traitor. I'm facing a whole other war when I find my way out of here.

It's like the situation with the Vannyks all over again, except this time I have no advantages. I have no weapons, no magic, nothing that could—

Wait.

Fingering the black cord around my neck, I think of Lex's words: *"If you ever need me, rub your stone between your palms. Mine will heat up in response, and I'll know to come to you."*

Everyone needs help at some point. It's time for me to admit that I need Lex's help.

"I'm not a damsel in distress," I growl as I roll the celestite between my palms, faster and faster until it seems to spark with life, glowing a dazzling blue.

A few minutes go by. Then a few more. I sit in silence on the steps and wait. I'm not sure what I was expecting exactly, but it wasn't this.

Sighing, I return to the cage where Enira stands. She's as uptight as ever. Even in these circumstances, she refuses to sit on the soiled ground. I wonder if she'll give in or continue standing there until she collapses with exhaustion.

Not my problem.

Wordlessly, I take a seat on the cold ground next to her cell, with my back pressed against the stone.

"Love makes you weak, Aife," she says, her icy voice slicing through the silence.

"Like you would know. Have you ever loved anyone other than yourself?"

She surprises me when she finally sits on the ground, mimicking my position with her back against her small section of wall and her knees bent. "Maybe."

"We're not friends. I'm not making small talk with you," I mutter.

It's strange really. I've begged her for years to pay attention to me. To talk to me. And yet, we've talked more today than we ever have in all the time I thought she was my mother.

The irony of it all.

I lean forward, resting my arms and forehead on my knees, and close my eyes, willing this nightmare to end.

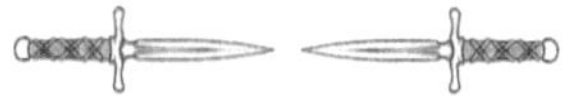

Thump.

I jolt upright. Somehow I managed to doze off. Probably not the smartest decision I've ever made, but I couldn't help it.

Enira stands in her cage, gripping the bars. Indistinguishable voices echo through the stone pit. I back up into the shadows, trying to conceal myself from whoever is approaching. If I have a chance of getting out of here, I'll have to attack them. It's not the smartest plan, but this might be my only chance to escape.

No one's coming to save me, and I can't wait around forever.

As soon as someone turns the corner, entering into the space, I sweep my foot out in an attempt to take them down like Dash once did to me.

I fail horrendously.

My foot collides with something solid, and I wince at the impact.

"Did you just kick me in the shin, luv?" a familiar, accented voice drawls.

"Lex!" It takes me a second to register him in the poorly lit space, but his sharp jaw and lean stature are unmistakable. I want to cry at the sight of him. I'm overcome with joy and relief.

"It's no wonder you thought I was lying when I told you that you're the goddess of death," he murmurs. I catch a hint of humor in his voice. "With moves like that, it is quite impossible to believe."

"Astrid, Kicker of Shins, Bruisebringer," Callan says, stepping beside Lex. "Hello again."

"Thank the goddess," I say. They came for me. It gives me hope, makes me feel *safe*.

"This scenario feels eerily familiar," Lex says. "I can't say I'm pleased to meet you under these circumstances." I wrap my arms around him and pull him into a hug. His masculine, pine scent greets my nose, and I inhale greedily.

"Did you just sniff him?" Callan asks, interrupting our reunion. I release Lex, moving to kick Callan in the shin, but he dodges my foot with a snicker.

"Lexyll, darling, how nice to see you again." Enira's taunt dissolves the lighthearted moment.

He's at Enira's cage in a flash, gripping her neck through the bars and holding a blade to her cheek. She looks wild with the shadow of dried blood from her head wound. She tries to speak, but only a choking noise comes out.

I place a hand on Lex's shoulder. "She—I need her alive to get my memories back."

"Is that what she told you?" Lex releases Enira, shoving her back like I did earlier, but this time, she falls to the ground with a pathetic whimper.

I can't believe I've been afraid of this woman for years.

"She fails to remember you. You poor thing," Enira mocks. "Maybe I can help with that. Maybe not."

Lex continues to stare at Enira with silent fury as Callan scouts the empty cells beside us.

"Or maybe it is a *good* thing for you that she does not remember?" Enira chuckles as she stands, fiddling with her skirts and brushing her hair over her shoulder. "Consider it a favor."

I'm ready to get the hell out of here and leave her taunting behind, but when Lex turns to face me, he's close enough that I can see the way his eyes shimmer with regret. My body stills.

"Oh!" Enira claps. "You *did* tell her the whole truth, right, Lexyll?"

"Enough," Lex says without breaking eye contact with me.

"What is she talking about?"

He doesn't reply, but he doesn't look away from me either. I take a step back, putting some space between us.

"We need to go," Lex snarls. "We can do this later."

Nodding, I follow Callan and Lex down the corridor toward the stairs as Enira's laugh rings out behind me.

"Love makes you weak. I did you a favor, Aife!" Her words are thrust into my gut like a serrated blade.

Gritting my teeth, I follow the men up the stairs. It irks me that I didn't get a straight answer about my memories, but at least now I have some direction.

In the meantime, I have a bone to pick with *King* Dashiel Dargan.

CHAPTER THIRTY

Lo and Sora are waiting for us at the top of the stairs speaking quietly. When they spot us, they nod and fly down the stairs in Enira's direction.

"They can't kill her," I say to Lex.

"They won't."

"And when the time comes, I want to be the one who—" My eyes widen as we step into the training room. A dozen bodies litter the floor around us.

The guards.

At first glance, it appears they have only been knocked out, like the people in the throne room during the storm. But upon closer inspection, I notice their faces are husks. Dried and hollow. Drained completely of their life force.

A severed hand lies discarded by the door, and I realize Lex got into the pit the same way I did when I first rescued him. Felipe's body lies a few feet away, a pool of blood beneath his severed wrist.

I'm both thrilled and sickened by Lex's tactics. I'm also finding it oddly satisfying that our relationship has come full circle this week. It's harmonious.

"You killed them all," I mutter. It's a *little* excessive.

Okay, it's a straight-up slaughter.

"Yes." Lex stares at me, his jaw tense. "I did."

"Why?" I ask. Lex can control his power, as he mentioned before. He could've taken them down without killing them. He *chose* to kill them.

"This is war," he says coolly. "There are two types of people in our world, Aife. Predators and prey. Both are terrible choices. Choose your terrible."

Of course. It's a war. His specialty.

I don't bother correcting him when he calls me Aife this time. It really doesn't matter. I consider his words for a beat and decide he's right. All my life—or what I thought to be my life—I've been preyed on. I know nothing of the woman I once was, but I bet she was never anybody's prey.

Lex must see the moment of realization in my eyes, because his lips slowly curve into a smile, and he reaches out a hand for me. "Come," he says. I eye his hand cautiously.

"Just accept his damn hand—he doesn't bite," Callan says from somewhere behind me.

"Why didn't you just do this in the first place?" I ask, ignoring Callan. I gesture toward the bodies.

"I am skilled in the art of war, but that doesn't mean it's my first choice," he says. "I gave them a chance to surrender." He tilts his head to the side, scrutinizing me.

"I can't go with you. I have unfinished business here."

"With Dash," Lex says, the disappointment obvious in his tone.

I shake my head. "Not exactly. But I can't be with you either. You might remember me as yours, but that's not who I am anymore."

"No. You aren't," he says, and I deflate. "But if I have my way, you will be in time." My body lights up at his words, buzzing with desire. I know in my deepest depths that he won't let me down, so tentatively, I reach for him. I let him interlace our fingers as our hands mold together. His eyes shutter, and I shoot Callan a confused glance, but he's too busy inspecting the weapons on a dead guard to notice.

Why does he even bother with weapons when Lexyll himself is a weapon?

My palm begins to pulse in Lex's grip, and I stare in awe as our hands begin to shimmer with a golden hue.

It's faint at first. Then the warmth blossoms into a delicious heat. It feels similar to when I absorb life forces. Pleasurable, all-consuming. I can't help but moan at the bliss of his energy coursing into my body.

As much as I hated taking lives, I missed *this* feeling.

This is when I feel most alive.

Suddenly, he breaks our contact. I mourn the loss of his touch.

"You said you weren't capable of transference," I say.

It's an accusation, but he chuckles in return, shaking his head. "That wasn't a transference."

He runs his fingers through his hair. I admire the way he wears it loose and wild today, the ends skimming his shoulders. "In all my years, Aife, you're still the only vygora I've met capable of transference."

I scoff. "If that wasn't a transference, then what the hell was it?"

"Power sharing."

"Power sharing? How?"

"Take a second to think about it. Maybe it'll come to you." He winks—a gesture that shouldn't be so disturbingly attractive yet somehow is—then heads for the stairs.

Callan follows him, flashing me a gap-toothed smile over his shoulder. "Maybe take that second later? We don't have time now."

Out of nowhere, something strikes me. A weird feeling flutters in my chest. I recall a moment I had in Nevaris with Lex:

"Power is only to be shared by the fated. Soulmates, if you will."

If Lex didn't transfer energy with me...did he *share* it?

Lex was awfully certain Dash wasn't my fated from the beginning, even before he learned about my defective magic. Lex and I also haven't been intimate...at all. At least not in many years. We've had time and space between us, yet he's still able to share his magic with me.

If after all this time, distance, and lack of intimacy, he can still share his magic with me, that can only mean one thing.

"Coming, Aife?" Callan calls down the stairs.

I bolt past the shriveled corpses and up the stairs, immediately leveling my darkest glare at Lex.

"Stop lying to me," I whisper-yell.

His eyes narrow, and he places his hands in the pockets of his slacks. "I've never *lied* to you. Not a single time."

"We're fated." The words sound ridiculous coming out of my mouth. I still don't believe in that nonsensical lore, but after everything that happened with Dash, it's hard to remain skeptical. "We kissed at the falls?"

"Yes." Lex steps toward me, pinning me with a dark look. His eyes flit to my lips, and his pupils dilate. There's no mistaking the lust there.

"And you didn't tell me?"

"We've gone over this, luv. Aren't you sick of people telling you who you are?"

"But this is different."

"Is it? Would you have believed me? Or would you have pushed me away, wondering if my words were the truth? You might be Astrid now, but you are still the same Aife at the core. *My* Aife. I *know* you. You needed to figure this out on your own without my interference."

My jaw tightens. I square my shoulders, trying to stand a little taller as he takes yet another step closer. There's only about a foot of space between us, and I incline my head to look up at him.

"So what? I'm just supposed to be with you forever? I have no choice over who I'm with?" I ask. Sure, I have an abnormal attraction to Lex—I am undoubtedly enraptured by the man—but I hate that my fate has been decided for me. I despise the concept of not having choice.

Lex is right: I need to feel in control.

"You can still make your own decisions," he says, running a thumb over his bottom lip. I yearn to reach for him, to cover his mouth with mine. I want nothing more than to taste him, devour him.

"This changes nothing," I say, though inside my brain screams that *this changes everything*. Fighting my indescribable need to touch Lex, to feel his skin on mine, I turn my back on him and head down the marble corridor.

"Where are you going? Let's get out of here," Callan says incredulously.

I pause, turning back to face him while avoiding Lex's penetrating stare. "I have something I need to take care of."

Lo and Sora emerge from the stairs with a shackled Enira in tow. Chains bind her arms together, and another set binds her ankles together. A sack rests over her head. She spits out a slew of profanities, and Sora elbows her in the gut to shut her up.

"What the hell is this?" I ask.

"Silenxstone chains," Callan says proudly. "A new addition

to our defenses, courtesy of that old abandoned prison. We had them made as soon as—"

"Short answers only," Lo interjects as she and Sora force Enira forward. Enira whimpers from underneath the sack, but I have no pity for her. "There's no way we're leaving her here."

Sora glowers at me, unsurprisingly, and I ignore him.

Fear prickles in my gut as I finally turn to Lex. "Did you kill Dash?"

"No."

"Then I need to find him." I don't have to waste time searching for him, because a moment later, Dash—looking absolutely irate—turns a corner with a half-dozen guards at his back.

"Astrid!" he calls out. "Get away from that bastard."

Callan and Lex flank me, and the guards mirror the movement, rushing beside Dash and leveling their elemental staffs at us. The orbs at the ends flicker with harnessed aethyn power: fiery red, watery blue, and golden lightning.

"What the hell is this, Dash?" I wince at his unnecessary show of power against us. Dash's face hardens; he's almost unrecognizable. "I need to talk to you" —I glance at all the guards around him— "alone."

"I'm sorry, Astrid. But that can't happen while they're in my palace." Dash shakes his head, inclining his head as he stares down his nose at Lex.

His palace.

Not mine.

Not ours.

Not even *the* palace.

He said *"my"* palace.

"That throne doesn't belong to you, Dashiel Dargan," I say, using his full name as a threat. Even if it's not technically mine either, Dash doesn't know that yet. At this point, it's the principle of the matter. "You used me to get here, didn't you?"

A look of confusion crosses his face. "I don't know what lies they've spewed, but you can't trust any of them."

"You're the only one spewing lies!"

"That's not even—" He shakes his head, a disbelieving laugh escaping his lips.

"Paramour Falls," I retort. "You and I both know the truth now."

"Astrid," he says, his voice pleading. His eyes dart between Lex and me. Clearly not caring about how dangerous Lex is, Dash takes a few steps toward me. "It's not what you think. Everything between us is real. Don't go with them."

"It's not about them!" I scoff. "It's about you and me. About *my* throne. My people."

"I'm doing *you* a favor by leading your people." His voice cracks, and it shatters a bit of my resolve. "I'm only doing this for Hakran. For you."

When I step forward toward him, his guards do the same toward me.

"What is all of this, Dash?" I wave at the guards beside him. "What is it really? Are you going to subdue me if I try to leave? Do they expect me to bow down to you?"

They take another aggressive step forward, as if they're protecting Dash from me. I growl, incensed by their audacity. A pulsing power—the new, exotic mix of Lex's and my magic— burns through my veins, begging for release. As potent as the pressure inside of me is, it's nothing like before when my emotions were unruly and dangerous. Now, I feel the same surge of power, but it's entirely commandable.

I am in control.

I follow the instinct, homing in on the energy of the guards.

I focus on drawing it out, pulling it toward me. At first, nothing happens, but then a small surge of energy jolts my body. I smile, giddy at the new ability.

Was I capable of this all along?

The intensity builds, and soon, the life force of all six of Dash's guards is flowing into me. They drop to their knees, faces contorting while I revel in the pleasure it brings me.

It's euphoric.

This right here is the most natural thing in the world for me. It fuels me, drives me.

This is who I am, no matter how it's labeled.

I've ignored it for too long. Been ashamed of who I am for no valid reason.

Right as they lose consciousness, Ilona steps into view.

I flinch, dropping the connection before the guards are entirely drained. Only Dash remains standing across from me, gaping at me with horror. A look of disgust crosses Ilona's face, and before I can call out to her, she shakes her head and bolts back down the corridor in the direction she came.

"What have you done?" Dash whispers. He takes a step back, and it's enough to confirm that he's afraid of me. A fact I find disappointing yet unsurprising.

"You did this, Dash," I accuse. "You caused this with your lies."

I wait for him to fight back, for his malicious, manipulating side to reveal itself. But it doesn't. It could be a trick of lighting, but I'm almost positive his eyes glisten with tears before he blinks them away. His face turns to stone.

"You are wrong. I meant it when I said I love you. You're going to regret whatever it is you're doing, Astrid."

Lex growls beside me, and my automatic response is to soothe him by interlacing my fingers with his. Dash's eyes track the movement, and I see the moment I break his heart. His gaze drops to the floor as a tear falls, and he rubs a hand over his face to cover it up.

"Don't go with them," Dash whispers so quietly that I almost miss it.

"Don't tell me what to do."

"Do you even know who that is? He's dangerous," Dash says, a murderous look on his face. "That's Lexyll, God of War."

I'm about to ask him how he knows that, if he's known it all along, but I don't get a chance.

Lex snarls, and it's a terrifying sound. "Do you even know who *she* is? Would you still love her, accept her, care for her if she wasn't who you thought she was?"

Dash searches my face for an answer.

"I'm not Astrid. I'm Aife. Goddess of Death."

He recoils, shaking his head in denial. "No you're not. That's not possible." He runs his hand through his hair, taking deep breaths. "You're Astrid, the love of my life."

"She's *mine,* jackass." Lex growls and my brows shoot up to my hairline. Normally, I'd be disgusted by such an archaic claim, but hearing those words come out of Lex's mouth is downright sexy. I just about melt at his feet.

I hadn't expected Lex to admit that so openly. Not that I think he's embarrassed of me, but he's normally so calculated. It seems Dash gets under his skin.

"I'm not giving up on you, Astrid," Dash says, ignoring Lex's declaration.

Enira releases a piercing laugh. At least Callan, Lo, and Sora have the decency to keep quiet.

"Shut the fuck up, Enira," I say.

"Or what? You *need* me, Aife," she says, goading me. "You

need me if you ever want your memories back."

"You know what? I am so sick of you controlling me, of you interfering with my life." I step away from the showdown with Dash, moving toward Enira. Sora and Lo are holding her under the arms. They watch me curiously, but don't interfere as I rip the sack off her head. "I am sick of being a pawn. I am *not* your prey."

"Being prey can be fun. Just ask your handsome *lover.*"

The thought of her touching Lex against his will ruins me. I buckle under the intensity of her claim. At first, I ignored her comments in the pit, assuming they were nothing more than a bluff, but she's a sick woman, and I wouldn't put it past her.

"You disgusting bitch!" Before anyone can register what I'm doing, I snatch the dagger from Lo's hip and run the blade across Enira's throat. It's a clean, killing blow, and blood gushes from the wound in ribbons of crimson. I watch as she chokes on her own blood, her face stretched with incredulity.

"I did not see that coming," Callan whispers. Lo tells him to shut up as Sora sighs and shakes his head. As Enira continues to bleed out, Sora and Lo release her body to the floor with a *thud.*

Holding the bloody blade in front of me, I turn back to Dash. "I am sick of everyone telling me who I am. More than that, I am sick of fearing that people will misunderstand me or hate me for who I am."

A brief glance at Lex causes the next wave of threats to die out on my tongue. His eyes, greener than the jungle, sparkle with approval. He watches me like I'm the most glorious being he's ever seen.

"There she is," he whispers. I swell with pride, and my stomach flutters at his praise. "I've missed you."

"This isn't you," Dash says.

I toss the blade aside with a resigned sigh. "It *is* me, Dash.

This is why we can never work. You need to let me go."

Before he gets a chance to reply, a shooting pain drives through my skull, and I drop to my knees with a panicked screech. Broken, distorted pieces of memories flood my brain. I can't fully comprehend them.

It lasts for only a brief moment, and when the pain subsides, I remember something. The image is foggy, and it's only one tiny missing piece. But it's something important.

Something that changes everything.

Lex helps me to my feet, concern marring his stunning features. "Are you okay, luv?"

Dash calls my name, looking torn between rushing to my side and keeping his distance. Lo, Callan, and Sora crowd around me, peering at me with unease.

I ignore them all. Instead, I look up into my fated's haunted eyes, a dark smile playing on my lips. "It seems that *some* of my memories have returned with Enira's death."

Lex swallows thickly, and his jaw tenses.

He's unsettled.

As he should be.

"I just remembered *why* it is that I hate you so much, my dearest, and I am downright done with all of these wicked lies." I fist his collar, pulling him toward me and violently pressing my lips to his.

He returns the kiss without hesitation, wrapping his arms around me and gluing our bodies together. It isn't a sweet reunion of a kiss by any means. It's a vicious thing, fueled by a passion I've never known before.

I moan into his mouth as our tongues dance. He matches my intensity like he was made for me, licking and nibbling in a way that drives me crazy. He tastes like mint and fire—a hauntingly delicious combination.

His hardness presses against me, begging to be touched. I'm desperate to remove our layers, to let him bend me over and slide into my slick heat, filling the aching hollow there.

The vague awareness of prying eyes is the only thing keeping me from ravishing him entirely. Instead, I settle for grinding against him as we kiss ravenously.

It's not nearly enough, but it's something.

It's a kiss birthed of old hate and new desire.

A kiss intended to devastate.

ACKNOWLEDGEMENTS

It takes a village. Truly. This book wouldn't exist if it wasn't for my support system. First, big thanks to my amazing husband Bryam for putting up with my chaos. I'm constantly spewing story ideas and reading random bits aloud, and he always listens patiently even when he has no idea what's going on. Thanks for loving me just the way I am and supporting my dreams!

Big thanks to my dogs: Lee the retriever mix and River the border Aussie. These two are the real MVPs. They help me manage my anxiety and sleep well enough that I have the energy to put my words down onto paper.

My alpha readers—Lia, Amanda, and Charity—were imperative to this project. Their feedback helped make the story a lot less awkward than it could have been. Trust me on that. You three are my OG hype team and I cannot thank you enough!

I also want to thank all of my beta readers and all the writers in my Write it Good group chat: Lindsay (extra thanks for formatting These Wicked Lies, too!), Abigail, Alex, Chip, Erin, Heather, Kelsey, Tia, Tricia, and Tori. You are all incredible and I'm so blessed to have you in my life. I'm thankful to have found a home in our group chat, and gosh do you make me feel normal, even though I'm anything but!

My amazing editor Emily (@litmosphereediting) deserves a

huge shoutout for being an absolute gem and helping me execute my vision with this project. You have a wonderful eye and are so perceptive.

Next up is the creative Fran (@coverdungeonrabbit) who made the most amazing cover ever; it's exactly what I wanted, even though I had no idea what I wanted! Thank you for your patience and kindness. You are unbelievably talented at what you do.

Finally, I want to give much love to my mother for encouraging my reading habits, setting an example with her own reading habits, and taking me to the library almost every week even in mid-winter storms and below freezing temperatures. Mom, when I told you I wrote a book, you said you were so, so proud of me. When I told you it had a sex scene, you asked "just one?" Here's to hoping I didn't disappoint you with my single sex scene. I love you!

ABOUT THE AUTHOR

Miranda is a fan of all things magical and romantic. She believes some of the best heroes come from dark pasts, and family is more than blood. She loves writing about strong characters who overcome unpleasant situations and find love along the way. She holds a BA in English and is currently pursuing an MFA. When she's not scratching out notes for her next story or devouring a book, she's petting her dogs. Bookstagram is a huge part of her life (@readwritejoy) and she loves to connect about all things bookish!

Follow Miranda on Instagram, Twitter, or TikTok @readwritejoy, and online at www.authormirandajoy.com